DEAD
We
HONOR

The DEAD *We* HONOR

WILLIAM W. JOHNSTONE
and J.A. JOHNSTONE

PINNACLE BOOKS
Kensington Publishing Corp.
kensingtonbooks.com

PINNACLE BOOKS are published by

Kensington Publishing Corp.
900 Third Avenue
New York, NY 10022

Copyright © 2025 by J. A. Johnstone

PUBLISHER'S NOTE: Following the death of William W. Johnstone, the Johnstone family is working with a carefully selected writer to organize and complete Mr. Johnstone's outlines and many unfinished manuscripts to create additional novels in all of his series like The Last Gunfighter, Mountain Man, and Eagles, among others. This novel was inspired by Mr. Johnstone's superb storytelling.

All Kensington titles, imprints, and distributed lines are available at special quantity discounts for bulk purchases for sales promotion, premiums, fund-raising, and educational or institutional use.

Special book excerpts or customized printings can also be created to fit specific needs. For details, write or phone the office of the Kensington Sales Manager: Kensington Publishing Corp., 900 Third Avenue, New York, NY 10022. Attn. Sales Department. Phone: 1-800-221-2647.

PINNACLE BOOKS, the Pinnacle logo, and the WWJ steer head logo Reg. U.S. Pat. & TM Off.

First Printing: March 2025
ISBN-13: 978-0-7860-5138-0
ISBN-13: 978-0-7860-5139-7 (eBook)

10 9 8 7 6 5 4 3 2 1

Printed in the United States of America

CHAPTER 1

The acrid smell of smoke drifted in through the open windows on a soft summer breeze. Ellen Branch, a life-long light sleeper, bolted awake. She shook her snoozing husband's shoulder.

"George. George!"

He stopped in midsnore and mumbled, "What?"

"I smell fire."

That one word had George up and out of bed, running to the window, and throwing the curtains aside.

"Dear Lord."

He bolted out of the bedroom in his boxer shorts and scraggly T-shirt faster than she'd seen him move in years. The pounding of his fist on their son's door echoed down the hallway. George yelled, "Jason, there's a fire!"

Ellen was on her feet, her face so close to the window her nose left a smudge on the glass. Orange and yellow flames clawed into the night sky, spreading deeper into their corn crop with each passing second. She barely noticed the pounding of feet down the stairs or the crash of the front door as it was flung open in a wild panic.

George and Jason sprinted into view, stopping dead in their tracks at the conflagration before them. Their heads turned to the east, and Ellen threw open the window to stick out her head so she could see what they could see.

Making the sign of the cross came naturally to Ellen, though she wasn't sure at the moment if God was open to her prayers.

The barn was on fire as well. Red embers smaller than fireflies danced in the air and peppered her face.

It was as if the devil himself had come to their home, leaving his hellish imprint on their land.

"Call the fire department!" George shouted up to her. Her gaze was fixed on Jason as he hurried to the barn. He was big and strong, one of the largest men in the entire town, but size and physical power were nothing compared to the destructive force of fire.

She banged her head on the sill when she dipped back inside. The pain didn't register. For a moment, she couldn't remember where she'd left her cell phone. There it was, on her night table atop a pile of old mystery paperbacks, right where she put it every single night.

You have to calm down, she admonished herself. *You won't be any help if you panic.*

That being said, it still took her three times to tap out 9-1-1 on her phone. Her call was picked up right away. She tried her best to describe what was happening and give her address, which eluded her for a frightening moment.

"We'll have fire on the way, ma'am," the woman said to Ellen. "Is anyone hurt?"

"Jason," Ellen whispered.

"Can you please repeat that?"

Ellen went back to the window, searching for her son. He was nowhere to be seen. George had the hose out and was watering the grass between the house and the cornfield.

"I . . . I don't know," Ellen said. "My son, he went into the barn, but the barn's on fire. I can't see him. I don't know where he is."

"Stay on the phone with me. Just describe what you see."

Four shots rang out. Ellen knew right away it was gunfire and not something popping from the heat of the fire. She dropped the phone on the bed, ran downstairs, and grabbed a shotgun from the cabinet in the mud-room. She made sure it was loaded and stuffed some extra shells in the breast pocket of her sleep shirt.

Without a care for her own safety, she ran through the open front door and stopped beside George.

"Someone's opening fire," she shouted above the roar of the conflagration.

George ran the hose back and forth, trying to create a soggy barrier that the fire couldn't cross.

"I didn't hear anything," he said.

That made sense. When Ellen was looking out their second-floor window she had a better visual and aural vantage point than down here on the ground. Now, all she could hear was the insidious fire as it inched their way.

"Where's Jason?"

"He went to get Jax."

She looked over to the barn. It was completely engulfed in flame. Squinting, she couldn't see Jason or his horse silhouetted against the flames.

"Did he make it out?"

George was sweating from head to toe, his eyes locked on the wall of flame. "Darn it, I don't know."

The hose slipped from his grasp. He joined Ellen in looking for any sign of Jason or Jax.

"I'll check the barn," George said.

"I'll go with you."

"It's too dangerous!"

Ellen nudged him aside when she ran past him, keeping the shotgun level and ready. George caught up to her and eventually passed her, heading for the barn. From the crack and groaning of wood, it sounded like it was about to collapse.

"Jason!" George and Ellen yelled at the top of their lungs. They ran as fast as they could, despite George's bad knee and Ellen's hips, which her doctor told her would need to be replaced at some time in the next few years. Adrenaline did what it could, but it wasn't a fountain of youth.

There were more shots behind them, followed by breaking glass. Ellen cast a quick glance over her shoulder and saw that the windows to their bedroom had been shot out. Without a second thought, she pumped the shotgun and fired. She was too far away to hit anyone near the house, but she wanted whoever was out there doing this to know she was armed and willing to shoot.

George must not have heard the exchange because he kept on running, right until he disappeared into the furnace that was their barn. Ellen pulled up short when a wall of heat sizzling enough to melt iron smacked her square in the face.

More shots rang out by the house.

Ellen returned fire, even though she wasn't sure they were shooting at her.

She spun back to the barn and shouted, "George! Jason!"

Despite the roiling fire, the interior of the barn was still too dark to see. It was as if a black hole had opened up dead center of the barn, refusing to allow the light to touch its inner depths. The roof, bathed in a spiraling wig of fire, canted to the left. The structure made a rending sound that weakened Ellen's knees.

Where the hell were George and Jason?

She couldn't wait outside any longer. The barn was going to collapse any second. If they were both hurt and unable to get out on their own, she had to at least try to help them. It had to be Jason first. She and George had made a pact that if anything should happen to their family, the children should always come first. Jason may be in his midthirties, but he would always be her child.

Ellen dropped the shotgun, took a deep breath, and headed into the fire with her head bowed and one arm draped across her face in a feeble attempt to stave off the heat and smoke. The wood of the barn popped and hissed, while the thrumming tornado of wind and flame threatened to make her eardrums pop.

When she took a breath to call out for her husband and son, the funnel of heat seared her lungs and punched all of the air out of her. The world spun and her vision wavered. Still, she plowed forward.

She pictured Jason on the ground near Jax, passed out from smoke inhalation, George unconscious beside him. Choosing to save her son over her husband would be heart-wrenching, but she knew full well that it was what George would want. Tears stung her eyes as thick black smoke enveloped her like a soft blanket.

The flames were now too bright for her to make out anything. For all she could tell, the entire world was ablaze. Her legs stumbled and she almost fell to her knees. Each inhalation seared her insides.

"Jason! George!" she screamed against the overwhelming pyre of destruction.

Her skin felt as if it were being burned away by an acetylene torch. She could feel her eyebrows and eyelashes reduced to cinders.

As she finally made it through the wide-open double doors, the roof made a sound like a hundred lions bellowing in agony. The left side of the barn filled with flaming boards as the roof collapsed. She felt it all hit the ground, the impact reverberating from the soles of her bare feet to her chest.

It didn't deter her. If she died alongside Jason and George, so be it. Surviving them was unthinkable at this point. And to think, just ten minutes earlier they were all sound asleep, exhausted from a day's work but eager, always eager, to start again just before sunup.

Unable to keep her eyes open for more than an instant, Ellen hunched as low as she could. She stepped into the disintegrating barn. Her head smacked into something hard. Before she could wonder what she'd run into, her feet were swept off the ground. Her torso was in the grip of a heavy vise. What was happening?

It wasn't until she was a good fifty feet from the barn that she realized Jason had ahold of her. He set her down as gently as he could before falling onto his rump, wheezing and holding his chest. Ellen wiped the thick film of tears from her eyes, trying to focus on her suffering son. Both of them coughed too hard to speak.

A hand on her shoulder startled her. It was George. He had his shirt pulled up to his nose as he hacked away. He was on his knees and looked ready to pass out.

The sound of approaching sirens was all Ellen needed to lay down on the hardpacked earth and lay a hand across Jason's bucking chest.

"I . . . I couldn't sa . . . save . . . Jax," he sputtered.

Ellen lamented the loss of his horse. They'd gotten Jax for him on Jason's twenty-fourth birthday. He loved that horse to no end.

But truth be told, Ellen loved her family more. And she was grateful beyond measure that they were together now, even though they were all in a sorry and serious state.

Red-and-white lights strobed around them. George reached out to grab her hand. Weak as a calf, Ellen did her best to pull him to her.

Men and women suddenly surrounded them, asking questions Ellen couldn't quite comprehend. The pain hit her a moment later and she once again gasped for breath.

CHAPTER 2

The new kid wiped the sweat from his brow and studied the huge gas tank for a bit. Bryan Branch watched him from behind the plate glass window that separated the office from the shop. He'd shown him how to drain the tank of any last remnants of gasoline just two days before. Now he had to see if the lesson stuck.

"You want to sign the checks?" Lori Nicolo asked as she sidled up next to Bryan. She dropped the pile of checks on his battered and cluttered metal desk.

"In a second," Bryan said, his attention fixed on the young kid.

Lori peered out the window. "Don't you think someone should help him?"

"I showed him how to do it twice on Tuesday," he said to his office manager of the past five years as well as a fellow wounded veteran and so much more. She'd lost an eye in Afghanistan during a nighttime firefight against a band of mujahideen fanatics. It may have taken her out of the shit but it never slowed her down. She'd been to more countries and been involved in more covert scraps than she could count postmilitary.

The loss of an eye only added to her will to fight. To most people she was just sweet-but-firm Lori who kept an orderly, Christian home and volunteered at the local animal shelter when she wasn't organizing fundraisers at the local VFW hall. Originally from Wyoming, she'd settled in Pennsylvania when Bryan decided it was time to set down some roots.

Without her, the place would be chaos, if not out of business.

"Yeah, but that's serious," Lori said with a worried frown.

Bryan rubbed the stubble on his chin. "We all have to learn sometimes."

"But not at the expense of other people. Or a whole damn building."

When he saw which hammer and chisel the kid picked off the tool cart, Bryan knew she was right. He jumped from his chair and nearly kicked open the door to the shop. With his damaged knee barking, Bryan hustled as fast as he could.

"Don't!" he shouted.

The kid had the chisel tip against the bottom end of the tank and was about to strike it with the hammer. The instant he saw Bryan, he stopped in midswing.

"Did I do something wrong?" the kid asked.

Bryan swiped the tools from his hand. "Almost. Remember how I told you there were very specific tools for puncturing the gas tanks?"

For a moment, the kid pushed his blond bangs from his face and looked as blank as a sheet of paper. Then his eyes scrunched up and he exclaimed, "Yes! I need to use the ones with the red handles."

Bryan held the tools in his palms. "You see any red?"

The kid shook his head.

"Exactly. If you used these and they sparked, you'd blow down the whole damn place." He was trying to be a calm teacher, but his frustration was getting the better of him.

A tow truck pulled up outside the open shop doors. The window rolled down, emitting the sound of laughter. "He almost make this block go kaboom?"

Bryan looked over at his friend and rolled his eyes. "Yep. Tell me I should blame myself."

Shane Perretti hopped out of the truck, squaring his greasy ball cap on his head. "You should blame yourself. When I started working for you, I wasn't allowed to touch the gas tanks for a couple of weeks. And I was a grown man who had just served his country."

The kid was the son of one of Shane's neighbors. His parents were alcoholics who had basically left him on his own. Shane had asked Bryan to give him a shot for the summer. There was no way Bryan could say no, especially when he saw the deep wounds in the boy's eyes. He was sixteen and on the verge of going feral. For the first month, Bryan had him doing smaller things around the shop, picking up parts and cleaning up. Now that they were into August, he thought it was time to expand his duties and teach him some things. A little hard work, sweat, and discipline for a couple of months could change his path.

Granted, if they survived.

Bryan set the incorrect tools on a bench. "You got me there." Then, to the kid, who looked about ready to bolt, he said, "Grab those red-handled tools from over there and let me watch you do it. Sound okay?"

The kid nodded and got the correct hammer and chisel. Bryan and Shane watched him work, giving him pointers along the way. Soon it was done, crisis averted, and Bryan slipped the kid a ten-dollar bill and told him to get five sodas from the deli around the corner.

"One thing's for sure," Shane said. "He'll never forget the right way to do it again. Nearly killing yourself and everyone else has a way of doing that."

"For the sake of my heart, and my knee, I think I'll keep him in the sanding room for the rest of the day." Bryan rubbed his kneecap as they walked back into the cool office.

Lori looked up from her desk and asked Shane if he wanted a coffee.

"Bryan's getting us all soda," Shane said, settling into an office chair with cracked leather and foam padding poking out from various cracks.

"Sweet." She picked up the phone and started dialing. Seconds later, she was in deep conversation with one of their vendors, insisting they make good on their delivery promise or else. No one wanted to find out what Lori's *or else* could pertain to.

Bryan flipped some papers around his desk and handed one to Shane. "After your afternoon tea you think you could swing by Bing's Motors to pick up some things?"

Shane looked at the order form and stuffed it in his

jeans pocket. "My pleasure. Hopefully some cars start breaking down. I hate slow days."

Bryan had known Shane since his second tour in the Middle East. Shane Perretti was in his unit, a hotheaded half-Italian, half–Puerto Rican from the Bronx who seemed to have a sincere death wish. He volunteered for every dangerous assignment the CO could dream up and never flinched when the guano hit the fan. He loved the action so much, Bryan was sure he'd still be serving, toiling away in some backwater for Uncle Sam. His military career was cut short when he was run over by a ten-year-old boy who stole a military Humvee. After double hip replacements, the removal of his spleen, and the installation of a plate in his skull, he was permanently excused from combat.

At least official combat. Shane had saved Bryan's butt on more than one occasion during secret ops missions they'd undertaken in some of the world's most dangerous and godless countries. The money was good, the rewards even better, and it kept them sharp. Plus, as the saying went, if you did what you loved, you never truly worked a day in your life. Keeping Shane busy meant helping him channel his controlled chaos, courage, and unique skills to endeavors that did a lot of good in this world that 99.9 percent of the population would never know about.

He also loved driving the tow truck, especially when there were big wrecks. Bryan had long ago stopped trying to figure out his friend.

"If this heat keeps up, there'll be enough busted radiators to keep you busier than a one-armed wallpaper hanger," Bryan said. He looked into the shop, watching Whiskey, his first employee when he opened the truck radiator/tow shop, as he soaked a radiator in the stripper tank. Whiskey was a man of few words, and when he did speak with his thick Jamaican accent, Bryan barely understood a thing he said. Luckily, Lori was an excellent interpreter. Bryan knocked on the glass and Whiskey turned around. "Take fifteen. Cold soda's on its way."

Whiskey gave him a thumbs-up and set the radiator on a hook so it hung above the tank.

Shane picked up the newspaper from the growing pile beside Bryan's desk and started right in with his jawing about the wrongs of the world.

"Well, we're officially done as a country. Did you know that math is racist?"

Bryan was busy signing checks that Lori had put on his desk earlier. "I saw that article. I still don't understand how these social justice flunkies came up with that one."

"According to this, we only teach Western math, which is the math of the oppressive, designed to keep down people of color. What in the hell? As far as I remember, the concept of addition and subtraction is pretty straightforward. It's so agnostic, even Bible thumpers and devil worshippers agree on the black-and-white logic of it."

"Maybe that's it. The whole black-and-white logic."

For a moment, Shane stared at Bryan dumbfounded. Then the corner of Bryan's mouth twitched, and Shane tore the page out of the paper, crumpling it into a ball so he could toss it in the wastebasket across the room. He missed. "That's not even worth lining a cat box."

"Well, I read the paper earlier this morning and it doesn't get much better. Save yourself the aggravation."

Shane set his work boots on Bryan's desk and slapped the newspaper back on the pile. "Math is racist. Unbelievable. Getting to be where breathing is offensive. We made it too easy in this country. Idle time makes for mush brains. If these people really had to struggle to survive, you can bet they wouldn't come up with horse crap like this."

Bryan shook his head. "I do agree, things are a little too easy now. Everything folks want is at their fingertips. I think it all happened too fast. As a species, we're wired to fight and scrap our way through life. At least here, in this country, we live longer and exert ourselves less and less. I guess it only makes sense that some part of our DNA has to create a crisis, no matter how ill informed."

"Maybe we can create one of those Outward Bound camps where we bring a bunch of these wackos with us next time we go to Yemen. That'll shut them up."

"For sure. If they survive."

The phone rang and Lori picked up. A few seconds later, she called over to Bryan, "It's Charlotte. She sounds upset."

Bryan's wife was no shrinking violet. Just like him, Shane, and Lori, she had served with them in the 10th Mountain Division in Afghanistan. To say she had a pretty tough skin was an understatement. She was discharged a year before him. They made plans to get married as soon as he got back to the States. They had everything lined up and ready to go until Bryan took on a hail of shrapnel from an IED his buddy had triggered while clearing out a house of suspected rebels. The blast left Bryan with compromised hearing, scars from head to toe, and extensive surgery to save his leg and eventual knee replacement. Charlotte had flown from her home in Pennsylvania to be by his side in Germany, where he was treated at the Landstuhl Medical Center on a US air base. It took months to get him to walk again, longer to overcome the mental damage at seeing his friend reduced to pieces. Almost as soon as they touched down in Pennsylvania, he found himself walking down the aisle in St. Peter's Church, feeling like the luckiest man in the world, cane in hand and hearing aid in his right ear. Charlotte was the most beautiful woman he'd ever seen, an angel in white with a will as solid as Mount Everest. Everything he'd become since his wounding was because of her, and he would never forget that.

If she was upset, it was over something serious.

He grabbed the phone, hoping she was okay. "What's up?"

"I just got a call from your brother."

"Jason? Why did he call you?"

"He was looking for you. Babe, your mom passed away last night."

Bryan felt a tightening in his heart that went all the way to his gut. He hadn't seen his mother since he left for basic training, but the long gap didn't ease the sudden pain. It did just the opposite. Grief and guilt rocked him to his core.

"Did he say what happened?"

Charlotte sighed heavily. "He said he wanted to talk to you about it."

"Okay. I'll call him."

"I'm so sorry."

"Yeah. I'll call you back after I talk to Jason."

"Do better than that. Come home and call him."

She wanted to be his rock again. "I'll be there soon."

"I love you."

"Love you, too."

He gingerly set down the phone. Lori and Shane stared at him, waiting to hear what had happened.

"Everything okay?" Lori asked.

Bryan ran his fingers through his close-cropped hair and took a deep breath. "My mom passed."

"Dude, I'm so sorry," Shane said.

"I'm gonna head on home. I need to talk to my brother to get the details."

"Take all the time you need," Lori said, walking over to give him a hug. "We can mind the store."

"Thanks. I'll call you both later, clue you in."

"Don't worry about us. We've got your back," Shane said.

"That I never doubt."

CHAPTER 3

That afternoon, after speaking to his brother, Bryan jumped online and made flight, hotel, and car rental reservations. Charlotte left him to himself because she was a mind reader when it came to her husband and knew he needed his space.

The story Jason told had left him feverish. At one point, his cell phone case started to crack because he was squeezing it so hard. He'd always thought he would eventually return to his family home in Iowa, just not under these circumstances.

He and Charlotte had never had kids for a variety of safety reasons. It also made things easier when they had to drop what they were doing and leave. There were no side jobs lined up at the moment, or at least none that had appealed to Bryan and his team of veterans. The world was still a hot disaster, and it would remain so until they were ready for another fray.

Charlotte would do everything she could to be his shoulder to lean on during the next few days. Bryan wasn't one to show his emotions, but this rocked him to his core. He'd always thought there would be time to mend the broken Branch fences.

Now, it had been taken away.

It was time to go home and not only grieve his mother's passing but see if he could repair his relationship with his father and brother.

Lori could run the shop just fine without him. He texted her to let her know he would be away for a few days, and she sent him back a heart emoji. Emojis usually exasperated him, but this was an exception.

When all of the plans were completed he went to the bar in their finished basement and poured a healthy serving of Basil Hayden, skipping his usual two cubes of ice. Slumped in his soft leather chair, he fought hard not to knock back the entire glass in one gulp. He didn't bother turning on the television or radio. He wanted the silence so he could let his thoughts run free.

After the second glass his dark thoughts turned a lighter shade of gray, and he went upstairs to his wife. She was in their bedroom with their large suitcase open on the bed. She wore a formfitting tank top without a bra underneath and very short gym shorts. His heart quickened, as it always did when he saw his beautiful wife, even when he was two whiskeys in and feeling as down as he had in a long while.

"What time do we need to be out of the house?" she asked.

"Right around five."

"I packed your good suit. You want to grab your toiletry kit from the closet?"

Bryan stood in the doorway, immobile for the moment.

"How many days do you think we should pack for?"

Head bowed, he said, "Three, maybe four." The words stuck to his tongue. Another Basil Hayden would fix that, help him move closer to slurring, which was where he needed to be.

Charlotte bustled about the room, pulling items from drawers and the closet and packing them expertly. It was one of her many skills. She could cram a week's worth of clothes in a four-day suitcase and everything would come out without a wrinkle. He remembered how immaculate her rack was at base camp. Everyone asked her what her secret was and to show them how to replicate it.

When she was just about done she sat on the edge of the bed and asked, "You want to talk about it?"

Bryan took a ragged breath. "I'm not sure I should."

She patted the mattress next to her. "Well, I think you should. Sit. Tell me what happened."

The bed sagged when he sat. Charlotte put her hand on his thigh and leaned her head against his shoulder. "I can only begin to imagine how you feel, honey. I know you've been thinking of patching things up lately. And I know how much you're beating yourself up about that now."

Staring straight ahead, he said, "It's not just that."

She rubbed his leg. "Then what is it? I've never seen you like this before. What happened out there?"

Bile gurgled at the back of his throat. He choked it back, felt the muscles in his jaw working overtime.

"She was killed," he said, so softly she almost didn't hear him.

"Oh, Bryan." When he looked at her there were tears in her eyes. Tears for a woman she'd never even met. "What happened? Did they catch who did it?"

It took him a bit to compose himself enough to tell the story. "According to my brother, some men went to the farm in the dead of night and set fire to it. He and my parents rushed outside. Jason went to get his horse from the barn because it was on fire. The smoke got to him, and my father had to pull him out. There was a shooter, or shooters, on the farm. My mother had been returning fire, but she couldn't see who was shooting or what they were shooting at."

"She was shot?" Charlotte gripped his arm.

"No. I guess the stress of the moment was too much for her. Jason said she had a heart attack just as the first responders got to the farm. She stopped breathing. My brother watched the paramedics try to revive her there in the dirt, all while the fire raged around them. They say she died at the hospital, but Jason and my father were with her all the way. He said she never came back."

Charlotte wrapped her arms around him. "That poor woman. I'm so sorry."

While his wife sobbed, Bryan chastised himself for not shedding a tear.

Crying would have to come later.

"You're not as sorry as the SOBs who did this to my family are going to be."

Charlotte sniffled and kissed his cheek. "Stay right there."

She hustled out of the room, leaving him with his dark thoughts. He was so inside his own head, he didn't hear her return. Not having his hearing aid in his ear didn't help, either.

His wife stood beside him holding two glasses with at least three fingers' worth of whiskey. She was also as naked as the day she was born. She took a sip from her glass and handed the other to him. Bryan set it on the dresser and took her in his arms, burying his face between her warm soft breasts. He needed to lose himself for a while, and there was no better person to do that with than Charlotte.

She moaned when he grabbed her buttocks, fingers probing.

Bryan didn't remember taking off his clothes. They made wild love on the bed, on the floor, finishing on the sink in the master bath. Collapsing on the bed, sweaty and breathless, Bryan was spent.

Though the embers of anger and need for vengeance smoldered, they would surely be there to grab ahold of him when daylight came.

Their flight out of Philadelphia International was delayed by two hours. When they were finally allowed on the plane they were told by the captain over the intercom that because of bad weather ahead, they would have to sit for a bit on the tarmac. That bit was another two hours. Bryan was about ready to chew through a horseshoe.

"Why do I feel like they intentionally make flying the most miserable experience possible?" he grumbled to Charlotte.

"Kind of makes me miss hitching a ride on a cargo plane," she replied, smiling as she thumbed through a magazine.

"They're about as comfortable as riding a bucking bull, but at least they're on time."

Less than an hour later, they were off. Bryan ordered a Bloody Mary as soon as the flight attendant came around asking about drinks. Charlotte ordered one as well, and the second round made the flight and all the delays a little more bearable. When they landed at Des Moines International, there was yet another delay getting their rental car. Bryan wasn't a member of their club so he was low man on the totem pole.

He took the keys from the rental attendant with a barely concealed snarl and stormed off to the parking garage. When he saw a Nissan waiting for him, his mood darkened.

"At least they're good on gas," Charlotte said with a shrug as she loaded her bag in the trunk.

"Yeah, well, considering how much it costs nowadays, I guess you're right."

He hopped on I-80, exceeding the speed limit considerably. Charlotte hung onto the strap by her door.

"Maybe we should get there in one piece."

Bryan looked at her, then the speedometer, and let up on the gas. "Sorry. Just feels good to be free."

"I know. But let's not be free of our earthly bodies."

He rolled down the window and let his arm hang outside the door. Where they lived in Pennsylvania, clear fresh air was never in short supply. But it was a long time since he'd smelled Iowa air. It was redolent of fresh crops, soil, and sun.

"Is it weird that I'm anxious to get there yet still hope we blow a gasket or something and have to turn back home?"

Charlotte laughed. "I'm glad I'm not the only one feeling that way. It's never been weirder not having met your family than right now. I don't know what to expect. I have to admit, I'm a little nervous."

"I have zero idea of what to expect, so we're on even ground there. My brother is the size of a bear, but he's a softy deep down. My father, well, he's another story. He's about as hard as old shoe leather and can be as pleasant as a rhino. I'm not sure how things are going to go when we meet. Our trip may be cut short. For all I know, he'll throw me out the second he sees me."

The last time he'd seen his father, the old man had wished him the best as he headed off to boot camp while reminding him to make the most of his second chance, because he'd burned the first one to the ground.

Charlotte looked straight ahead at the road, deep in thought for a moment. "Death has a way of changing things. Of changing people."

Bryan grasped the steering wheel tight enough to whiten his knuckles, thinking, *She may be right. Guess we'll see if time has changed us for the better.*

Charlotte played with the satellite radio, bouncing from station to station until she settled on a hair metal channel. Bryan focused on the road, trying to keep his mind as clear as possible. They passed by a never-ending wall of cornfields. Most people would quickly become bored with the view, but for Bryan it was calling him home to the place where he'd spent the first nineteen years of his life.

The sign for Maverick had only one discernible bullet hole in it. "Looks like they upgraded," he said, smiling for the first time all day.

"What do you mean?"

"Me and Jason and our buddies shot the hell out of that sign one night when we'd had a little too much to drink. The new sign looks a little more respectable."

Charlotte shook her head. "You really were hooligans."

"I was chief hooligan. Jason tagged along every now and then, wanting to impress his big brother. Luckily he was smart enough not to follow in my footsteps."

He took the exit, navigating the sweeping ramp that went on for almost a mile. His heartbeat quickened. Bryan rolled down all the windows when he pulled up to the stop sign. It was hot and muggy, but he felt the need to not have anything separate him from his mission. If he was going to be home, he wanted to experience all of it.

It was another mile or so before the cornfields gave way to the town proper.

Bryan had pictured his return to Maverick many times

over the years, wondering how the town would look and
how he would feel.

His wildest imaginings couldn't have prepared him
for what was before him.

CHAPTER 4

"I thought you said Maverick was like Mayberry," Charlotte said, wide-eyed as she took in the grim tableau.

Bryan drove slowly down Broad Street, the main thoroughfare of the town. A car horn blasted behind him, and he stuck out his arm to wave the driver to go around. He couldn't believe his eyes.

Bryan thought he'd somehow taken the wrong exit and ended up in another state that was somewhere in the vicinity of *The Twilight Zone*. Storefront after storefront was shuttered closed, and in many of them, homeless people slept or sat amid piles of accumulated detritus. In one shadowy doorway, he spotted an entire family. He stopped to get a better look at them, wondering if they were someone he might have known.

Back when he was a teen, Maverick only had one homeless person, an itinerant they called Leather on account of his tanned face and weathered shoes. Leather walked all across Iowa, from what he'd tell them, stopping in town once a year for a week or so before moving on. Leather never asked for a thing, was quick with a smile and always happy to talk. Folks looked forward to Leather's return like they would the coming of spring, and on account of his amiability, he was fed quite well, though he never accepted offers for a new pair of shoes. "I got these broke in just the way I like 'em," he'd say. To repay folks for their kindness, Leather had worked on most of the farms at one point or another and helped out in the various shops. He'd spent two days on the Branch farm one year, planting corn and telling stories. Bryan and Jason hung on his every word, entranced by the man who lived by his own rules and experienced everything life had to throw at him with a smile and a thank-you on his lips.

Bryan wondered if Leather was somehow still alive and part of the mix of homeless who dotted every street. If he was, he'd have to be at least eighty by now. Bryan knew damn sure the sight of Maverick would wipe that permanent smile from Leather's face.

The father of the family of four—if he was the father—jumped to his feet and said, "Can you spare a few dollars? My family could use a meal." He looked to be Mexican or from somewhere in Central or South America, but his English was near-perfect. He gestured toward his family, which consisted of a sad-looking woman and a young boy and girl.

Bryan stopped the car, pulled out his wallet, and fished out a twenty-dollar bill. "Have you gone over to St. Matthew's Church? I remember they used to have a pretty good food pantry." He wished he had more cash on him. With the state of the economy and rocketing food prices, he wasn't sure how far twenty would take them, unless a McDonald's had opened up since he left, and even then, they'd need to stick to the value menu.

The man took the twenty and bowed. "God bless you. You don't know how much this means. There is very little food in the pantry. Most days it is empty. Father Rooney, he tries, but . . ."

He let the rest hang in the air. So, Father Rooney was still in the parish. When Bryan was an altar boy, the Irish priest with the booming voice had been his favorite. When he'd strayed miles from his altar boy days, it was Father Rooney who had tried hard to intervene and help him get his life back on track.

"I get it," Bryan said. "I'll come back around tomorrow, see what I can do. Will you be here?"

"Yes. We sleep in the lot behind the building. Thank you so much."

Bryan made a note to check out the lot. It used to be a parking lot for the nearby stores, but he could see tall grass growing and makeshift shelters made out of plywood, tin, and even car doors. There was a time Bryan and his friends would play Wiffle ball in that lot when there weren't many cars around. The best thing about a Wiffle ball was that it was so light, it wouldn't bust a window no matter how hard they hit it.

"What's your name?"

"David."

He stuck out his hand. "I'm Bryan. Nice to meet you." They shook, David staring at their joined hands as if he were witnessing a miracle.

The man ran back to his family and Bryan drove on.

"That just breaks my heart," Charlotte said. "If I had any cash, I would have given it all."

"I had to do something to make sure what I was seeing was real. Babe, this isn't Maverick. It's like driving down skid row in L.A. What the hell is going on?"

"I don't know, but it looks like Mayberry never existed here."

They passed the old playground, which was now piles of rusted swings and seesaws, the benches filled with people who appeared to be stoned or looking for a fix. No mother in her right mind would bring a child within a thousand feet of what was once his favorite place to be with his brother and their friends.

Most of the stores of his youth were gone, but the pharmacy was still there, as was the dry cleaner. The toy store had been replaced by a pawn shop, which seemed downright wrong. The Maverick Diner was now a dollar store that, at a quick glance in the windows, was overcharging its customers.

Almost nothing and no one looked familiar. How could so much have changed?

He was happy to shoot past the town and turn right onto the road that would take him four miles out to his family home. Neither of them spoke as they processed the travesty that Maverick had become and wondered how the fast approaching reunion would proceed. The only bright spot were the flags hung out at most of the homes they passed. Many looked worse for wear, but at least American pride wasn't dead in Maverick.

When Bryan braked in front of the house, a plume of dust washed over the car, obscuring the view of the house and blackened barn beyond it. Charlotte covered her mouth as she coughed. Bryan waited for the dust to settle and took deep steady breaths. High rows of corn rattled as a warm breeze drifted over the farm. At just under four hundred acres, it was on the small side for the average Iowa farm but just big enough for his family to manage, with seasonal help, and pay the bills.

The Branch family had raised feed corn on this plot of land for four generations now. Unlike the sweet corn, mostly grown in Florida, that filled grocery store shelves, feed corn was produced to provide animal feed and ethanol. The land had been good to them most years, but small family farms like theirs were being consumed by conglomerates by the fistful. Bryan hadn't anticipated the choke of pride and nostalgia that tightened his chest at the sight of the farm.

His brother and father were nowhere to be seen. It was going on four o'clock. They should be done for the day, especially with the rising heat.

The air still smelled like smoke. The barn was nothing but a pile of blackened beams and ash. Bryan and Jason used to work hard and play harder in and around that barn when they were kids. The barn, like those memories, was just a thing of the past now.

Beside it, corn rows had been burned to the ground, leaving a black smudge on otherwise orderly and pristine farmland. Jason had told him on the phone that the crop damage was limited to just a quarter of an acre.

"Wow, this place is massive," Charlotte said.

"Believe it or not, it's far from it."

"Does your father raise any animals?"

Bryan thrummed the steering wheel. "We always had chickens. My mother would sell the eggs at the farmers market on the weekends. Sometimes we'd sell the chickens, too. We had some pigs that we raised for ourselves. One of those sows could feed us for months. There might still be some dairy cows and goats. My parents made sure there was just enough to keep us self-sufficient in case things went bad."

"You going to teach me how to milk a cow?"

Bryan's gaze roamed over the farmhouse and the fields, but what he saw were visions of the past. His mother standing on the porch calling him and Jason in for supper. Working beside her in the smelly chicken coop, collecting eggs that were carefully placed in baskets lined with straw. Seeing the grief-stricken look on her face the first time he was brought home in the back seat of a squad car.

"You okay?" Charlotte asked.

"Nope. But since that's not going to change any time soon, we might as well rip off the Band-Aid."

They got out of the car and walked up the creaking wooden steps to the front door. Bryan noticed plywood installed in several windows.

He'd left all those years ago without a key to the house. He'd have to knock and wait, just like any stranger. Charlotte slipped her hand in his as he knocked.

For a breath or two, there was nothing. Then he heard heavy footsteps approaching.

"Has to be Bigfoot," he said under his breath.

"Who?"

The door swung open and there was his brother filling

the opening. He'd put on a little weight, most of it seemingly muscle, and added a couple of inches since Bryan had last seen him. Jason still had a baby face that hadn't figured out how to properly grow facial hair. He was dressed in dirt-stained dungarees and a black T-shirt.

"Hey Bryan." Jason held onto the doorknob, not bothering to open the screen door.

"Hey Jason."

They looked each other up and down for a bit.

"Nice hairline," Jason said. Bryan's had receded a touch over the past couple of years. He'd opted for a close-cut mohawk to hide the fact.

"You know, ice cream isn't meant to be eaten at every meal," Bryan quipped back. As they stared at each other, Charlotte squeezed Bryan's hand hard enough to make his knuckles crack. "You want to let us in?"

A tiny smile played on Jason's lips. "Yeah."

He pushed open the screen door and stepped aside so they could enter. Bryan took a quick sweep of the living room to his left and the dining room to his right, with the stairs and hallway leading to the kitchen in back smack in the center. After all of the changes he'd witnessed in town he was relieved that time had stood still in the Branch house.

"Jason, this is my wife, Charlotte."

His brother took Charlotte in for the first time and was visibly flabbergasted. "Nice to meet you. Wow. Talk about a guy playing way above his league. If you're a captive, just blink twice."

"I don't think I've met the man yet who could hold me captive. Alive, at least."

Jason crouched down and pulled Charlotte into a bear hug. "It's nice to finally meet you."

"Same here," she managed to croak.

The brothers locked eyes again, and this time they embraced, hitting each other hard on the back. In the past, all of the fighting and bitter disappointment had been between Bryan and his parents. He knew Jason had looked up to him. It was a shame that he had to be caught between it all and, in the end, make the choice to stay with their parents, which meant severing the bond they'd had.

They had stayed in touch, just barely, with a brief but amicable call right around Christmas.

Now, reunited after almost two decades, it was as if no time had passed, except Bryan wasn't carrying all the baggage of his troubles on his back.

"I never thought I'd say this, but it's good to see you, Bigfoot."

Jason looked down at Bryan's leg. "Better that than Gimpy."

"I'm lucky I'm able to walk at all."

Jason shook his head. "Remember, there's no such thing as sympathy points. A gimp is a gimp."

Bryan laughed. "Fine. I can still kick your ass with my bad leg."

"Keep telling yourself that." Jason turned to Charlotte. "You want something to drink? I have beer, wine, water, soda, harder stuff, you name it. Come on over and have a seat."

"It's good to stand," Charlotte replied, stretching her

arms above her head. "We did way too much sitting getting here."

"Beer for me," Bryan said. "And since when do you have wine in the house?" No one in the Branch family was a fan of the fruit of the vine. Even their mother drank whiskey neat when she wanted to sit back and relax, which wasn't often.

Jason clomped down the hallway to the kitchen. "Since I knew we had a lady of sophistication with poor taste in men arriving."

"A glass of wine is fine," Charlotte called after him.

"Okey dokey."

Bryan and Charlotte perused the living room. He was shocked to see his high school graduation photo still on the mantel, along with the family picture they had taken at Sears on a very hot Sunday afternoon right after church the day Bryan had made his first Communion. He'd always assumed once he was out of sight, as far as his parents were concerned, he was out of mind. It stung to be so wrong.

The seat of his father's ratty La-Z-Boy chair had sunk a little deeper since he'd last seen it, and had gained a few new stains. His mother's matching recliner still looked practically new. A couple of used paperback mysteries, their spines cracked and corners missing from the covers, were on the table by her chair, along with her readers and a box of tissues.

Good God, I've missed so much, he thought. *What was I thinking?*

Jason came back with drinks and handed them out.

They were about to toast when a voice behind them said, "Bryan?"

George Branch was freshly showered and shaved and in his Sunday best, which was a clean pair of dark blue jeans and a white button-up shirt with one of the two ties he owned. The lines in his face were deeper, his skin bronzed from the sun. When he fiddled with his tie Bryan saw how arthritis had swollen his knuckles. He may have been older, a little more stooped, but he was still a formidable man. His body was forged by years of toiling in the fields.

Father and son stood on either side of the room, neither of them knowing what to say next or what to expect once those words finally came out. Jason edged closer to Charlotte, as if to keep them both out of the way of an oncoming collision.

Bryan's father cleared his throat, then said, "I wasn't sure you'd come."

"There's no way I wouldn't have." Bryan's entire body tensed. "I just wish . . . well, that I'd come a hell of a lot sooner."

Silence enveloped the room again. No one moved. The grandfather clock in the hallway ticked on.

Finally, his father said, "Well, I guess there's a lot both of us wish we'd done different." He paused and looked at the floor. After a deep breath he looked Jason in the eye and said, "What's done is done."

"Yeah. I guess it is."

"You look a lot different. Seems the army was the right choice."

"It sure was. Though there are parts I wish I could change."

His father took three steps and extended his hand. "We all wish that. Welcome home, Son."

"I'm sorry, Dad."

"I think it's safe to say we're all sorry. Sorry for being so hardheaded. It's not one of the best Branch traits. I only wish," there was a catch in his voice, "that your mother was here."

The instant they shook hands, the atmosphere in the house immediately changed. Jason and Charlotte's shoulders slumped a bit as they exhaled. George's bright eyes set upon Charlotte.

"This my daughter-in-law?"

"Sure is. Dad, meet Charlotte."

His smile went a mile wide. "Well, you're just the breath of fresh air we've needed. It's mighty fine to meet you."

CHAPTER 5

Dinner consisted of a smorgasbord of delicious dishes that neighbors had been dropping off the past few days. They filled up on lasagna, chicken pot pie, fresh green beans sautéed in garlic and oil with sesame seeds, a tuna casserole, and fried chicken. Dessert consisted of homemade blueberry pie with whipped cream and chocolate pudding. A bottle of whiskey was placed in the center of the table, making the rounds until it was empty and Jason had to get another.

Bryan was shocked at how well things had gone. The old hurts were still there, but there was no sense in bringing them up now . . . or maybe ever. His father was a tough nut to crack. If there was still any beef between them, he wouldn't have hesitated to bring it forth as directly as possible.

Most of the early talk was about Bryan's mother. No one went too deep into the night she died. Despite the somber undertones of the day, Bryan couldn't keep himself from laughing out loud, along with his father, when Jason regaled Charlotte with the story of the day their mother had caught them playing cards with pictures of naked ladies on them out by the doghouse that was no longer there. Bryan had found them in the alley beside the market. He was twelve and Jason was nine, and they got one hell of an education that day.

They also got one hell of a whupping when their mother grabbed the cards and found the nearest stick to tan their hides. Except that time they ran into the cornfield, ignoring her command for them to stop. She'd silently waited them out, even making their favorite dinner, spaghetti with meatballs, letting the aroma pull them from their hiding places. When they saw her sitting out back, they resigned themselves to their fate.

"As soon as she wacked Bryan, the stick broke and caught me right in my cheek," Jason said. "Bryan thought it was funny, so you know what my mother did?"

"No, what?" Charlotte asked as she sipped her whiskey.

Jason had to pause to get out his laughter. "She . . . she clobbered him with those meatballs! Every single one of them ended up in his hair."

"I smelled like an Italian restaurant for days," Bryan said. "Our shampoo didn't stand a chance against it. Let me tell you, a meatball thrown at you from close range is both unpleasant and kind of hysterical."

"When it was over all three of us were bent over laughing," Jason said.

"I watched it from the kitchen window. I thought you had all lost your minds," George said.

Bryan and Jason cleared the table and they retired to the living room. The windows were open, the white lace curtains billowing from the soft evening breeze. The sun was just starting to dip over the horizon. The acrid smell of woodsmoke filled the room, a stark reminder of the horror that had visited their home days earlier.

"Will the wake be at Hodder's?" Bryan asked.

"It's the only one left in town," Jason replied. He stood by the mantel nursing a can of beer. "We're just doing a one-day viewing. Not enough of the old guard left to merit any more than that."

"Is there anything that still needs to be done that Charlotte and I can help with?"

Their father's gaze turned inward, and a sheen filtered over his eyes. "Your mother, God bless her heart, prepared everything for both of us when the day came. Always the planner. Except I was supposed to go first."

Bryan recalled the last time he'd seen his mother face-to-face. It was right here in this room. He'd had his bags packed to head off to basic training. She'd said, "I hope the army can do what your father and I can't." And that was that. She'd briefly, softly put her hand on his shoulder, then turned and gone upstairs to her room. At the time, Bryan had thought it was a cold send-off from a woman who only saw him as her biggest disappointment.

Now, standing in almost the same spot, he realized how much it must have hurt her to see him go. What a blind fool he'd been. He thought he'd done them all a favor by keeping away. Lord knew he was no Boy Scout. You couldn't remove the wild streak from some men, like Bryan, but it could be harnessed for good. No matter what he'd done, he never felt that he'd fully atoned for his past sins, that he'd never measure up. If only he could turn back time.

Feeling himself starting to choke up, he said, "Did either of you see the men who set the fire?"

Jason wiped a tear from the corner of his eye. "I was busy trying to save Jax, but I thought I saw a couple of men. Shadows, really. It was dark, and the fire and smoke only made it harder to see. And then I was just about passed out from the smoke."

Their father just shook his head as he stared into his whiskey glass.

"Cops have any leads?"

"The cops? It's not much of a priority for them. More than half the department is gone thanks to all the budget cuts and the veterans retiring early because the system has been rigged against them. You've seen what downtown has become. They let people commit crimes right there in broad daylight. A little arson isn't worth their time."

"Yes, but your mother," Charlotte said.

"As far as the cops are concerned, the arsonists didn't kill her. At least not directly, so it's not a murder." Jason took a sip of beer and snorted in disgust.

Bryan paced the living room. "Do you have any idea who it could have been? Something like this seems pretty deliberate."

"I know exactly who did it," George said. "Trouble is, I don't know where the hell they've hidden off to."

Bryan spun on his heel and looked down at his father. "Why is this the first I'm hearing this?" He cast an accusatory look Jason's way. "Who are they, Dad?"

His father polished off his whiskey. "Drifters. Probably illegals. You know how we hire day laborers during planting and harvest season."

Bryan was well aware. They were usually Mexicans making the rounds at all of the farms, and sometimes you'd get a man like old Leather.

Jason chimed in when their father lapsed into silence. "There were six of them. They came to the farm looking for work. Maybe Mexican, or a mix of South American. Hell if I know. When I told them we couldn't afford to hire on any help, things got kind of strange."

"Strange?" Bryan said. "Strange how?"

"They started talking to one another real quiet. In Spanish. I couldn't understand what they said, but I really didn't like the way they looked at me while they spoke. All of them stared right at me while they chattered away. Not a one of them came up to my chest, but I felt like they were challenging me. When I told them to get the hell off my property, they laughed. Before I could say anything else, they just walked away, still laughing."

Charlotte hugged herself. "That is strange."

"When did this happen?" Bryan asked.

"About a week before the fire. Trust me, I know it's them. Who else would do something like this? A fire I can see some kids or junkies accidentally starting. But shooting up the place, too? No, that feels too much like a message to me."

Bryan felt his blood rushing through his veins. He wanted those men here, in this very room. "What's the message?"

"'Go to the devil, Americans,'" their father said with steel in his voice.

"You think you'd know them if you saw them again?" Bryan asked.

Jason nodded.

"Like I said, they're long gone," George said. "Like cockroaches."

Bryan said, "You forget, Dad. Roaches come back when the lights go off."

As his mind churned, Bryan realized he was going to have to call Lori to let her know his stay was going to be extended. This was now more than just a return home to see his mother laid to rest.

Bryan wouldn't be happy until he found the men who did this to his family. And if the police wouldn't help, he had no reservations taking matters into his own hands.

He also wasn't going to leave and stay in a hotel miles away. What if they came back to finish what they started? Bryan pulled out his phone and canceled his reservation.

"Hope you don't mind putting us up?" he asked his father and brother. "I'd rather be here than the Holiday Inn."

"Fresh sheets on the bed in your old room," Jason replied.

Bryan was tired and his head a little fuzzy from the whiskey, but he knew damn well he wasn't going to get much sleep tonight.

CHAPTER 6

George and Jason were right; there weren't many people left to see the Branch matriarch off to her final resting place. Bryan remembered funerals from his youth, Hodder's Funeral Home having to utilize both viewing rooms to accommodate the crowds for one wake. Back then, everyone in Maverick turned out when someone was in need, or a member of their community had passed. The procession of cars to the cemetery would require a police escort.

The first viewing had just a dozen or so friends and old neighbors come in, almost all of them looking worse for wear. Jason had to remind Bryan who a few of them were, taking great pleasure in introducing him as Bryan the Exiled. Recognition would flash on their faces, then consternation, at least until Bryan introduced Charlotte. He assumed they thought any man who could land such a sweet and personable woman had to have something good about him.

If only they knew her own past. It was part of what had drawn them together.

They ate at Mannion's between viewings. It was just

the four of them. The old restaurant, which specialized in excellent meat and potatoes, was practically empty. The waiter spotted their father and remarked how he hadn't seen him in a dog's age. When he heard of their mother's passing, he offered his condolences and gave them a bottle of wine on the house.

Bryan was surprised that the food was still as good as ever. "How come the place is empty?"

"Wait'll you see the bill," his father said between spoonfuls of creamed spinach. "Mannion is getting hit with rising costs for food and overhead. Folks around here can't afford to eat out anymore. Sad to say, but this will be gone by next year, if not sooner."

Mannion's was where everyone went to celebrate special events. Or somber ones, like this.

"Looks like nowhere is safe from the nonsense going on in this country," Bryan remarked.

"Maverick is a high-water mark," Jason said as he placed his linen napkin on the table. "If we're drowning, everyone's drowning."

The bill was a shock. The total looked like something you'd expect in a New York restaurant, not out here. The waiter saw Bryan's reaction and his face turned apologetic.

George took the bill from him.

"I've got this, Dad."

"No, sir. Your mother will come back and haunt me if I let you foot the bill."

The second viewing saw more people as they were freed up from their chores on the farms. Father Rooney came in to give a final blessing and lead them all in prayer. He seemed shorter, had definitely lost a good amount of weight, and his still wavy hair was pure white. As he was leaving, he pulled Bryan aside and said, "Good to have you back home, Son. You planning to stick around a while?"

"We'll see how it goes. Going to take it as it comes."

The priest looked down at his leg. "Heard you got wounded over there in that sandpile."

"I took my licks. But I gave them, too."

Father Rooney patted his shoulder hard enough to dislocate it. "I'm so sorry about your mother. But I have to confess, I'm happy to see how you've turned out."

The weather was perfect the next day and the sun seemed to shine directly on his mother's casket as they dropped roses on it to pay their final respects. The Branch men shed silent tears as Father Rooney conducted the service.

Ever since he'd gotten the phone call about his mother's passing, Bryan had wavered between sorrow, loss, and anger, sometimes, impossibly, feeling all three at once. Now, here before his mother's final resting place, knowing he'd never see or hear from her again, what he felt most was regret. All those years, wasted.

"I'm sorry, Mom," he said, so softly only his wife could hear.

Charlotte held onto Bryan's arm and tried to be stoic. She'd told Bryan before they'd left the house that she didn't want people wondering why a total stranger to the woman was blubbering at her gravesite. Bryan and Charlotte were unfortunate pros at funerals. Not all their friends made it back home, and even those that did weren't long for this world thanks to their wounds—some physical, some mental, most both.

"You still want to help me?" Jason asked after the casket was lowered and they'd said their goodbyes to those who had attended the gravesite vigil.

"Yeah. Come on."

They raced back to the farm ahead of everyone else. Jason led the way to the burned barn, carrying two shovels. They'd found the remains of his horse, Jax. All that was left were charred bones.

Together, they dug a hole behind the barn. When they made it a few feet deep, they picked up the bones and placed them in the blanket that Jason would cinch over Jax's back on cold nights. Reverently, they lowered the blanket of bones into the grave.

"Jax was one hell of a horse," Jason said. He had tears in his eyes that refused to fall.

"We'll find the ones who did this," Bryan said, wiping the sweat from his brow with his tie.

"I don't see how that'll even be possible." Jason tossed a shovelful of dirt on the blanket.

"In my life, I've found that everything is possible. It all depends on how deep you want to dig."

They buried Jax's remains in silence.

"One more thing," Jason said. He rummaged through the rubble and retrieved a burlap bag. He reached inside and pulled out the tattered and burned remains of the American flag their father always flew on the flag-pole next to the barn. It was a huge flag that could be seen way out on the road running parallel to the fields. George Branch had served in the marines for six years and was damn proud of it. One of their chores growing up was raising the flag at sunrise and lowering it to take it inside at sunset.

Now, it was reduced to a ragged patch with a few burned stripes and far less than the fifty stars.

"If you want, you can bring it to the VFW so they can dispose of it," Jason said.

Bryan held what was left of the flag and felt his insides boiling. "We need to keep this. And we need to get the flagpole back up. Not just to remind us, but to remind everyone that we'll never back down to the people who hate us."

Jason rested a meaty paw on Bryan's shoulder and gave it a squeeze. "Dad'll like that. Mom would have, too."

Bryan folded it as best he could and slipped it back in the bag.

When they were done they saw a line of cars parked along the road leading to the house.

"I miss Mom," Jason said, leaning on the handle of his shovel.

"I've missed her for more years than I can count." All Bryan felt at the moment was rage. He wanted to tell his little brother everything about his life post-service but decided this wasn't the time.

He would avenge their mother. Of that there was no doubt. For now, all he could do was put his hand over Jason's shoulders, take the shovels, and walk him back to the house. There was a time and place for everything.

* * *

The reception back at the house was a crowded affair. Once again they were inundated with home-cooked meals. Bryan had a hard time remembering everyone. How had they gotten so old? Most of his time was spent introducing Charlotte and giving a surface account of what he'd been up to since he'd left town to join the army. Naturally, he left out anything that would raise an eyebrow.

At one point Bryan excused himself from Charlotte's side and grabbed Jason along with a couple of beers and went out behind the house.

"When's the last time you heard from the police?" he asked his brother, taking a long sip from his beer.

Jason loosened his tie and sat on the picnic bench. "The night of the fire."

"Are you kidding me?"

"Nope. I've been meaning to reach out to them, but things have been kind of crazy, what with the chores and arranging the funeral."

"Anyone we know on the force?"

"You remember Aaron Chisolm?"

"Wasn't he in your class? Dorky kid with glasses and braces?"

"That would be him. He wears contacts now and his teeth are straight as a new picket fence. He's a solid guy, but he's overwhelmed. The governor defunded the police without actually using those words. Budget cuts outside of the bigger cities laid waste to a ton of police precincts."

"Who's the governor now?"

Jason's face broke into a cross between a grin and a grimace. "Benedict Arnold? She's a real piece of work. She's got more nicknames than we have corn. Wolf in sheep's clothing describes her best. She ran as a Republican, then switched to a Democrat six months into her term, but is really a progressive with an agenda that seems to be hell bent on the total destruction of the state and everything Iowa has stood for. Talk about buyer's remorse. We have to wait two more years to send her packing, but I'm worried that she'll be reelected."

"What's her name?"

"Alexa Bennington. Easy on the eyes, harder to digest than Mom's meat loaf."

Bryan patted his stomach, warmed by the memories of his mother's meat loaf and how he and Jason used to stuff bits in their pockets to feed to the pigs. "Now that's saying something."

"Yeah. I really don't give a damn about politics, but I've been paying more attention because I see now how bad policies can wreak havoc on a place like Maverick. It almost feels like they're intentionally ruining it."

Bryan stared off into the cornfield, his gaze flicking on the pile of blackened timber that was the barn.

"Let's go pay Aaron a visit." Bryan chugged his beer and put it down on the picnic table with a heavy thunk.

"Now? We've got all those people."

"They're mostly here to see Dad. Come on. Waiting for the right moment is for slackers."

"But Bryan . . ."

Bryan walked inside and found Charlotte. "Jason and I are going to head on over to the police station."

She looked deep into his eyes, trying to ferret out his reason for leaving in the middle of the reception. "Go. I'll take care of everything here." He kissed her, loving that he rarely if ever needed to explain himself to her.

Jason trailed after him. Their father was surrounded by people. They were laughing and smiling, recounting better times. He didn't even notice them leaving.

"You drive," Bryan said.

"Why? You don't want to be seen in your little foreign rental?"

"Exactly."

Jason's RAM truck roared to life. It was so big, a step needed to be installed so passengers that weren't the size of Bigfoot could climb aboard. Bryan wasn't quite as hulking as his brother, but he wasn't in need of assistance, either.

"This way I can also take my time looking around," Bryan said above the deep bass thrum of the engine and the souped-up exhaust.

"It sure won't be a tour of the Riviera."

Jason opened all of the windows and mashed the accelerator. Their ties flapped in the wind, at least until they took them off, tossing them in the back seat.

Downtown Maverick looked just as forlorn and depressing as it had when Bryan had first rolled in. In fact, it seemed as if there were even more homeless people begging for change or sleeping among the piles of their throwaway possessions.

"Make a pit stop at the bank," Bryan said.

"You're the boss."

Bryan hopped out and made a withdrawal from the ATM. "We need to go over by the old Wiffle ball lot."

Jason arched an eyebrow. "That place is a homeless camp now."

"I know."

Bryan looked for David and his family, wondering if they were out and about, begging for spare change. When he didn't see them, he rapped his knuckles on the truck door and asked Jason to stop.

"Why are we here, man?" Jason asked.

"I have someone I need to meet."

"I better come with you," Jason said. "You might need backup, you know, with that gimpy leg and all."

"Just stay here. I don't want people running away because they think a Sasquatch is in town."

Bryan walked back to the lot and saw a few tents but mostly poorly constructed shelters filling almost every square inch. The place reeked of human waste and weed smoke. He got a lot of leery looks as he walked through the illegal camp.

An old woman sat on a car seat, knitting. She could have been someone's grandmother making a baby blanket for the newest addition to the family.

"Excuse me, do you know where a man named David and his family would be?"

She eyed him suspiciously. "*Policia?*"

"No, ma'am."

She took her time measuring him from head to toe. In heavily accented English, she said, "Over there. The one with the blue tarp."

"Thank you." He offered her a fifty-dollar bill, which she flatly refused, telling him in Spanish that she wasn't his charity case.

You should be someone's, he thought. *This is no place to spend your golden years.*

Before he could knock on the corrugated tin door to David's shelter, the man opened it wide. It took him a moment to register who Bryan was.

"Hello, David."

"Hi, Mr. Bryan. I didn't expect to see you again."

"Well, you'll learn I always keep my promises." Bryan handed David a wad of twenty-dollar bills.

David shook his head. "No, I can't accept that. It's too much."

"Actually, it's not enough. It was all I could get from the ATM just now. My brother and I have an errand to run. Should only take half an hour or so. I want you and your family to meet me out front. We'll take you to a hotel and put you up for a few nights."

David's eyes shimmered with tears. "This is crazy. Why would you do so much for us?"

"Because someone helped me when I needed it most. And it looks like you and your family could use a little streak of good luck."

David made the sign of the cross and called to his family to come out. He spoke to them in rapid Spanish. All of their eyes lit up. Then came an avalanche of thank-yous.

"Just get what you need and, like I said, we'll be back before you know it."

"God bless you." David put his arms around his family. Bryan looked around and realized they had attracted a lot of attention. Some of it unwanted, judging by the curious and wolfish stares.

"Better yet, come with me now."

"Now?"

Bryan eyeballed a particularly surly trio of men who he knew would pounce on David the moment he left.

It only took a couple of minutes for the family to get their stuff together. There wasn't much to gather.

"Okay, what now?" Jason asked when he saw the procession. Bryan helped them load their things in the truck's flatbed and opened the back door for them to climb in.

"Just doing the right thing."

During the short drive to the police station Jason said, "What do we do with them when we're in the station?"

"Put them on a bus to Albuquerque. Your precious truck will be fine. Is the Country Inn still open?"

"It's a Best Western now."

"That'll do."

"I take it that's another stop."

"You were always the intuitive one."

CHAPTER 7

Aaron Chisolm wasn't on duty. Bryan and Jason were sent to the desk of Detective Meyer, an obvious transplant from somewhere around New York judging by his accent. He was in plainclothes with slicked-back salt-and-pepper hair. The detective chewed gum loudly with his mouth open.

Bryan knew right away they weren't going to get anywhere with this guy.

The big room was empty, most of the desks having been emptied out. Jason hadn't been exaggerating. The budget cuts were loud and clear as a foghorn.

As they sat down, Jason said, "I'm Jason Branch. You don't look familiar. Are you new here?"

Meyer settled himself into a squeaky chair. "Kinda. Got here about six months ago. I thought I was going to get a quieter life. Man, was I wrong."

Alarm bells went off in Bryan's head. The man was probably exiled here from some big city precinct out East. That likely meant Internal Affairs had offered him a deal: scram or face the consequences.

Bryan was all too familiar with that kind of ultimatum. Except in his case he was young and had time ahead of him to get his head straight.

He and Meyer were not the same.

Jason nudged Bryan's knee, as if to say he was thinking the same thing. "This is my brother, Bryan. Our barn and a portion of our crops were set on fire and the house vandalized."

Meyer paused his aggressive chewing. "I heard all about it. I was out of town when it happened. I'm sorry about your mother."

"Not as sorry as we are," Bryan said as he leaned his forearm on the detective's desk. "I assume this means you're not the person assigned to the case."

Meyer leaned back in his chair as if to establish his personal space zone, which Bryan had breached. "I am not. Detective O'Bannon is investigating what happened."

"The reason we're here," Jason said, "is to get an update on the investigation. I also wanted to see if we could talk a little more about the migrant workers who came to the farm over a week ago. They should be your prime suspects. Maybe someone could come down and do some sketches to help find them."

"They all look alike," Meyer said, popping another stick of gum in his mouth. "I don't see how a sketch would make a difference."

Jason's face reddened. "Trust me, they did not look alike. There were distinctive differences, especially with the one who spoke to me. He had a very low hairline that almost came to his eyebrows. And a scar across his nose."

"Uh-huh."

After an uncomfortable silence Bryan asked, "Do you think you could check the files, maybe give us an update?"

Meyer only moved his jaw. "No need to check anything. Small department, and we all talk. So far, we've got nothing. Since they let the border crumble, we get immigrants shipped up here on the regular. Some stay for a few months but most eventually move on. I know they sure as heck aren't going into Canada. Those Canucks seem nice on the outside, but they'd put them all in a hole twelve feet deep before they let them ruin the place."

Bryan's patience wore thin. Talking to a potentially crooked or at least tarnished cop who was clearly lazy and racist was a recipe for disaster. He stood up before he exploded.

"You think you could ask Detective O'Bannon to call me when he gets a chance?" Bryan handed him his business card. Meyer studied it for a moment.

"You heading back to Pennsylvania?"

"Not while I have unfinished business." Jason got up from his chair. Meyer craned his neck as far as it would go. The brothers leaned over the desk, looking down at him. It was an intimidation move they'd perfected back in high school. "Also, please let Officer Aaron Chisolm know to call us. He's an old friend. It would be nice to catch up."

Meyer tipped back his chair, his eyes wide, furiously

gnawing on his gum. "Sure. No problem. Again, I'm sorry about your mom."

"Don't be sorry," Bryan said. "We just need you to find the men who put her in the ground."

Bryan and Jason stormed out of the precinct.

"That was a waste of time," Jason said.

"You never know. Meyer looked scared of us, which is good. Maybe it'll light a fire under his keister."

"Maybe. Or maybe he won't tell O'Bannon or Aaron that we were there."

Bryan grinned. "That's not a problem. Because we'll be back. The squeaky wheel gets the grease."

After their frustration with the police they took David and his family to the Best Western, on the edge of town by the highway. Bryan checked them in for three nights and paid. He told them he'd swing by on checkout day to see what they could do from there. The wife hugged him until his back cracked. The children were too taken in with the clean hotel to speak.

Back on the road home, Jason said, "What are you gonna do with them? You can't adopt a whole family."

"I'll think of something. Can you take me down Broad again?"

"You know everything's closed up by now. And what's up and about is nothing you want to see.

"Exactly. I want to see how much worse things are at night now."

"We should really get back to the house. Dad's prob-ably wondering where the heck we went."

"You afraid of some junkies and pushers?"

Jason kept his eyes on the road. "Most definitely not."

"You feel as aggravated as I do?"

"Yep."

He asked Jason to stop in front of the playground.

"Remember when you got to the top of the monkey bars and started crying because you were too scared to come down?"

"Dude, I was like three," Jason said.

"I'm not saying it's a bad thing. Just one of my earliest memories is all." Pointing at a bench in the pink and dark of dusk, he said, "Mom used to sit right there and read her mystery novels. She'd tell us to get it all out of our systems before we got home. She'd always have money for an ice pop when the ice cream man came around."

Jason rested his forearms on the steering wheel, staring at the bench. "She never stopped reading those mysteries. We have boxes at home. I wonder if the library will take them."

The playground may have been closed for the day, but it was far from empty. Small gatherings of shadow people were everywhere. Marijuana wasn't legal in Iowa yet, but the plume of smoke hanging over the playground was rank enough to make Bryan gag.

"God, I hate that smell," Bryan said.

"You and me both. They say weed may be legalized by next year. That's been enough to get every pothead in town blazing like it's Mardi Gras."

Bryan suddenly got out of the truck.

"What the heck are you doing?" Jason asked as he locked up the RAM.

"Just some snooping."

He approached the first group he saw. They were gathered around the swings. Up close, he saw they were mostly teens. One of them noticed the two men saunter up and went running.

"They're not cops," a boy called out to him, the rest of the gang of girls and boys giggling. "What a wuss."

All of them had their own joints. Bryan wondered whatever happened to sharing.

A blond girl with her hair in dirty dreads turned her glassy eyes to them and asked, "You guys looking for something?"

"Maybe," Bryan said.

She looked over his shoulder. "He your bodyguard?"

"Him? Nah. He's just my driver."

Another girl said, "What are you, like rich or something?"

"Something."

One of the boys, his baseball cap on backward and wearing jeans pulled so low Bryan could see his underwear, said, "We ain't holding. Just out for a good time, you know?"

"I do. Who is holding in this little wonderland?"

They all pointed to a man sitting on the low end of the seesaw.

"He take kindly to strangers?"

"If they have money."

"Good enough."

As he walked to the dealer, the boy said, "You need a backup driver?"

"I do. But I drug test all my employees."

He got confused silence in return.

"Seriously, Bryan, what are you up to?" Jason whispered.

"Just getting the lay of the land."

They approached the dealer. Bryan walked with his hands low and palms open so the man could see he didn't have anything to hide. "Hey brother."

"You can stop right there," the man said. This part of the park was near pitch-black. Bryan would bet all the lights had been blown out on purpose. Dirty deeds needed dark corners. The man wore a hoodie despite the heat. It was pulled over his face. By his build, he was no teen. "What you need?" he asked with a voice that spoke of too many cigarettes, joints, and booze.

"Just looking for a dime bag." Bryan wasn't sure if dime bags were a thing anymore. He'd dabbled briefly with pot as a teen before deciding he liked his lungs and brain too much to fry them.

"You got cash?"

This guy sounded like a grade A sleazeball.

"My driver does. Show him."

Jason sighed behind him, fished for his wallet, and took out some cash. It was impossible to tell how much in the dark.

The man stood up and his hood fell back.

Bryan cocked his head, trying to make out his features in the dark. When the moon hit his face just right, Bryan said, "Jimmy?"

"What'd you call me?" The man took a step back from Bryan.

"Jimmy Youngblood. You smoke so much of your stuff you lose your memory?"

It took a moment for the light of recognition to turn on. "Bryan Branch? And is that you, Jason?"

"That's us," Jason said.

Jimmy Youngblood was an expert at stealing car radios back when Bryan ran with his crowd. He was also adept at shoplifting, always talking a big game about one day becoming a bank robber.

Now he was dealing drugs to kids. Robbing banks would have been nobler.

"Holy shit," Jimmy said. "I heard you got locked up. Never thought I'd see you again."

"I got locked up, but not the way you're thinking. So, how have you been?"

"Same old, man. Just hustling as always. You?"

"Got my own business back home. Got a wife. And some shrapnel in my leg that'll be with me until I die."

That tickled Jimmy, who was most definitely high.

Bryan swept his arm around the dark playground. "So, I see you've branched out."

Jimmy sniffed and rubbed his nose. "Easy pickings, man. Almost too easy. Cops today won't even look my way, much less bust me."

"Bigger fish to fry, I guess," Bryan said.

"They ain't fryin' anything but doughnuts. I'm not complaining. Makes my life easier."

Bryan motioned with his hand behind his back for Jason to move so he was behind Jimmy. Bigfoot moved with surprising stealth. He didn't even catch Jimmy's attention.

Jason stepped closer to Jimmy. "You just dealing weed now?"

"Nah. I got everything. These kids start with weed, but they eventually come sniffing around for benzos and fentanyl."

These kids.

Bryan let that sit for a moment.

Then he put his arm around Jimmy's shoulders. "We used to have a hell of a time back in the day, didn't we?"

Jimmy snickered. "We sure did."

Bryan tightened his hold on his old friend. "Man, I remember that time you went on that radio spree. You broke into how many cars that night?"

Jimmy shrugged. Bryan could feel his body stiffen. "I don't know. Ten, maybe twenty."

"Crazy. And all that time I was with Cherice, you were hiding them in my trunk."

"I needed a place to stash them."

Bryan nodded. "True. You did. You did. I took the rap for that when the cops caught on and searched my car."

Jimmy tried to pull away, but Bryan pulled him closer. "I . . . I remember."

"I didn't narc on you then. I took the hit. Just one more nail in my coffin with my family, but I didn't care. Friends before family, right?"

"Heh, yeah, right."

"I did you a solid then. And I'm going to do you a solid now."

The blow to Jimmy's solar plexus knocked the wind right out of him. Jimmy dropped to his knees, desperate to catch his breath. While he was down, Bryan grabbed the back of his head and brought his knee into the dealer's nose. The crack could be heard across the playground. Jimmy tried to crawl away but found his head butting into Jason's legs instead.

"Not long after your stunt I had to leave town. Because of that, I missed a lot of years with my family. Now I'm going to give you a similar choice, Jimmy, just because we're old friends. Pack up your stuff and get out of Maverick. Tonight. If I catch you selling that poison to kids . . . to anyone . . . I'm going to put you next to my mother. And believe me, you don't want to go there."

Jimmy blubbered as he tried to get on his feet. His hands covered his broken nose. A few of the kids in the park started to walk over. Jason barked, "Back off. This isn't your business."

"I can't believe you broke my nose, man!" Blood seeped out from between his fingers.

"I can't believe that's all I broke."

Bryan grabbed him by his hoodie and lifted him to his feet. "Are we clear?"

Jimmy slowly nodded. "You think you're going to clean things up around here?"

"Doesn't hurt to try."

"Then you're screwed. You think I'm the big fish?"

Bryan chuckled. "Jimmy, you wouldn't be a big fish if you were the only one in the pond."

Jimmy staggered away, bumping into Jason and stumbling. "You're a dead man, Bryan. You want to be a hero? You're gonna end up just like your mother. You and your whole family."

"I look forward to someone trying. Now get the hell out of here."

The dealer lumbered his way out of the playground. Jason cupped his mouth around his hands and said, "Playtime is over. Go home or end up like Jimmy."

The playground cleared out in under a minute.

Bryan rubbed his bad knee. "Should have used the other one."

"That was kinda fun. We done here?"

"For now."

"You feel better?"

"A little."

As they walked to the RAM, Jason said, "Jimmy never saw that coming."

"He will the next time. If there is a next time. I'll be ready. You can count on that."

CHAPTER 8

The next day they all woke up early to take on everything needed to keep the farm running. Bryan's father had yet to ask how long he and Charlotte intended to stay. He also didn't ask for their help, but they lent a hand anyway.

Bryan was no couch potato, but he'd forgotten how backbreaking the work could be. It was a good thing his father had Jason. That wouldn't be enough in the years to come. At some point, the bodies of old farmers betrayed them. There had always been temporary help that would be taken on in late August and stay on until the end of September. With no one around, Bryan assumed money was an issue. He'd make a note to offer some assistance to his father later, not that he thought the old man would accept it.

Charlotte clearly enjoyed it all. A CrossFit junkie, she tackled every task with a grunt, then a smile. By the end of the day Bryan's knee was barking louder than a junkyard dog. They sat on the front porch, escaping the sun and nursing cold glasses of iced tea Jason had made.

Between sips, Bryan set the icy glass on his knee, hoping it would lessen the pain.

"Charlotte," George said, "you're handier than a pocket on a shirt. I think you outdid your husband today. Thank you."

"It was a pleasure. I think we made a pretty good team." She leaned into Bryan, her eyes on the horizon, skimming the stalks of corn.

"You thought about what you're going to do when we leave?" Bryan asked. "Mom could outwork any two men and still have dinner on the table. You and Bigfoot, here, can't do everything."

After a pause his father said, "That might not be an issue soon enough."

Without expanding on his comment, he got up from his chair and walked inside, the screen door banging behind him.

"What did he mean by that?" Bryan asked his brother.

"I'm not entirely sure, but I think I know just from seeing what's gone on around us. Dad doesn't let me in on the big stuff. I'm almost forty. Still a kid to him. It's high time he partnered with me, since I'll be the one running this place when he's gone. But he's right; there may not be a future, whether we like it or not."

"Fill me in,"

Charlotte got up and stretched. "This sounds like Branch family business. I'm going to go inside and make your mother proud by whipping up some dinner."

"You don't have to do that," Jason said.

She waved him off. "It's no problem. So, I didn't see

any when we came to town, but is there a pizza parlor or Chinese takeout in Maverick?"

The brothers grinned. "Menu for Lucky Son is tacked to the side of the fridge. Dad always goes for the number four dinner special. I'll have a five."

"You got it. How about you, Hubby?"

"I don't know the numbers, but I don't like Chinese food. Make it pizza."

After Charlotte left to place their order Bryan asked again, "So, what's the deal?"

Jason scratched at where he should have stubble on his chin. "It's bad. A lot of people have been losing their farms the past few years. I have no reason to assume we'd be immune."

"People have always been losing farms. It only takes a bad growing season or a blight."

"This is different. It's institutionalized theft of private land by the government who are in service to foreign and domestic corporations. They use WOTUS rules against us, knowing we don't have the time or money to navigate all of the red tape and legal review."

Bryan had wanted nothing more than to finish his iced tea and take a shower. Now, that shower was the farthest thing from his mind. "Hold on. What's WOTUS?"

"Waters of the United States. It's part of the Clean Water Act. Basically, WOTUS was designed to make sure we provide clean uncontaminated waterways. But the rules change all the time. I hear they're going to include water that only comes about during heavy rain. Which means the farms need a total EPA review, along with enough paperwork to choke a rhino. And since Dad and every other farmer in Iowa isn't a lawyer on the side, we have to hire one to make sure we don't get fined up the wazoo. The government just sits back and waits. Farms are either fined to death or bled out by legal fees. Once that happens, in comes some corporate schmuck to snatch it all away like thieves in the night. Except these thieves do it in broad daylight with full approval from the people we elect to speak for us."

Jason was on his feet and pacing, his heavy footfalls making the wooden porch sing.

"Sorry for getting on my soapbox. But it's true. The government is coming for us. That's a fact. It's only a matter of when and how long we can hold out."

Bryan was as shocked as he was incensed. He'd come back to the farm because he'd lost his mother and now his family might lose the farm?

"If it's a matter of money, I can help," Bryan said.

"In perpetuity? Because that's how this is going to play out. Besides, how much can you possibly be making at a repair shop?"

"And towing," Bryan said, wagging a finger. "I made a lot of lucky investments early on. I'm not hurting for money." If only Jason knew how he really made his money, taking down bad actors in foreign countries.

"Please don't tell me you're one of those crypto guys."

"Give me some credit." Bryan walked to the end of the porch and leaned his back against the rail. He'd forgotten how beautiful the farm was, especially at dawn and when the day's work was done. The land had been in his family for four generations. He may have abandoned the farming life, but maybe that choice helped him gather the resources they'd need to keep the farm with the people who loved it. "We need to talk to Dad, find out exactly what's going on, and let me help. It's all about living to fight another day."

Jason peeked inside the house, as if to make sure their father wasn't listening in. Charlotte was in the kitchen laying out plates while listening to a podcast on her phone. "You know Dad. If he doesn't want to talk about it, he'll seal right up like a clam. And there's no way he'll agree to take charity money from you."

"I know I haven't been around, but I'm still family, dammit. It's not charity if it's the family pulling together."

"All right, keep it down. Dad had a good day today. Let's not spoil it. Right time, right place. Okay?"

Bryan sighed and shook his head. His old man was as immovable as a mountain. He didn't relish having to have this conversation. No matter. It had to be done. "Fine."

The sound of a car crunching up the road drew their immediate attention. Both balled their hands into fists.

The sight of the plastic pizza sign atop the beat-up Ford put them instantly at ease. A kid, no more than seventeen with long hair squashed under a trucker cap, slid out carrying a box of pizza with a brown paper bag atop it.

"Delivery," he called out to them.

"No foolin'," Jason said.

Bryan went inside to get some cash out of his wallet. "Pizza's here?" Charlotte asked. She was holding a glass of red wine.

"Yep. Nobody fixes a dinner quicker than you," he replied, smiling wide.

"I'm a woman of many skills."

When Bryan walked back onto the porch, the delivery kid was talking to Jason while still holding the box with both hands. His head swiveled to Bryan and said, "You really the guy who sucker punched Jimmy?"

Bryan stared down at the kid. "Who wants to know?"

"Me?"

Jason took the food from him. "I just wanted to tell you, that was pretty cool. Jimmy has his uses, but he's kind of a creep. Sells cheap weed at a high price, too."

"How much?" Bryan asked.

"Oh, ah, twenty-one."

Bryan handed him twenty-five. "Keep the change. And keep away from people like Jimmy. Being stoned and stupid is not a life choice."

The kid didn't appear the least bit offended. "Thanks for the tip. And I got a tip for you. Word is that Jimmy's boss is pretty pissed."

"Who is Jimmy's boss?"

Scratching under his ball cap, he said, "We all figure it's some narco kinda stuff."

"Cartels in Iowa?" Bryan said with a heavy note of sarcasm.

"All drugs come from a cartel. Mexico, Colombia, the CIA. You just gotta follow the money. Anyway, I'd be on high alert if I was you. If Jimmy knows where you live, his boss will, too."

Jimmy had spent innumerable days with Bryan at the

farm when they were young. He could probably drive there with his eyes closed.

Jason patted the kid on the back, guiding him back to his car. "Well, thanks for the warning. We'll be sure to keep an eye out." He pulled a twenty-dollar bill from his pocket. "And here's a little extra. Don't tell anyone about this conversation."

"Um, yeah, okay, sure."

After the kid pulled the car away Jason said to Bryan, "Any chance he keeps this to himself?"

"Not a single one."

"Should we be worried about some cartel dude showing up?"

Bryan looked around and took a deep breath. "Better safe than sorry."

"About what?"

They turned around and saw Charlotte behind the screen door. Bryan said, "I'll tell you inside, later. When's the last time you pulled night watch duty?"

Rather than being shocked and worried, Charlotte seemed excited. "A couple of days in and we already have to watch our backs? Wow. This could be more fun that I thought."

Jason cast a quizzical glance at Bryan.

"She married me for my charm. I married her to keep me safe from trouble."

"Oh boy," Jason said as he opened the door, balancing the pizza with his other hand. "The terror of Maverick has definitely returned."

* * *

"Busy day?" Todd Bennington said as he looked over his tablet at his wife when she entered the room.

"When is it not?"

"When we both retire."

Alexa Bennington, the current governor of Iowa, tossed her computer bag on the sofa and went straight to the wet bar. She poured herself a vodka on the rocks and sat in the chair opposite her husband, crossing her left leg over her right, her foot bouncing to a rhythm only she could hear. "Well, it had better be sooner rather than later, before the stress kills me."

Todd set aside his tablet. He'd been reading through a series of heavily encrypted emails from a very wealthy foreign investor. "You have a little less than two years left in your term and then we just need a second to get everything where it needs to be. After that we can get one of those luxury huts on the water in Bora Bora, where the most exciting thing we'll do all day is watch the sun set."

Alexa took a huge swallow, almost emptying the glass. "I don't want to be a tanned vegetable, either. By the way, we found the little pissant who sent those death threats to my office. I plan to stick him in the deepest hole I can find in the state. Do you know how many video meetings I had today?"

When he didn't answer she said, "Fourteen. Fourteen! How am I supposed to get anything done when I sit behind my desk like a veal staring at a screen?"

"You have to look at it this way. It's better than in person. At least you can shut it down and blame it on your Wi-Fi."

Alexa flicked a lock of dyed black hair from her face, clearly unamused. "Have I told you how much I hate this job?"

"Just about every day."

"Some days I don't know what I dislike more, being governor or the state of Iowa itself. You know, I left here right after college for a reason," she said, jabbing a manicured finger in his direction.

Alexa came from a long line of conservative Iowa politicians. Her grandfather, father, two uncles, and one aunt had all held varying positions serving the state over the course of the past century. Her own values were forged in rebellion against her cloying, flag-waving family and hadn't changed one whit as she got older. She managed a full ride at Harvard, became a successful lawyer who lived in Manhattan, and had a summer house in the Hamptons. Her Christian megaconservative family labeled her the black sheep, and it was a name she cherished. On the rare occasions she spoke to her parents or came to visit family during holidays, she kept her lips zipped when conversation inevitably turned to politics. There was no point trying to bring enlightenment to the blind.

It was Todd who had convinced her to move back to Iowa and run for governor as a perceived continuation of a strong party-loyal lineage. Her parents had passed on and polling showed the people of the state needed— no, *wanted*—to fill the void with the successful daughter of a political dynasty. The carrot Todd dangled was the grand opportunity for her to transform the entire state to her liking, sticking a shiv in the side of her family. So she ran, and won pretty handily; Todd had built an enormous war chest with donations from powerful people and lobbyists far and wide who, like them, saw a different vision for America. She'd watched the Chinese take control of New York without a single shot fired, using real estate as their weapon. They made people very rich as they handed over their land ownings to those who despised them.

Alexa and Todd's plan was to play into China's hunger to devour America from within, while also handing over the state on a plate to the richest man in the world. He had big plans for Iowa that consisted of taking over the farms and converting them to dumping grounds, ultrarich resorts, or GMO plants to topple the meat industry and control the diet and food supply of the nation.

And that was where Alexa Bennington's true allegiance lay: the almighty dollar. If she could get insanely wealthy *and* have her parents spinning in their graves while doing it, all the better.

The one day Alexa did not hate her job was when she announced she was changing her party affiliation. In years past, such a move would have seen her being run out on a rail. With the influx of people from big cities all around the country and now a flood of migrants, the political landscape had changed just enough for her to make good on all of their plans without worrying about the villagers coming for her with pitchforks and torches. Just give the sheep their access to social media and the latest nonsense from the Kardashians and all would be well.

Thanks to the crisis at the border and the city dwellers who clung to remote work as if it were a cure to all ills, there were more than enough new sheep in Iowa to keep her in power long enough to see her and Todd's plans come to fruition.

Todd Bennington rose from his chair, already weary of their nightly ritual. He poured a double scotch for himself, neat.

"Are you getting closer to the environmental initiatives we outlined?" he asked.

The *we* was an assortment of exceedingly wealthy backers who had propped up her campaign as well as her bank account, who had a vested interest in the fertile land Iowa had to offer.

She finished her drink and held out her glass so he could refill it. "It's going to be close. This isn't exactly a state that embraces electric cars and all the climate change policies I've set out. Did you see the editorial about our push to ban gas stoves and gas-powered outdoor power tools?"

Todd leaned against the desk. "I did. Just a lot of neocon lip service. The only sphere where they hold power is talk radio. Look at all the good it does them. You're smarter and stronger than any of them." He set down his drink and massaged her shoulders. The tension in them made it feel as if she were made of stone.

She leaned back her head and closed her eyes, a small smile playing on her lips. "We'll be long gone before most of the changes take full effect, but who cares? Though it would be nice to see the faces of all those hausfraus and Mexican landscapers who have to deal with their electric stoves and leaf blowers. Maybe we should buy a stake in the electric suppliers."

"Who says we haven't?"

Alexa purred. "We snatched up two more farms today. Let your pal Ying know: It's his for the taking."

"That will make him very happy. He plans to set one of them aside for electric car battery waste disposal with the help of the governor clearing all that red tape."

The batteries in the electric cars that were coming sooner rather than later were toxic as hell. Just like nuclear waste, they would need to be buried deep. Corporate entities who could secure the land and stand up the operation to make the dark side of climate concern disappear stood to make the kind of money that would give a Saudi prince pause. Unfortunately for the Saudis, the Chinese had the jump on that cash cow. And one other very noteworthy person.

"Yeah, yeah, yeah," Alexa said, flicking her wrist and spilling some vodka on her lap. "Just make sure he knows I need to see the reward for my efforts *before* I roll up my sleeves. Right now, my team is working on a story to explain just why the farms are being lost. Oh, and there are four more in the hopper for Ganz. He can make all the horrible fake meat he wants on them."

"Can you have Colin send the locations and details to me tomorrow?"

Alexa typed on her phone. "Why wait for tomorrow? Colin is still at the office."

Nostrand Ganz was the richest man in the world, soon to be its first trillionaire, having had a hand in early online technology, advanced weaponry for the military, aerospace, and now the front lines of artificial intelligence.

Because Nostrand Ganz could never have enough money, he ultimately wanted to control the food supply, all in the name of saving the planet by eliminating those gaseous cows and immoral meat eaters. He was scooping up small farms by the dozen every month, all throughout the farm belt, reappropriating them for plant-based food production while making himself even richer. Todd knew for a fact that Ganz loved a rare rib eye possibly more than his third trophy wife. Hypocrisy meant little to Todd and Alexa so long as the money rolled in.

Ganz had his eye set on Iowa because, like the Chinese, he knew all those future dead batteries would need a tomb. With a huge stake in making those batteries and electric cars, getting governments and private industry to pay up for a place to bury them was a matter of closing the circle.

He also had major plans for building sprawling resorts set within the wondrous nature that was Iowa. Admission to these resorts would require one to be a multimillionaire.

Keeping Ganz happy was a priority for them. Four more farms in Iowa alone would put a big smile on his face. The man had more money than their Chinese business partners, and a larger ego than the entirety of the communist nation. That was one man you did not want to cross.

"Speaking of Ganz, would you like a plant steak for dinner?" Todd joked.

Alexa laughed coldly at the thought, then flicked on the television to watch CNN and nurse her drink.

CHAPTER 9

Three days passed without incident, but that didn't make Bryan let down his guard. Charlotte was proud of what he did and happy to face any dealer who thought they'd get the drop on them. She said this in front of Jason, whose mouth hit the floor.

"You forget, I met her at that lovely resort town in Afghanistan," Bryan reminded him as he pulled her close. "If there's something she can't handle, I've yet to see it."

"Do you have any guns?" she'd asked.

"We don't just farm, we hunt," Jason said with a beat of his fist on his chest. They had four rifles in all.

It was decided that they wanted to keep this latest development from their father. He was still grieving in his own stoic way, plus they didn't want him to get upset at Bryan for potentially bringing disaster back to the family. At least not now when things were going so well.

They worked the farm by day and took turns doing watch at night.

The goodwill food was running low, and they needed

to go to town. Bryan said he would take Charlotte while Jason kept an eye on things. There would also be a detour to the Best Western to pick up David and his family. He had an inkling what to do with them, at least for now.

He picked a good day to head out because the temperature suddenly shot up to the high nineties, with enough humidity to hatch an egg.

"Does it always get this hot?" Charlotte said as she pulled her shirt away from her body and fanned herself with her free hand.

"Sometimes," Bryan said. "There's plenty of changes around here, but I don't see climate change being one of them. I spent a lot of summers looking for shade before I melted. And even then it didn't help much."

They tucked one of the rifles in the back seat and covered it with a blanket. You could never be too sure . . . or safe.

First stop was the Best Western. David's family was waiting for them in the lobby, looking clean and freshly pressed. Their adorable daughter wore a new pink dress and had her long hair in a French braid. It was a far cry from the scruffy street kid he'd met just days before. Bryan introduced them to Charlotte.

"I can't thank you enough for your generosity," David's wife said. Bryan was surprised. She had barely spoken before, and he had wrongly assumed she couldn't speak English. In fact, she could, quite well. Living on the street with her family must have had her in a state of shell shock. "If you could take us back to the lot, we would be very grateful."

"I have a proposition for you, but I need something in return," Bryan said. The last thing he was going to do was drop them off in that tent and lean-to city.

"Sure," David said. "Anything."

"I need to know all of your names. And your last name."

"That's all?"

"That's all."

Their last name was Cruz. David's wife was Pam—she said she was named after her grandmother, who was a white woman from Texas—their son Tomás, and their daughter Lola. They hailed from Juarez, one of the most dangerous towns in Mexico, coming to America to keep the kids safe and give them a chance at a future.

"You all speak very good English. Almost better than me," Bryan said jokingly.

"We've been preparing to come to America for many years now," Pam said. "We took classes, but mostly we learned by watching American television on the internet."

David grinned. "We watched every episode of *Dancing with the Stars*. *Mi esposa* here loves the dancing. I preferred *The Sopranos*."

"Well, it's a wonder you don't sound like a Jersey mobster. Dave, Pam, Tomás and Lola, have you ever done any farming?"

Charlotte cocked her head at him. He hadn't told anyone of his plan. Better to do it and ask for forgiveness than permission.

"Pam and I have, when we were younger."

"That's good because we have a farm that needs

some help right about now. We also have a farmhouse with too many empty rooms. If you'd like to help us, you've got room and board. And I'll pay you for your work."

David and Pam beamed. "Are you sure?"

"I'm always sure. Right, honey?"

"Oh, of course." Charlotte playfully slapped his arm.

"We would love to help you. But you do not need to pay us," Pam said. "A place to stay is all we need."

Bryan put a hand on her shoulder. "For the short term. The kids are going to need a lot to get started with their new life. I'll make sure of that."

As they loaded up the truck with the Cruz family and their meager possessions, Charlotte whispered to him, "Are you sure your father will be okay with this?"

"If our past is anything to go by, he'd be happier with them than with me around. We took in workers all the time. Besides, how can we let a girl as cute as Lola back on the streets?"

Charlotte stopped him in his tracks and gave him a bear hug. "Do you know how much I love you?"

"I think I have a pretty good idea. Besides, it kills two birds with one stone. My dad gets extra help and I'll have some free time."

"Do I even need to ask what for?"

He kissed her cheek. "I don't think you do."

They stopped at the supermarket, wading through men and women straggling in the parking lot and at the store's automatic doors with hands out or signs asking for money or food.

"What are we in, San Francisco?" Charlotte asked.

"Looks like it's well on its way." Bryan grabbed a shopping cart and gave it to Lola. He passed out singles, knowing it wouldn't do much good, and for most, by the looks of them, just get them a little closer to the next bottle of booze or hit. He'd yet to meet the addict who had set out to end up that way. As much as he wanted to help everyone, he had an entire family to care for now.

And unfinished business.

The cart was loaded to the top and then some. Pam promised to make them some authentic Mexican meals. Bryan had to coax Tomás and Lola to buy treats like a bag of chips and a box of Pop Tarts. Lola's eyes especially lit up when he put in a box of colorful sugary cereal she'd been staring at.

"You'll spoil her," Pam said.

"Good. That's exactly my intention."

At the register, he was a bit set back at the grand total for their excursion. "What did Iowa do, make fun of inflation's wife?"

The girl at the checkout didn't acknowledge his bad joke. He was sure she heard complaints all the time. Prices had been soaring in Pennsylvania, but this was a California tab. What did the locals who didn't grow fresh fruit and vegetables do to feed themselves? He could only shake his head in disgust as he swiped his card.

It was just going on lunchtime when they returned, which was what Bryan had planned. His father was on the porch, eating his obligatory ham-and-cheese sandwich with a glass of milk set on the ground beside his chair. Jason had a sandwich fit for a gorilla. They were both visibly confused when the truck's doors opened and an entire family emerged.

"Dad, Jason, I want you to meet the Cruzes. This is David, Pam, Tomás, and Lola. They're here to lend a hand."

His father said nothing. He set his sandwich on his plate.

"Hey guys," Jason said, his voice heavy with trepidation. They waved back at him.

"I figure we can put them up in the guest rooms. If that's okay with you."

Charlotte and Pam grabbed some bags from the flatbed. All eyes were on George, even Jason's.

The handle of Charlotte's bag broke and out spilled everything. Lola ran over to retrieve her box of cereal.

"Look what Mr. Bryan bought me!" she said directly to George, her smile brighter than the sun. "It's so pretty. Do you have milk? I've always wanted to try cereal with milk."

George Branch just about melted. He crouched a bit and held out his hand. "Why don't you come inside with me and I'll fetch you a bowl and some nice cold milk."

Lola looked back at her parents for permission. "Go on," her mother said.

She placed her small smooth hand in George's thick callused mitt, and together they walked into the house. Bryan heard his father say, "Your name is Lola? That's very pretty."

After everyone exhaled Jason said, "He always wanted a girl, but he got stuck with us."

"Put down your Sasquatch sandwich and help us unload the truck," Bryan said.

"It's better than watching you limp back and forth."

When they were just about done and it was only Bryan and Jason outside, they heard a loud crack, immediately followed by the ping of metal. They dropped to the ground, Bryan trying to locate where the shot had come from.

Charlotte was coming out of the door when Bryan shouted, "Get back inside!"

"Was that a shot I heard?" she said, crouched down behind the screen door.

Another rang out, this time kicking up gravel a few feet from Bryan.

"Yep," Bryan said.

"I think they hit my truck," Jason said, fuming.

"Lucky that's all they hit so far."

They were out in the open with only the truck to protect them. Bryan heard someone rustling through the tall stalks of corn. He took a quick peek over the hood to see which stalks were swaying. A breeze came out of nowhere, as if to assist the shooter.

The front door slammed shut. Bryan could hear Charlotte through the window telling everyone to get down.

"What do we do?" Jason said.

Bryan pointed at the house. "Sit tight and see."

The door suddenly burst open. Charlotte strode onto the porch, firing into the cornfield from left to right. When she was done she hit the deck, but not before tossing another rifle to Bryan.

Whoever was out there fired back. Bryan motioned for Jason to stay put, got to his feet, and stepped out from behind the truck, firing blindly, hoping to see some movement other than the wind.

More shots sounded behind him. He spun around to see Charlotte back on her feet a moment before she slipped into the house.

Two more rounds came from the corn. This time, Bryan saw the wood splinter in the front of the house. That was good. It gave him an angle he could follow to help zero in on his target.

"He's at your two!"

Bryan's father was at the upstairs window, rifle in hand. He pulled the trigger once, twice, three times. Charlotte opened the downstairs window and fired in the same direction.

Emboldened by their suppression fire, Bryan stepped away from the truck, approaching the cornfield carefully. He didn't want to get shot by whoever was out there, or, more importantly, his father or wife.

Rustling up ahead told him he was close. Bryan looked back at the house and waved his arm down.

The cornstalks were higher than his head, tilting into the suddenly relentless breeze. He crouched as low as he could go, following the sound of someone on the move, though it wasn't easy with the hearing loss he'd suffered while on tour.

He breathed slowly through his mouth, keeping his finger on the trigger. Their assailant had apparently stopped moving and was lying in wait. Or he'd somehow gotten away and was halfway to the access road by now.

Bryan bet on the former. Besides, if anyone had gotten to the road, they would have been picked off by Charlotte. She was a decorated markswoman. The only thing he could do was sit as still as possible and wait him out. Or her out. He knew full well that both sexes were fully capable of murder, though in his opinion men seemed to relish it more.

A few minutes passed by. He prayed Charlotte, Jason, and his father would not enter the cornfield. It was better they stay out of harm's way and kept an eye on everything.

And poor Lola and Tomás. They hadn't been at the house for more than five minutes before all hell broke loose. There would be time to worry about the traumatic effects on them later.

After another few minutes Bryan grew tired of waiting. He estimated where the shooter had stopped, lifted the rifle, and pulled the trigger. The bang of the rifle was quickly followed by the crash and rush of someone bashing their way through the corn.

Mother Nature decided to side with him, pulling the plug on the wind. Bryan looked at the tops of the stalks to track his quarry. He fired where he thought the shooter would essentially walk into the bullet.

By the sounds of the man wailing in pain he'd done a pretty good job of estimating.

CHAPTER 10

Charlotte came with the first aid kit and her rifle, worried that it was Bryan who had been shot.

"I've been shot at, and I don't think I ever hit that high a note," he said when he saw her.

The man writhing on the ground was covered in sweat. A bloom of red was spreading out on the thigh area of his jeans. When he saw Bryan, he spat a slew of curses at him in Spanish. Bryan stepped over him and put his boot on the man's wrist, forcing him to release his hold on his weapon. Keeping pressure on his wrist, Bryan grabbed the rifle and slung it over his shoulder.

"We need to stop the bleeding," he said.

Charlotte stared at the dark-skinned man. His crow's-feet were etched deep and his mustache was peppered with white hair. "Or we could just let nature take its course."

"And I could be charged with murder in this backward world."

"There is that."

Charlotte dropped to a knee and ripped off her belt.

When the man tried to push her away Bryan put his boot to his neck. "You nearly shot my family," he seethed. "You should be thankful I don't shoot your other leg."

The man didn't appear to understand him. But Bryan knew some of the choice words hurled his way. He was grateful when Charlotte roughly applied the makeshift tourniquet, causing him to yelp once and pass out.

Crashing in the corn at their backs had them both at the ready with their rifles.

"Are you all right?" Jason asked, slightly winded, Bryan was sure more from the excitement than a jog through the corn. His father was right beside him.

"Better than him," Jason said. "You call the police?"

"Just now," his father said.

Bryan got down on his good knee and lifted the unconscious man's head. "He look familiar?"

Jason and George studied the man's face. "I have no idea," George said.

"I don't think so," Jason said. "He does and he doesn't."

"Was he one of the men who came looking for work that day?"

Bryan worried that if his brother said yes, he was going to undo the tourniquet and let the fool bleed out.

"No. I don't think so," Jason said.

Bryan's lips pulled into a tight line. If this wasn't one of the laborers who wanted to finish what they started, could this be a stooge sent by the man who was Jimmy's boss? It was a fifty-fifty toss-up at the moment.

When they heard the wail of sirens George and Charlotte ran out to the road to flag down the cops.

They returned with two officers in tow. When the man on the ground saw them, he attempted to get up and run. Bryan and Jason each grabbed a shoulder and set him back down.

"Hey Aaron," Jason said.

"I didn't expect a call like this today," Bryan and Jason's childhood friend said as he looked down at the man's bleeding leg. He was trim with a square jaw and light brown hair. Even when they were in grammar school they used to tease him that he looked like a cop. Apparently, they'd been right all along.

His partner was a middle-aged Black man with the physique of an NFL linebacker. The name tag on his shirt said *White*. His gaze darted between Bryan and Jason, clearly wary. They had made sure to set their rifles on the ground before they arrived.

"He needs better medical attention than I can give," Charlotte said.

Chisolm got into a crouch and examined the wound. When he touched the tourniquet the shooter yelped. "You did a pretty good job. May have saved him from bleeding out." When he got back up he looked Bryan's way and paused. "Wait. Bryan?"

Bryan put up his hands halfway. "Came back for my mother's funeral. And before you ask, I was the one who shot him."

White's meaty paw went to his handcuffs.

"You care to tell me why?" Aaron Chisolm asked.

"Because this devil started shooting at us!" George exclaimed. "There are children inside the house. He could have killed them. For all I know, he's the one who shot up my house and burned me out. He's lucky he's still this side of the dirt."

"Is that true?"

Bryan nodded. "We were defending ourselves. Who he is and why he did it, you'll have to ask him. I don't think he speaks any English."

The shooter had his head down and had gone very still.

"You speak English?" Chisolm asked. When the man didn't answer Chisolm tapped his wounded leg with his shoe. The man's head shot up and his eyes flew open. He cursed at Chisolm, all in Spanish. "I guess that answers my question."

White got on his radio and called for an ambulance.

"Was anybody hurt?" Chisolm asked.

Jason turned to his father.

"The Cruzes are okay. A little shaken but okay."

"And who are the Cruzes?"

"A family we took in to help with the harvesting," Bryan said.

"Let's all go back to the house so I can speak to everyone," Chisolm said. He turned to his partner. "Keep a close eye on him."

"I don't think he's running anywhere anytime soon."

"You never know. He could be a world champion hopper from Tijuana."

As they walked back to the house, Chisolm said to Bryan, "Keeping a low profile was never your thing."

"It wasn't much yours, either." Many folks wondered which side of the law Bryan and Aaron would end up on. They had both chosen the right path, though for the moment Bryan couldn't help but feel he was still on the wrong side of the tracks.

"I'm really sorry to hear about your mother. And your wife," he said to George. "It was a senseless tragedy."

"This easily could have been, too," Jason remarked. "Now I need to know why men have come to shoot up our home twice in a little over a week. If someone tries again, maybe we won't get so lucky."

Bryan looked back to the spot behind the corn where the shooter was laid out. "Or maybe *they* won't."

Chisolm let it slide. When they got to the front porch David and his family were outside, huddled together. "Did you get him, Mr. Bryan?" David asked.

"It's just Bryan. And yeah, he's in custody."

"Are you all okay?" Chisolm asked.

"We're fine," Pam replied. Her arms were draped over Lola's chest. The little girl seemed unfazed by the recent events. "We've seen worse. Far worse."

Chisolm reached into his back pocket and took out his black notebook. "I think I'd be better off with a court stenographer."

"This is why they pay police the big bucks," Bryan said.

"Oh yeah. I don't know what to do with all the money coming my way. I hear you served in the Middle East."

"I did. So did my wife. It was every bit the paradise you've heard."

Charlotte put on a fake grin.

Aaron Chisolm took a deep breath, seemed to do a mental count of all the statements he'd need to take, and opened his notebook. "All right, who wants to go first?"

CHAPTER 11

The still-anonymous shooter was in custody and had yet to speak a word. So far, Bryan wasn't in imminent danger of being arrested. It was clearly self-defense. The thing that nagged them all was who the man was and why he went out to the farm with a gun in his hand and murder in his heart.

Even though the heat and humidity kept on mounting, the Branch and Cruz contingents worked tirelessly under the blazing sun. Bryan and Charlotte's tolerance for the heat had been forged overseas. The Cruzes, having lived in Mexico, didn't bat an eye. Even George and Jason plowed forward with little complaint. They knew days like this were inevitable and what good did whining about something you couldn't control do you?

Some corn farmers harvested at night when the heat was this bad. Bryan's father said the lighting that was needed for a night harvest was on the fritz. The look he shot Bryan said there would be no welcome offers to replace the light rigging.

Bryan checked in with Lori and Shane every day, just to give himself some sense that he was needed back at the shop. Apparently, he wasn't. He told them about his altercation with Jimmy and the shooter they'd captured. They offered to shutter the doors and head to Iowa, but he reassured them that he and Charlotte had things under control.

David and Pam made for great farmhands. Tomás and Lola were also pretty adept at working with the chickens and tending the vegetable garden. Each night Pam made a feast fit for kings, though some of the spice was getting to George. Jason broke a little sweat at dinner as well.

Five days into the heat wave, they lost power.

Bryan and Charlotte weren't even aware of it until Lola came out to tell them that none of the appliances would turn on.

"I knew that was coming," Jason said. His hands and forearms were nearly black from working in the soil all day. "Happens all the time. Last year we had a rough heat wave. Electricity was out for a week. Seven people died in Maverick alone, including Mrs. Bateman."

"Mrs. Bateman?" Bryan said, visibly shocked. "She made the best key lime pies."

"I hear her living room was wallpapered with the blue ribbons she won from all those pie contests. She had a heart attack brought on by heat exhaustion. A couple of others died because their insulin went bad and they were too sick and isolated to get help."

"She was one of the few adults who was always nice to me, no matter how far my head was up my butt. That's a terrible way to go for a woman who did so much for others all her life."

"If there's a pie heaven, Mrs. B is there, rolling out some dough as we speak," Jason said as he wiped the sweat from his face and head with his bandanna.

Work called, clearing their minds of anything but the task in front of them. When they got back to the house the lights were still out. Any kind of breeze disappeared with the electricity. They ate cold sandwiches on the porch, fanning themselves with their paper plates.

Bryan went to his car to check out any updates on the blackout on his radio. It also felt good to turn on the air-conditioning for a spell. Charlotte was in the passenger seat, letting the cool air dry her sweat-soaked hair. "Oh, that feels good."

"Don't get too used to it or it'll feel even worse when we get out."

It didn't take long for the news to report that some-one had shot up one of the substations just outside Maverick. There was no estimated time to get the power back online, but it was safe to assume it would be a few days. They then listed local cooling stations, along with the warning signs of dehydration and heat stroke.

"I've been hearing that way too often," Charlotte said. "Check tomorrow and they'll say they have no suspects, no witnesses, no leads. It's like our power grid is being assaulted by phantoms. And what kind of diseased animal would wipe out power during a heat wave?"

Bryan was on his phone, checking out other recent reports of substation and power grid attacks.

"You and I both know there are plenty to go around." He pointed at his phone's screen. "It says here that vandalism and assaults on the US power grid are up over one hundred percent in the past two years. And you're wrong, it's not phantoms, at least not according to the news. It's white nationalist groups."

Charlotte leaned over the middle console to get a better look. "Which ones?"

He scrolled down to find mention of any particular group. There were plenty out there, and many of them had names assigned to them either by themselves or the authorities. When he didn't find any he clicked into several more articles, wondering how this had escaped his notice all this time.

Because you've had your mind and sights set on plenty of other things, he reminded himself. Those things were equally insidious, but a man could only attend to and put out just so many fires.

"Can't find a single name. But there are a couple of Islamic terrorist suspects that you'd recognize. How has no one been caught? There are cameras literally everywhere but around substations. Does it feel like folks don't want to know, or am I reading too much into things?"

Charlotte shut off the car and opened the door. "The powers that be count on people not to read into things at all. It's how they get away with literal murder." She came over to his side of the car and gave him a kiss. "Now, save your phone's power. Who knows how long this is going to last."

"This is starting to create an itch in my brain. And you know what happens when I get itchy, babe."

She entwined their fingers as they walked back to the house. "People tend to get scratched. Let's take care of the more immediate issues at hand first. I say we take a break from the farming life and start digging around to find out who has it in for you and this place."

For a moment, Bryan's heart skipped a beat. He could have looked the world over twice and never found a woman better and more suited for him. They were each other's ride or die, and both knew that actions spoke louder than words.

"A day in town it is," he said.

When he first got the news of his mother's passing Bryan thought the trip would be short-lived, with an uncomfortable reunion with his father and a nostalgic ride around town before heading right back to the airport.

He never once dreamed that he and Charlotte would need to employ their unique skills to get them through a war zone.

Maybe I should give a shout-out to the others, he thought as he sucked in a damp lungful of night air.

He and Charlotte would have to do some digging first. Help was always just a call away.

If only the people messing with his family knew what that call would mean to their short and bleak future.

But that was for another day. For now, they joined everyone on the porch, staying outside until the sun melted into the horizon and the moon and darkness brought little relief. Lola and Tomás were the only ones with a lick of energy, playing tag in the front yard as if the air wasn't a stifling, hot, wet blanket. Bryan and Charlotte turned in early. They would need their rest for tomorrow . . . if there was any chance for a peaceful night's sleep in the cloying heat.

At breakfast, which was prepared by Pam and Charlotte just before the sun came up, Bryan pulled Jason into the living room.

"Charlotte and I are going to head into town today. Can I borrow your truck?"

Jason narrowed his gaze. "What are you planning to do with my truck?"

"Just drive it. I'll even top off the gas tank. I hate that damn Nissan."

After what seemed like an eternity of consideration Jason said, "Fine." Just as he was going to hand over his keys, he pulled them back from Bryan's reaching grasp. "Wait. What are you gonna do in town?"

Bryan stayed silent.

"Are you crazy? You're going there to stir up more trouble . . . with your wife?"

"You're just getting to know Charlotte. There's a lot to peel with that onion. She can handle herself better than just about anyone I know."

Jason shook his head. "This isn't right. Let me at least come with you."

Bryan put a hand on his chest and snatched the keys out of Jason's hand. "Stick to what you do best, Bigfoot, and we'll do the same."

Before he could leave, Jason grabbed him by the arm and practically spun him around. Whispering so their father wouldn't hear, he said. "Would you like to clue me into what *you* do best?"

Bryan smiled and patted his brother's cheek. "Not really."

In the kitchen, George knocked back the rest of his coffee and tucked a biscuit with bacon in the front pocket of his overalls, an old habit that his deceased wife had long ago given up trying to stop. It was important to him to be the first out the door and the last in it. "Thanks for the grub, Charlotte and Pam," he said on his way out.

The screen door smacked the frame in his wake.

David and the kids were at the table eating scrambled eggs and toast. Bryan filled a plate for himself. He'd forgotten how something as simple as a farm-fresh egg could taste as good as anything prepared by a Michelin chef.

When everyone was finished Charlotte and Bryan stayed behind to clean the table and wash the dishes. The Cruz family didn't ask any questions about why they weren't heading out with everyone else. Lola was anxious to check on the chickens and Tomás seemed half asleep. David and Pam would be in the cornfields all day, knowing their children would finish all their chores without the need of adult supervision.

Jason pointed at Bryan and Charlotte before he left. "Don't do anything I wouldn't do."

"I've lived my life pretty much doing things you won't do," Bryan said.

"Whatever."

Bryan offered his arm to Charlotte. "Ready to paint the town red, my dear?"

She locked arms with him. "I can't wait."

CHAPTER 12

What they got when they drove into the downtown area was not what they expected. Yes, many of the stores were closed on account of there not being any power. It was a scorcher of a day, so Bryan assumed most people would be laying low in the shade or staying indoors with all the windows open. The unrelenting summer sun had a way of infusing small towns with a generalized lethargy. There was little hustle and bustle to begin with. Add a heat wave to the mix and cut off ways to cool down and you had a downright ghost town.

Not so on this day.

Everywhere he looked, the homeless were up and about, some lugging bulging trash bags with cans and bottles over their shoulders, others pushing stolen shopping carts crammed with all of their possessions, while many others begged for money or food. There was one exception. A man with a boxer's nose and cauliflower ears held a sign that said: I NEED WEED. BEING SOBER IS FOR QUITTERS.

When they stopped at a light a man approached

the car on Charlotte's side and a woman knocked on the window to get Bryan's attention. Both looked strung out, probably in their early thirties but aging rapidly from that poisonous cocktail of addiction and poverty. Charlotte handed them each a ten-dollar bill while Bryan studied their faces. The woman looked awfully familiar. The man was clearly from some South American country, most likely here illegally and finding the grass wasn't always greener. The woman accepted the money graciously, looked almost embarrassed, and shuffled back to the intersection.

The man looked at the money and said to Charlotte, "If you can spare ten, I'll bet you can give a little more."

Charlotte snatched the bill out of his hand. "And I can also taketh away. Besides, you couldn't handle what I can give."

She rolled up the window a second before he spat at her. His expectoration ran down the window, thick as a slug's trail. Bryan pulled away before she could open the door.

"I refuse to reward people for being rude," she said, turning away in disgust from the wad of spit on her window.

"It was a good call. I'm pretty sure I know that woman. Just can't remember where. I have a feeling we went to school together."

"Don't think about it. Let your subconscious figure it out. Is there a car wash somewhere?"

"Yep. It's called the hose back home."

"Lovely."

The park was pretty active, though Bryan didn't see

one young child playing on the swings or zipping down the slide. There were plenty of older teens and twenty-somethings either actively procuring what they needed to get high or full in the throes as they sat on park benches or lay in the grass.

"Did we just drive into the summer of love?" Charlotte asked as he slowed down the truck and stopped.

"Where the hell are you, Jimmy?"

He couldn't find anyone who bore even a passing resemblance to his old friend, which meant putting him out of business for a while had zero impact on the drug trade in town. The fact that it was being done so brazenly out there in the open in the light of day burned him up inside.

It was easy to spot the dealers because they had nothing to fear. One hand went into a pocket, the other accepted money, then the hand came out of the pocket with a baggie in its palm, which was slickly handed over to the buyer. He spotted two dealers. They were young, maybe early twenties. Jimmy's street team.

"So, what do you want to do?" Charlotte asked. Unlike his brother, he knew his wife would be game for just about anything he suggested that didn't involve sitting around.

"We could take their supply away from them, wait around for the boss to demand we give it back. Hope we can engage in a dialogue at that point."

Charlotte leaned her head against the window, the air conditioner flipping back her hair. "It would be better if we had our full arsenal. You know how there are many ways to . . . dialogue." Meaning the guns they'd left at home in Pennsylvania because they never thought they'd need them during this trip.

She was right. Without knowing who they were dealing with, it didn't make sense to volunteer to be sitting ducks.

"I could grab one and stuff him in the back so we could converse in a more private setting," Bryan said.

"Now you're thinking."

"Which one? You pick."

Charlotte pointed to her right. "The one with the hoodie. Who wears a hoodie when it's hot enough to melt steel outside?"

Bryan grinned. "Solid choice. Even more solid reasoning. Let's go."

As soon as they opened their doors, the tinny clang of an alarm went off. The door to the stationery store across the street flew open as two men casually walked out carrying cardboard boxes. The man who either owned or worked in the store came running out after them.

"Get back here! You think you can just rob me blind? I called the cops."

One of the men laughed. "You do that, *papi*. Call me when they get here."

The thieves proceeded to walk down the street as if they didn't have a care in the world. Taking a quick glance over at the playground, Bryan noted not one single head turned to witness the brazen burglary. They either didn't care or it was such a common occurrence, it had become background noise. Probably a bit of both.

Bryan had seen this kind of devil-may-care robbery in

news reports from places like New York, San Francisco, Chicago, and Seattle.

But in Iowa?

"Detour?" he asked his wife.

"Without a doubt."

They jogged to the man from the store. He was perhaps sixty, slightly overweight, and sweating profusely.

"Are you okay, sir?" Charlotte asked.

"Not by a long shot." He wiped the sweat on his brow with his forearm.

This close, Bryan recognized him as the man who used to manage the bowling alley. He couldn't remember his name, but he did recall the kids nicknaming him Cue Ball on account of his having no hair.

"That's the third time this month," Cue Ball said. "Same guys, too. If this keeps up, I'm gonna go broke! And the police don't give a damn."

"What did they take?" Charlotte asked, keeping one eye on the sauntering thieves.

Cue Ball threw up his hands. "Every pack of cigarettes and lottery scratch-off in the place! My insurance company is gonna cancel my policy for sure this time."

"Hold off on calling them," Bryan said.

As he and Charlotte walked down the block, he heard Cue Ball say, "Don't I know you from somewhere?"

"Last time I saw him, he chased me out from behind the bowling alley he ran for smoking," Bryan whispered to his wife.

"You really did need an ass whupping, didn't you?"

"That's what the army and you supplied in abundance."

They didn't run after the thieves because they didn't

want to alert them. Besides, it was too hot to do anything more than a semifast walk. And these guys were in no hurry to get to wherever they were going. In fact, just two blocks away from the scene of their crime, they set down their boxes, opened a pack of cigarettes, and took a smoke break.

When Bryan and Charlotte caught up to them, Bryan looked down at the boxes briming with cigarette packs. "Spare a smoke?"

The man who had laughed at Cue Ball blew smoke in his face. "Take a hike."

"I only asked because it looks like you have plenty to spare."

"Not for you. Now get outta my face."

His partner, who was as pale as he was dark, tittered until he coughed.

Bryan stood with his hands on his hips. "I asked you nicely. Why can't you be nice in return?"

The thieves looked at each other as if they had just seen an alien pop out of a spaceship. "Can you believe this guy?" the white one said. Then he turned to Charlotte and said, "Why is someone as fine as you with someone as dumb as him?"

Charlotte didn't give him the satisfaction of a reply.

Bryan squatted to get closer to one of the boxes. "I'm smart enough to realize you didn't buy these cigs and lottery cards."

As he reached out to touch the box, the dark man's hand flew from his pocket, a switchblade firmly in his grasp.

"A switchblade? What is this, *West Side Story*? You do realize that is the most ineffective knife to bring to a fight, right?"

Before the man could try to stick Bryan with the business end of the switchblade, Charlotte brought the full force of her elbow on his wrist. The crack of breaking bones had long since lost their ability to repulse Bryan. In situations like this they were more like music.

The blade clattered to the floor. Before the thief could grab his broken wrist, Charlotte delivered a savage punch to his throat. He collapsed against the wall, gasping for air.

The other thief was on the edge of fight-or-flight.

Bryan decided to make the decision for him. He slapped him hard enough to make his head jerk violently to the side. His eyes fluttered and he went down hard.

The wounded thief's mouth opened and closed in pained silence, like a fish that had been dropped on land.

"Just settle down," Charlotte said to him. "If I meant to break your windpipe, I would have."

Bryan patted the unconscious man's cheek until his eyes opened. He waited for them to clear.

"Now, my wife and I are going to return these to the man you stole them from. And if we hear of you stealing from anyone again, we're going to hit you hard enough to make sure it's the last thing you ever do. The police may not care, but we do. Do you understand me?"

Both men stared at them, wild-eyed and confused.

Bryan shouted loud enough to make them flinch. "I said, do you understand me?"

One man nodded vigorously, the other with the damaged throat barely, but the message was clear. He then croaked, "Hospital."

"You weren't worried about the police coming," Charlotte said. "I wouldn't worry about an ambulance, either."

She and Bryan picked up the boxes and turned their backs to them. Cue Ball was huffing down the street with an enormous grin. "Thank you! Thank you!" When he looked at the thieves on the ground, his upper lip curled and he spat, "Serves you right. How do you like a taste of your own medicine?"

They looked at Bryan and Charlotte and seemed to think better of making any kind of reply.

"We'll bring these back to your store," Bryan said.

"Really, I can't thank you enough. I've been terrorized by those two for the better part of a year. They knocked out two of my teeth the last time."

A smattering of applause suddenly broke out around them. Bryan's attention was so fixed on the thieves that he hadn't noticed the crowd that had gathered around as shop owners and pedestrians came out to see what was going on.

"Way to go!"

"That'll show them!"

"It's about time!"

"Can I hire you?"

"There's more where they came from."

He also noticed that the playground had emptied out

to watch the spectacle. They were not clapping. Rather, they looked worried.

All he and Charlotte could do was smile and give polite nods as folks patted them on their backs on their way to the stationery store. Before they went inside to help put the pilfered items where they belonged, Bryan took the moment to address the stoners and dealers from the playground.

"Enjoy watching, because you're next. You tell Jimmy when you see him that I want to meet his boss at the gazebo tomorrow at three. If he doesn't show, you *all* will have a problem."

Glassy and venomous eyes glared at him.

Inside the store, Bryan and Charlotte got behind the counter with Cue Ball and placed packs of cigarettes in their slots on the wall rack while Cue Ball told them about the wave of unpunished crime that had become a daily occurrence thanks to district attorneys who refused to punish criminals.

"They say society failed them so they've been punished enough already. Is that the most asinine thing you've ever heard? We need to lock these DAs away for dereliction of duty and failure to protect fully functioning, God-fearing citizens." Cue Ball picked up one of the cigarette packs that had been crushed when they were pilfered. He threw it on his counter in disgust. "I'd pack it in and move, but I've lost so much money over the last year, I can't afford it. So now I get to sit here and let these criminals whittle me down until I die broke and alone. It breaks my heart what's become of this place. I'm only glad my mother isn't alive to see it."

Bryan put a hand on Cue Ball's shoulder. "One thing I've learned is to never give up hope. District attorneys get elected. With what I see, there's no reason anyone in their right mind would vote them back in."

Cue Ball waved a hand in disgust. "With that turn-coat governor leading this state, she'll only coerce the next one to her will. These people are in it for money and power. Bennington will find a way to dangle that in their faces if they play by her rules." He stopped his ranting to study Bryan's face. "Hey, I know you. You used to run with that wild crowd. Always up to something when I owned the bowling alley."

Bryan's cheeks reddened. "Guilty as charged. Name's Bryan Branch." He thrust out his hand and they shook. "And this is my wife, Charlotte."

"Branch. You related to George Branch? I read what happened out at the farm in the paper. I'm sorry to hear about that . . . and your mother."

"Yeah, I'm sorry, too."

After an awkward pause Cue Ball said, "Well, I guess you're proof that a person can turn their life around."

"I like to think so. You won't catch me stealing smokes behind the bowling alley."

That brought a smile to the man's face. "Those were good days. Even when I had to chase you kids. You may have been up to no good, but you weren't like those wastes of space." He pointed out the window to the park across the street. The stoners had returned to their usual spots, flaunting their disrespect for their community and the law. "Well, the bowling alley is just an empty building now. But seeing you, you give me hope. Let me do something for you."

"That's really not necessary," Bryan said.

"Free paper and a coffee anytime you come in at least," Cue Ball said.

"That's nice of you to offer, but you don't have to do that."

"It will make me feel better."

"Then fine. We're just happy to help."

Cue Ball huffed. "Help has been something in short supply here. You come back to Maverick to stay?"

"For a while longer than I initially thought." Bryan found a pen on the counter and wrote his cell phone number on a lottery slip. "You have problems again, call me. I'll see what I can do."

"I definitely will. Thank you, Bryan. Thank you, Charlotte. This started out as a terrible day, what with the heat and the power out and those goons. You're the silver lining I think we all needed."

They shook again, and Bryan and Charlotte headed back to the truck.

"'Local boy makes good on redemptive return to small-town America in peril,'" Charlotte said in the voice of a newscaster.

Bryan opened the RAM's door for her. They were both a sweaty mess and couldn't wait for the cool kiss of air-conditioning. "Headlines are not a good thing."

"Not in our line of work. But this is different from our, uh, usual."

He started the RAM, his gaze sliding over to the park filled with lost youth. "I'm beginning to think it's not all that different. In fact, we have a call to make."

CHAPTER 13

"Are you serious?" Shane Perretti said on the other end of the line. "What kind of crap storm did you get yourself into?"

Bryan and Charlotte were back at the farm. She and Lola were going through a workbook that Jason had found in the attic to help her with her spelling. Their mother used to bog him and Jason down with workbooks during the summer break before, as she put it, their brains turned to mush.

The cornstalks were as still as terra-cotta soldiers and the sun felt like it was hanging about ten feet over the porch. Bryan's glass of cold tap water had turned tepid in seconds.

"It wasn't something I went looking for. But it's kind of hard to miss," Bryan said.

"In Iowa?"

"Yep. In Iowa."

Shane sighed. "Looks like the drive'll be about fourteen hours. Very doable. How much do you want me to bring?"

That was a good question. Bryan had a feeling it

would take a while to close the Pandora's box that he'd just opened.

"Prepare for the worst," he said.

He could almost hear Shane's smile. "You got it, Boss. I'll hit the road in about an hour. Factoring in gas and bathroom and food breaks, I should be there by early morning. Just in time for a good old country breakfast."

Shane's appetite was a force of nature.

"Don't set your hunger jets to full throttle. We have no electricity, so perishables are starting to perish. I can charge my phone in the car, so you'll have no problems getting through to me."

"Too bad this isn't a paying gig."

"It is in a way. A paying *back* gig."

"I'm always looking for karma points. Got a lot to make up for."

Bryan laughed. "Well, this is a chance to maybe even the books. See you tomorrow."

Charlotte walked onto the porch just as he hung up.

"The cavalry is coming," Bryan said.

"Good. He can help take shifts on night watch while he's at it."

Bryan pulled her close. "Not that anyone can sleep in this heat."

Just then the door opened and Bryan's father came out sipping from a warm bottle of Coke. He was still wearing his overalls. The man didn't have a drop of sweat on him.

They don't make them like that anymore, Bryan thought. Even his band of veterans who had been forged in that damn desert in the Middle East weren't as stoic as George Branch.

"What cavalry is coming?" he asked as he settled into his chair.

"Just a friend of mine," Bryan said.

His father flashed him a look that told him he didn't believe it was *just a friend* coming for a visit.

David and Pam came out as well, smiling despite everything. "That was very kind of you," Pam said to George.

"It only makes sense. Kids shouldn't have to suffer. They'll do enough of that when they're older."

"What did you do?" Bryan asked.

David answered. "He set up cots in the basement for Lola and Tomás."

Bryan was confused.

"A lot cooler down there." And that was all George was going to say about the subject.

"I'm going to make some sandwiches," Pam said. "I hope peanut butter and jelly is good. The cold cuts went bad."

"That sounds good," Bryan said. "You can go heavy on the PB, light on the J for me. In fact, let me help you. I feel like a third wheel today."

As he and Pam made the sandwiches, he wondered how much longer the jelly would hold out before it soured, too. If the power didn't come back on soon, they'd be down to bread and water.

He also thought of all the people who might not even have this much. What was going to happen to them if this went on much longer? There was still no definitive word on what had happened at the substation, but one report briefly mentioned that a white nationalist group was a chief suspect. No shock there. Again, no specific group was named.

"You see this?" Jason said. He came in the back door with a newspaper in his hands. With the Wi-Fi out and data getting low, he'd gone old school. Bryan assumed he picked it up at Cue Ball's place. "They found five teenagers dead in a bedroom last night."

Bryan's ears perked up. "Were they murdered?"

Jason scanned the article. "In a way. Fentanyl overdose. They think the pot they were smoking was either laced with it, or they added it and didn't take into account how little of it was actually needed." He continued to read, then his eyes closed and he dropped the paper on the table. "One of them was Henry Goodkind's kid. Good Christ. She was his only child."

Bryan hadn't heard the name since he was a kid. Henry was the brainiac of Jason's grade. He did everything right back then. Aced his grades, played basketball with the CYO, sang in the church choir. Bryan always assumed Henry would end up a priest or a scientist. It was hard to imagine young, innocent, and naïve Henry all grown up and with a child that he'd now lost.

"The sad thing is," Jason continued, "it seems like a whole generation is smoking weed, and sometimes they get more than they asked for or can handle. Why would a drug dealer kill his own cash cows? It makes no sense."

Pam looked horrified. Bryan spied her looking out

the window at Lola, most likely imagining the nightmare of losing her daughter. She made the sign of the cross and made another sandwich.

"It's not the dealers," Bryan said. "It's the countries behind the drug trade. When it comes to fentanyl you can lay a lot of that blame on China. My buddy Shane swears it's a concerted effort by China to wipe out a generation that would normally be called on to fight in a war. Me, I just think they like to see Americans die. Either way, you can bet it's no accident." He wiped the sweat from his forehead before it dripped on the sand-wiches. "All the more reason that we need to root out the drug trade in Maverick from the source."

Jason leaned against the counter, swapping the news-paper for an apple. "You're still not going to clue me into what you and Charlotte are up to?"

Pam's eyes went from Jason to Bryan.

"We'll talk later. Shane will be here tomorrow, so you might as well know."

"Where's he gonna sleep, the porch?"

"He's got an RV. Shane's all about self-sufficiency." *Among other things*, Bryan thought.

"You're gonna have to talk to Dad, you know. All that stuff you did behind his and mom's backs when we were kids? That's something you don't want to repeat, even if you're not some adolescent miscreant this time around." Jason finished the apple in three bites, includ-ing eating the core. Bryan was surprised his brother still did that. Back in the day, their mother would tell him an apple tree was going to grow in his stomach if he didn't stop.

Bryan set the sandwiches on plates and put a handful of potato chips next to each.

"Trust me, I will. I didn't come here to go backward."

I also didn't come here with the expectation of calling Shane in with his war wagon.

"That reminds me, I have to make a call to a lawyer friend of mine. If Dad's going to keep the farm, he's going to need some help."

Jason grabbed some plates. "Good luck with that."

"He can't lose this place. Maybe we can get the government to declare it a Bigfoot sanctuary."

"Ha ha. Limp your way to the porch, Funny Guy."

Pam walked between them. She asked, "What is this *Bigfoot* you keep calling your brother?"

Despite the stress of everything going on, Bryan laughed. "Bigfoot is a big, hairy ape-man. Like him."

Pam looked Jason up and down and giggled. "Now I understand."

"Wow. Now I'm being ganged up on. When is your plane supposed to leave?"

They ate their sandwiches out on the porch, lingering outside until the brutal sun went down. Even in the dark of a half-moon night, the heat and humidity didn't take their foot off the gas.

Still, Bryan enjoyed the night with his family and the Cruzes. Lola and Tomás eventually went down to the basement to cool off and sleep. The adults were reluctant to go inside the cloying house, so they remained on the porch, reminiscing and learning more about David and Pam and the many hardships they'd endured in Mexico and America. Even George Branch became loquacious at one point, filling Charlotte in on some of the gritty details of Bryan's teenage years that, in light of the real life-and-death issues they were facing today, seemed almost trivial. There was a lot of laughing at Bryan's expense. He didn't mind it one bit.

It was close to a picture-perfect evening. The only thing that could make it better was if his mother was there, crocheting a blanket while talking about the old times and laughing.

It would be the last moment of peace for all of them for a long, long time.

CHAPTER 14

Shane Perretti called ahead when he was about an hour away from the farm. Bryan told him that he and Charlotte would meet him by the pharmacy in town.

"What, no farmer's breakfast?" Shane said.

Bryan paced in the kitchen. The creaking of floorboards above told him that his father and brother were up and getting ready. "Not today. Most of the food is spoiled here anyway. I have to do something first, and I don't think you showing up in your RV will make things any easier."

"This is no way to treat a guest."

"You're more of a house *pest* than a guest. Just cool your heels."

Bryan hung up the phone. Pam startled him when she slipped into the kitchen.

"I'm sorry," she said. "I wanted to make breakfast, but I don't even know if there's anything left to cook."

Bryan went through the cabinets and pulled out a can of beans. "My old man always loved beans on toast. Trust me, he's not a picky eater. Just needs some calories to get through the day."

Pam rolled her eyes when she took the can. "Canned beans. I'm just glad my *abuela* isn't here to see this."

"And eggs. We'll always have eggs."

Already breaking a sweat, Bryan poured himself a cup of coffee and waited in the living room. When his father came down he said, "Can we talk for a second?"

And that was when he told him about encountering Jimmy, upsetting the drug runners in town, and wanting to find the men who had attacked the farm. He let him know he'd called his friend Shane to come lend a hand, and that Shane was a veteran as well.

George Branch sat taking it all in without saying a word, his face as unreadable as a stone wall. Bryan had been through this dance before, but in the past he was either lying or pleading.

When he was done they sat in the cloying living room for what seemed an eternity, neither speaking, gazes locked.

Finally, his father said, "You think you and your friend can find the men who did this to us?"

"I do."

"And as if that isn't enough, you plan to stop the drug trade in Maverick?"

"I can try."

"Then do it." His father got up from his ratty chair.

"I'll do my best. And trust me, I'm very good at what I do."

George huffed. "There was a time I'd treat your promise like a balloon. All empty inside." He stared at Bryan with an intensity that felt as if he were measuring his soul. "You came back better than I hoped you'd be. I'm just sorry your mother wasn't here to see it."

"Look, Dad, I'm no angel."

"I know it. I went to church every Sunday with your mother for going on forty years. If there was one thing I learned, angels were not pretty boys with wings. When bad people encountered angels, it was the worst day of their lives. I see you, Son. I see it in your eyes. You've been through things I can't even contemplate. We need you to be an angel, Bryan. Be the most terrifying angel you can be."

With that, he went into the kitchen and was greeted by Pam with a plate of hot beans and dry toast beside a hard-boiled egg. He ate quickly and was out the door, off to another day of harvesting corn.

David and Jason came down next, both eating in silence before heading out.

Jason said, "I heard you talking to Dad. You're going to have to cut me in. I'm bigger than you, and stronger than you, too. And I was here when Mom died. If, while you're kicking up trouble, you find those men, remember it's a family affair. You good with that?"

Bryan sat with his elbows on his knees. He slowly nodded.

"Okay, then. See you later."

Twenty minutes later, Bryan and Charlotte were in town. It was hard to miss Shane's RV in the early dawn light. It was dirty and dented and twice the size of any vehicle parked on the street.

Before Bryan's knuckles could rap on the door, it swung open. Shane was holding a bowl full of eggs. He looked exceedingly refreshed and alert for someone who had driven all through the night to get there. His infectious smile was present and accounted for.

"Sorry, I'm no witness for Jehovah."

"Hey Shane," Charlotte said. She gave him a quick kiss on the cheek when she walked through the door. It was cool inside the RV. The smell of fried bacon and pancakes was this side of heaven.

"Grab a plate and have a seat. When you told me about the power being out I stocked up on food. Also brought a generator we can hook up to your house."

Bryan was appreciative of the cool air. He put some eggs and bacon on a plate and plopped down on a bench, knowing that under the cushion was a cache of weapons. The interior was a stark contrast to the exterior. Just like its owner, the RV was a study in contrasts. "How was your drive?"

Shane munched on a strip of bacon. "Fine. Just me, the road, and an endless supply of Willie Nelson. You know me. I could drive to Alaska and be happy as a kid on Christmas morning."

Bryan's war buddy and current tow truck driver may have grown up on Long Island, but he was obsessed with all things Southern. After his discharge he'd lived for a few years in a little South Carolina town called Springerville. It didn't take much for him to convert into a country boy. He kept talking about going back to Springerville, especially when the town was in the news. It seemed the townies had taken their home back from less-than-desirable big-city interlopers. Shane bemoaned the fact that he hadn't been there to take part in it. Bryan couldn't help feeling a correlation between Springerville and Maverick.

"We should bring the leftovers home," Charlotte said between bites of a pancake. "You made enough to feed a church social."

"That was the idea," Shane replied, tapping the side of his head. "By the way, what's up with your slice of Americana? I've had seven people knock on my door begging for money, food, even booze, since I parked. I keep thinking I took a left and wound up in San Fransicko."

"Just another symptom of a deep, underlying problem. I can't decide what I feel more, mad or sad," Bryan said.

Charlotte patted his arm. "I'm the one who has to listen to you grinding your teeth all night. Trust me, I know the answer."

Shane sat down opposite them, the small table piled with plates of food. "So, you expecting a shoot-out at the O.K. Corral? Meeting in the middle of the afternoon isn't exactly your brightest idea. We're still here because we like the shadows."

"You may be right. I just think this needs to be done in the light of day so everyone can see. There are people here who need hope. And there are others who need to learn fear. Hard to do that under the cover of night."

"We have before."

"Yeah, but this is my hometown. It's different."

After breakfast Shane opened the small safe in the back bedroom and gave Bryan and Charlotte their favorite pistols. Bryan's was a Glock 19X and Charlotte's was an expensive Staccato 2011 CS. Each was an extension of their arm. Just holding them brought them comfort.

"Cleaned them for you before I left," Shane said. "So, what's the plan?"

Bryan tucked his gun in the back of his waistband. "Like always, we hurry up and wait." He looked at Shane's getup. He wore camo cargo shorts, a sleeveless T-shirt, and a fishing cap that had seen better days. "You already look like you fit right in here. This was always a place where everyone knew everyone. Now it's just strangers looking for trouble." He pulled out a map of the area he'd drawn the night before. "The playground seems to be the heart of the drug trade in town."

"That's sick." Shane cringed at the thought.

"The only people on the swings now are high as kites," Charlotte reassured him. "Not a child in sight."

"Come three o'clock, I plan to walk right to the center of the playground. There's nowhere to lie in wait to ambush me in the playground itself. But there are plenty of places around it. That's where you two come in. About a half hour before I head out, I need you to sweep the area and then watch my back."

Shane tapped the map with his thick index finger. "You mentioned there might be some cartel stuff going on. This could get out of hand."

"If anything, it's cartel light. Any dealer using a loser like my old friend Jimmy doesn't exactly ooze managerial confidence." He knocked back a cold glass of orange juice, knowing it was going to be hard to force himself out of the RV. The unending heat was wearing on him. "One last thing. Shoot only if you have to, and if you have to, shoot to maim, not kill."

"That makes things a lot harder," Charlotte said.

"I like a challenge," Shane said.

"And if you do shoot, you need to disappear. Fast."

"Like ghosties," Shane replied, waving his hand in the air. "Though I have some ideas that don't involve guns. Charlotte, you interested?"

"Of course."

"Remember that job in Nigeria?"

Charlotte laughed and slapped her knee. "You still have them?"

Shane kicked the floor. "Got them stashed right under our feet."

Bryan had been on that Nigerian job but couldn't recall exactly what they were referring to. He just remembered how it had almost gone belly up at least half a dozen times. They were lucky to make it out alive, much less have something to laugh about. He said, "I also want them alive in case they can lead us to who shot up and burned my parents' farm. Cops have a recent shooter in custody, but he's not talking. We get enough of them, one is bound to break the Cone of Silence."

Charlotte popped her knuckles. "To be honest, I'm not a fan of this plan. Why don't you skip it today and we can take them by surprise? At night, when no one is around."

"Because it's not just about them." He pulled aside the curtain and pointed to the shops across the street. "It's for them, too. And those five teens who overdosed.

This has to stop today. Now, let's hide this RV. I know just the place."

Shane snapped off a crisp salute. "Aye, aye, Captain."

The RV rumbled, and Bryan and Charlotte had to grip the edge of the table to keep from slipping off the bench. Bryan fought gravity until he was in the passenger seat, telling Shane where to go.

"Doesn't sound like this is going to take long," Shane said as he turned on the stereo. "Everything's Beautiful," a sappy duet by Willie Nelson and Dolly Parton, blared out of the speakers. "What kind of fun do you have planned for tomorrow?"

Bryan set his boot against the dash. "That all depends on how loose we can make some lips today."

It was minutes before three o'clock. Bryan had scoped out the playground and knew where he could stash his Glock if necessary. Iowa recognized conceal carry permits from other states, but there was no sense taking a chance if he didn't have to.

The playground was empty, which implied that word of his demand had spread. That was a very good thing. He didn't want anyone getting hurt who didn't need to.

Without being obvious, Bryan tried to find out where Shane and Charlotte were hiding. Although he couldn't see them, he knew they had his back.

Standing alongside a bench in the middle of the park, Bryan checked his watch. Seven minutes after three. He kept expecting to see Jimmy come waltzing in, waving a proverbial white flag as a means of distracting him while the real dealers behind the drug trade ambushed him. The sun felt as if it was crouched on his shoulder like an expectant vulture. Every pore of his body leaked sweat. When it came to showdowns like this Bryan was as cool as the other side of the pillow. He'd looked death straight in the eye too many times to panic.

Five minutes later, three men approached him from the other side of the park. They wore long black jackets in the sweltering heat, which meant they were packing some serious weaponry. If they had just handguns, a hoodie or windbreaker would have sufficed.

Or maybe they'd watched too many gangster movies and thought this made them look intimidating.

Bryan could see the fat beads of sweat running down their faces from twenty yards away.

Posing idiots, he thought. The heat would slow their reflexes, as would their bulky jackets. More than likely they were sporting shotguns under said jackets. By the time they managed to pull them up and point, he could put a bullet dead center in each of their foreheads.

"You can stop right there," Bryan said when they were around ten yards from him.

"We stop when I say we stop," the man in the middle said. All were Mexican, the leader about six inches shorter than his bodyguards, who looked like they'd just broken out of some dunghole prison in Tijuana. They had terrible tattoos on their necks and faces, the fleshly décor of society's flotsam and jetsam.

Bryan reached behind his back, his fingers tightening around the grip of his gun.

"It's in your best interest to drop the tough guy act," Bryan said, his throat scratchy because he was parched. "I came here to talk, but I'm more than happy to let this go down a different way."

The man in the center looked at Bryan, then at his goons, as if to say, *Can you believe the stones on this guy?*

"If you want to test me, I'd say you have about two seconds before you're choking on your own blood."

That stopped them.

The leader considered him for a long moment, then wiped sweat from his threadbare mustache. He grinned like a jackal with indigestion. "That's some big talk from a man who is outnumbered."

"You'd need to call a whole lot more of your stupid friends if you wanted to outnumber me."

The insult wiped the smile from the man's face. Bryan was no linguist, but he had managed to learn ways to offend people in at least a dozen languages. He found it often came in handy.

"What did you just say to me?"

The flanking bodyguards stretched their necks and made a big show of trying to look menacing. Their hands had also disappeared inside their coats.

"You heard me just fine. Which means you can hear this. I want you and your drugs to disappear from Maverick. Not tomorrow. Not next week. At this very moment."

"And what happens if we don't?"

"You don't want to find out. If I could connect you

with the afterlife, I have a lot of people who would be happy to advise you to do what I say."

The man spat on the ground and took two steps behind his goons. They moved forward until he was almost completely shielded. "I don't know who the hell you think you are, but this is *my* town," he said. "And no one tells me what to do in my town."

Bryan kept his eyes locked on the goons. "Well, I grew up here and I'm pretty sure I never saw you around the schoolyard. Which means this is actually *my* town. I don't allow drug pushers and murderers in my town. You dig it?"

There was a long silence as both sides stared each other down.

One of the goons finally spoke up. "The only thing we're going to dig is your grave, *hijo de puta!*"

When the goons opened their mouths that was usually the sign that things were about to get hot and heavy.

The one who hadn't spoken grabbed the side of his neck as if he'd been stung by a wasp. A splash of crimson squirted through his fingers. He dropped to a knee with a panicked look in his eye.

The talking goon twitched this way and that as great blotches of red exploded all up and down his great coat, and then the side of his face.

Before their fearless leader could turn tail and run, both sides of his head burst with fountains of scarlet. In a matter of seconds, all three men were on the ground, writhing in agony. Bryan raced toward them, his old friend adrenaline letting him forget he had a bum reconstructed knee. He relieved them of their weapons with the speed of a hummingbird taking a sip of water on a summer afternoon.

Shane and Charlotte came running into the playground carrying guns in one hand and a fistful of zip ties in the other.

Bryan spotted the cylindrical containers set on top of each of their guns.

"Paint balls?" he said.

"You wanted them alive," Charlotte said as she applied zip ties to the nontalking goon's wrists.

"Except you don't want to get hit with these paint balls. I modified the CO_2 cartridges. They'll have bruises for a month," Shane said breathily.

"I don't think they need to worry about how things will be a month from now," Bryan said gravely. There were consequences to the things they did, but he had made peace with himself and the life he'd chosen long ago.

The goons were woozy and their leader was out cold from the shot to his temple. The talking goon saw all the red and started to panic. Shane clobbered him with a left hook to his jaw and put him out.

"I'll get the RV so we can load them up," he said. "You two okay to babysit?"

"I think we'll be fine," Charlotte said, flashing a wink Bryan's way.

Shane ran out of the playground, remarkably fast for a man who had put on some extra padding the past couple of years.

Charlotte sat atop the unconscious leader. "That was almost too easy."

"Yeah, well, I don't think they were expecting paint-ballin' soldiers of fortune to pee on their picnic."

His wife smiled wide and beautiful. "Nobody ever does."

"So, you two paintballed your way out of that Nigerian village?"

"There were a lot of kids around. Trust me, it hurts enough to lay a man down, and when he sees red, he assumes the worst."

Several minutes later, Shane pulled the RV up to the park's entrance. With a little bit of difficulty, they loaded the three men inside while the shop owners and citizens of Maverick watched.

No one said a word.

But the smiles on their faces spoke volumes.

CHAPTER 15

Everyone was busy at work on the farm when the RV and the rental car pulled up to the house. Bryan flicked the light switch the second he walked in the door. Still no power. The air inside the house was practically unbreathable. The thermometer outside was nearing ninety-five degrees. He wondered how many people were close to dying at this point.

One problem at a time, he reminded himself.

"Still dead?" Charlotte asked when he came back out.

"Yep. It's like a pizza oven in there. Might be better to sleep outside tonight if we can't get the genny Shane brought up and running. I'll have to check if my father saved our sleeping bags and tents later."

There wasn't even a hint of a breeze. He worried about his father. Going on seventy, he was still tougher than leather, but he was human, too. He dialed Jason on his cell.

"What's up?" Jason sounded winded.

"Can you come over to the house now? We'll be in my friend's RV."

"Be right there."

Bryan and Charlotte went back into the cool RV. The three men now also had zip ties around their ankles and duct tape wrapped around their mouths. They looked like they had waded through a river of bright red blood. They were wide awake now and shooting daggers at Shane, who had an AR15 trained on them.

"Don't make a move," he said. "I guarantee you there ain't no paint in this bad boy."

A few minutes later, there was a knock on the door.

"Before I let you inside, I need you to realize what you see is paint, not blood," Bryan warned his brother.

Jason looked puzzled. "Oookay. That sounds bizarre."

Bryan waved him in. Jason's eyes went wide for a moment when he saw the three captives.

"You recognize any of them?" Charlotte asked as she offered him a cold bottle of water. Jason was drenched in sweat, but he didn't even try to take a drink. His eyes were glued to the men on the floor.

"Who are they?"

One of the goons started flexing in an attempt to break out of the zip ties around his wrists. Shane tapped him hard on the head with the barrel of his gun. "Calm down, buddy."

"Were any of them at the house looking for work or on the night Mom died?" Bryan clenched and unclenched his fists.

Jason stepped closer, squatting so he could get a better look at their faces. "Um, I'm not sure."

"I need you to be very sure."

"Give me a second."

The leader mumbled something against the duct tape. His narrow eyes radiated fury. It didn't seem to bother Jason one bit.

After a quiet spell of studying them up and down Jason said, "I don't think it was them. These two are too big. This guy, he's about the right height, but nothing about his face rings a bell. Seems a little on the older side, too."

Bryan released a breath he wasn't aware he'd been holding. "Okay. Thanks."

What he thought was, *Son of a mongrel. I should have known this wouldn't be easy.*

"So, who are they?" Jason asked again. Now he twisted the top off the water bottle and downed half of it in a loud series of gulps.

"We're pretty sure they're the guys behind the drug trade in town," Charlotte said. "We'll find out more in a bit."

Bryan patted his brother on the shoulder. "Let's let Shane and Charlotte do their thing." He ushered Jason out the door. The heat felt like a punch to the face.

The RV motor hummed, and it made a wide turn, heading down the driveway.

"Wait, where are they going?"

"Someplace remote where they won't be disturbed."

Jason watched the RV disappear around the bend. "But what are they going to do?"

"Charlotte has very special interrogation skills. She's going to try to extract as much from them as she can. And Shane, well, he does whatever needs doing."

They walked to the picnic table, sitting on opposite edges.

Cicadas chirped mercilessly all around them.

"Are they going to, you know, kill them?" Jason said after finishing his water.

"They'll do whatever needs to be done. If history is a good indicator, I wouldn't set a place for them at the dinner table tonight."

A look of grave concern fell over Jason's face. "But that's your wife."

"You have to stop looking at her as some soccer mom/housewife. Yes, she's my wife. She's also one of the best, brightest, and bravest soldiers you're ever going to meet."

"Heck, dude, what exactly are you guys into?"

Bryan looked up at the broiling sun, slicked the sweat from the back of his neck.

"I'll tell you. But you have to promise not to interrupt me. And it will help to keep a very open mind."

Everyone had looked worse for wear after a day of toiling in the cornfields. Even Lola and Tomás were listless after dinner. Shane was the electrical expert, and he was still who knew where with Charlotte and their captives. Bryan and his father attempted to get the generator hooked up, but it was difficult in the dark with only some flickering candles to work by.

"At least we can't electrocute ourselves," Bryan joked at one point, sweat stinging his eyes and pouring down his face.

"Save it for tomorrow," his father replied. "I don't want to keep fiddling with this and say some words that'll make your mother come straight down from Heaven and give me a what for."

Bryan and Jason found their old tents and sleeping bags and set up a minicamp in the backyard. The kids were delighted. The adults, without giving voice to it, were less enthusiastic about sleeping on the ground. George said his hips had outgrown sleeping bags and chose to sleep in the living room with every window thrown wide open.

When Bryan was asked where Charlotte was he told them she was with a friend who'd come to visit. His father looked as if he had many more questions to ask but decided to let it drop.

It was near three in the morning when Bryan got up from his sleeping bag and settled into a wicker chair on the front porch.

He wasn't worried about Charlotte and Shane. They were somewhere close to town, and fearing for their safety never crossed his mind. He'd left his wife in hostile territory with no means of communication before. She always came back to him. And it wasn't as if the three men they'd captured were exactly pros. They'd been taken down by paintballs, for corn's sake.

What had sleep evading him was wondering what intel they were getting from their captives, if any. The crickets kept him company, as did the fluttering and chirping of bats as they flitted over the field.

Jason's heavy footsteps broke his train of thought.

"Can't sleep?" Jason asked.

"I think that goes without saying," Bryan said, snappier than he'd intended.

"I'm sure Charlotte is all right," Jason said as he sat on the top porch step. The sweat on his face glistened in the moonlight.

"Of that I have no doubt. I'm just anxious to hear what she gets out of them."

Jason looked back at him. "The things you told me. I mean, they sound insane. Like stuff out of a movie. Why on earth do you do it?"

That was one question Bryan had never bothered himself with. "For one, it pays well. But that's the bottom of the priority list. It's what we were trained to do. It's what we're very good at. One thing I learned during my time in the Middle East is that there's no short supply of very bad people doing terrible things to very good people. None of us are saints. We all share a checkered past. The military reshaped us, made us what we needed to be. Maybe we're trying to atone for past sins. More than that, I just believe we're doing what's right. Taking care of the dirty work so others don't have to."

Shaking his head, Jason said, "My big brother, the vigilante."

"Charles Bronson was a vigilante."

"So, do you subscribe to *Soldier of Fortune* magazine?"

"Do *you* subscribe to *Combine Weekly*?"

Jason raised an eyebrow. "Is there such a thing?"

"I don't know. You tell me. How about *Bigfoot Quarterly*?"

"Well, at least you're still an impossible idiot. Glad to see that some things haven't changed."

They sat listening to the crickets for a few minutes, hoping for a breeze that never came.

"Yes," Bryan said.

"Yes what?"

"I read *Soldier of Fortune* magazine. But I don't subscribe. That's traceable. Always buy it from different places with cash. Lesson one, Grasshopper."

Jason's mouth opened to throw something his way when they heard the RV come rumbling down the road to the farm. The lights preceded the dented bus before it stopped well before the driveway. The headlights flashed three times, a signal for Bryan to come to them.

Bryan's knee ached when he stood up. "You stay here."

"Not a chance. If those guys had anything to do with what happened to Mom, I'm in."

"But they may not have."

"Either way. Unless you want to try to stand in my way."

It was said part in jest, but also partly serious because Jason was in the erroneous mindset that size mattered when it came to hand-to-hand combat. Bryan was in no mood to wrestle with his brother.

"Fine. You're a big boy now. Just remember to keep what you hear and see to yourself."

"Lesson two for Grasshopper?"

Bryan walked past him, heading for the RV. The door swung open just as he got there. Charlotte waited for him on the top step with her hands on her hips. Her hair was a little out of place, but otherwise she looked fine.

"Did you miss me?" she asked.

"Always." They hugged until Jason tried to squeeze through the door. "I thought you wouldn't be back until later."

Shane was in the driver's seat with his booted feet propped on the steering wheel. He had a *Fantastic Four* comic book on his lap. "Did you forget how good your wife is?"

"That's one thing I never forget."

"Oh, hey Jason," Charlotte said, stepping back to make room for him. He had to hunch to avoid hitting his head on the RV's ceiling.

"Shane, this is my baby brother, Jason. Though the only thing baby left about him is that smooth round face."

Shane shook his hand. "Damn, corn does a body good, doesn't it? You should have stayed on the farm a little longer, Brother," he said to Bryan.

Bryan was too hot and tired for small talk, even though the temperature in the RV was this side of wonderful. "So, what did you get out of them?"

He noticed a small smear of blood on the floor, and some more on the edge of the foldout table. Jason saw it, too.

"They were exactly who they said they were. Just low-level dealers being supplied every month by some runners employed by the cartel. The runners are illegals who owe the cartel for getting them into the country. They operate out of fear rather than any sense of loyalty."

"Did you find out where they hold the stuff?"

Charlotte extracted a piece of paper from her back pocket. "Got it right here."

"Good. We'll go destroy it all in the morning. Did they have anything to do with the day laborers who came here?"

Charlotte looked crestfallen. "No. And trust me, they were pretty quick to talk. We gave them a good incentive. They had no idea who they were but had heard about them because word gets around in a small town. They would have given up their mothers at that point if they knew who burned up the farm. Trust me."

Bryan trusted Charlotte implicitly. No one could drag information from a captive better than his wife. She was also incredibly adept at reading people. At times it bordered on the spooky. It was why Bryan knew lying or being evasive with her was futile.

"Hey," Jason said, "where are the guys?"

"Where they belong," Shane said.

Jason looked to Charlotte and then his brother. "Wait, you killed them?"

"It's a dog-eat-dog world, man," Shane said. "We can't afford to have them blabbing to their bosses. Besides, no one will miss them. Yeah, people in town will miss their dope, but that's all the more reason to take them off the board."

Jason looked like he was on overload. Bryan was

glad he'd clued him into some of the details of their secret life earlier. If he hadn't, the man's head might have blown clear off.

"You two, get some shut-eye. We have more to do later," Bryan said.

"I'm actually freezing in here," Charlotte said.

"Well, get ready to enjoy sleeping in the great outdoors." Bryan turned to leave. "I'll introduce you to the gang if you don't mind getting up in a couple of hours," he said to Shane.

"Sounds good. I'm just gonna finish this comic, clean up those stains, and hit the hay for a bit."

Bryan, Charlotte, and Jason crept to the back of the house so they didn't wake anyone. They had all worked so hard the previous day, it probably would have taken cannon fire to jar them from their sleep.

Jason wordlessly went over to his sleeping bag, processing everything he'd learned over the past twelve hours.

As Charlotte nestled next to Bryan atop the sleeping bag, she kissed his neck and whispered in his ear, "There's a lot of good we can do here, you know?"

"I know."

"I told Shane about the power outage. He wants to investigate."

"Me too. Something's up. It's taking too long to get fixed. Maybe we add that to tomorrow's agenda."

She set her head atop his chest, and even though it made the warm night even warmer, he didn't complain.

"I have a feeling this is going to be more than the three of us can handle," she said between yawns.

"That's a bridge we'll cross another day. Just close your eyes, hon. You earned it."

They quickly drifted off to sleep under a half-moon and a symphony of night critters. Bryan never felt more at home.

CHAPTER 16

It rained late the next morning. Instead of bringing
relief, it only made the atmosphere more humid. Breathing had become a chore. Work on the farm stopped just
after noon. Bryan's father grumbled to himself as he sat
on the porch.

Meanwhile, Charlotte had asked Jason to make a list
of any elderly, single, or ill neighbors in town. It was
her idea to ride with Jason to do some wellness checks.

The need to save a life after taking one had always
been part of her nature, even when the lives she took
saved others. Jason drew up his list and plotted out the
best route to take. He and Charlotte headed out in his
truck, promising to be back by dinner.

It took a lot of cursing and false starts for Shane to
hook up the generator and get some power restored
to the house. "Damn old wiring!" he lamented time
and time again. He had five full gas cans to keep the
power running for a while. For now, they would use
the power to run the refrigerator and a minimum of
lights and fans.

Bryan found out that the downed substation was just

ten miles away. When Shane was done he tapped him for a little recon. They used the awful Nissan rental car because the RV would have been too conspicuous. Before they left, Shane encouraged everyone to use the RV as a cooling station but advised the kids not to poke around. Pam and David seemed to understand what he was getting at and spoke to the kids in Spanish before hopping aboard.

"You should take a spell in there, too, Mr. Branch," Shane said. "Take a nice nap. The bedroom's all yours. I promise you, the sheets are clean."

George waved him off. "That air-conditioning will only make this feel worse later. I'll nap right here on the porch."

Bryan tugged Shane's arm. "No sense arguing with him."

They drove to the substation with the AC on high while Shane fiddled with the radio. On a local conservative talk show, the host called out Governor Bennington for not opening a proper investigation into the latest attack on the power grid. It was the fifth in Iowa this year.

"I've been to some of the substations," the host said with a gravelly voice. "There's more security around shopping carts at a supermarket. Some aren't even fenced-off properly. It's almost as if we're encouraging our enemies to cripple us, especially when it's dangerously hot or cold. I haven't heard of any authorities taking a deep dive into what's going on here. I guess it doesn't matter to our turncoat governor because I have taken great notice that these power outages have never occurred by any of her four homes. When the lights are on and the white wine is chilled, the health and safety of the people you were elected to serve becomes a low priority. What a joke."

"I like this guy," Shane said.

"I'm sure the governor doesn't."

Bryan drove past the substation, studying it from the corner of his eye. It was next to a small industrial park that appeared to be vacant. There wasn't a car in the lot and the state of the buildings and grounds said no one had been around for quite some time.

He drove another mile, then made a U-turn, this time parking behind one of the buildings so he and Shane could approach the substation on foot. A sign on the lawn noted that it had once housed a telemarketing company, two law offices, and a Realtor.

There was a fence around the substation, but it wasn't all that high or topped with concertina wire. The gate had one padlock on it, which could easily be picked or simply chopped away with bolt cutters.

What wasn't there was what had him mad as hell.

There wasn't a single person working on fixing it. The rain had stopped hours ago. Why the hell weren't they working overtime to get it repaired?

"Well, this is unexpected," Shane said, looking around for hide or hair of a single repair person.

"You have got to be kidding me."

They walked up to the fence. Bryan checked the padlock on the gate. It wasn't even closed all the way.

"No signs of any cameras," Shane said as he looked all around.

"I think in a courtroom they would call this criminal negligence."

He slipped out the padlock and opened the gate. They walked around the transformers.

"Look at that," Shane said, pointing ahead. "That's where they shot the place up."

Bryan slipped his finger inside one of the holes. The circumference of the metal was dented inward. "Heavy round, too."

"So, not just some yokels with their daddy's rifles having a bit of idiotic fun."

Bryan ground his teeth until his temples ached. "Nope. Not a chance."

"I ask because I don't know the kind of firepower you Iowans walk around with. Okay, then it's gotta be white nationalists."

Bryan slapped his friend on the back of his head. "Idiot."

As they inspected the other transformers, they found more gunfire damage. At least one of the transformers looked like someone had been working on it. A box of tools was left beside it, as if whoever was repairing it had to run without giving his or her tools a second thought.

Or they were removed without notice.

If there was one universal law, it was how much anyone who repaired just about anything for a living valued their tools. He knew men who wouldn't bat an eye if their truck was stolen but would scream bloody murder if anyone tampered with their toolbox.

"Makes me wish I could find out who needs to fix

this and bring them down here by their ears," Bryan said.

They walked out of the substation. Bryan left the padlock hanging on a link in the fence.

Shane reached for the pistol he had tucked at his back when they saw a man standing ten yards from the enclosure. Bryan put his hand on Shane's chest to get him to cool down.

The man must have sensed the potential for danger because he took a frightened step back and raised his hands. "I didn't do anything," he said defensively.

"Nobody said you did," Bryan said in as reassuring a tone as he could muster. "We're not cops, if that's what you're worried about."

"Cops would be the least of my worries," he said. He was young—maybe in his late twenties—and, judging by his complexion and accent, of Indian descent. He wore a Taylor Swift concert shirt and cargo shorts. He slowly lowered his hands. One of them held a phone that looked like it would grow into a tablet someday.

"We're not anything you need to worry about. Just concerned citizens who wanted to see what's going on with the power."

The man exhaled as if he'd been holding his breath since he hit puberty. "Okay. Same as me. At least, I hope. I saw you guys walking around in there and got curious."

"Curious about what?" Shane asked.

"If you were there to assess the damage, fix it, or make it worse. So, which are you?"

He'd regained a little bit of composure, but Bryan was sure it was on shaky ground.

"D: none of the above. You work for the power company?"

He made a face, as if he'd just bitten a ghost pepper. "Not a chance. Too corrupt for me."

"Corrupt how?"

"You've seen it for yourself. We're in one of the worst heat waves in twenty years and nobody gives a damn. Have you seen any live footage on TV?"

"Power's out, so that makes it kinda hard," Shane said.

The man snapped his fingers. "Exactly. But for people who do, they talk about the power being down, but not a single reporter has been allowed near the place. Whoever is pulling the strings doesn't want anyone to know what's going on here, and the power company isn't in any hurry to fix it. This is all just part of the big con."

Bryan extended his hand. "I'm Bryan. This here is my buddy, Shane."

The man's grasp was weak and sweaty. "Sam Mishra."

"So, what exactly are you doing here, Sam Mishra?" Bryan asked. The earlier clouds had departed. The blue skies and angry sun were making him feel like an ant under a microscope.

"I have a podcast called *Lying for Dollars*. It's relatively new, but I've got a pretty good following. I'm just trying to expose the truth about what's going on in modern-day politics, and how everything wrong can be tracked by a path of dollar symbols. This hoax is just another example."

Bryan sighed inwardly. Why did everyone under thirty-five feel they needed to have a podcast? But seeing that they were already conversant, he asked, "This doesn't look like a hoax to me. I can show you the bullet holes."

Sam grinned. "No, no, the sabotage is real. It's who's behind it and why the glaring problem is not being addressed that makes this a hoax."

"And you know the who?"

Wiping sweat from his forehead, Sam said, "Not yet. But all of this seems awfully suspicious to me. I aim to get to the bottom of it."

"You mean you don't buy that it's the work of white nationalist domestic terrorists?"

The podcaster shook his head. "The only white nationalists within a hundred miles of here are made up of about a dozen guys barely out of their teens who probably still need their shoes tied by their mothers. This isn't them. You ever notice how any bad stuff that goes down in our country is always the work of *domestic* terrorists? We went from suspecting the entire world to turning on ourselves in under twenty years. Makes you start to question things. No, whoever did it had the permission of some people in high places because no one's looking for them or working to make things better." He peered at Bryan and Shane as if trying to read their minds or auras. "Which leads me to ask, which side of the fence are you on?"

Bryan looked back at the substation. "This side." When Sam didn't get his joke he added, "The side that's concerned that nobody seems to give a lick that people are suffering while this place sits empty."

That appeared to reassure Sam. He plucked something out of his pocket and handed business cards to them. It had the name of his podcast, website, and email address, as well as the social media links for his show.

"If you find anything out, let me know. Maybe we can blow the lid off this thing."

Bryan studied the card briefly before tucking it in his shirt pocket. "I'll think about it. Nice to meet you."

He and Shane walked away.

Sam called after them. "Hey, if you're not cops or one of *them*, who are you?"

Shane turned around and replied, "We're the guys who get things done when no one else can or even wants to try. If you want to keep poking the bear, get yourself some bear spray and be prepared to use it."

As they drove back to the farm, Bryan worked overtime trying to figure out what was going on. Sam was right: always follow the money. Whose bank account had grown larger since the attack on the substation?

Shane was on his phone the entire time. "Kid's got almost thirty thousand followers. I was just looking at some of his stuff. He's not a complete moron. He's actually right more times than wrong."

That gave Bryan an idea. Though he'd sit on it a while before giving voice to it.

CHAPTER 17

Governor Alexa Bennington reviewed the video that had been forwarded to her by the state police for the third time. She paused it on the frame of the two men as they examined the damage to one of the transformers. Zooming in only made the image worse. She could clearly tell they were men but couldn't make out their faces. That was no help at all.

"Is this the best we have?" she asked Penny Hastings, her young personal assistant, whose only perceivable skills were with phones and videos, just like everyone else her age.

The strawberry blonde who graduated from Harvard leaned across the desk to get a look at the image. "I guess so."

"You guess so?" Bennington felt her acid reflux act up. She would have fired her within the first hour of her first day of employment when she arrived forty minutes late and wearing jeans with rips in them and sandals. However, her hands were tied, as the young dunderhead was the daughter of a major contributor. "Is there another angle? Another video?"

"Um, no. At least, not that I know of."

"Well, for the rest of the day make sure you know. Call the trooper who filmed this. Maybe he had a partner who was closer."

The girl settled deeper into the leather chair and crossed her legs, as if she was going to stay there for the afternoon, maybe take a nap.

Measuring her tone, Bennington said, "Now would be a good time to get started."

"Oh. Yeah. Sure."

Penny walked out of the office with all the urgency of a sloth looking for a place to nap.

"If we can get a better image, we can run them through the database and see if we get a match," Colin Farmer, her chief of staff said. He'd stood pensively by the window, eyes fixed on her and the tablet's screen. Unlike Penny, Colin was the farthest from a blue blood. He had to work his way up to his position. With his graying hair and slight build, he looked far older than his thirty-five years. He had no family or romantic ties and was usually the first one in and the last one out of the office. When Bennington had asked him if he could whip Penny into shape, he'd rolled his eyes and said, "I'm many things but a miracle worker isn't one of them."

The governor scrolled the video back. Who were these clowns and what were they doing there?

Now, the third one outside the perimeter, the trooper had recognized. He was a podcaster already on her radar. She'd listened to his show once and decided he was a pest at best.

The trooper who had filmed them from his hidden position had done his job as he'd been asked: simply observe and record. Call in for backup only if someone actually came there to double down on the damage. Not that the further destruction of the substation would upset her, but catching some fools red-handed after the real dirty work had been done by her handpicked team would be good PR. She toyed with the idea of rustling up a couple of patsies for just such a thing.

These two lookie-loos had Bennington wondering. Sure, some people had driven by the substation since the power went out and took a slow roll to get a look at things. A few got out of their vehicles to get a closer peek. But no one had actually dared walk inside.

Members of her private security detail had been tasked with keeping an eye on things over the past week and urge any onlookers to keep moving. Aside from the podcasting idiot, there had been no return visits. Unfortunately, the man she'd had on watch had fallen ill from the heat and left his post today. He'd have a cardboard box waiting for him at his desk tomorrow.

Repair work had partially begun, but the devastation to the transformers had been extensive and the needed parts were on *back order*. Said parts were made in China and were taking a slow boat to get here. The slower, the better. Blaming the Chinese for things like this was actually good business with the Chicoms. They insisted on suffering some slings and arrows as a diversion to their real crimes and misdemeanors.

"Do you think these could be some actual white nationalists?" she asked. "Maybe they want to get a closer look at the damage so they can sound credible when they lay claim to it."

Colin flashed a sly grin. "That would be very advantageous if it were the case. I would be lying if I said the odds were good, though. You know how people are. It's probably just two bored yokels with nothing better to do now that their televisions and air conditioners don't work. Odds are we've captured them somewhere else on camera. A facial recognition match will be a piece of cake. *If* they come back and we get a sharper image."

She watched the shaky phone cam video again, unable to explain to herself why this had her on alert. Call it a hunch.

One of the men walked with a limp. The other was shorter and broad as a barn. That wasn't much to go on. Most of the farmers in the state profiled as either one.

"Did the state police get a license plate number?"

Colin shook his head in dismay. "He thinks they had the car parked somewhere out of sight. He tried to sneak up on them when they left, but they were gone before he could find out where they'd stashed their ride."

"Any chance they came on foot?"

That would make things a little easier. A search perimeter for the two wouldn't be a wide net. Who would walk far in this heat?

"Most likely not."

Bennington tapped the tablet's screen. "I need a closer watch on this area. If they come by again, I want them arrested."

"I'll let the state police know." Colin put some manila

file folders on her desk and spaced them apart. "Now, onto other business."

Governor Bennington listened with half an ear, signing where he pointed to and agreeing with his suggestions. She trusted Colin implicitly.

She also trusted her instincts. The blurry images of the two men were going to nag at her to no end. She hoped they couldn't keep away from the substation.

Curiosity killed the cat. And more times than most, they did not come back.

CHAPTER 18

After their recon at the substation Bryan and Shane went back to the farm to pick up the RV. Their timing was perfect because Charlotte and Jason were just returning from their round of wellness visits. She had withdrawn a few hundred dollars from their bank account to buy food and water at an ATM outside the dead zone. Bryan wished they could provide everyone with a generator, but he wasn't lottery rich.

"How did it go?" Bryan asked his wife.

Sweat ran down her face and neck. "We did the best we could. You have quite a few old-timers out here, most of them not-so-merry widows."

"Farming has a way of whittling a man down," Bryan said, casting a glance back at the house as if he could see his father through the walls.

No matter how much gas the generator went through, air conditioners were going on tonight. Everyone needed a break if they were going to be of any help to themselves, the farm, or the community.

"Well, we got some food, brought others into the truck to cool down for a bit. I have a list of things that they'll need tomorrow. Jason and I picked up a few things at the supermarket. The prices here are insane. How are people supposed to live? I even offered to make travel arrangements if they wanted to stay with family and escape the heat. Flying them out of here would be less expensive than grocery shopping!"

Bryan wiped the sweat from Charlotte's forehead. "Let me guess. They all turned you down?"

"They sure did."

"I think Iowa is Latin for *stubborn*. We're born with it."

"With no exceptions in this family," Jason said. He carried stuffed KFC bags. "Look, I cooked!"

"Better that than you tying on an apron in the kitchen," Bryan said as he took Charlotte's hand. "We'll be back in a little bit. Got something that needs doing."

"Should I ask?"

"Nope."

Shane held the RV door open for Bryan and Charlotte. It was hotter than the center of a fresh-baked apple pie inside, but the AC would eventually make it bearable.

"What's the address again?" Bryan asked her as they settled into the small booth that was part of the dining area while Shane set the hulking RV into a three-point turn that rocked them back and forth.

Charlotte slipped the paper from her back pocket and slid it over the table to him. "Does it look familiar to you?"

165 Grossinger Road.

That was the address she'd gotten out of the cartel creeps before they shuffled off this mortal coil.

It wasn't the swankiest part of town. Mostly blue-collar workers in that section, and a lot of families, too, at least back in the day. Bryan remembered going pool hopping with his friends in that neighborhood on hot summer nights just like this.

Bryan flicked the paper with his finger. "Smart of them. They deal out of crack houses and the streets, and store in unassuming locations so as not to arouse suspicion. Want to bet somewhere in the wind those guys had a woman accomplice so they could give the appearance of down-home domestic bliss? I'll bet she skipped town the moment they didn't come check in. Hopefully we get to the stash before any cleanup crew comes along."

"If they do, that could be more fun," Shane said.

"Too many innocent civilians around. Those houses are packed close together. Cartel lowlifes use locations like that as human shields. It discourages law enforcement from going balls-out to storm the place. Too risky."

Bryan angled himself so he caught a cold breeze blowing out of the air vent. "Just be ready for anything, but let's keep whatever we do quick, close, and quiet."

Charlotte and Shane knew exactly what he meant. They were used to working in close quarters, where precision work married with brutal efficiency and minimal noise were the difference between success and failure, life and death.

Bryan moved up front so he could guide Shane to the

house. On the outskirts of the town proper, they entered a grid of streets with similar-looking houses all in a tight row with postage-stamp front lawns and covered porches just about big enough for a couple of chairs.

Everything looked the same but different. Many of the houses were in need of paint and/or repair. Every third lawn cried out for attention, with grass grown ankle high. Back when he was a kid, he recalled how a lot of the houses were adorned with potted plants that displayed a riot of colors come spring. That was their version of keeping up with the Joneses.

It didn't look so much like Maverick's own botanical garden anymore, though a few owners kept the tradition alive.

The stash house was a single-family home that straddled the line between nice and starting to turn. In other words, nondescript. It was neatly nestled between two identical houses, though the color was different for each. Bryan spotted three small bicycles leaning against the porch of the olive-green house on the right and a wheelchair ramp on the maroon house on the left.

"Morons," Bryan grumbled. "Housing their poison between children and a disabled person."

Shane drove past, keeping his foot on the gas. He would make another pass before finding a place to park the RV out of sight but not too far away. "I was hoping it would be more in the open so we could just torch it."

"If it's too easy, it ain't worth it," Bryan said, studying the house from the side-view mirror. "Besides, we can't burn that crap in a packed neighborhood. We could get a lot of people sick or worse. We'll have to be a bit more tactical than that. You know the drill."

With that, he opened a plastic baggie he'd stashed in the RV earlier. It had three sets of surgical gloves and masks. If there was fentanyl in the house, they had to be extremely careful. Even the slightest touch could give them a fatal overdose. They had Narcan nasal spray on hand in case there was an accident, but avoiding accidents made life a lot simpler.

Charlotte scooted to the back bedroom to take a peek outside the tinted back window. "Hard to tell if anyone's there," she called out across the RV. "All the blinds are drawn. No car parked in the driveway."

Bryan instructed Shane to the easiest way to make their way around again. When they got to the house Shane eased up on the gas just a bit. The RV was not the best recon vehicle. Bryan had him pull behind an abandoned store three blocks away.

They each tucked a pistol at their back and clipped knife sheaths at their waists. Shane preferred a bowie knife, Charlotte a tactical knife like the KA-BAR she sported in the military, while Bryan stuck with a very plain hunting knife that had helped him do his fair share of hunting in the past.

"Shoot only if it's your last resort," Bryan said to them. "I don't want any strays hitting one of the kids next door."

When they got out the heat kicked them in their guts, stole the breath from their lungs.

Bryan looked at the vacant storefront and remembered it being a corner store that sold household essentials, cold beer and pop, cigarettes, and, come Independence Day, smoke bombs for fifty cents apiece. The owner had been an old-timer named Charlie who was known to give a few extra pieces of candy to the kids when they came armed with pockets full of coins.

The sign that used to read CHARLIE'S in bright red letters, with YOU NEED IT, WE GOT IT, underneath, was long gone. As was Charlie, Bryan supposed.

He led the way.

"We'll check things out from the back. I used to pool jump in the yard behind it. I know that spot pretty well."

"Is pool jumping just another of your petty crimes?" Charlote asked jokingly.

"It's a crime to have an empty pool on a hot day or night. My friends and I were just helping make things right."

The Cape house behind the storage house looked to be vacant. A long-dead potted plant, its leaves and stalks as brown as a camel's hide, wilted in a pot in the center of the porch steps. The windows were bare, and when Bryan made to look as if he were going to ring the bell, he peeked inside and saw there was no furniture.

"Okay, we have that going for us. Let's go."

They walked around back as if they owned the property. Overgrown weeds had taken the ovular spot of the aboveground pool. A low metal fence separated the two yards. They could easily hop it.

Just as Bryan was about to make his way over, a woman's voice called out to him, "You with the police?"

She startled him. He looked around, finding a woman

in a wheelchair smoking a cigarette and holding on to a can of beer in the adjacent yard.

"Not exactly, ma'am. Why do you ask?"

She took a deep drag on her cigarette. "Because I've been calling the cops about this place for three months now. Apparently no one listens to an old disabled lady."

There was no sense trying to be stealthy now. Bryan, Charlotte, and Shane went over the fence. She looked to be well into her eighties, wearing a white-and-yellow housecoat. Her wheelchair was motorized and decorated with streamers on the handles, just the way little girls would adorn their bicycle handlebars.

Bryan would bet one of his secret bank accounts that this woman was the unofficial neighborhood watch. Nothing would get past her, even in the dead of night.

"You mind me asking what you were calling the police about?" Bryan asked.

She looked them each up and down and a mischievous smile broke out on her face. "Oh, I think you know." She pointed to Bryan and Charlotte. "You the ones that stopped those thieves over on Broad Street, ain't ya?"

"I wouldn't know about that."

She pointed at them with her beer hand. "I think you do."

"You see anyone come by this house?" Charlotte asked.

Shane's eyes darted from window to window. His hand was in his pocket, curled around the grip of his pistol.

The old woman shook her head. "It's been quiet the

past few days. Not that things ever get rowdy there. Just suspicious. Something's up in that place. A couple moved in there less than a year ago. Not exactly from around here, if you get my drift. They wouldn't so much as say hello to you if it would cure cancer. But I seen a lot of cars and vans pull up to the driveway late at night. And grown white men in hoodies sniffing around, sometimes going inside. I'm old but not stupid. I know drug trouble when I see it. I was born and raised in Baltimore, you know."

"I think it's best for now if you go inside," Charlotte said.

She flicked her cigarette butt into a squared section of dirt that must have been a planter at one time. Now it only grew yellow cigarette filters. "You going to shut down whatever's been going on in there?"

"If you can keep it between us, yes," Bryan said.

"They have someone watching the place," she warned them. "Comes around in a different car. Windows are always tinted, so I can't see who's inside. You be careful. And if you don't mind, give me a knock when the coast is clear."

With that, she spun around her wheelchair and rolled up the ramp and into her house, but not before crumpling her beer can and tossing it into a plastic pail by the door.

"Now that's a broad," Shane said. "And I mean that only in the best possible way," he added, looking at Charlotte. She was too busy looking down the narrow alley between the houses.

Bryan put his hand on the back door handle and gave

it the slightest turn. "A broad with good intel. What do you think?"

"I'll bet my grandmother's *pernil* recipe it's booby-trapped," Shane said. He looked in one of the windows. "So are the windows."

Looking up at the second floor, Bryan said, "There's a good chance they didn't bother with those."

Shane grunted. "Okay, I'll be the base."

"First things first," Bryan said. They quickly slipped their hands into the gloves and put on their masks.

With Shane's help, Bryan stood on his friend's shoulders. Their bodies were pressed close to the house. Charlotte climbed up them with practiced ease. Bryan's knee barked when she got onto his shoulders, but the pressure didn't last long as she quickly opened the window and slipped inside. Bryan hopped down, and he and Shane stood on either side of the back door.

The wait for his wife to open the door felt as if it took hours. When it finally clicked open she appeared in the doorway with her palm up.

"There are trip wires everywhere. Watch where you step."

He noticed a chair opposite the door with a shotgun affixed to the back and wood blocks nailed to the chair and floor to keep it from tipping backward when the gun went off. Whoever opened the door would have gotten a face full of buckshot.

They went inside and gently closed the door.

"You see any stash?" Bryan asked, eyes taking in every corner of the kitchen. There were a few dirty dishes in the sink. A scarred metal folding table with three rusted folding chairs sat in the center of the kitchen. On the table were three full ashtrays. The entire room smelled like smoke and neglect.

"Nothing upstairs. I haven't given a sweep of this floor," Charlotte said.

Bryan spotted a trip wire by the basement door. "Wanna bet it's down there?"

Shane was about to disarm the trip wire when they heard steps on the front porch. The trio froze. Bryan snuck out of the kitchen, lighter on his feet than a cat, and hustled to one of the front windows. He pulled the closed blinds aside to give himself less than an inch of viewing space.

Two men were on the porch, with two others walking up the steps. They were trying to be cautious without looking conspicuous. The only problem was that physically, dressed in tracksuits and all sporting long, jet-black hair tied back, they stood out like clowns at a wake. Proof they didn't really care if they were spotted. When one of them moved, Bryan spotted the dark handle of a pistol poking out of the holster on his hip.

Timing was everything. It appeared the movers had come to squirrel the stash to another location. Or maybe they'd been spotted. An old woman in a wheelchair had gotten the drop on them, so why not some cartel thugs?

Can't be this sloppy, Bryan scolded himself.

Charlotte and Shane popped up beside him.

Bryan held up four fingers and pointed at the door.

Shane nodded and positioned himself against the wall so he'd be concealed when the door opened. Charlotte crouched behind a love seat while Bryan stayed hunched by the window.

The door opened.

A flurry of Spanish wafted into the room. The first man to walk inside looked around the room while pulling a hand cannon from inside his tracksuit. He paused for a moment before giving the all clear.

Shane allowed three of the thugs to enter the house. As the fourth was about to walk inside, he slammed the door in his face.

Before the other men could react, Bryan and Charlotte burst from their hiding places. Charlotte buried her tactical knife into the lead man's carotid artery. Blood sprayed the walls in steady pulses as he spun around and fell, clutching his neck. She twirled away from him like a ballerina, ducking under the stream of blood.

Bryan delivered a brutal kick to one man's kneecap. The bone broke with the sound of snapping a handful of dry spaghetti. As the other fumbled for his weapon, Bryan drove his hunting blade into the soft spot under his chin, pushing it to the hilt until the light went out in his eyes. He collapsed when Bryan extracted the knife. His body went into twitching spasms on the floor, his sneakers beating an erratic tempo.

Charlotte clasped her hands over the mouth of the man with the shattered kneecap so the neighbors couldn't hear his cries. She cut his throat and held him until he stopped struggling.

All the while, Shane had pulled the dazed man into the house, closed the door quietly, and twisted his head until his neck snapped.

It took all of fifteen seconds to wipe out the cartel movers.

Breathing heavily more from adrenaline than exertion, Shane said, "You don't suppose they were just some Jehovah's Witnesses, do you?"

"You ever see a Witness wear a tracksuit?" Charlotte said as she went through the pockets of the man in front of her. She came up with a wad of cash, all hundred-dollar bills, wrapped in a rubber band.

They went through all of their pockets. Not an ID to be found among them, though one had ten credit cards, each bearing a different name.

When Bryan peered out the window he saw a non-descript blue van parked in the driveway. "Talk about timing. If we'd been here an hour later, this place would have been cleared out."

"I'm gonna chalk this one up to blind luck," Charlotte said, pulling her mask away to take a few deep breaths.

Though they each had a sizable list of people they had killed, they never took joy in it. On the other hand, they didn't shed a tear, either, because when they did kill, it was for the side of right. As far as they knew, since their time postmilitary, they had claimed no innocent lives. Far from it.

A quick recon of the basement revealed boxes and bags of just about every drug imaginable. There was enough there to overdose every living soul in Maverick five times over.

"I could get some bleach and destroy it all," Shane said.

Bryan's eyes flicked to the ceiling. "With those bodies up there, I'd rather get out of Dodge."

They went upstairs, and Bryan collected the newspapers that were strewn about the living room, balled them up, and threw them in the fireplace, along with their masks and gloves. Making sure the flue was closed, he set a match to them. Gray smoke coiled out of the fireplace.

Next, they disabled all of the booby traps, crudely constructed as they were.

"Time to go."

Back outside, Bryan stepped over the fence separating the drug den from the old woman's house next door. He rapped on her door, and she answered right away. She must have been waiting by the door the entire time.

"All clear," he said, noting the fresh beer and cigarette in her hands. "You won't have any more reason to reach out to the police, but only after you make one last call. Tell them there's a fire next door."

The woman grinned. "I saw those fellas come out of the van. I thought of yelling over to you, but I figured you had it handled. Looks like I was right. I'll call 9-1-1 right now."

"Just give us a two-minute head start."

"Want one for the road?"

Before he could answer, she handed him a plastic holder with three cans of beer. "It's the least I can do."

Bryan took the beer, looping his finger in an empty

ring. "What you can do is tell no one about us. Not anyone."

She shrugged. "Who do I have to tell? My doctors? All my friends are either dead or senile. You got rid of the scum of the earth. Your secret's safe with me." Wheeling past him, she looked at Charlotte and Shane, then the house, where smoke was beginning to escape from a side window. "You best get going."

"We best. Thank you."

"No, thank *you*. And I'm speaking for everyone here. God bless all of you."

Shane snapped off a salute and Charlotte waved. They left the way they'd come in, keeping their heads low so no one could describe their faces if they'd been seen.

When they were back in the RV Shane asked, "What about all the drugs? If the cops are crooked, it'll just make it back onto the streets."

Bryan settled into the passenger seat, cracked open the beer, and took a long swig. "I'm going to count on the force having some good cops left. Like my old friend, Aaron Chisolm. That stuff is going to be locked in an evidence locker for a long time."

"This is gonna cause a stir," Shane said. "Cops will be looking all over for who did this."

Bryan shook his head. "They'll assume it was just some rival dealer. Out with the bad, in with just the same. I don't think they'll be looking very hard at all. It'll probably be a case of bag 'em and tag 'em and don't be late for dinner."

The sound of approaching sirens came just as they were leaving, blocks away from the action.

As they drove back to the farm, Bryan and Charlotte both agreed that what they'd done would put a serious dent in Maverick's drug trade, but it would come back eventually.

Unless they took care of a lot of other business and restored his hometown to what it used to be. If such a thing were even possible was anyone's guess. The only way to find out was to try.

CHAPTER 19

Another day of blistering heat, even though the thermometer said it was five degrees cooler. It was stickier than flypaper, with air thicker than molasses.

George Branch said the harvesting would stop at eleven in the morning. He'd come across an old transistor radio in the attic and found a local AM station that broadcast the news and weather. They said a storm was coming in the early afternoon and would break some of the heat and humidity. When the storm passed they would head back out and hope things were more agreeable.

While sitting around the porch with the radio on, Bryan heard a quick report on the murder of four unidentified men in a house containing one of the largest caches of drugs in the county's history. The story was more centered on the size of the bust and the hard work of the police rather than the death of what were four obviously guilty men, just as Bryan had suspected. Charlotte cast him a knowing glance between sips of lemonade.

"Where'd you sleep last night, Dad?" Bryan asked.

George looked at the graying skies and replied, "The living room. Doesn't seem right to sleep in air-conditioning when everyone else is suffering."

Bryan wasn't sure if that was a dig at him. There was a lot about his father he didn't entirely know. Too much time had passed. Best to go with the gut feeling that it was just his father being a stubborn old coot.

Shane had driven to another county to get fresh food just as the sun came up. The now-working refrigerator was full, and Lola and Tomás enjoyed ice pops as they chased the chickens around. Shane was with them, running around like a ten-year-old, seeming not to have a care in the world even though he'd helped kill those men the day before. It was a form of compartmentalization that was necessary in their line of work.

"Come on," Charlotte said as she tapped Bryan's shoulder.

Pam elbowed David. "Call the children."

David reluctantly got up from his chair and whistled loud enough to perk every dog's ear within a country mile. His children didn't protest as they waved to Shane and the chickens and headed into the house to change.

The noon mass at St. Matthew's Church was set to start in half an hour. The Cruz family were devout Catholics and had asked Jason if they thought there would be any trouble if they went to church. It had been a while since their last Sunday mass and they were feeling both guilty and grateful. Jason assured them that Father Rooney's congregation would welcome them with open arms.

Charlotte had coerced Bryan into going, too. Whenever they came back from an overseas mission, the ritual was to go to church and silently atone for their sins, hoping God would understand the work they did and why it had to be done. Rather the blood be on their hands than others who didn't possess their will or special skill set. Bryan had long ago learned not to hem or haw when Charlotte said it was time for church.

His father and brother, now that his mother was gone, were in no mood for one of the priest's sermons. They were still hurting and didn't feel much of God's grace at the moment. Bryan hoped that would change. His mother would be furious at them if they stopped going to mass altogether.

After a quick change, Jason tossed the keys to his truck to Bryan.

"That looks familiar," Jason said, noting Bryan had on the same suit he'd worn to their mother's funeral.

"I left my Brooks Brothers wardrobe at home. Sure you don't wanna come?"

"I'm not ready. Not yet." Jason looked over at Shane. "You going with them?"

Shane grinned. "Forget lightning. If I walked into a church, the earth would swallow up the whole place. Me and the chickens have unfinished business."

The Cruzes looked their Sunday best, with Tomás in a sport coat that wouldn't fit him much longer and Lola in a pretty flowered dress. On the drive to the church, Tomás told them he'd been an altar boy at his church in Juarez and how he thought at the time that he might become a priest.

"What about now?" Charlotte asked him.

His eyes were suddenly downcast. "I don't know. Do you think God is angry because I haven't been to church for so long?"

His mother put her arm around him. "God is our Father, right?"

"Yes!" Lola chirped.

Tomás nodded.

"And just like your *padre*"—she put a hand on David's lap—"he has seen everything you have been through and been with you every single minute. He loves you. He loves all of us, without condition. He is not mad at you, Tomás. You always make Him happy. And I know he is extra happy to see you in His home today."

Charlotte gripped Bryan's hand. He saw a tear in her eye.

They made it just in time and found seats in a center pew. Back in the day, St. Matthew's was standing room only, even for the noon mass. Now, it was barely half full.

All of the stained-glass windows had been propped open as well as the double front doors. Paper fans were left in the pews to help folks get some minor relief from the heat.

Father Rooney gave Bryan a nod as he passed them down the aisle.

As the mass progressed in rapid fashion lest half the congregants pass out, Bryan couldn't help running what Pam Cruz had said over and over in his mind.

Was it possible that *he* always made God happy? Bryan had serious doubts.

He prayed for forgiveness, barely hearing the readings or even Father Rooney's short sermon.

Bryan also prayed for what was to come. He'd been thinking a lot lately and had decided to take things a step further. It was time to call in the cavalry. The job of setting things right in Maverick was too big for just him, Charlotte, and Shane. He was a firm believer in fighting fire with fire. And what he projected needed to happen required a lot more fire power.

He and his team had always done their work on foreign soil. This time around, he needed to tend to his own backyard.

He hoped the Lord would understand.

The older members of the church looked washed-out and exhausted by the time mass ended. Father Rooney had wasted no time, getting them out of the stifling church in just under thirty minutes. Fat beads of sweat poured down his pale face as he shook hands after mass.

"So happy to see you and your lovely wife," he said to Bryan. "It's proof that miracles do happen." He had a playful twinkle in his eye when he said it.

"I bet you can't wait to get out of those robes," Bryan said.

"And set my keister in a folding chair outside and listen to the Cubs game on my radio. See you next week? You planning to stay a while?"

Bryan shook his hand. "We'll see, Father. Stranger things have happened."

Tomás looked like a fifty-pound weight had been lifted off his shoulders. He dipped his finger in holy water and made the sign of the cross three times. David handed Pam his handkerchief so she could dab the sweat from her brow and upper lip.

"Thank you for taking us," David said. "It means a lot to my family. For the first time since we came to America, we feel whole."

"Happy to," Bryan replied. "Now, let's get home and get out of these duds."

Back at the farm, Bryan was elated to ditch the monkey suit and put on his jeans and a white T-shirt. Charlotte slipped off her dress and underwear, turning on the fan and standing before it with her hair billowing in the breeze. The sweat that dotted her skin made her look like a model in a wicked photo shoot.

"Damn, girl, you can't do that to me just after church. What would Jesus think if he could read my thoughts?"

"He can, and I think He'd approve if you did your husbandly duties."

It was logic he couldn't argue with. Just as soon as he'd dressed, he undressed and took her against the dresser.

When they were done they were drenched in sweat and had to take a cold shower. As Charlotte soaped his back, she said, "Now your mind should be all clear."

He laughed. "My mind is clear, but my legs are a little shakier than normal." She massaged his neck as water sluiced down his back. "I figured all three of us should have a kinda sit-down."

"Pam is going to teach me how to make authentic tamales. You and Shane make your plans and clue me in later."

He turned around to face his beautiful wife. "Wait. How did you know I have plans to share with Shane?"

She went to her tiptoes and kissed his nose. "I know you better than you'll ever know yourself."

After toweling off and getting dressed for the second time, Bryan went outside and found his father with Lola by the goat pen. There were only three goats left— there had been over a dozen back when Bryan was a kid—and Lola was excited to feed them by hand. The old man loved to show her around and teach her all the little chores that needed doing on the farm, and Lola seemed to cherish being with him and learning

Shane was in his RV, taking a nap. He jumped awake when Bryan opened the door.

"You know, not knocking could get you hurt," Shane admonished.

"I'm willing to take my chances. The chickens tire you out?"

"Yeah. Then I got bored. Please tell me you have something that can make me unbored."

Bryan wiped the sweat that was already collecting on the back of his neck. "You been listening to that kid Sam's podcast?"

"Sure have. Pretty good stuff. I'm sure most people think he's just some conspiracy wacko, but there are times he gets it right."

"Do you still have his card?"

Shane flipped down his visor and the card fell in his hand. Bryan scanned it. "No phone number."

"He has a podcast, not some late-night call-in show. You want me to reach out to him?"

"Yes. Find out if he has enough listeners in the area that he thinks can be mobilized in a couple of days."

"You enlisting a podcast army?"

"Just witnesses. I'm going to call Norm Hendricks to see if he can get here today." Norm was with Bryan on several assignments over the years, including Yemen, Iran, Somalia, and a particularly tricky op in North Korea. He was a mechanical wizard and superior engineer with a degree from Cooper Union under his belt. After graduating, he'd enlisted in the army because he came from a military family and truly wanted to do his part.

A big grin broke out on Shane's face. "Norm! I think I know where you're going."

"That's just a start. We're going to need some muscle. I'm thinking Easy Campisi, Bruno Rocchio, L.G. Iverson, maybe Amy Thomas. Definitely Lori. She must be getting antsy, running the shop alone."

"The Yemen crew. You think this place is as bad as Yemen?" Shane asked with a note of incredulity.

"Not many places on earth are as bad as Yemen, but this is important. Not just to me or the people of Maverick. This is going to have a bigger impact when we're done. At least, I hope so. Our cover might be blown when the dust settles. This may put us out of business for good."

Cracking his knuckles, Shane said, "We're getting real close to aging out of what we do, anyway. There's always the shop."

Bryan patted his shoulder. "But won't you be too bored?"

"Maybe it's time I found a pretty *mamacita* and made some little Shanes."

"Little versions of you will keep you busier than a one-legged man in a butt-kicking contest," Bryan said, laughing. He may have been laughing on the outside, but inside, he was feeling the weight of what he was considering. This could blow up everything they'd taken great pains to create.

He looked out the RV's front window and spotted his father walking around the house with his shoulders hunched, looking very alone.

Everything from here on out was going to be done for his father, to return his town, his state, to the way it was so he could spend the rest of his years in the comfort of what he'd always known. And it would be for the memory of his mother, and all those years wasted between them. She was looking down on them from her rightful place. Lately, he'd felt her presence all around him, especially at church today.

It was time to give the people who were ruining Maverick, and Iowa, a little hell, so he could make his mother smile in heaven.

While Shane sent a message to Sam the podcaster, Bryan dialed Amy Thomas, his best intelligence asset. She answered on the first ring.

"Mercury Hats Manufacturing."

"Funny," Bryan said. Amy never answered the phone the same way twice. "You have some free time on your hands?"

"I can always make free time. What's up?"

"I need you to look into the governor of Iowa, Alexa Bennington, and her husband."

"Anything in particular I should be looking for?"

"She's a politician, so there's that. She also pulled a switcheroo and got elected as a Republican, then changed her party affiliation to Democrat with an ultra-progressive agenda."

Amy huffed. "So, she's either an idiot or bought and paid for."

"Or both."

"Dangerous combo. I'm on it."

"One more thing. You think you can be in Maverick, Iowa, by tonight?"

"Maverick? Isn't that where you're from?"

"Yep."

"Did you find trouble, or did trouble find you?"

Bryan considered the question. "Maybe both. Check out the latest news and you tell me."

He heard the frantic tapping of keys in the background. "If I haul ass, I can be there by ten tonight. Anything else?"

He stared off into the swaying corn rows, watching storm clouds gather on the horizon. "We'll discuss that when you get here."

CHAPTER 20

Norm Hendricks hailed from Upstate New York by way of Guam. He came from a long line of military men and lost a foot in a skirmish outside Kandahar. Hendricks swore he moved faster and better with the prosthetic. Bryan countered that even before the accident he had legs made of redwood logs. Tall and what he liked to declare himself as ruggedly handsome, he was the definition of the person you'd want to share a foxhole with, which was why he didn't so much as flinch when Bryan asked him to come.

Before he'd checked into his hotel—an establishment that was outside the no-power zone—he stopped by to check out the damage at the substation. Careful not to go inside the fence, he was able to take pictures with his zoom lens camera to make a fair assessment of the damage.

"You said no one was working to repair the place?" he asked Bryan once he'd settled into his hotel room.

"At least not when we were there."

"You'll be happy to know it's emptier than a movie star's head. Though I did spot a state trooper and a blue sedan keeping an eye on things. Guess they want to supervise the dust and air around it."

Bryan said, "They're probably there to keep the workers out," he joked. "I wonder who was in the sedan."

"Beats me. I could go back and tail them, but I have tools to buy. Couldn't bring what I need on the plane. I won't know the full extent of what's needed until I get into the guts, and I'm sure there are parts that I won't have access to. But maybe I can do something to at least get partial power back on."

"I remember what you did in Qalāt with what seemed like only a screwdriver and a hammer. I have faith in you."

"That was easy. Here in America, we make things complex as all get-out so folks can charge a lot of money for parts and repairs."

"I'll send a meetup location to you later. See you around oh-eighteen-hundred?"

"See you at six."

Norm Hendricks just had to throw that in. It was the little things that kept him smiling. What he was about to attempt was no little thing. In fact, it was the kind of thing that could get him arrested. But he'd long ago learned to trust Bryan and Charlotte.

It was time to go tool shopping. He'd make it a quick trip. The hotel's cute bartender looked lonely, and a potentially condemned man by all means should have a little fun.

* * *

When Amy Thomas landed in Des Moines International, she texted Bryan an encrypted message. She thought it best to meet somewhere they couldn't be seen or heard. Bryan sent back coordinates right away.

She picked up her rented yellow Mustang and laid down some considerable rubber when she left the Hertz lot. She'd wanted a convertible, but the muscle car was a fine substitute. Opening the windows, she fiddled with the radio as the wind whipped her jet-black hair into a frenzy.

Her GPS said it would be a forty-minute drive to their meeting point. That gave her more time to digest the information she'd learned about the Benningtons and their various associations. The farthest thing from naïve, she was still a bit taken aback by some of the things she'd discovered calling in a few favors from her intelligence network to get her up to speed in record time.

Everyone knew that the vast majority, if not all politicians were about as crooked as the letter *L*. The policies, false narratives, and manipulation of the media and those who consumed it were evidence to some shady intent on the part of the local, state, and federal government. This Alexa Bennington and her wealthy snake of a husband were in a league of their own. Twice, Amy was warned not to dig too deep. That only encouraged her to find out as much as she could. She still needed more time to corroborate some of what she'd learned.

"You don't want to mess with them," her ex from the NSA had said. "They have friends in very high places.

Like, you'll get a nosebleed just by trying to look at how high."

"I'll bring tissues."

"I'm serious. There's a vacuum around them. You'll get so far, then fall into a black hole. When I see those black holes it's time to steer clear. You know what happens when you get sucked into a black hole?"

"You end up with that astronaut in *2001: A Space Odyssey*."

He breathed heavily with frustration into the phone. "You never come out, Amy. It's as if you were never here."

"I'm fine with that. You're only two generations away from being completely forgotten anyway. Unless you manage to do something epic. Surviving a black hole seems pretty epic to me."

She pulled into the mostly vacant lot of a laundromat about twenty miles east of Maverick. Shane's RV was parked amid the smattering of cars. Amy shielded her eyes from the sun to look inside the laundromat window. There were three middle-aged women inside, all of them glued to their phones.

Shane opened the door before she knocked. "Hola, amiga."

She climbed up the three steps into the RV. Bryan was sitting by the fold-down table.

"Gentlemen," she said.

"That we ain't," Shane said as he wrapped her in a bear hug. Bryan got up and settled for a quick pat on the back.

"You want something to drink?" Shane asked as he opened his minifridge.

"Perrier with a twist of lemon will do."

He plopped a bottle of store-brand water on the table. "Perrier with lemon at your service."

The three of them settled around the table. "I can't see why we couldn't do this at my place," Bryan said.

"I'm just being extra cautious. People on the inside I spoke to got pretty spooked when I mentioned the Benningtons. Considering what's gone on at your family farm, I can't be sure that they don't already have eyes and ears on you."

Bryan waved her off. "That's another matter entirely. I'm going to deal with that, too."

"Don't be so sure," Amy said, holding up a finger. "These two are dangerous, and from what I gather, they have their fingers in just about every rotten pie in this state. If you have foreign thugs burning the place up or pushing drugs, your governor is somewhere in the background, pulling strings."

"There's not a lot of love for her from the locals," Bryan said. "*Turncoat* is just about the nicest thing I've heard her called."

"*Satan* might fit her better. This is a woman who hates this country, and Iowa especially. The only reason she would ever come back here was to cause chaos and make money. Apparently, she's done quite well on both fronts."

Settling back into his seat, Bryan said, "I feel like I need bourbon for whatever you're about to tell me."

Amy nodded sagely. "It would help." She didn't

have a folder of papers or notes on her phone. With the type of intel she gathered, electronic or paper trails could mean death. She had an excellent memory and used it to her advantage. "Alexa Bennington is the product of political royalty in Iowa, but I assume you already knew that."

"I left here when I was nineteen not giving four shits about politics, but even I knew her family. Sometimes it seemed like they held every available office."

"The Taylors have been in seats of power since the late 1800s. Clue number one that our pal Alexa is the black sheep is that she happily took her husband's last name. Tradition in the Taylor family was for the women to keep the family name, especially if they were running for office. Not Alexa. She went to a liberal college and took part in quite a few demonstrations for radical left causes. At the time it seemed like a typical case of spoiled rich girl rebelling against the family that gave her everything. Colleges have a way of preying on women like her and grooming them for a future of pain-in-the -butt-ery."

Shane laughed until he spat out his drink. "Is that even a word?"

"It is now," Amy replied with a grin. "Her father did an admirable job of keeping her exploits out of the news, but we all know that Uncle Sam has a way of tracking things, especially when one of their own starts to go off the reservation. After college Alexa went to law school and graduated at the top of her class. She may be an asshole, but she's not stupid. She practiced out of a firm in New York, had an apartment in the city and a house in the Hamptons."

Shane shook his head. "That's all I need to know about her. Freaking Hamptons."

"Then you'll like this. Do you know where she met her husband, Todd?"

"Are you going to tell me it wasn't at the Dairy Queen in Tallahassee?" Bryan quipped.

"China," Amy said. "She was there for a month-long holiday and spent a lot of time attending fundraisers for various wealthy members of the CCP. Todd Bennington was there, too, as a bottom-feeder looking to curry favor, and gather as many yen as he could to boot. From what I hear, it wasn't love at first sight. More like a meeting of the damaged minds. They found out they had a lot in common—that being a love of money and a hatred of democratic ideals."

Bryan got up and stretched. Listening to Alexa Bennington's life story was making him tense. "What about Todd Bennington? What's his pedigree?"

"He comes from old money, but he was not a favorite son. Word is he was mostly cut out of the will when his father passed. He wasn't exactly broke. In his world, their version of *broke* is ours of *rich for life*. You know folks like him can never have enough, which is why he found himself in the world of Democrat fundraising for a while. Turns out he was very good at it. Somewhere along the way he was added to the boards of a few private equity groups, then real estate and hedge fund manager." Amy took a break to down half the bottle of water.

"The guy must blow his nose with hundred-dollar

bills," Shane said. He was picking under his nails with the tip of his Swiss Army knife.

"He could if he wanted to," Amy said. "I could go on and on, but basically we have two rich and determined people who have secret and not-so-secret ties with other rich and determined Chicoms. Both are castaways from patriotic families with an axe to grind. Almost everyone that the Benningtons have helped get positions of power are people of dubious character. I could list all of the district attorneys they've assisted who raise red flags with just a casual peek under the covers that would make your head spin."

Bryan cracked his knuckles. "Which is why crime is rampant in Iowa."

Amy winked. "You catch on quick. Now, the DA in Crawford County who has thrown Maverick into the dumpster is a career boot licker called Eric Donnegan. He's in deep with the Benningtons. He was a terrible lawyer and an even worse DA. If you want change here, you have to change the DA."

"Oh sure, we'll just find a candidate and get the whole election process rigged," Shane joked.

"We all know there are easier ways," Amy said.

"That we do," Bryan replied.

Amy continued, "I've saved the best for last. The heaviest branch of the Bennington tree of traitors is none other than Nostrand Ganz."

She let that one sink in for a bit. Bryan looked at her, then at Shane, and shook his head. "That guy is one piece of work," he said. "I read recently that he might become the world's first official trillionaire. And he has ties with these two chuckleheads?"

"Mmm-hmm. And don't forget China. If it weren't for the Chinese, he'd only be a billionaire."

Shane had put away his knife and grabbed a beer from his refrigerator. "How did this woman get elected in Iowa of all places? Sounds like she's a walking talking red flag."

"Because most of what I told you is not public knowledge."

"Okay, then why would the powers that be even allow a commie worm like her to run for office?"

Bryan answered, "Consider who our president is. He's not exactly running around brandishing an America flag. President Mathers makes that progressive loony congresswoman over in New York look like Ronald Reagan. He's turning a blind eye to what goes on in Iowa because he approves of it."

Now it was Amy's turn to get up and do a little pacing. "Which is why I was strongly warned to walk away. Oh, and don't forget who was Jackson Mathers's biggest supporter."

"Nostrand Ganz," Bryan said with a note of dejection in his voice.

"Give the man a prize!" Amy shouted.

"Talk about a David and Goliath situation," Bryan said as he gazed out the window, deep in thought.

Amy nudged him with her elbow. "Don't forget what they taught us in Sunday school."

"What's that?"

"Little ol' David won."

They sat in silence for a spell. Amy was sure Bryan and Shane were wondering what they had gotten themselves into. A crooked politician was one thing. A crooked politician with ties to the most powerful man in the country, if not the world, was another. If Bryan called it off, Amy would walk away. If he didn't, she was all in. They'd done so much dirty work righting wrongs in foreign countries, she couldn't help feeling this was worth the fight, despite the risk and considerable odds.

Bryan's phone broke their contemplation.

"What's up, Bigfoot?" Bryan said. He nodded a few times and then went from confusion to anger. "Okay. Is he at the hospital?"

Shane gripped the edge of the table, leaning closer to Bryan so he could hear the other end of the conversation.

"It never ends, does it?" Bryan said. "Yeah. See you at the house soon." Bryan skipped the phone across the small table. It hit into the wall and clattered to the floor.

"Is it your father?" Shane asked.

"No, he's fine. But Maverick, it's on life support. Come on. I'll tell you on the way back."

CHAPTER 21

Before she left the RV, Amy asked, "Who else is in on this?"

Shane had gunned the engine while Bryan rolled down the passenger window. "I've got Easy, Rocchio, Iverson, Lori, and Hendricks on the roster. In fact, Norm is already here. He's staying at the same hotel as you."

Amy rolled her eyes. "Great. I know where to find him. I'm sure he has some barmaid in his sights by now."

"Of that I have no doubt. I'll be in touch. And thanks for the intel."

"It's just the start. I have plenty more favors to call in." She slapped the side of the RV as Shane backed it out of the space.

They turned out of the lot. Shane asked, "So what's the deal?"

"My brother just heard through the grapevine when he went into town that my cop friend was put in the hospital by a gang of mail thieves."

One of Shane's bushy eyebrows shot up. "Mail thieves? They still have the Pony Express out here?"

"It seems groups of mostly men like to swarm delivery trucks in the middle of their routes. The drivers have been advised to step aside and let them take what they want. My friend Aaron happened to be driving by in his patrol car when about ten people hit the truck. The driver this time tried to stop them and got a brick in the face for his trouble. Aaron pulled up alongside the truck and was immediately attacked by a bunch of them. They said he got beat pretty bad. They grabbed his gun and badge in the process, as well as his car. A witness said they took the truck a couple of blocks before intentionally driving it into a wall."

Shane shook his head soberly. "With all the crap people order online, those trucks are little gold mines. I hope your buddy is okay."

"Yeah, me too. Apparently, this is a regular occurrence in Maverick. Sometimes the police bust a few of them, but they always end up walking. Maybe now that they attacked a cop, something will happen. I hope his dashcam was on and there are some local doorcams that caught it from several angles. Jesus. I never thought I'd see the day when delivering the mail wasn't safe."

When they got to the farm Jason met them on the porch. He was drenched in sweat with bits of cornhusks peppering his clothes. The heat had backed down a couple of degrees from the day before. With any luck the late summer heat wave would pass. Bryan wondered how long it would take some people to recover from the damage the power outage had done.

"You hear anything else?" Bryan asked his brother.

"Nah. Just what I got from Edna Stearns over at the IGA."

Edna Stearns had been the town gossip for as long as Bryan could remember. She may have been a snoop and a busybody, but she also outscooped the newspaper on a regular basis.

"Where's Dad?"

"Finishing things up with David and Pam. Your lovely wife is by the barn with the kids and has something to show you."

"This should be interesting."

Charlotte's surprise was hard to miss. While he'd been gone, she'd installed a new flagpole right where the barn used to be. She had the burlap bag with the remains of their father's flag under her arm.

Bryan looked up at the towering flagpole. "Wow. I can't believe you did this."

Charlotte beamed. "You said you wanted to do it, and I had such great helpers." She ran her fingers through Lola's hair. Tomás was beside his sister, his hands and jeans caked with smears of concrete.

"Miss Charlotte let me help pour the concrete," he said.

"Me too," Lola added.

"I can see that," Bryan said.

Charlotte held out the burlap bag to him. "I know it's late in the day, but there's still some sunlight left. Care to hoist it up?"

Jason popped up behind him. "Want to do it together?"

"You bet."

The tattered flag snapped in a warm breeze that seemed to come out of nowhere. Everyone, even the kids, paused to watch it wave. Shane stood ramrod straight, taking in the burned and battered symbol of their country, and the spirit of the Branch family.

"I'm sure glad we saved it," Jason said.

Bryan clapped him on the back. "Me too, Bigfoot."

When they walked back to the farm Bryan saw his father admiring the flag from the porch. The old man looked at him and Jason and Charlotte and gave an almost imperceptible nod before heading inside. Bryan swore he saw a tear in his father's eyes.

"It looks beautiful," Pam Cruz said. David Cruz even snapped off a salute. They both looked bushed.

After Bryan sent the kids inside he said to Charlotte, "Amy dropped some bombs on us."

"How big?" Charlotte asked with concern.

"EMP bomb big," Shane said.

She looked to Bryan. "Tell me."

"I will when everyone gets here, which should be in a couple of hours. Let's just say that if we do this, we're going to have to throw ourselves a retirement party when it's over. And maybe disappear entirely."

She sucked on her teeth and twisted her lips a bit, considering the potential outcomes. "If that's the case, we have to make it worth the risk."

Bryan cast his eyes back to the burned flag. "It will be, honey. We'll make sure of it."

* * *

After a dinner of leftover fried chicken, fresh biscuits the size of Jason's considerable paw, creamed corn, string beans, and applesauce, Bryan asked Jason to help him wash the dishes.

"Me, Charlotte, and Shane are heading out to meet up with some people we know."

Jason was drying a dish. "Well, thanks for leaving me out."

"Yes, I'm leaving you out for a good reason. One of them being that someone needs to stay here to keep an eye on things. We shouldn't be back late. Keep your rifle close."

Since the attack at the farm, they'd been on high alert. Without knowing who had shot at them or why, there was no reason not to believe that someone would be back to finish what had been started.

"I can do that," Jason replied, sounding a little less hurt. "I forgot to tell you. I heard Mr. Winokur and Mrs. Bruck died today. They were both very sick, but I hear it was most likely caused by the heat. They were both at home."

Bryan squeezed the sponge until bubbles flowed over his hand. Two more reasons to carry through with his plan. Mr. Winokur used to be the town pharmacist until he came down with MS. And Mrs. Bruck had been the nurse on duty when Jason was born. They may have been old and ill, but they shouldn't have died just because the governor didn't want to turn the power back on.

David set some dirty bowls in the sink. "I can help, if you would lend me a weapon. I want to protect my *familia*, and yours. I'm very capable. I served in the army in Mexico for four years. I was an expert marksman."

Bryan set the dish he was washing back in the sink. David Cruz was kind, a bit doughy, and a very religious man. He couldn't picture him in the military. Yes, all eligible Mexican men had to serve part time in the military for a year. It was usually weekend warrior kind of stuff. But that David served for four and was a marksman was a surprise.

Without hesitation, Bryan said, "You can use mine. I'd take it out and fire off a few rounds just to get the feel of it if I were you."

David smiled and nodded. "Of course. Thank you. I have to help Lola with her math, and then I'll practice."

When he left Jason raised an eyebrow.

"It's the quiet ones that you have to look out for," Bryan said with a grin.

The meeting was set up at a busy bar two towns west of Maverick. Bryan had never been there before, but Jason had assured him the crowd skewed toward their age and was rambunctious enough not to take notice of any nonregulars who popped in for a drink.

The Last Rodeo Bar and Grill was loud and crowded, with a DJ playing Luke Combs loud enough to force Bryan to adjust his hearing aid. They asked the pretty waitress, dressed in a tight red-and-white-checkered top with Daisy Duke shorts, for a corner table for nine. She flashed her too-white teeth and pointed over her left shoulder. "You wouldn't happen to be in the same party, would you?"

Norm Hendricks was alone at a table with a mug of beer and a shot. He spotted the hostess and gave her a wink. Bryan thought he detected a blush blooming on the girl's cheeks. Or it could have been the heat.

"Yep, he's with us," Bryan said, not shocked that Hendricks had already taken a shot with the waitress.

"Oh, he's one to watch out for," she said playfully.

"You don't know the half of it," Shane said as he walked between Bryan and the hostess.

"We'll see ourselves over," Bryan said. She handed him a stack of menus.

"Brittany will be your server. Hope y'all enjoy yourselves."

Charlotte took Bryan's hand. "Maybe we can dance later?"

They walked by a square dance floor where about a dozen couples dressed in jeans, boots, and a lot of cowboy hats did some boot scootin'.

"If you're still in the mood after everything, sure." Bryan was as tense as an alligator wrestler at the moment. He wasn't sure how everyone would take to the plan. Even worse, if they all agreed to it, he wasn't sure he wanted them to. This was *his* hometown, not theirs. And it wasn't as if there was a payday at the end of it all, either.

Another pretty young girl, this one a brunette with violet eyes that would have made Elizabeth Taylor jealous, was taking Shane and Norm's order. The name tag on her shirt said she was Brittany.

"Can I get you something to drink?" she asked Bryan, ignoring Charlotte because she was experienced enough to know men were bigger tippers for pretty waitresses.

"Two pitchers of Bud will do."

"And nine glasses," Charlotte added as she slid in the booth next to her husband.

Hendricks got up and came around to give Charlotte and Bryan a hug. "Still married? Charlotte, I keep hoping you'll come to your senses."

She couldn't help laughing. "Hope springs eternal, Norm. How've you been?"

"Keeping busy, as always."

Bryan pointed back at the hostess. "We gathered that."

Hendricks gave a wolfish grin. "Talk about corn-fed goddesses. I may never leave Iowa."

Shane poured the beer when the pitcher arrived, along with shots of Jack for him and Norm. They made small talk until Amy Thomas arrived, looking tired but bursting with energy at the same time. That meant she had more intel she was hopped up to share.

Ten minutes later, Jack "Easy" Campisi came in with L.G. Iverson. Easy was always quick with a joke and a master of trivia, in addition to an expert bomb maker and recipient of a double knee replacement when the Humvee he was in was hit by a rocket-propelled grenade.

L.G. was compact, with a bald head that looked as if it had always been freshly shaved and shined. He'd lost some hearing and had permanent nerve damage when he was shot storming a Taliban hideout. Quiet and thoughtful, his best talent was listening and planning, on top of being a hell of a soldier. They all shook hands, and Easy and L.G. settled into chairs opposite the booth.

"I hope hearing you guys isn't a requirement tonight," L.G. said as he fiddled with both of his hearing aids.

The music had gotten louder as more people streamed in.

"I've got you covered," Easy said. "I've been learning sign language." He proceeded to flip L.G. the bird, eliciting laughter from Shane and Hendricks. L.G. simply shook his head and grabbed a pitcher of beer. He poured a glass for Easy first.

Last but not least, Lori Nicolo, Bryan's expert assistant, and Bruno Rocchio, her on-again, off-again partner both in the war and at home, parted the sea of revelers, hand in hand.

"Guess they're back together," Charlotte said before they got to the table.

"I give it three days, tops," Shane said as he knocked back his shot of Jack.

Bruno Rocchio was built, as the parlance went, like a brick outhouse He fought like he didn't have a care in the world. Land mine fragments had taken bits of several organs from him, but you'd never hear him complain about it. He could also be a bit of a hothead, and had no inclination to cool down. As far as he was concerned, it had gotten him this far and through too many scrapes to count. Bryan wasn't in a mind to disagree.

"My favorite Irish couple," Shane said when they sat down.

"You need new material," Bruno said, reaching for the beer.

Seeing all of nine seats occupied, Brittany came over with her pad. "Can I get you any appetizers?"

Shane took charge of the food, as always. He ordered enough appetizers to feed an army, which was exactly what they were.

After everyone got caught up with one another—it had been two years since this particular group had been under the same roof—Bryan knocked on the table and said, "You all ready? Because this is going to be a big ask."

CHAPTER 22

When he had everyone's undivided attention, Bryan said, "How often have we talked about the declining state of this country? Our political system is broken. There's only one party, and they are self-interested ego-maniacs who intentionally divide America while they make themselves wealthy. Our financial system is corrupt, feeding as much as it can to those who already have more money than they'll spend in ten lifetimes, while leaving the poor and middle class having to choose between a meal, gas, or necessary medication. All of this while they tell us everything isn't just fine but trending to get even better. You all know the justice system is a sham. And the media? They open up and say *ah* as they're spoon fed whatever the powers that be want them to say. All of this—and I mean *all* of this—has one root cause. Greed."

Bruno Rocchio slammed down his empty beer glass. "How much did we give to foreign countries fighting their petty wars just last year? I can't even count the billions. You see the line for soup kitchens or food pantries lately? It looks like Germany after WWI. It's a joke!"

Rocchio's face was red. At least the music and general noise didn't let his small tantrum leave their table. Lori patted his arm to get him to take it down a notch.

Bryan continued. "The infection started in big cities long ago. Unfortunately, it's spreading like a virus everywhere the big-city people have touched. When I came back here for my mother's funeral, I honestly thought I somehow blacked out for a day and drove on instead. Maverick is infested with drugs, illegal immigrants, poverty, and corruption. Like a fish, it's rotting from the head on down. Amy, you want to fill them in on our governor?"

Amy leaned close to L.G. so he could hear as she recounted everything she'd laid out to Bryan and Shane earlier in the day. Even Norm Hendricks had pulled back his wandering eye to listen. When she brought up the name *Nostrand Ganz*, Easy sat back in his chair and shook his head.

"That bag of ego is a whale hunter with his finger in just about every pie on every windowsill. What does he want with Maverick, or Iowa for that matter?"

"Ganz is in league with the Chicoms. He wants the land. Supposed leaders like Alexa Bennington are happy to give it. When he has the land he can set the rules as to what gets grown on it, what gets harvested. And what doesn't. He's in talks right now about buying Monsanto. He also wants to destroy family farms with toxic electric car batteries. Seemingly whatever is bad for the land, and Iowa, and the people who live there, he wants to do it."

Charlotte poured herself another beer. "They used

to say if you control the oil, you control the world. I guess the food supply is the new oil."

Lori Nicolo looked disgusted. "Don't forget all of the oil wells Ganz owns. It won't be just our country that will have to bow down before him. Think about all the food we export."

Norm Hendricks tapped his finger on the table. "And the more chaos you create, the more people will look to you as a savior. A world of law and order and principles doesn't need a man like Nostrand Ganz. So, he and the power elite, like your illustrious governor, through their policies and dirty dealings, throw everything on its head. Fear makes for obedient sheep. They won't rock the boat as long as Big Poppa throws them some scraps in between doom scrolling on their phones or watching TikTok clips. The problem is, Ganz is becoming too big to fail . . . or topple."

"Especially when he and President Mathers are so close. I'll bet as soon as Mathers finishes his term, he'll be brought on as a high-paid adviser for a bevy of Ganz's companies. We have a president who will make sure Ganz can't fail. And even when Mathers is gone, the next one will be in the pocket of Ganz or someone in that circle. A winning candidate would need their money just to get there," Amy said.

"So, what the hell can we do?" Rocchio said with a note of irritation in his voice. "At least on our prior missions, the target was narrow enough to be achievable in a short period of time. Go in, smash things up, then get the hell out. Going after the governor, Nostrand

Ganz, and the leader of the free world is like trying to eat a T. rex in one bite."

Brittany the waitress came over to ask them if they wanted to order a meal. Shane asked her for more beer. She went on her way, appearing to have no clue what they had been discussing.

"Forget a T. rex," Bryan said, looking to L.G. "What should we have for dinner instead?"

"An elephant," L.G. replied. "So we can eat it one bite at a time."

"Exactly. If we can somehow take back Maverick and restore order, that can spread just as much as the cancer that's trying to kill it. We need to show people that they don't have to lie down and take it. The cure is waking up." Bryan pointed at Rocchio. "And I'm not talking about being woke. We start with restoring power. And then we take the next bite. And the next, and the next."

Hendricks said, "To that point, I'm pretty sure I know what we need. I'm getting the parts tomorrow from a guy I know. He's driving here right now from New Mexico to deliver them. The problem is, how do I get the work done without getting arrested? Or my face on the evening news?"

Bryan said, "We do what we do best. We work in the shadows. Leave that part to me. I also have a twist that I think will help you. All you need to do is get the repairs started. We'll shame the power authority to finish it."

"First step is, we poke the bear," L.G. said.

"And then see what the bear does," Easy said. "Other than crapping in the woods."

"We poke all of the bears," Bryan added. "Which means things will get ugly in a hurry. We may find ourselves compromised. That's why if you're in, you have to be ready to put your retirement plan into action." It must have been someone's birthday because a line of clapping waiters and waitresses marched their way to a table on the other end of the restaurant. The DJ paused the music so they could sing to the birthday boy. Bryan couldn't see through the crowd. The DJ punctuated the song with a loud, "Yee-haw! Happy birthday, buckaroo!"

Bryan couldn't help laughing. "I guess that's apropos of us all to consider this might be our last rodeo together. Sleep on it, then let me know first thing tomorrow."

Shane threw up his hands. "I don't need to sleep on anything. You know I'm in, hoss."

Charlotte leaned into Bryan. "And you all know where I stand."

Without hesitation, all of Bryan's friends and fighters voted to poke some bears.

It was time to set things straight and reclaim Maverick, and if they did their job well, turn back the tide of evil.

When they returned to the farm, with Shane staying in the RV to get his beauty rest, Bryan and Charlotte found his father sitting on the porch in the darkness. The orange glow of the cigarette in his hand was the only thing that gave away the fact that he was even there.

"I thought you gave up smoking?" Bryan asked him. Charlotte gave his hand a squeeze.

"I did. Right around when you were five and your mother begged me to quit so I'd be around to raise you and Jason. The two of you are full grown and . . . well . . . your mother's not here now, is she?"

It wasn't a question meant to be answered or the start of a confrontation. It was simply a matter of fact. What Bryan also heard in the somber notes of his father's voice was that if smoking shortened his life, so be it.

"I'm heading up to bed," Charlotte whispered in his ear. "Good night, Mr. Branch."

"If you're comfortable with it, you can call me Dad."

Charlotte opened the screen door with a sharp squeal. "I believe I am. See you in the morning . . . Dad."

Bryan leaned against the rail, taking in the smell of earth and sky, of the harvest and home.

"Where's Bigfoot?"

"He and David are somewhere around, keeping an eye on things. You think that's something they'll have to do much longer?"

Bryan took a deep breath. "I sure hope not."

"Me too. It's no way to live."

"No, it sure isn't. But sometimes it's a necessity."

The silence between them seemed to stretch on forever.

"You're about to stir things up," his father said.

"What? Why do you think that?"

"You've changed a lot, but I can still tell when you're up to something."

Bryan held up his hands in surrender, even though

there was no way his father could see. "Okay, you got me there. Yes, I have some people in town who are going to help me."

"You trust them?"

"With my life."

"They like you and Charlotte?" Meaning, Bryan assumed, veterans.

"Yep."

The wicker chair creaked as his father adjusted himself.

"Some of them will be coming by in the morning. Then Charlotte and I are going to pull out with Shane."

"This is your home. You don't have to leave."

There was a time Bryan never thought he'd hear those words come out of his father's mouth. It shook him, but in a good way.

"It's best to keep you all safe. Just need to keep distance between myself and here for a little while." He was willing to sacrifice his newfound connection with his family and home if it meant giving them back the life they deserved.

"Okay, then. Just know the door is always open."

His father lit a new cigarette with the stub of the one in his mouth. Bryan had no intention of admonishing him.

"See you in the morning?" Bryan asked.

"I was thinking of getting a late start anyway. Harvesting's almost done."

Bryan patted his father's shoulder and went to bed.

* * *

At nine a.m. sharp, L.G., Amy, and Easy showed up at the ranch in Amy's rental Mustang. The entire Branch and Cruz families, along with Shane, were on the porch, waiting for them.

L.G. wiped the sweat from his smooth head. "It's hotter than a sweat lodge out here. Did Iowa somehow move closer to the sun?"

"I kind of like it," Easy said. "Feels like Cabo, without the margaritas, pools, and good times."

"All the more reason to do what we have to do tonight," Bryan said, shaking L.G.'s hand when he made his way up the steps. Introductions were made all around. Lori Nicolo and Bruno Rocchio were with Norm, waiting for the delivery. The man behind it was of dubious character, and there was safety in numbers.

"You're Bryan's *little* brother?" Easy asked Jason.

"Chronologically speaking only," Jason replied with a big grin.

Amy was immediately taken by Lola and Tomás. She'd been told she would never have children of her own on account of her injuries. She shifted into maternal mode effortlessly. He wondered, if this was their last go-around, if she would adopt a child and lean into her second nature.

Bryan's father was in his clean overalls, taking everything in, answering any questions asked of him with his usual bare bones simplicity. Bryan swore his father was happy to see them. It made sense. The sooner they got to work, the sooner things in Maverick got better and, possibly, they would find the men who had taken out the Branch matriarch.

"Well, time for us to get to work," George Branch announced after several minutes. He nodded toward Jason, Pam, and David. He walked off the porch with a backward wave, heading to the cornfield.

"You need me for anything, just call," Jason said.

"Maybe," Bryan said, clearly joking.

As they went inside, Amy remarked, "Your dad's a bit of a hottie."

"You talk too much for him," Bryan said. "He'd be out the door in under five minutes. Now, let's get to work."

They sat at the dining room table and went over the plan for the night.

"You talk to Sam?" Bryan asked Shane.

"All set."

"He give you any numbers?"

"Nothing definitive. He'll know when they come."

"Who's Sam?" L.G. asked.

"A podcaster," Bryan replied.

The wood chair protested lightly when Amy leaned back. "Where in the world does a podcaster fit into all of this?"

Bryan knew this question was coming. "He has a pretty big following and he's beholden to no one. Shane said he won't even accept sponsors because he knows that eventually money and influence tie you down. For once, we need a way for what we do to see the light of day."

Even with the fan on, it was stifling in the house. Sweat dripped down everyone's faces.

"Tell me what you need him to do. I don't want any surprises," L.G. said. Bryan laid it all out, and when L.G. didn't protest, he felt he could move on.

They went over every detail so there were no gaps, no risks that hadn't been accounted for. By the time they were done it was lunchtime.

"I'll grill us some burgers and dogs," Shane said when he pushed back his chair. Bryan could tell he was anxious to get out of the house.

"There's no turning back once we start," Bryan said.

"Good," Charlotte said. "Let's kick these sons of devils in the teeth."

CHAPTER 23

Easy had procured a car for them after they had lunch. They couldn't use Shane's RV because it was too recognizable, nor Bryan's rental car because it could be tied to him. Easy had assured them he'd nicked it from someone who deserved their car being stolen and would most likely not report it as such.

Turning off the headlights a quarter mile before the meeting point behind the abandoned corporate park, they pulled alongside the van that Norm Hendricks had told them his supplier had given at a fair price.

It was dark and cloudy with few visible stars. Bryan secretly thanked Mother Nature for working on their side.

Hendricks, Rocchio, and Lori jumped out of the side door of the van.

"You see anyone?" Bryan asked Hendricks.

"Just one state trooper in his car across the street from the substation. With so few cars coming around here, I'll bet he or she is half asleep."

"Good. You have everything you need?"

"At least to get the ball rolling."

Bryan clapped him on the back. "Hopefully that's all we need." He then turned to face his crew. "Shane and Easy, you'll assist Norm. Amy, Bruno, Lori, L.G., Charlotte, we'll guard the perimeter. Everyone good?"

"I don't know if I've ever been good, but I am ready," Easy quipped.

"Fine. Go!"

Everyone pulled down the black masks that were rolled up on their foreheads. It was damn hot for a mask, but they needed to suck it up so their identities were kept a secret. Shane had brought an assortment of assault weapons from his RV. Bryan was almost 100 percent sure they wouldn't have to use them. For now, they were there as a show of force.

If they had to use them tonight, the plan was over before it began.

Hendricks, Easy, and Shane grabbed heavy bags from the van and ran to the substation. Rocchio and Lori headed for their assigned positions at the rear of the building. L.G. and Amy jogged to the side gates while Bryan and Charlotte made their way to the front gate, along with the repair team.

Someone had added a new padlock and a thick chain since their last visit. Rocchio extracted a bolt cutter from his bag and made quick work of it. The three hustled inside, Norm leading the way.

Bryan shut the gate and fixed his attention on the state trooper's car across the street. Inside was dark. He didn't see any movement. In the still of the hot and humid night, Bryan heard the clatter of tools as Hendricks, Shane, and Easy got to work.

Charlotte waved to Bryan to step into the shadows with her.

"Let's hope our night watchman snoozes long enough for Norm to get something back online," Charlotte said.

"Even if he doesn't, that's fine. We can't leave without making a visible fuss."

They maintained their position for the better part of an hour, neither of them moving very much. They were used to interminably long waits in their line of work. The key was to make sure your legs, feet, and hands didn't fall asleep so you weren't anything less than your best when action called.

Hendricks, Easy, and Shane did very little to conceal their work. The trooper had his windows up and air conditioner on. They'd have to do something to make the ground quake to get his or her attention. Try as he might, Bryan couldn't make out the features of the person in the driver's seat.

He keyed his walkie. "How are things going?"

Hendricks replied, "Meh. This thing was shot to hell man. What time is it?"

Bryan checked his watch. "Almost eleven."

"Showtime soon. I know we said eleven thirty. We'll be cutting it close."

The next thirty minutes felt like an eternity. Only one car drove past them, a pickup truck with two men in the front and two men in the flatbed. It sounded like they were having a lot of fun. They must not have noticed the trooper's car because Bryan didn't see the red flare of brake lights.

Charlotte and Bryan remained completely silent.

When he looked around the substation's perimeter he couldn't see any of his team. That was good.

"It's time," Charlotte whispered.

Bryan checked in with Hendricks. "Yeah, we're good."

Bryan tapped his walkie three times to alert his team that the game was about to begin. He picked up a rock and threw it across the street. It hit the roof of the trooper's cruiser. The door immediately flew open. A tall man emerged, squaring his cap on. He looked up and down the street.

Then he peered into the substation and went for his gun. Bryan turned his head. Hendricks had Easy and Shane shine their lights at whatever he was working on.

"Hey!" the trooper cried out. "What the hell do you think you're doing in there?"

He jogged across the street, saw the cut chain on the ground, and raised his gun.

"Stop what you're doing right now! You're trespassing on private property."

"Don't I know it," Hendricks called out. "Someone's gotta get this thing up and running."

"Get on the floor! All of you! Now!" The trooper put his free hand on the gate, about to open it.

Bryan and Charlotte swept out of the darkness, AR15s up and pointed at the trooper. "It's best you stay out here," Bryan said.

The trooper swung his gun hand toward them, his feet kicking up dust as he pivoted on his bootheels.

"Put your gun down," Charlotte said coolly. "We don't, and I repeat, don't want to shoot you."

"Drop your weapons!" he shouted, seeming to overcome his shock, though his voice quavered a bit. Having two people in black masks with high-powered weaponry appear out of the darkness was enough to shatter most men's reserve.

Bryan took a tentative step closer. "You should listen to her. But she forgot to add, as much as we don't want to shoot you, we will if you force us to."

"He's right about that," Easy said from within the substation.

"Who the hell are you people?" the trooper asked. His free hand started to go for the mic attached to the shoulder of his jacket.

"Just concerned citizens who pay a lot of money for electricity and would like it turned back on. And I wouldn't call for backup if I were you. If you think we're the only ones out here, you'd be very wrong. No need to make a scene."

The trooper's eyes flicked back and forth between Bryan and Charlotte. His chest puffed up a bit and he now had both hands on his gun. "You and your terrorist friends need to cease and desist right now."

Bryan shook his head. "You ever hear of a terrorist *fixing* things?"

"I don't need to explain myself to you. I'll say it again. Put your weapons down! Now!"

Bryan was impressed. The man's bark was pretty good. He bet he used it to great effect on speed zone violators and drunks.

"You don't stand a chance."

The trooper whirled around when Amy stepped out

of the shadows behind him. "Three against one doesn't bode well for you," she said.

For whatever reason—whether it was bravery or shock—the trooper would not back down. In fact, he fired his weapon into the air and blurted out, "Everyone drop their weapons. Enough!"

Charlotte nudged Bryan. If they let this go on much longer, someone would get shot by accident if not intent. Bryan keyed his walkie four times. It was a signal for Sam.

"Everyone calm down," Bryan said. "We're just here doing our civic duty. You know, a lot of people are very ill or dead because of the delays on this."

"That's not my problem," the trooper said, spinning to face him.

"It should be. You are sworn to protect and serve the people of this state," Amy said.

"I'm going to count to three," the trooper said.

Suddenly, a brilliant white light turned on from the street, startling the statie. On cue, Sam Mishra appeared, along with a couple of dozen of his podcast listeners. All had phones in their hands, recording everything.

The trooper looked exasperated. "Get that damn light out of my eyes! And put down those phones."

A few of Sam's followers gasped when he turned to face the source of the light, his gun swiveling to face them.

"You need to put down your gun," Bryan said. "Pointing it at innocent civilians is not advisable."

The trooper looked at Bryan with exasperation. "Can you please explain what is going on here?"

"Holster your weapon," Charlotte said. Then added, "Please."

He took in everything going on around him and then holstered his gun.

Bryan let out the breath he'd been holding.

"I told you before, we just want to get the power back on. Seeing as someone obviously doesn't want that to happen, we decided to take matters into our own hands."

"And what about them?" the trooper said, jerking a thumb at Sam and his tribe.

"They're here to get the word out," Bryan said.

"We're live streaming everything," Sam said. "We have almost five hundred people watching now, and growing exponentially. Is there anything you want to say to them?" He pointed his cell camera at the trooper.

Bryan walked over and took it from Sam's hands. "Don't be a fool. It's not his fault."

"He's part of the corrupt system," Sam protested.

Shutting off the phone, Bryan leaned close and whispered, "He's a man with a job who probably needs it to support a family. Just do what we asked you to do."

He returned the phone to Sam's palm. Sam's followers took a couple of steps back.

"It's cool. It's cool," Sam said to his people, most of them in their twenties and predominantly men. Then he focused his camera on Bryan.

"Getting the power back on for a town during a heat wave should never have come to this," Bryan said. "We've started the repairs and will finish them if need be. Unless the powers that be finally do the right thing.

People have suffered. People have died. For what? That's a question with an answer we all need to demand. So, if you're with the power authority or know someone who is, get your ass here and *do your job*. You already have blood on your hands. This is your chance to begin to atone."

A string of expletives wafted from within the power station. It sounded like Hendricks was not having an easy time of things.

"Tonight is a first step to setting things right. If you're in a position of authority who has been turning a blind eye to the decay that has set in here in Maverick—or Iowa, for that matter—well, know this: We're not going to play your game anymore. We're not going to hold more funerals and hear your empty words about keeping the dead in your thoughts and prayers. It's time we take back our town and the American way of life. If you want to stand in the way of good and decent people, you best get ready."

Bryan turned away and took the trooper by the arm, leading him away from the crowd.

"I don't know how you think you're going to get away with this," the trooper said. Up this close, Bryan saw his name tag.

"Trooper Gaines, same as I guess the folks who have played games with the lives of the people of Maverick have these past few years. We're going to do what's right and not worry about whose feathers we ruffle."

"I should have known some militia wackos would eventually pop their heads out of the sand," Gaines said.

"Hell, I'm not even zip-tying you and forcing you on

the ground. If you equate us with some misguided militia, you're going to grossly underestimate our intentions . . . and abilities. For now, let's just get the power back on."

"We're almost at four thousand viewers," Sam announced. There was a light cheer from his followers, who were still filming with their own phones.

Bryan nudged Trooper Gaines with his elbow. "You look hot. Let's go to your car so you can cool off. In the back seat, of course."

Fifteen minutes later, a phalanx of police cruisers arrived.

Bryan and his team had pulled out after he set Trooper Gaines in the car. They watched it all on Sam's live feed, when they were almost ten miles from the substation.

The police tried to swipe the phone out of Sam's hand, but he was wily.

More important than the arrival of the police was the trio of repair trucks from the power authority. As the police tried to disperse Sam and his followers, seven men and one woman wearing overalls with massively heavy tool belts walked through the gate into the substation.

By the time Bryan and his team had split up and he and Charlotte were in Shane's RV, he got word from Jason that the power was back on.

CHAPTER 24

Governor Alexa Bennington furiously kicked over the small wastebasket in the conference room. She'd called everyone in her inner circle to an all-hands meeting in her office. Colin Farmer was seated on the right side of her empty chair. There were fifteen staff members in all seated around the oblong table. Her dimwitted office admin, Penny Hastings, was assigned to coffee duty. The young girl yelped when the basket hit the wall.

Bennington shot Penny a glowering look, driving her out of the room with her empty tray.

On the large television screen behind Bennington was a still image taken from the *Lying for Dollars* podcast live feed that Colin had recorded. It showed two armed people standing before the substation gates with the defanged state trooper off to the side.

"What the hell are we dealing with here?" she asked her mute staff. "This is obviously an act of domestic terrorism. Who are they? I need to know now!"

She cast her gaze to Damien Arnstadt, a veteran chief of police who had served two governors. She knew he wasn't happy with the policies of her administration, but he accepted his paycheck every two weeks, so that meant he still had to do his damn job.

Arnstadt was dressed in a tight-fitting blue suit, his bull neck spilling over his shirt collar. He wasn't fat so much as he was just plain thick all over. He met the governor's reproachful stare for a moment before clearing his throat. "As of this moment, we have over a hundred individuals or groups claiming responsibility for the incident. After speaking to Trooper Gaines we ascertained certain information that was not caught on camera or released to the public. So far, no one has matched our intel. We did find tire tracks of what must have been a large vehicle not too far from the substation. It's difficult to tell if the tracks were made last night or days ago."

Tapping her nails on the screen, Bennington said, "I don't care about tire tracks. We have crystal clear images of the terrorists right here. It looks to me like there are two women and two men. What groups do we know of that are possibly a fifty-fifty mix of men to women? It shouldn't be a very long list." Bennington spoke to Arnstadt in a tone a jaded teacher would adopt when talking to a particularly confused child.

Arnstadt sat straighter in his chair to show he wasn't intimidated. "Contrary to popular belief, there are quite a number of underground militia groups with an almost equal mix of men and women. However, what none of them have done in the past is take action under the gaze of social media just to get something *fixed*." He looked around the room. "Terrorism implies doing something to strike terror. In this case, getting the lights back on would seem to be the polar opposite."

"I think the state trooper would look at it differently," Bennington said icily.

"He wasn't harmed in the slightest, except possibly his ego," Arnstadt reminded her. "Groups that we know would at least cuff him, if not hog-tie him just for the fun of it and to prove a point. What we're dealing with here is something entirely different, in my opinion."

Bennington paced around the room. "Who authorized those trucks to waltz into a war zone?"

Her chief of staff consulted his tablet. "Someone who saw the live stream called the dispatch manager. After he had an internal conversation the decision was made to send out the repair crew, under police supervision, of course." Colin kept his eyes glued to the table. He did not want to incur any more wrath than was already suffocating the room.

"I want everyone responsible for that boneheaded decision to report to my office this afternoon. Is that clear?"

"Yes," Colin said, tapping on his screen.

"Do we know how many terrorists were there?" She was going to keep using the word *terrorist* until everyone bent to her way of thinking. A band of people with military-grade weapons storming a public utility were not to be considered anything less.

"There were the three by the front gate, and Trooper Gaines said he thought there were two or more inside the substation doing repairs. He was also told there were others surrounding the facility. We have no way of knowing the total. By the time backup arrived they were gone."

"Useless. Just absolutely useless!"

Bennington relished the looks on everyone's faces as they were clearly trying to decide if she meant Arnstadt's evaluation was piss-poor or they themselves were useless. The truth was, she meant both.

"I think you should see this," Colin Farmer said. He set down his tablet and reached across the table for the remote control. After a bit of fidgeting with the menu options he settled on the local morning news. It showed a pretty Hispanic woman standing outside the substation. The area was mobbed with other news vans and reporters. Alexa Bennington spotted a few national networks in attendance. Her acid reflux went into high gear.

"I'm standing outside the Maverick substation that was the scene of a domestic terrorist attack just over a week ago. Last night at around midnight, it was taken over by a mystery band of armed intruders who also utilized a local and popular podcast to live stream their takeover. After subduing a state trooper who had been guarding the substation they proceeded to demand that the power authority fix the essential component of the power grid immediately. Stranger still, it appears that members of the group were inside beginning repairs as the drama outside the gates unfolded."

The live feed cut away to some of the video from the *Lying for Dollars* stream. Bennington fumed when she saw a promotion for the podcast on the stream. That little idiot who ran it must be dreaming of fame thanks to this stunt. Bennington made a note to make sure his fifteen minutes were about to come to a close.

After a twenty-second snip of the overnight stream it cut to the reporter talking to citizens who had come out to the substation because the uneducated masses couldn't resist a scene. A middle-aged woman with a bob haircut who couldn't stop fanning herself with her hand said, "I don't know who did this, but I'm just thankful. My husband has COPD and we were about to take him to the hospital because he doesn't do well in the heat. He's already feeling better."

An African American man probably in his twenties was next. "We were about to run out of food, man. These guys just might have saved our lives."

Then a senior citizen wearing a Navy ball cap said, "It's about time. You mean to tell me this all could have been fixed within a few hours? Why were we left to suffer for so long? The people who did this are heroes in my book."

A cut back to the reporter. "Everyone I've spoken to so far is grateful for the actions of the men and women who forced the power utility's hand overnight. Better yet, no one was hurt during the altercation."

When the report went back to the studio the anchorman interjected, "Jessica, is anyone concerned that this was a brazen act of domestic terrorists? If they were there in the town's best interests, why bring guns?"

Bennington had caught that particular anchorman groping a young girl at a party thrown by the network's president last summer. Alexa didn't know if the girl was underage or not, but she knew his wife wouldn't approve. He'd been in her hip pocket ever since.

"That's a question we can ask them if we get the chance in the future," the on-site reporter replied. "Until then I think it's safe to say the town of Maverick can breathe a cold sigh of relief that what could have been an ugly situation turned into a solution to a very big problem."

Narrowing her eyes at the screen, Bennington took note of the reporter's name. If that lady thought the Maverick beat was small town, she'd have a whole new appreciation of what she'd lost once Alexa spoke to her boss.

Bennington swiped the remote control from Colin's hand and turned off the television.

"If I hear more talk of these terrorists being heroes . . ."

She let that hang in the air.

"Now go do your jobs and find them And let's get the narrative straight. I will not have the people of my state looking up to armed lunatics. Is everyone clear?"

Fifteen heads nodded. Papers were shuffled and cell phones appeared in palms.

Bennington looked to Arnstadt, who she swore had the beginnings of a grin on his face during the news report. She would have to keep a very close eye on him.

"I want you to arrest that podcasting punk for aiding and abetting a terrorist group."

"I assumed you would, which is why I sent several cars to his address first thing. It appears he's in the wind. He'd clearly taken a lot of clothes with him and there wasn't a single bit of technology in his apartment."

Bennington put her palms flat on the table and leaned close to him. "Well, we know exactly what that little Indian twerp looks like, so go find him. On a good day he sticks out like a sore thumb. If you don't get him soon, today is going to be a very, very bad day for you."

Chief of Police Arnstadt's jaw flexed for a bit before he nodded and abruptly rose from his chair.

CHAPTER 25

Bryan woke up with his back and knees barking from sleeping in the passenger seat of the RV. They were parked inside an abandoned barn in Pistol Creek, two towns east of Maverick. Jason had told them about it when Bryan asked him for an out-of-the-way location to hole up for a while. The farm had belonged to someone Jason went to school with until the parents became too ill to run it a couple of years ago and the sons had left town for bigger cities. Jason was sure some conglomerate was ready to get its dirty hands on the property, but for now it was a perfect spot to lay low.

He looked back to see Charlotte still asleep in the pull-out sleeper in the kitchen/living room. Shane's snores rattled the walls from his bedroom in the back.

Quietly, he slipped outside to stretch his back and limp around the old hay until the pain and pins and needles lessened. The morning was hot and sunny, but the humidity had dialed back a bit.

Yawning, he checked his watch. Almost seven. His father and everyone else would be working the fields now. Bryan had asked Rocchio to lend a hand so he had someone professional keeping an eye on the place.

"Why me?" Rocchio had asked.

"Well, with your swarthy Southern Italian looks and physique, you're a natural choice. No one will raise an eyebrow if they see you there."

Rocchio got the implication and laughed. "Fine. I get it. I won't be able to go to a gym, so the work will do me good."

Bryan had called ahead to let Jason know they would have a new farmhand/security detail. For once, his little brother didn't ask any questions. He'd seen full well that there was a potential for danger everywhere. Hopefully he now understood that Bryan knew what he was doing and was, in fact, in his element.

He also hoped Sam Mishra was safe. They had made arrangements to contact each other at ten that morning. Bryan had made plans with Sam to pack up and scram. His face and podcast were quite prominent last night. Sam said he was a late sleeper, which was why Bryan had to wait. How anyone could sleep late after what had happened was beyond him.

For now Sam was holed up with one of his listeners in Denison. Bryan had told him to hunker down and stay out of sight for now. They would need him later. He'd be of no use if he was arrested, which he surely would be if caught out and about.

Bryan checked out various news reports, shocked to see the overwhelming positive reception to their actions. That would change once the media bosses got their marching orders to flip the narrative.

He turned when he heard the door open. Shane came striding out still dressed in his fatigues.

"Morning, Boss. You sleep okay?"

"I got about three full hours, which is fine by me. Being awake just allowed me the privilege of listening to you saw wood like a world-class lumberjack."

Shane used both hands to scratch at his head. It looked almost as if he were screwing it back into place. "Hey, to pull off what we did last night without a shot fired? That was pretty good. That was the sleep of a satisfied man."

Bryan handed him his phone. "At least for now the morning news people are calling us heroes. You know that won't last."

Shane scrolled through the various headlines. "I prefer being the villain anyway. They have more fun."

"You read way too many comic books."

"It keeps me young." He sniffed the air. "Do I smell bacon?"

Bryan followed Shane's nose back into the RV. Charlotte was up frying a pound of bacon.

"Morning," she said. Her hair was all over the place. She had a pot of coffee on.

"I'll take over while you read through these," Bryan said, taking the tongs from her and replacing them with his phone. Charlotte sat down and read for a good ten minutes, her brows knitted the entire time, with just a hint of a smile on her face.

When she was finished she went to the mini refrigerator and took out a carton of eggs. "That's all well and good. But that was also the easy part. We're in no position to get cocky."

Bryan set three pieces of cooked bacon on a paper towel and kissed her. "We most certainly are not."

The trio tucked into their breakfast as if they had just ended a hunger strike. The adrenaline spikes from the night before had left them famished. When they were done Bryan and Charlotte cleaned up and changed into fresh clothes.

Shane was in the driver's seat reading a *Captain America* comic book.

"You good?" Bryan asked his friend as he opened the RV door.

"I brought about fifty comics from my collection so, yeah, I'm good."

Bryan and Charlotte walked across the empty barn to the blue Chevy sedan that Easy Campisi had procured for them. He'd used one of his fake IDs and shadow bank accounts to rent the vehicle for them.

On the road Bryan made a quick call to Sam Mishra. He simply said, "All square?"

To which Sam gave the previously agreed upon reply, "And fair."

Good. Sam was okay. For now. He'd better be good with directions and keep his head buried. With traffic cams and front-door cams everywhere, any venture outside could spell disaster. Being young and potentially drunk with success, Sam was considered a risk for the moment. Shane was in charge of checking Sam's accounts to see if he was posting anything over the next few days. Bryan had explained to Sam the meaning of *radio silence*. He hoped the youngster fully grasped it.

The first stop was to Maverick United Hospital. The nice receptionist gave them each a visitor sticker to affix to their shirts and told them where the elevator was located and what floor to get off. Charlotte picked up a small bouquet of flowers in a glass vase in the lobby store.

When Bryan saw the state of Aaron Chisolm sitting in his hospital bed, staring out the window, he thought he might grind his teeth to dust.

The top of Chisolm's head was wrapped in gauze. His entire face was a mélange of black, blue, purple and yellow. His eyes were practically swollen shut and his split lips looked like plumped hot dogs. One arm was in a sling and he had a wrap around his ribs. When Chisolm saw them he attempted a smile that clearly hurt.

"If I'd known I'd have such distinguished visitors, I would have gotten into my good pajamas."

"Hey Aaron," Bryan said. "How are you feeling?"

Bryan and Charlotte grabbed a couple of chairs, pulled them near Chisolm's bed, and sat. Charlotte set the flowers on the lone spare space on the window ledge.

"Thank you for the flowers," Chisolm said, his voice sounding stuffed and nasally. It didn't look as if his nose were broken, but there was clearly damage they couldn't see. "Truth is, I'm not feeling much of anything. They've got me hooked to this morphine drip to keep me comfortably numb." He held up the small trigger that he could control to get his next hit. "I'm thinking of asking them to take the damn thing out today. You know how many people, how many kids, I've had to call the coroner for because they were addicted to stuff like this? Having this here thing is making it too easy to fall into that trap. I'd rather they just get rid of it and let me deal with the pain."

Bryan put one hand on the bed rail. "Did they catch the creeps who did this to you?"

Chisolm's swollen eyes blinked slowly. "Four of them were picked up. That leaves about six others in the wind. Not that it much mattered. The judge let those thieving punks right out without bail. You know, no one wants to make these poor thugs' disadvantaged life any harder than it already is."

Charlotte was outraged. She shot up from her chair. "That's ludicrous. Look what they did to an officer of the law. Doesn't that mean anything to anyone?"

"Yeah, it means I'm just another cop who probably had it coming to him. How did we come to a place in this world where the police are lower on the scum rung than lawyers? If my father was alive now, this would kill him."

Aaron Chisolm's father had also been a police officer in Maverick, as had his grandfather. They would surely be shocked to their cores if they could see the prevailing attitude to peace officers not just in Maverick but all over the country.

Bryan couldn't help thinking how quickly these progressive fools would fumble to call 9-1-1 the second there was a hint of trouble. When the tide had begun to turn against the police countrywide, Bryan wished there was a way to make everyone who denigrated the cops or called to defund them sign a waiver that forbade them from asking for police help in an emergency. Why bother wasting time or even lives helping people who said publicly they didn't want your help?

"You married? Have a family?" Bryan asked.

That brought a small gleam to his eyes. "Married to Sue Pellone for seven years now. We have a three-year-old daughter, Maisey."

"Sue Pellone? Wasn't she the president of the student council in high school?"

"You're thinking of Anna Kimbers. Sue was shy back then. I don't think I talked to her once in school. Then one day she called in a noise complaint. Some parents were away and their teen sons threw a party. I was the lucky one sent to the scene, and we've been together ever since." His thumb hovered over the button for morphine. Chisolm let the device slip from his fingers. "Sue said she'd be by around noon. I haven't seen my little girl since this happened. I miss her. I just want to get out of here and get back home to her."

Bryan almost patted him on the shoulder but pulled away. He didn't want to add to Chisolm's pain. "You will, buddy. You will. We just wanted to come by to see you and also let you know we're heading back to PA."

"So soon?"

"My father and brother have everything in hand. I'll just get in the way. It was good seeing you again."

Chisolm winced when he raised his arm to shake Bryan and Charlotte's hands. "Don't be a stranger for so long again." Looking at Charlotte, he said, "You seem like a lovely woman, but I do have to question your taste in men. Before you go, you should know those men we picked up that took shots at you on the farm . . ."

"Did you get one of them to crack?" Bryan asked.

"The opposite. They were released. God knows where they are now."

Bryan felt his veins fill with ice. "So, people can shoot at my family and get away with it. Is that what you're telling me?"

"Unfortunately, yes."

"Yeah, well, thanks for giving me the news. Take care of yourself," Bryan said, rising to go.

"Thanks for what you did," Chisolm said.

"You don't have to thank us for visiting you in the hospital, man."

Chisolm shook his head. "No. Not that. For the town. I know it was you who stopped those smash-and-grabbers. And cleared out the playground. Hell, we haven't seen that lowlife Jimmy since you came to town. Sorry to see you go. I'm sure he'll pop out of whatever dingy hole he's been hiding out in the second you leave. Hopefully you gave folks just the little extra courage they need, though."

Bryan and Chisolm locked in a long silent stare, feeling each other out.

Finally Bryan said, "Wasn't us. We've been busy on the farm. I'll see you."

When they turned their back Chisolm had one more thing to say. "Well, someone also took out the cartel that's been poisoning our town. And they did it without having to waste taxpayer money. As an officer of the law, I'm not supposed to condone vigilante behavior. But as an American trying to work within a broken system, I'm pretty damn appreciative."

Bryan looked back at him one more time. Chisolm had turned his head and resumed looking out the window.

They drove from the hospital in silence, each chewing on Aaron Chisolm's words. When Bryan and Charlotte had stopped those thieves they had done so in broad daylight with no desire to conceal their identities. Same when Bryan confronted his old pal Jimmy the drug dealer.

Chisolm was no dummy. He'd managed to put two and two together. The silver lining was his approval of what they'd done in that drug den. Maybe nearly being beaten to death and watching your attackers walk free and clear was enough to change your opinion on how things should be.

Bryan still had to be cautious about his old friend. He may have been able to turn a blind eye now, but how would he react when the escalation began? Aaron was a lawman, that was certain. But a lawman had his limits when it came to right and wrong and the rules that governed them.

They got to the farm just after noon. Everyone was in the fields, including the kids. David Cruz had said he

. wasn't going to take his eyes off them. That was smart thinking. Bryan hoped David and Jason found a way to keep their weapons close at hand while they did their harvesting. Plenty of room in the harvester to store them.

An unfamiliar Ford pickup was parked near the house. It belonged to Bruno Rocchio by way of Easy Campisi. Easy was busier than a Miami luxury car dealer.

Charlotte grabbed their packed bags from the upstairs bedroom while Bryan poured them each an iced tea. When she came downstairs they drank them standing by the sink.

"Follow me?" Charlotte asked.

"To the end and back," he replied with a sly grin.

It was a silent and lonely goodbye. Bryan took a long look at the family house and farm and got into his car.

They made the long drive back to the airport so Charlotte could drop off their rental car.

When they left the parking garage in the Chevy sedan Easy had gotten them, they made sure to keep their visors and heads down so any security cameras wouldn't get a good shot of their faces.

They made it back to the abandoned farm in Pistol Creek later in the afternoon. The sun was high in the sky, delivering another body blow of brutal heat. At least this time the people of Maverick could get relief from their fans and air conditioners.

Shane stepped out of a swatch of shadow within the barn when they pulled up. He was carrying an AR15 pointed at the ground.

"Experience any trouble while we were gone?" Bryan asked.

"Yeah. Those damn heat bugs never stop. I like noise to drown out the tinnitus, but this is ridiculous."

"Everyone check in?" Charlotte asked him.

Shane opened the RV door. They were hit with a wave of cool air. "Sir, yes sir. Bruno just called me five minutes ago." When they sat inside Shane looked at Bryan. "He wanted me to ask you why anyone would want to be a farmer."

Bryan chuckled at that. "I have a feeling we'll be around long enough for him to get used to it. You ready to take first shift?"

Shane's eyes lit up. "Hell yeah. I'll give Lori the signal."

"Okay, then," Bryan said as he set his boots on the seat across from him. "Let Operation Return to Sender begin."

CHAPTER 26

Shane Perretti met Lori Nicolo behind the ice cream shop just off Broad Street. It was going on suppertime, still sunny and warm. There were very few people about.

Actually, there were very few *legitimate* people walking around. Most of what Shane and Lori saw were either homeless, recent immigrants, or shady characters.

Lori was dressed in a pair of mom jeans she must have found at a thrift shop, with a yellow T-shirt that had the logo of some seed company on the front. Shane had opted for his oldest pair of jeans and a flannel shirt with the sleeves cut off.

"You look like Larry the Cable Guy," Lori quipped when they came together. Both had wide, happy smiles on their faces as they hugged.

"That's because we're gonna get 'er done."

Posing as a harmless couple, they held hands as they walked down the street, taking in what they could from their periphery without looking like out-of-towners with their heads on a swivel.

Lori said out of the corner of her mouth, "Really? Do you have to hold my hand?"

"I didn't write the script."

"I would love to see Bruno come walking down the street."

"You two haven't broken up yet?" He checked his watch. "I'll give it another two hours."

"You're not as funny as you think you are."

"No one can be as funny as I think I am."

After walking a couple of blocks they stepped inside an independent pharmacy. The place was a disaster. Two men were finishing installing plastic cages over the shelves. All of the shelves in the front of the store were empty for the moment. Work tools and scraps of metal were everywhere.

"Please forgive the mess," an elderly man wearing a white lab coat called over to them from behind the counter. "If you need anything, just ask. As you can see, we're doing a little remodeling to, ah, discourage the rash of thefts that never seem to end."

"I don't blame you," Shane said, wanting to sound like he was someone local who knew what the Maverick merchants were going through.

Lori asked the pharmacist for deodorant and a bottle of shampoo. It took the man a bit of time to find them within the plastic crates crammed into the back of the store. He thanked them and told them when they came back, he would have someone in the aisles who could unlock the doors to get what they needed in the future.

When they walked out Shane couldn't stop shaking

his head. "They're locking up toothpaste in Iowa. The world is ending, Lor. Just so you know."

Lori eyed a pair of suspicious men walking across the street. Despite the heat they wore hoodies. What was it with the criminal element and hoodies? At least it made them easy to spot, especially in the summer. Their hands were shoved deep in their pockets. "You know they're up to no good."

"Hopefully we meet them on the way back."

They dipped into stores that looked like perfect spots for a smash-and-grab, taking their time to see if anything developed. So far, things were quiet.

When they went into a beverage mart—because what thieves could resist liquor?—they saw a large man with a shopping cart at the counter. The problem was, the cart was marked as belonging to the IGA supermarket a couple of blocks away, and it was filled with random items found in a supermarket, not a beverage mart.

Shane and Lori sauntered over to a display of hard seltzers close to the counter.

"How about this?" the man said. He pulled out a digital meat thermometer from the haphazard pile. "I'll sell it to you for three bucks. Price tag says it'll cost you fifteen at the store."

The young man behind the counter scanned the contents of the cart with suspicion. "Where'd you get all this stuff?"

The scruffy man waved his hand. "It's just things I've had in my house I've been meaning to get rid of." He dug into the pile, extracting a handful of razor blade cartridges. "Ten bucks! You won't have to buy razors again for a couple of years."

"Dude, I don't want your stolen stuff. You need to get out of my store."

The thief picked up a box of cereal and tossed it at the clerk. The box bounced off his raised forearm.

"You don't call me a thief! You hear me? How about I make you *buy* those razors?"

To his credit, because the shopping cart crook was six inches taller and about fifty pounds heavier, the clerk reached under the counter. "How about I make you get to walking?"

They stared at each other until the thief violently pushed his cart out the door, clipping the edge and rattling the glass.

Lori approached the counter. "That was . . . unpleasant."

The clerk put both hands on the counter, turning his head so he could watch the man walk away. "Just another day in paradise. When he's not stealing from here he's hawking stuff he stole from other stores in town. He's roughed a few people up, too. If you see that guy on the street, steer clear of him. He's trouble."

Hugging herself as if to appear shaken up, Lori said, "I definitely will."

With a phony stammer, Shane said, "I'll, uh, t-take a small bottle of rum. Phew, that was scary."

"It never ends, man," the clerk said dejectedly.

With his rum tucked in his back pocket, Shane took Lori's hand again and headed outside. He looked around and then pointed down the street to their right. "There."

The pilfered shopping cart had a bum wheel, so the

thief was having a hard time pushing it down the sidewalk. Shane and Lori didn't have to walk very fast to catch up with him. They waited until he walked across an alley to grab him and his cart and toss them out of sight. Shane shoved him as hard as he could. The big man stumbled but didn't go down.

"Hey, what the hell's wrong with you?" he complained, quickly regaining his footing. "You lookin' for trouble?" He reached into his jacket pocket. "You just found it."

Before he could pull out whatever weapon he had, Lori kicked his wrist. The sound it made confirmed she'd broken it. The thief grabbed his damaged arm and staggered into the wall.

"You little bi—"

He kicked at Lori. She easily stepped back and out of range. Seeing as the man had opened himself up, Shane nailed him in his crotch with the business end of his steel-tipped boot.

Gasping for air, the large thief crumpled to the ground.

Shane stood over him with his hands balled into fists. "You like taking things that aren't yours?"

The man's eyes were wide, his mouth opening and closing, unable to make a sound.

"I bet you thought you had it pretty good here. Not anymore. Once your balls come back down from your throat, you're going to find the next bus out of Maverick. And if we see you again . . ." Shane paused to laugh. "Let's just say you don't want to know what will happen."

With surprising quickness, the thief jumped up and went to tackle Shane. Lori punched the man in the left ear just as Shane hopped out of the way. Stunned but not stopped, the thief grabbed the front of the cart and rammed it into Lori. She doubled over as it smashed into her midsection.

Shane gave a swift chop to the side of the man's neck, stopping him from running out of the alley. He then crushed his heel into the back of the man's leg, dropping him like a bag of hammers.

"You okay?" Shane asked Lori.

"I'm fine," she replied breathily with her hand on her stomach.

"You shouldn't have done that," Shane said to the prone man. When he tried to scream Shane punched him in the throat. "Now my friend has to show you what happens to people who steal in countries that don't care about the rights of criminals." He nodded at Lori.

While Shane kept his hand clamped over the thief's mouth Lori proceeded to break every finger on both of his hands. The man stopped trying to squirm away by the third broken finger.

When Lori was done Shane said, "Do you understand what you have to do now? That if we ever see you here again, you won't be as lucky as you are today?"

He shook his head rapidly. Tears leaked from his eyes.

"Good." Shane took out his wallet and tucked a fifty-dollar bill in the thief's shirt pocket. "And look, I'm even doing you a solid. Now get the hell outta here!"

Shane got off the man so he could totter out of the alley, holding back tears of pain. They watched him stumble down the block until he turned a corner.

"Another one bites the dust," Lori said as she put the items that had spilled out of the cart back.

"And a lot more to go," Shane said. "Let's bring these back to the IGA."

L.G. and Easy drove past the substation just to check on things. There was a new lock on the gate and concertina wire had been looped around the top to prevent people from climbing over it. They even detected a mounted camera on a pole.

"Better late than never," L.G. said.

"They featured the security improvements on the news today. Unfortunately it won't keep out the real saboteurs who can waltz in there with permission to wreak havoc."

"I think they'll leave this place alone for a while. The trick is knowing where they'll strike next."

Easy opened the window to get some fresh if not baked air. "I've been thinking about that. We're going to need some insider information. Only Bryan's from here, and he has as many connections to the corrupt politicians and one-percenters as we do."

L.G. turned onto the road that would get them into Maverick proper. They knew Shane and Lori were on foot somewhere in town. "I'm way ahead of you. I've been putting together a list of people who work in the governor's office. There has to be a weak link somewhere."

"Or a strong link that we can bend."

"Or that."

"I've asked Amy to run some background checks on the list. I should have more tomorrow."

They drove through a wall of cornfields, the stalks reaching seven feet or higher. It was like going through a maze where the only things they could see other than the corn was the road and the broiling sun overhead, though it would be setting within the hour.

Easy said, "It seems strange to be doing an op like this in our own country."

"That's because there are too many people in power trying to take our country from us." L.G. looked at his friend. "Be honest. When we call it quits where were you deciding to retire?"

"Either Switzerland, or I was thinking someplace warm, like Costa Rica. How about you?"

"I've been planning to ride out the back nine in Denmark. One side of my family came from there."

The downtown area popped up in the distance as the fields gave way.

L.G. tapped the steering wheel. "That's kind of the problem. Why would we work so hard only to want to leave our home country in the dust when we have time to sit back and enjoy it? The hell of it is, if things keep going the way they're going, even with the money we set aside, we might be broke when we're too old to go out and hustle. It's a freaking mess that I don't see any way around. Maybe we can make a difference here, now, but in the long run, while we let the maniacs remain in power, there's no hope."

They drove down Broad Street, careful not to appear

obvious that they were taking things in. When darkness set they would get to work.

"You're a real ray of sunshine," Easy said.

"I'm practical, and honest with myself."

Easy gave a mock shiver. "Practical? Not for me, Brother."

L.G. smiled. "Trust me, I know."

They parked in a deserted lot down the block from the IGA market, easing next to an empty dumpster so they couldn't be seen from the road. Easy spotted Shane and Lori walking out of the store.

"Shane looks happy," Easy said. "He must have gotten into it with someone."

"He's not here to buy groceries."

When dusk came and went L.G. eased out the car so it was more visible. He knew it would only be a matter of time until they attracted the unsavory of Maverick. A few homeless people shuffled by and gave the car a look. A woman pushed a shopping cart loaded with bags bursting with cans and bottles. She looked to be about the same age as Easy's mother, though life on the street could age you dramatically.

Less than an hour later three men stopped at the edge of the lot, had a brief powwow, and approached the car. They all wore backward baseball caps, two of them sporting Cubs jerseys. The other wore a wifebeater and long shorts. One was white, one was Black, and one was Asian.

"It's good to see that criminals are now so multi-cultural," Easy quipped.

L.G. rolled down his window as a signal that he was willing to accept whatever they were offering.

"You lost, man?" the white guy wearing the wife-beater said, leaning on the doorframe.

"You tell me," L.G. replied.

"You cops?"

"Would it matter?"

The three men got a kick out of that one. "Nah, it really wouldn't. I just don't like to waste my time. But what wouldn't be a waste of my time was taking a little old test-drive of your car."

The white guy's companions started walking around the car, admiring it the way lions sized up their prey.

Unperturbed, L.G. asked, "I was wondering if you might have any pills. My friend and I are looking for some Molly. We have a party to go to later and, well, you know."

The man sucked in his bottom lip, then shook his head wearily. "Unfortunately I don't got no pills for you. But I do have this."

He thrust a small pistol into L.G.'s face.

"Get out of the car, cracker!"

L.G. put his hand on the door handle.

Easy said, "Cracker? Do you not own a mirror?"

The Black man tapped on Easy's window. "Hey. Funny man. Open your door."

"But this is my car. I just got it a month ago," L.G. protested, sounding scared out of his wits.

"Well, they do say timing is everything. Now step on out before you make me have to go through all the work of cleaning your brains out of it before I take it for a nice long joyride."

The Asian man was standing back by the trunk. He had a thick chain wrapped around his hands. The Black man pulled his Cubs jersey aside to reveal a holstered gun.

"All right. All right. I don't want any trouble," L.G. said, ducking his head.

"Then you shouldn't have parked in my town," the white guy said.

"I told you this was a dumb idea," Easy said.

"Just shut up!" L.G. snapped. "You were the one who wanted the Molly. Where was I supposed to go? Walmart?"

The Black guy tugged on the door handle. "You ladies can argue about your poor choices later. Out!"

L.G. looked to Easy.

Both men grabbed the door handles and put their weight into pushing the doors open with enough force to knock the punks down.

The white guy raised his gun hand so he could take a shot at L.G. For his efforts, L.G. had his own weapon out and used it to shoot the man in the forearm. He cried out in agony as the gun jumped from his hand.

On the other side of the car Easy kicked his man under his chin, clacking his teeth shut and knocking him out, all the while keeping an eye on the Asian chain wielder. When L.G. shot at the white man, the Asian man took one look at his wounded partner in crime and started to run.

With two fake knees, there was no way Easy would be able to catch him.

Luckily, the crook was just within reach of Easy's taser. The twin metal probes buried themselves in the man's back. Fifty thousand volts froze the man, sending him face-first to the ground. When the taser shut off Easy turned over the man with his foot. His nose was broken and it looked like he'd left a few teeth on the pavement. He'd also wet himself. His eyes fluttered before falling closed.

"Never bring a chain to a taser fight," Easy said.

"My arm! You shot me!" the white guy wailed. L.G. dropped to a knee and clamped his hand over the punk's mouth.

"I grazed you. You're a tough guy. Suck it up." He found the man's gun and stuffed it in his waistband. "You won't be needing this anymore." The white man was having trouble drawing a breath, so L.G. pulled away his hand. "If you scream again, I'm going to snap your neck. We clear?"

The man nodded, his eyes going to the ragged and bloody wound on his arm.

"Now, when your buddies regain consciousness, you're going to go back with them to whatever hole you crawled out from. This is *my* town now, and I don't want it cluttered up with trash. If I ever see any of you again, even if it's to help an old lady across the street, me and my friend here are going to have a fun time burying you . . . alive."

He stared the would-be thief in the eyes, making sure his words sunk in.

Easy poured water from a bottle on the faces of the Black and Asian men. They woke up sputtering. Easy handed the Asian man his teeth. He pointed to their wounded leader, who was on his feet, cradling his arm and sniffling. "All of you, get lost. Your buddy will fill you in."

Just as they were leaving, L.G. called out, "Hey. You tell anyone about what just happened here and I'll know. Remember what I told you would happen to you next time."

The Black man mumbled something surely derogatory, but the white man told him to shut his mouth. The trio staggered out of the parking lot and out of sight.

"Well, that was fun. You ready for round two?"

L.G. couldn't stop smiling. "Now that I'm all warmed up. Let's go."

They got back in the car and headed for the rendezvous point.

CHAPTER 27

After Shane left to meet up with Lori, Bryan called his brother and asked to speak with David Cruz. They were still working in the field, but Rocchio would make up for any labor lost while David was on the phone.

"How can I help you, Mr. Bryan?" he said a little breathlessly. It was still hot as a clambake in July.

"Please, Bryan is good enough. I wanted to ask you about that tent city you and the family were living in. Be honest with me. How bad is it?"

Without pause, he said, "Very bad. Pam and I took turns staying awake at night to protect the children." Before Bryan could speak he quickly added, "But not everyone was bad."

"That I know. That you and your family were there is testament to that."

"We came here because Juarez is a dangerous place. Others, they came here for different reasons. When you've run out of people and places to rob, to corrupt, you need to find a new place to spoil."

Bryan grabbed a pen and paper. "Can you tell me

who is there for the right reasons? Describe them as best you can."

They were on the phone for the better part of fifteen minutes. When they were done Bryan moved the papers across the table to Charlotte. "David thinks there have to be almost a hundred people there. Almost all are illegal immigrants. He didn't know everyone, but of those he did, we have about twenty folks that he swears are good people. Most of them are older, or children. There are a lot of young single men prowling around who make life more difficult than it has to be."

Charlotte studied his notes, no doubt setting them into her incredible memory.

"Looks like we have our work cut out for us."

"Yes, it does. Which is why I went and bought us both some nice steaks while you were napping."

"That's awfully nice of you."

"An army can't march on an empty stomach. And we Iowans know our way around a cut of beef. Now, kiss the cook."

She threw her arms around his neck. "With pleasure."

After their steak dinner with a side of potatoes and corn on the cob, naturally, they packed the car with what they needed. Bryan set aside a plate for Shane and put it in the refrigerator for when he returned.

After checking in with Rocchio to make sure all was quiet on the farm Bryan and Charlotte got into the car and hit the road.

He had his hand on the gearshift. Charlotte rested her hand on his as he stayed within five miles of the speed limit so they wouldn't get pulled over.

"We're doing a good thing," she said. "This is the best I've felt about an op in, well, maybe ever."

"I feel the same way, babe."

They pulled behind the old hardware store that had been left to rot after the owners moved to a new space a few years before. There were three other cars parked there. As soon as Bryan pulled into a spot, doors opened, and his team were on their feet and waiting for him.

Dusk had passed and the night sky was awash with a brilliance of splashes of starlight. Bryan looked up, then down the alley to Broad Street. There should be light pollution from various streetlights, but they were not on, either from neglect or outright vandalism because the unsavory preferred the darkness.

When Bryan saw Shane, Lori, Easy, Hendricks, and L.G., he asked, "How did it go?"

"Like shooting morons in a barrel," Easy quipped. "We had three would-be carjackers who, if we scared them good enough—and I think the whole pants-wetting thing was proof— should be hightailing it outta Maverick as we speak."

"Good. And you?"

"We had a nice talk with a local terror and repeat offender. Let's just say it's hard to shoplift or mug people when your fingers are pointing different ways," Lori said.

"And we returned some stolen goods to the IGA. Well, at least we left the cart of stuff inside. Hopefully some clerk ends up putting it all back on the shelves."

Norm Hendricks added, "I took a great nap."

Everyone laughed.

"It seems like just a drop in the bucket," Charlotte said.

"A bucket we're going to try to fill right now," Bryan reassured her. "Everyone set?"

Five heads nodded.

"Okay, let's serve some eviction notices."

Everyone took an assault weapon from their trunks, along with nylon masks to hide their faces. They stayed in the shadows behind the mostly derelict storefronts, keeping parallel to Broad Street.

Charlotte had suggested they infiltrate as stealthily as possible.

Bryan saw things a different way. They were outnumbered by almost ten to one by David's calculations. There was no way to know how many of the literal bad hombres in the tent city were armed. If a shoot-out started, the innocent majority would be at risk. Using an old phrase from the first Iraq War, his plan was to deliver a little shock and awe. Catch everyone unawares with a tremendous show of force in the hopes of inciting a kind of mass paralysis. He knew they wouldn't catch everyone they needed to and made his team aware not to break ranks and chase those who darted into the night. There was a hope that they would get the message that this place, and maybe all of Maverick, was off-limits.

When they got to within sight of the lot turned refugee camp Bryan gave the hand signal to break up. Hendricks teamed up with Shane and Lori, while L.G. and Easy slipped away. The idea was to approach the camp from all sides. They only needed three teams because one side was blocked by an abandoned building.

Bryan could smell the fires burning in barrels, along with the savory scent of food cooking. It reminded him of how much he missed Pam Cruz's delicious home-cooked meals.

He also saw a lot of shadows walking about. They had their work cut out for them.

He checked his watch. The team had synchronized all their watches and set an alarm for when it was time to make their presence known.

"I just hope no one gets hurt," Charlotte said. "When I say that, I mean no one who doesn't deserve to get hurt."

"That's why we have these," he said, tapping his AR15. "When they see these they'll be less likely to take a potshot with whatever stolen pea shooter they have tucked at their backs."

Bryan and Charlotte's watches beeped three times.

They pulled down their masks and sprang out of the shadows, striding confidently through the broken fence lining the back of the lot. A few men who had been playing cards on an upturned milk crate saw them and froze. There was a lot of cash in the center of the milk crate.

"Get up slowly and move to the middle of the lot," Bryan said in a gravelly voice. All eyes were on the weapons he and Charlotte were carrying. The men quickly complied, so taken aback that none of them thought to grab the cash.

He heard L.G. shouting at the other end of the lot.

Bodies were in motion everywhere.

Two men in their late twenties sprinted through the growing unrest, heading for the back. When Bryan and Charlotte spotted them, they raised their rifles. Both had facial and neck tattoos. Bryan assumed they were most certainly on the naughty list.

"Turn around or tell your head goodbye," Charlotte spat.

They raised their hands and stepped backward, a mix of anger and fear on their faces, lit by the firelight.

An older woman with tears in her eyes was scooping her belongings into a blanket. Bryan said to her, "We're not going to hurt you. We just need you to stay where you are."

When she looked at him with incomprehension he repeated himself in Spanish. Everyone on his team spoke multiple languages because of the many places they'd had to go over the years. The woman looked like she didn't quite believe him, which was natural, but she did stop gathering her things.

Hendricks, Easy, Lori, and Shane were barking orders. Children wept. Adults cried out or yelled back at them in Spanish or a bastardized form of Spanglish.

A young man, maybe in his teens, shot past Bryan and Charlotte. Before they could turn around they heard the clatter as he hit the chain fence. Bryan saw him clamber over it with the dexterity of a squirrel and disappear.

"On your knees! *Ponte de rodillas!*" Hendricks barked over and over. One man stupidly whipped out a butterfly knife and lunged at Hendricks. He got the butt of a very heavy rifle to the face for his misguided efforts.

As the three teams slowly advanced, trying to push most of the people into the center of the lot, more and more of the illegal residents tried to escape. Some were stopped by a threat or tripped up. Others fled to Broad Street.

One of them hit into a burning barrel on his way out. He knocked it over, spilling flaming wood everywhere. The barrel rolled next to a pair of wood pallets with makeshift tents set up on them. They ignited quickly. Charlotte rushed over to make sure no one was in the tents.

People screamed, on the verge of panic.

Bryan saw the fire as an advantage. It blocked others from trying to flee in that direction. However, if it wasn't stopped, the whole place was going to burn down. He wanted to remove the bad elements from the encampment, not burn it to the ground. There were scared and lost people like the Cruzes here, and they had to keep them safe.

"Keep pushing forward," Bryan said to Charlotte.

Charlotte shouted in English and Spanish for everyone to calm down, move away from the fire, and get on their knees.

As Bryan darted for a pair of blankets, he saw Lori kick a man in the groin. He'd had a thick cord of wood in his hand. Now he was on his knees, gasping for air.

Bryan grabbed a blanket and attacked the flames, kicking loose dirt onto the burning wood from the barrel. He did this while keeping an eye on things. A small girl came trotting over to the fire.

"*Vuelve!*" he shouted at her, urging her to get back. She had a cup of water in her hands. Ignoring him, she dumped the water on one of the tents. He could hear it sizzle. She ran back into the huddled mob as quickly as she'd come.

This was madness.

He continued to fight the flames while some of the men recovered from their initial shock and made threatening gestures toward Bryan's team. To their credit, they managed to get most of them to stand down, sometimes with a little help from the butt of their rifles or a well-placed punch or kick.

When the flames finally subsided Bryan saw that there were about fifty or sixty people in the center of the lot, all on their knees.

Easy and Charlotte went through the crowd, picking out people who didn't belong. First all of the children were moved to the front of the lot, most of them weeping. Bryan felt terrible for putting them through this, but in the end, it would be for their own good.

Next came the elderly, then other adults who Charlotte recalled from David's description.

When all was said and done, there were fortyish people left, all of them males, some of them clearly not Mexican—more Arabic—and not a one of them looking the least bit innocent. The Arabic men sported short, wiry beards that had been unprofessionally groomed. Bryan supposed they had cut them back to blend in. It hadn't worked.

Charlotte and Lori ushered the "nice" list people out of the lot, their soothing voices getting them to comply where Bryan was sure his would not. Once they were out, he, Easy, L.G., and Hendricks bore down their rifles on the collected men. A few of them wept and winced, clearly thinking they'd hit the end of the line.

Bryan wished they'd snagged more, but this would do.

"Do you know why we're here?" he asked. Only a few of the men appeared to understand him, so he spoke the rest in Spanish. "Tonight is your last night in Maverick—or Iowa, for that matter. If you have an issue with that, you can take it up with God when you greet him."

Easy took out his phone and proceeded to take close up pictures of every man. Their eyes blinked in the harsh flash. Bryan enjoyed the confusion on their faces.

"We now know who you are," Bryan said. "And we will track your every move while in this country. I strongly urge you to leave and never return." He then focused his attention on three Arabic-looking men who made little effort to disguise the hatred in their eyes. He said in English, "You're going to come with us."

He motioned for Hendricks who grabbed one man and kicked the other two in the back, forcing them out of the circle. "Keep looking at me that way and I'll shoot you in the eyes," he said to them.

One of the men spat on Hendricks's leg. "Go to hell, you American dog!"

"Well, now you get to learn this dog's bite is worse than his bark." Hendricks pulled a handgun from his holster and pistol-whipped the man. He fell onto his side, unconscious. The other two shouted curses and leaped to their feet. Hendricks used the nonbusiness end of his AR15 to set them down.

The rumble of a truck caught Bryan's attention. A big rig pulled up on Broad Street. Amy Thomas was in the driver's seat.

In Spanish, Bryan said, "I'd tell you to grab your things before we take you on a ride, but from what I hear you've taken enough of other people's things already. So, slowly get up and form a single line. When you get to the truck climb inside. Anyone who doesn't do exactly what I tell you will be shot."

The men reluctantly got to their feet. While Hendricks stood watch over the three Arabs, Easy, L.G., and Bryan forced the rest of the men to get into the truck. Amy looked up and down the street for police or other potential witnesses. Bryan assured her that since Broad Street had gone to pot, no one wanted to be there at night. He was pretty confident that even the Maverick PD steered clear of the main thoroughfare. It was late, so all of the stores were closed.

Some men cursed at them as they got to the truck, at least until they were roughly forced inside. When they were done Amy closed and locked the giant double doors.

"Nice truck," Easy said, handing Amy his phone. "I got a picture of every one of them so you can run their faces. If you want fingerprints, I'm sure I can get that, too."

Amy pocketed the phone. "This is good. Thanks. There's a bag inside with teriyaki beef jerky, pork rinds, barbecue chips, chewing gum, and a few bags of mixed nuts. I also got you a half dozen bottles of water. You'll need it after eating all that salt."

Easy jumped into the driver's side of the rig. "You're better than Santa. Thanks." He looked for Lori and waved her over. "You coming? We have a long road ahead of us."

Lori Nicolo walked around the truck, checking the lock on the door one last time, and clambered into the passenger side.

Bryan patted the side of the truck. "See you in a few days."

Easy almost tooted the loud horn but stopped himself. Smiling as always, he gave a thumbs-up before putting the rig in gear.

Bryan, Charlotte, and L.G. watched it rumble down the street.

"What do you want to do with these guys?" Hendricks asked from the lot.

"I think we need to introduce them to the trunk," Bryan said. "I'll help. And while I do that, Charlotte, you, Amy, and L.G. start shuttling everyone else to St. Matthew's. I know Father Rooney will be overwhelmed at first, but he'll do whatever he can to help. Appoint someone who speaks English to be their spokesperson. You know what to tell them."

Charlotte tapped the side of her head and said, "It's all up here. That's why we rehearse. Let's go." She jabbed L.G. in the ribs with her elbow. The ex-soldier winced.

"You still don't know your own strength."

"Oh, I know it," she replied with a sly grin.

Bryan and Shane went over to Hendricks, who stood guard over the two conscious and one unconscious men.

"I get the feeling they won't go quietly into that good night," Hendricks said.

"I agree."

Before the men could protest, Bryan and Shane put them in sleeper holds until they passed out.

CHAPTER 28

Nostrand Ganz stepped out of his hundred-thousand-dollar sensory deprivation chamber nude as the day he was born. One of his health and wellness team, a former nurse named Gaye, toweled him off and helped him slip into his robe. She knew not to speak to him when he emerged from the chamber. To do so would find herself on the unemployment line before the day was out.

He dismissed her with a flick of his hand, sauntered to his meditation garden, and assumed a lotus pose. With only the sound of running water from the stream that had been built to run into his home, he cleared his mind, concentrating on his breathing.

After an hour of meditation he opened his eyes, stretched, and rose to his feet. He went to his glass refrigerator and took out a small bottle of probiotic juice, downing it like a shot of whiskey. Next came a shower and a change into comfortable clothes.

He loved being here in this part of his sprawling, twenty-thousand-square-foot mansion in New Canaan, Connecticut. The shame of it all was that he didn't get to spend as much time here as he wished. There were too many things to attend to all over the world. All told, he owned over twenty homes, from Provo, Utah, to Monte Carlo, Monaco. New Canaan was his favorite.

Despite having enough room to wander throughout for an entire day, he preferred keeping to his wellness rooms and adjoining office.

His wife was currently in Milan for fashion week. Later that night he was scheduled to meet with a woman he'd used to release his carnal desires for going on five years. She was betrothed to a billionaire who lived in Darien, Connecticut. Her husband despised Ganz and made sure everyone knew it. That was why Ganz had to have her.

With too many irons in too many fires to count, Ganz focused on the goings-on in Iowa for the moment.

He didn't like what he was seeing.

So many much larger cities had been conquered already. Places like New York, Los Angeles, Chicago, San Francisco had gone down without a fight, the citizens blind to their manipulation.

Not so with Maverick.

Something was going on there that threatened to eradicate the peace and calm he'd spent a morning cultivating.

Who was behind this uprising?

Ganz, having an iron grip on countless politicians and other elites, didn't fool himself. They were allies by force or blackmail or plain weakness. That didn't mean they weren't potential enemies as well.

Alexa Bennington better get it together, he thought.

There were very big plans in play for Iowa. From the

conversion of farms to battery graveyards, he stood to earn billions.

There was no way he could allow a town of losers like Maverick to spoil everything.

Bennington was on a short leash.

If the people of Maverick knew what was in store for them should Bennington lose, they would stop and comply right away He would break their backs one way or another and have what he wanted. No one defied Nostrand Ganz.

No one.

CHAPTER 29

With Easy and Lori driving the full rig down to the border, where the captives would be released with a weighty threat to go back to where they'd come from, the rest of Bryan's team kept busy.

First things first, they had pooled their money together to make an anonymous donation to St. Matthew's Church. Father Rooney had just taken on a lot more responsibility with the illegals from the tent city. He would also need help tending to the homeless who would be sent his way by Bryan's team as well. Using a considerable amount of cash procured from a Taliban warlord they'd eliminated eight years earlier, they made sure the priest would have one less thing to worry about while tending to his growing flock.

Next, Amy Thomas was able to get a solid ID on two of the Arab men they had pulled out of the tent city. Both were known terrorists. Aamil Zaman, the oldest of the three, had attempted to set off a homemade bomb in Times Square on a busy summer day. He'd also been involved in at least a dozen successful bombings across the Middle East. Usman Malik had claimed responsibility for blowing up a preschool in Israel as well as masterminding an attack at an army base in Iraq. The third man was a ghost in the system, but if he was aligned with these two pieces of filth, it was a matter of guilt by association.

They were currently strapped down in the dilapidated barn where Shane was keeping his RV, lashed to thick pillars and covered in moldy hay. Bryan, Shane, and Charlotte took turns keeping an eye on them.

"I'll kill you and your entire family when I get out of here," Zaman had snapped at Charlotte.

To which she coldly replied, "What makes you think you're getting out of here?"

Bryan thought about turning them in to the feds, but doing so would surely compromise their identities and jeopardize their plan to save Maverick.

Instead, Bryan brought back a veritable feast from a barbecue joint he'd found several miles away. He undid the bindings on the right hands of each man and let them chow down. It had been the first real meal he'd provided them since the night of the raid. While the men ate ravenously, they stared daggers at Bryan, Shane, and Charlotte.

When Shane, who gnawed on a rib, walked too close, Malik spat a mouthful of corn bread at him.

Shane looked down at his pants, which were speckled with yellow crumbs. "That's a sad waste of good corn bread."

"You and all Americans are a waste of the life breath given to you!" Malik blurted out.

"Well, then, you should take that up with Allah," Shane said.

"Pig!" Zaman added. The third Muhammad Doe remained silent but watchful.

Bryan motioned for Shane to stand down before things escalated.

When everyone had finished eating Bryan announced to the men, "I know you're all not from around these parts, but have you ever heard of a last meal?" When no one answered he said, "It's what we feed inmates the night before they're going to be put to death. I know, the prisoner is usually allowed to choose his or her last meal, but that *was* one hell of a barbecue."

The eyes on the men went wide as reality started to sink in.

Turning to look out the barn doors at the fallow field, he said, "Maybe someday this place will bounce back. But to do that, the soil needs nourishment. Now, I know bright men like you understand fertilizer. I'm sure you're very familiar with it for building bombs. Out here in Iowa, we use it to replenish the soil, help the crops grow."

Aamil Zaman struggled against his bonds. He cursed at them in Farsi, his face gone beet red, spittle flying from his yapping mouth.

When Charlotte responded in Farsi his ranting stopped.

"I should have known," he said. "The only Americans who speak our language are those who came to destroy us. You reek of the invading scum who spoiled our land."

"My reek is perfume compared to what you're going to smell like in about an hour."

Bryan stood before Usman Malik. His arms were folded against his chest. This man he liked least of all, and it took all of his restraint not to hit him. Anyone who boasted about slaughtering what were essentially babies deserved a special hell.

"I hear you took great pride in the death of those innocent children you murdered in Jerusalem."

Malik's face broke into an evil smile. "There are no innocents among the Jews."

"Buddy, where you're going, there won't be a stack of virgins waiting for your dirty manhood."

Laughter bubbled up from deep within Malik's chest. "At least I will die a hero."

Bryan ground his teeth. "Hope they have dictionaries in hell. You might want to look up the definition of the word *hero*."

While they spoke, Shane had snuck up behind the men. He put a bullet in the back of each head with skilled efficiency. All were dead before they fell.

Staring down at the bodies, Bryan said, "The world just got a little bit brighter."

"I only have two shovels," Shane said.

"You guys dig first," Charlotte said. "I'll get the wheelbarrow loaded and start picking up the bloody hay. You can save the last grave for me."

It was an hour past nightfall by the time they had buried the men and incriminating hay. They walked across the field, sweating and exhausted.

"Never thought I'd kill an actual terrorist on a farm in Iowa," Shane said when they were back in the RV and drinking beer.

"It had to be done," Bryan said.

There were no regrets among them. It wasn't as if they hadn't taken out their share of terrorists in the past, both in wartime and after.

After showering together—to conserve water because the RV was too close quarters to do anything else with Shane reading a comic book just feet away—Bryan and Charlotte went outside to get some air and look at the stars. The night was noticeably cooler than it had been the past few weeks.

Standing beside each other, they silently gazed at the stars. For the moment all was calm and quiet.

Until their burner phones started chirping as coded messages came in from Amy, L.G., Rocchio, and Hendricks. They had been very busy as well.

Amy had met Bruno Rocchio at a gas station, where the gas prices were out of the realm of sanity. She gave him the phone Easy had used to take pictures of each of the men they'd rounded up. Rocchio then gave it to Jason Branch and his father to look through to see if they recognized anyone.

No solid hits.

When word got back to Bryan, he vented his frustration by snapping a rotted board from the barn over his bad knee. His anger had him beyond feeling any pain.

"You know, we may never find the people who attacked your parents' farm," Charlotte had said soothingly once he'd settled down.

"Part of me realizes that's probably the truth. But

I still have this feeling they're out there, close enough to grab."

"We're not going to stop trying."

He patted her hand, which was on his shoulder. "I know. I'm just not feeling much in a hurry-up-and-wait mood right now."

"Then it's a good thing we have a lot of work to do."

Over the next several nights, Bryan and his team slipped into Maverick at nightfall, patrolling the streets while keeping to the shadows. On the first night L.G. Iverson had stopped two men from breaking into a house over on Hyatt Avenue. He hog-tied them on the front lawn and rang the bell, leaving a note for the owners to call the police to make a pickup.

Bruno Rocchio went to the local dive bar, Freddie's Lounge, after a hard day working in the field. Amy spelled him keeping an eye on the farm. He said he needed some action before he went crazy. He found it in the guise of four men who were bragging about a smash-and-grab they'd done at the laundromat earlier that day. They had gone in while it was mostly full of women washing their clothes, armed with sledge-hammers. They proceeded to smash the place up, collecting money as it spilled from the broken machines. One of them joked about how he'd tripped an elderly woman as she rushed out the door in a panic. Another said he'd grabbed one of the MILFs before she could scoot just so he could cop a feel.

Rocchio listened to them as he nursed his beer, his eyes locked on the TV screen above the bar, which was showing a rerun of a Bears game from the mid-80s, when

Walter Payton was at the top of his wizardry. When he spotted them leaving the bar—minus a tip, which irritated the bartender—he went to the bathroom located at the right side of the bar. Having scoped it out earlier, he easily climbed out of the window and met the foursome just as they were breaking into an SUV.

"Can you guys spare any change?" Rocchio asked.

One of them looked him up and down for a second, then said, "Get outta here, bum."

Rocchio turned his back for a moment, seemingly dejected, then spun around with a collapsible baton in his hand. He made quick work of them, shattering arms, noses, and knees.

Pulling their bodies behind some bushes so no one going in or out of Freddie's could see, he said, "Where did you put the money?"

"I don't know what you're talking about," one man said. He was cradling his right arm and his flesh was waxen, a sign he was going into shock.

Rocchio bashed his fingers with the baton, cracking several. He slapped his hand over the man's mouth just as he started to yowl in pain.

"If you make me ask you again, I'll just keep breaking things until the only thing left is your jaw so you can tell me where the money is."

"Just tell him, man!" the one with the shattered knee-cap pleaded.

The man complied. Rocchio coolly whispered exactly why they should head out of town permanently before he went to the apartment they had been squatting in to retrieve the money. He left it in a black plastic bag outside the laundromat just before dawn, keeping an eye on it until the distraught owner came by. The look on his face was worth the lost night of sleep.

Meanwhile Norm Hendricks had checked to make sure the tent city was still clear. Father Rooney and the parishioners of St. Matthew's Church had taken in everyone they had rescued and set up a living space for them in the church itself and the middle school's gymnasium.

Hendricks found three men standing around a fire.

"What you got on you?" one of the men asked.

He looked himself over and threw up his hands. "Beats me. Other than God's gift to pretty and single women everywhere."

One of the men had a teardrop tattoo at the corner of his eye. Hendricks bet if the man removed his shirt, his body would be a veritable artist's canvas of bad prison tattoos.

Teardrop sauntered his way to Hendricks, stopping when there were just a few inches of space between them. The thug was much shorter than Hendricks, though he didn't seem to mind having to crane back his neck to give him the dead eye.

"Empty your pockets," he said in heavily accented Spanish.

The other two approached in an attempt to flank him.

"I'm not sure I appreciate your tone."

Hendricks had danced with death so many times over the past decade plus, a trio of common punks barely moved the fear needle. These three may have served some hard time, but in the end they were just street fighters, which meant they were undisciplined and emotional.

"What did you say to me, *pendejo*?"

Teardrop saw the fist coming for his lower jaw, but he was too late to avoid the blow. As his head snapped back, revealing every square inch of his throat, Hendricks whacked his Adam's apple.

The other two made for him.

He stepped back and out of their path. Then he grabbed them by the hair and smashed their heads together with an ugly crack. All three were down and out and Hendricks wasn't even out of breath.

Knowing that Bryan was specifically looking for men like them, he tied them up and wrestled them into the trunk of his car. Then he took a picture of their faces and sent them to Rocchio, who quickly showed Jason, who then woke up his father.

Rocchio called Hendricks. "He thinks the guy with the face tattoo might have been one of them. He didn't notice the tattoo at the time, but he's pretty sure this guy hung around the back when they came looking for work."

"Copy that."

Hendricks disconnected the call, ground the phone under his bootheel, and kicked it into the sewer.

One of the men started stirring in the trunk.

"Let me out!"

"Oh, I will. Though I think once I do, you're going to ask to be put back in the trunk." With that, he slammed the lid shut.

Half an hour later he pulled up to the abandoned farm

and flashed his lights. Bryan popped up from seemingly nowhere and rapped on the driver's side window.

"Cut your lights and follow me."

He drove slowly over a bumpy field, pulling into a barn that looked like it might collapse under a whisper of a breeze. Shane's RV was parked inside. He and Charlotte sat on bales of hay, waiting.

Hendricks knew all of his captives were awake from all the banging and cursing they had been making over the past two miles of the trip. He opened the trunk to a slew of invectives.

"Hey, you're hurting my feelings," he said. Then he, Bryan, and Shane roughly pulled them from the trunk and unceremoniously dumped them on the ground before Charlotte.

"Which one?" she asked.

"The one with the tattoo on his face."

Charlotte got up and walked around the three men, who called her every bad name in the book in both English and Spanish. She looked to Bryan. "You and Norm hang out. Shane and I have this."

Hendricks understood why she was leaving out her husband. One of these men could be the reason his mother was dead, robbing him of any reconciliation. There was no telling what Bryan might do if he got angry enough. Even someone with his level of discipline had a breaking point.

"Come on," Hendricks said, almost having to pull away his friend. "I hear Amy has a job for me tomorrow. Why don't you fill me in?"

Bryan reluctantly followed Hendricks to the RV, only turning away once he stepped inside.

One of the men cried out in pain as they closed the door.

Bryan looked like he wanted to leap back out the door. Hendricks blocked the way and said, "I hope you all have cold beer because I'm thirsty as hell. Now tell me, what's Amy got me doing?

CHAPTER 30

Iverson met the podcaster, Sam Mishra, at a bustling coffee shop in Omaha. Mishra was staying at a second listener's house outside the Iowa state lines as an extra precaution. The idea was to keep him moving for now. L.G. came bearing gifts.

"What's in the bag?" Sam asked when L.G. pulled up a chair at his too-small table. The rattle of conversations made it a perfect place for them to meet. It was also a challenge for the wounded vet to hear Mishra amid the babble.

"Some extra equipment to help boost the quality of your little show."

Sam went for the bag. L.G. pushed it away.

"Don't open it up here. Wait until you get home. Your temporary home."

"Right. Got it."

"How is your show doing?"

The podcaster's face was split by a mile-wide grin. "The numbers are through the roof, which is good for all of us."

L.G. nodded. "In the bag is a list of some of the

things we've managed to accomplish over the past few days. It might be a good idea to let your listeners know that someone not only cares about Maverick but they're also making it a point of doing something about it."

"When can I go back there?"

"We'll let you know. For now, your safety and the ability to keep broadcasting your show are a priority." He took a sip of his coffee. It was delicious, which meant it wasn't for him. After his years in the military any coffee that couldn't take varnish off a wall was a no-go.

"You know, the governor will have that place crawling with cops sooner or later."

"That's to be expected. Don't you worry about us. We know how to take care of ourselves. We've been in places and situations that would make you forget your pronouns and ask your momma if you could crawl back inside."

Sam rolled his eyes. "Not everyone in my generation is fixated on pronouns."

"Good for you. Keep swimming against the tide. One of my buddies left clear instructions on how to use the stuff in that bag. If you follow them, no one will be able to get a bead on your location. The key is to make you a ghost with a platform. Do everything it says and you'll be fine."

L.G. got up and tossed his coffee in the nearest trash receptacle.

"When will I see you again?" Sam asked.

"Me? Maybe never. Just keep doing what you're doing. And keep your head low."

"Maybe one day we'll all have a beer and laugh about this," Sam said, smiling.

L.G. did not return the smile. "Doubtful, kid. Head low."

He left to make the drive back to Iowa. That night, before it was his turn to go out on patrol, he tuned into Sam's podcast.

"Tonight on *Lying for Dollars*, I have some breaking news coming out of our favorite small town in crisis, Maverick, Iowa. It appears that the unknown group that brought power and life back to the town has been extremely busy cleaning up the mess that was intentionally created by Governor Alexa Bennington and her elite cronies. If you're in Maverick right now with anything but goodness in your heart, you might want to consider getting some expensive running shoes." There was a long pause. L.G. leaned closer to his phone, as if that would hurry the kid up. "The Night Warriors are out there, and they're waiting for you to make your move. We the people dare you."

"Night Warriors?" L.G. didn't remember seeing anything like that in the notes that had been written up for Mishra. It was too late to take it back now. He wondered how long it would take the kid to start making T-shirts with a Night Warriors logo.

Governor Alexa Bennington heard the helicopter before she saw it descending toward her front lawn. By the time it was hovering over her house she could feel the churning of the powerful rotors vibrating in her chest.

Swiping her phone off her desk, she dialed her husband. "Todd, where the hell are you?"

"On my way home. I got a text that I need to be there ASAP."

"How far are you?"

"Five minutes tops."

"It looks like Ganz is going to beat you. And destroy our lawn."

Before Todd Bennington could say anything else she swiped the screen to end the call.

An impromptu visit from Nostrand Ganz was not a joyous occasion. Not after everything that had been going on in that little back-water town he desired so much.

She checked herself in the mirror, brushed her hair, and took a series of deep, calming breaths. The last thing she wanted to appear was nervous and taken aback, even though that was exactly how she was feeling.

Colin Farmer was on his feet and rushing to her when she opened her office door.

"What do you need from me?"

The state-of-the-art helicopter looked like it might hold two dozen people, which it probably did. Nostrand Ganz never traveled without his small army of security. Some of them were ex–secret service, the best and brightest who had guarded presidents lured to Ganz's employ by promises of money they had never seen before and a chance to see the world.

"Just be ready," Bennington said. "I think we're about to get our marching orders."

Penny Hastings was working on organizing files in the governor's mansion. She came darting out of the bedroom turned storage room with a worried look on her face.

"Did you know there's a helicopter outside?" she said worriedly.

"I had no idea," Bennington shot back. "It doesn't concern you. I believe you have a lot of work to do."

Penny blushed and apologized before slipping away.

Ganz didn't ring the bell or knock on the door. He had one of his men open Bennington's front door for him. Alexa had just made it to the vestibule when Ganz walked into her house as if he owned it. He wore blue jeans and a white button-down shirt. A simple ensemble that she was positive had been custom made and cost more than any other man's suit allowance for the next three years. He was very tall and lean, his youthful face shiny from the fillers and Botox shots that he received on a regular basis.

"Alexa," he said when he spotted her, as if *she* were the one intruding in *his* home.

"Good to see you, Nostrand. You always excel at making grand entrances."

A phalanx of men in dark suits followed him into her house, others sweeping the front yard. All wore dark glasses and earpieces.

"I was on my way to a tech summit in Chicago and decided to pop in."

Alexa put on her best fake smile. She'd bet her bank account there was no tech summit.

"Well, make yourself at home," she said, her voice dripping with sarcasm. "Would you like a drink?"

Colin peeled off for his office as she led Ganz and his men to her study.

"I haven't had alcohol in three months. Part of a six-month cleanse my wife has us on."

Bennington poured herself a vodka on the rocks. "You want a juice or water?"

"I'm fine. I have my own water."

One of his men handed Nostrand a metallic thermos as he settled into a chair. She could only guess what was in it. Probably water from some rare aquifer on a remote island he'd most likely bought. Anyone living near it would have been quickly displaced. Those who had enjoyed the bounty the aquifer brought them for generations could now have bottles of tap water imported from Detroit. One thing Nostrand Ganz did not like to do was share. As the middle son of five boys in a dirt-poor family, Alexa often wondered how miserable his childhood must have been to make him the monster he was now.

A monster to whom she was content to hitch her wagon if it made her rich enough to finally put Iowa in her rearview mirror for good.

Alexa took the seat opposite the almost trillionaire and sipped her drink. The man was impossible to read. He always had a look of vague curiosity, as if he'd only recently landed on Earth and was tasked with figuring out how it all ticked. She was about to ask him what brought him to her home when Todd burst through the door.

"Nostrand!" he said with too much enthusiasm. Ganz rose from his chair so they could shake hands.

Once Todd sat, Nostrand got right to business. Pleasantries were never his forte.

"I'm concerned about what I'm hearing in Maverick. It sounds like you have a vigilante problem on your hands. What are your plans to deal with it?"

Todd leaned forward in his chair and clasped his hands together. "We don't quite think these are vigilantes. They could be just an offshoot of the criminal element we've flooded into the town."

Nostrand paused for a beat, tilted his head, then said, "Criminals *preventing* other criminals from committing crime? I've never heard of such a thing. Now, *vigilantes* marshalling their efforts to rid their home of a criminal element, that's a very real thing that predates Charles Bronson's *Death Wish* franchise. That Bernhard Goetz subway shooter fellow in New York even made it into a Billy Joel song. No, you have a vigilante issue. They even have a name: Night Warriors. I'd say if you don't get control of the situation immediately, you're going to find yourselves in a very tight predicament."

The threat was loud and clear. Alexa tried to tamp down her flaring anger. How dare he invade her home and make threats?

"My people and I are working on plans as we speak," she said as casually as she could.

Ganz arched an eyebrow. "Plans that will be put in place . . . when?"

She knew deference to Ganz was always the best move, but something about this intrusion and his attitude had her dander up. Alexa smoothed an imaginary crease in her skirt and took another sip of vodka to buy herself time to compose herself. "Right at this very moment."

"Would you care to share those plans?"

It was not a question.

Todd started to speak until Alexa held up a hand to silence him. If it weren't for Todd, she wouldn't be here kowtowing to a sociopath in a state she detested.

"By the nature of their childish monicker, the Night Warriors strike at night. To that end, I've had night vision cameras installed throughout the downtown. I also have forty officers and state troopers on duty tonight. Many will be in plainclothes. If we don't catch them on camera, we will catch them in the act. Even if we only manage to get one tonight, I'm sure he, or she, will be the first domino to fall. The rest will come easy."

"What if they are some militia? Are your people armed enough to face them?"

"Armed and ready," she replied, looking at Ganz over her crystal glass. That part may have been a stretch. It wasn't as if she had an army under her command. But she was confident tonight would be the start of the Night Warriors' downfall.

Nostrand Ganz got up from his seat with the urgency of someone who had just heard a fire alarm.

"I don't think it will be as easy as you believe." One of the dark-suited men came forward carrying a briefcase. He opened it, and Ganz removed a manila folder.

"Nothing worth doing ever is. I'll be watching closely. You don't mind if I leave a few of my men here, do you?"

Biting her tongue, Alexa said, "Not a problem." The last thing she wanted was one of his men-in-black minions mucking about. To be honest, they gave her the creeps. She'd yet to hear one speak.

Ganz handed the folder over to Todd. "Some papers I'd like you to review. I have some schematics for the resort we'll build in Maverick, and the support system that needs to be constructed around it."

Todd Bennington opened the folder to give the documents a cursory glance. "I'll read everything this afternoon."

"Good. Nice to see you both. I'll see myself out. You both have enough to do."

Ganz turned on his heel and headed for the study's exit. When he got to the doorway he turned back and said, "I have a contingency plan in place should your efforts fall short. They are in that folder as well. After you read them please pass them over to Stuart. He'll dispose of them properly."

As if Alexa and Todd didn't know how to shred sensitive documents, especially those that could land them in prison.

She didn't bother asking who Stuart was.. Whatever silent suit stayed close to them would be him.

She heard Ganz close the front door and the helicopter's engine rev. The house rattled just enough to cause concern.

After it pulled away a man entered the room.

"You must be Stuart," Alexa said.

He gave an almost imperceptible nod.

Todd and Alex stared at Stuart. The ensuing silence was more than uncomfortable.

"I take it I need to review everything right here and now," Todd said.

Again with the slight nod.

Alexa swiped the folder out of Todd's hands and rifled through the papers. A particular sheet with the title HUNGER STRIKE caught her eye. She scanned the proposal and felt her stomach drop.

She understood why Stuart was in the room with them now.

CHAPTER 31

Charlotte and Shane entered the RV just as Bryan got off the phone with Easy.

"I think we need to call Jason over," Charlotte said.

Bryan's stomach soured. "He's one of them?"

"He so much as admitted it. But sometimes people will say anything just to make the pain stop. I know it won't be easy for your brother, but it's important."

"Where is he now?"

"You'll know when Jason gets here," his wife said. She knew him well. If he had his way, by the time Jason arrived there'd be nothing left of the man who killed his mother.

Charlotte and Shane knew to give him space while they waited. Bryan spent the time sharpening his hunting knife, focusing on the task at hand to prevent his mind from running wild.

Jason's truck pulled into the barn thirty minutes later. He wore stained overalls and heavy boots.

Bryan met him at the door. "We need you to confirm something."

"Or do you mean *someone*? Is it that guy in the picture?"

"Yeah. Come on."

Charlotte led the way, with Shane trailing behind the brothers. The cicadas performed a manic symphony as they trudged across the field, wending their way through the overgrown grass. They came to a pair of double doors set in the ground. A heavy chain was wrapped around the handles, held together with a thick padlock.

"You got them in the storm shelter?" Bryan asked.

"And it is not pretty. And hot as hell," Shane said.

Charlotte undid the lock and pulled the chains loose. When Shane flung one of the doors open, choice phrases in Spanish wafted up from the fetid darkness.

Bryan went down the rotted steps first.

The three men had their arms tied behind their backs and zip ties around their ankles. As soon as they saw Bryan, they started screaming for help.

"You realize we didn't bother to gag you because no one can hear you here, right?" To make sure they understood him, Bryan repeated it in Spanish. It quieted them down immediately.

"Come on down," Bryan said to Jason.

His brother had to stoop to avoid banging his head on the shelter's wood-slat ceiling. Charlotte had brought a flashlight. She shone it directly in the men's faces. They squinted and turned away. Bryan grabbed the man with the face tattoo by his jaw and jerked his head so he could look at him straight on.

"Tell me, Jason. Was he at the farm that day?"

His brother looked around nervously, which was understandable. Bryan gave him time to compose himself.

"I mean, I think so."

"I need you to be sure."

Charlotte trained the light on the tattooed man. Bryan forced him to his feet and grabbed him harshly by the back of his greasy hair.

As soon as the man stood, Jason took a step back.

"That's definitely him. He was taller than the rest. He didn't say anything, but I remember him towering over the other guys."

Bryan threw him to the ground.

"What about these two?"

Jason crouched to get a better look at them. Then he shook his head.

"Their hair is too long. All the others were pretty clean-cut."

The tattooed man threatened Charlotte, telling her he'd have the time of his life when it was just the two of them.

Bryan punched him in the temple. "No one talks to my wife like that. *Comprende?*"

The man tried to wriggle up from his side, but Bryan kicked him back down. He looked to Charlotte and said, "Find out what you can. Shane, I'll help you get these other two out of here."

"I got it," Jason said, lifting one of the smaller men

like he was a bag of potatoes at the market. Shane and Bryan wrestled the other one up the stairs. He protested loudly until Shane popped him in the mouth. Then he was too busy spitting out teeth to complain.

Once they set the two men in the grass Bryan said, "I'm going in with Charlotte."

"What are you gonna do?" Jason asked.

"What needs to be done."

"Then I'm going with you."

Bryan put a hand on his brother's chest. "Not a chance. Just help Shane keep an eye on these two."

Jason pushed off his hand. "She was my mother, too!"

Bryan took a breath. "I just need you to trust me."

"It's not a matter of trust. I need you to stop treating me like a child."

"You don't understand. I'm trying to protect you. Charlotte, Shane, and me—we came back from the Middle East different people. That's a whole world of shit I don't need you exposed to."

"I get it. But you need to get this. We're in this together or not at all."

They stared long and hard at each other as the wind swept across the field.

"Help Shane tie them up first," Bryan said as he handed some zip ties to his brother. "Then you can come down."

Jason got right to work while Bryan climbed back down into the storm shelter. Charlotte had the man on his knees with the back of his hair balled up in her fist. He could tell by the sweat pouring off the man's face that she had been very busy in the brief time she'd been left alone with the criminal.

Charlotte pulled a pair of pliers out of her pocket. If the man was worried about what she would do with them, he did a very good job of not showing it.

"It's time to get right with Jesus," Charlotte said. "Why did you set fire to the barn and shoot up the house?"

His upper lip curled and then he spat on Charlotte's boot.

She dropped to a knee, grabbed his middle finger with one hand, and tore the nail clean off with the pliers. The man screeched like a bird that had been caught in a trap.

"Start talking!"

Charlotte held the pliers up to his face so he could see his bloody nail.

"I'll keep going until there are no more left."

The man was breathing heavily, the shock of having his nail ripped off fading.

"You can both go to hell!"

"Oh, I'd say you're already in it," Bryan seethed.

"I didn't burn no farm."

Bryan nodded at Charlotte. She took the man by the wrist and splayed his hand on the ground. Bryan ground the heel of his boot on the man's injured finger.

"Technically, I guess you're right. You did burn the barn down and a part of the farm, nowhere near the whole farm. Why that farm?"

Spittle ran from the man's lips. "*Pendejo.*"

"You're evading my question. Honey?"

Charlotte snapped the pliers together. The man flinched.

There was a tremendous thud at Bryan's back. Jason had just jumped into the shelter.

His brother made it to the kneeling man in two strides, picking him up by his neck with one hand.

The man's legs pedaled in the air as he fought for breath.

White-hot rage radiated from Jason's eyes. "You killed my mother! You killed my horse! You tell me why, right now, or I'm going to snap your neck!"

The man kicked Jason in the midsection, but it did nothing to loosen his grip. Bryan worried that Jason would choke out their prisoner before he had a chance to speak.

Jason lifted the man even higher, until his head bashed into the ceiling.

"Jason!" Bryan shouted.

Turning around, Jason met Bryan's gaze, and a level of mute understanding passed between them.

His brother dropped the man to the ground, kicking up dust and dirt.

The captive gasped for air and clutched his throat. Bryan hoped his Bigfoot of a brother hadn't done irreparable damage to the man's windpipe.

Squatting next to the man, Bryan said, "Here's the deal. You answer every question I'm about to ask . . . without hesitation. If not, I'm going to let my brother finish what he started."

"F . . . f . . . fine," he croaked.

Charlotte turned on the audio recorder on her phone.

Bryan patted his brother's shoulder.

"Okay, let's get started."

They emerged from the storm shelter an hour later. Shane was sitting in the grass reading a comic book he'd had rolled up in his back pocket. The other two captives were on their rumps, tied to each other.

"How'd it go?" Shane asked.

"Good and bad," Bryan said. "At least with Bigfoot over here, it was quick." He looked to his brother. "That was some Jason Voorhees stuff, man."

Jason rolled his neck and cracked his knuckles. "I'm not sure what came over me."

"I am. I get it."

Shane tucked away his comic and got to his feet. "So, what are we dealing with?"

"It wasn't random," Charlotte said. Jerking her thumb at the shelter door, she said, "He and five other men were sent there to scare off Jason and his family. They were supposed to pay similar visits to other farms, but four of the men took off when the fire got out of control."

"Why would they target your family's farm?" Shane asked.

"We don't know who is ultimately behind it, but I have some guesses. The government has been trying to take the land from my parents for years now. Same with all of the other family farms. Government red tape takes too long. Looks like they wanted to speed up the process."

Ominous thunder rumbled as dark clouds filled the horizon.

"What do we do with them?" Shane asked.

"Keep them locked up down there for now," Bryan said. "Best place to be when a storm hits."

Bryan wanted to drag every detail from the man like pulling corn off a stalk. But there was a pace to everything, and he wasn't entirely sure the piece of garbage had much more to give.

They were one step closer to finding out who had killed his mother. Time to both tread carefully *and* wield a big stick.

Needing to vent his mounting anger, Bryan, Charlotte, and Shane drove to Denison, the center point of Crawford County. The overcast skies at dusk made for a pitch-black night. Amy Thomas had gotten them the address of the county's progressive district attorney, Eric Donnegan. This was the creep who was letting criminals skate out of the justice system for the past two years. He wasn't alone in Iowa, but Bryan had to concentrate on his county first.

Donnegan lived in a sprawling Victorian house on a corner lot with plenty of surrounding property.

Bryan wished he had a truckload of the criminals Donnegan had set free so he could let them swarm the expensive home like locusts. Unfortunately he knew people like Donnegan. He'd stick to his progressive ideals and use the incident as proof that more needed to be done to help those who couldn't help themselves.

It was going on midnight when they parked several blocks away. Wearing all black, Bryan, Charlotte, and Shane stuck to the shadows as they made their way to Donnegan's house. There was a placard on the lawn letting any would-be trespassers know the place was protected by an alarm company Bryan had never heard of.

They cased the house. Charlotte studied the alarm panel on the wall by the front door through the glass panes on either side.

"Piece of cake. Love these wireless systems."

Crouching behind a bush by the door, Charlotte took out her tablet and went to work. Five minutes later she said, "We're good."

Having jammed the wireless system, she nodded to Shane, who used his lock picking kit to open the door.

Donnegan was a single man who had an appetite for younger professionals who worked in the courthouse. Bryan hoped there were no lady friends spending the night.

Soundlessly, they crept up the stairs to the master bedroom. Donnegan was asleep atop the sheets, all three hundred–plus pounds of him naked and exposed. Charlotte cringed.

Slipping on their masks, they stormed into the room. Shane smashed the light by the bedside and swiped Donnegan's cell phone so he could crush it under his boot.

Donnegan awoke floundering, trying to get himself upright.

Charlotte stood on one side of the bed with her

Staccato to his head while Bryan was on the other side brandishing his Glock.

"Wh-wh-wh—" Donnegan stammered.

"Calm down, big fella," Bryan said as he clamped his hand over the DA's mouth. "We're just here to deliver a message."

Despite the cool central air, the corpulent man was covered in sweat. His eyes rolled in their sockets as he fumbled for a sheet to cover himself.

"Don't move," Charlotte said coolly.

"When I take my hand off your mouth you're going to do everything I say," Bryan said. "Are we clear?"

Donnegan, still stunned, nodded.

"Good. You're going to decide that the life of a DA is no longer worth the trouble. We'll give you time to pack your things and get in your car. You're going to take a long trip out of Iowa. Once you've settled somewhere you're going to write your letter of resignation. Plan to stay out of Iowa for the next several months."

Donnegan went to push Bryan's hand off his mouth. Charlotte pressed the barrel of her gun deep into his temple. The DA froze.

"This isn't a discussion. This isn't a debate. You either leave tonight with a suitcase or we take you out in said suitcase, except you'll be in pieces." He took a long look at Donnegan's prodigious flab. "Make that three suitcases."

When Bryan slowly pulled away his hand Donnegan tried to scream. Shane knocked out two of his front teeth.

"You can't threaten me," he said with blood spilling from his mouth.

"I believe we can. Though to be clear, these are promises. Threats are just empty words. You, being a lawyer, would know all about that."

The next half hour was spent supervising the DA as he gathered his things, sobbing quietly. They followed him to his BMW and reiterated their promise.

"In the old days I'd tie you to a horse and set it to galloping. Be thankful you get to leave here in such a nice car. Know this. Someone will always be watching you. If you come back to Iowa, this will be your final resting place. And your parents in New Mexico? They'll be the first to go so you die an orphan."

Donnegan was pale as a ghost as he started his car. They watched the BMW roar down the street and out of sight.

"One DA down," Bryan said. "We'll see how many more we have to go."

CHAPTER 32

Bryan wasn't too keen on the whole Night Warriors name that Sam Mishra had stuck them with. At least not until Charlotte pointed out that putting a name to something helped people get behind it. The idea was to start righting a lot of the wrongs that had befallen Maverick, with the hope that the people who lived there would eventually take up the torch. Bryan and his team couldn't stay in town forever.

As usual, his intelligent wife proved him wrong when she showed him the news after he'd come in from a short run through the farm with Shane. The terrain was uneven and had his knees barking, but he needed the exercise.

Charlotte, who had been up before both of them for a five-mile run, was already cooking up breakfast, looking fresh as a blossomed flower.

"Check it out," she said, pointing to the small television. "It's on a ten-minute cycle. The Night Warriors are getting some serious press."

On the screen a man who looked familiar to Bryan stood outside his store, a place that repaired computers, and extolled his thanks to the Night Warriors. "Since they've come around, I don't have to have eyes in the back of my head when I close up at the end of the day. I also don't need to step over passed-out junkies getting into my shop. I'm not at the point where I'm going to take the locks off my display cases, but it's definitely a step in the right direction."

"Aren't you concerned about a band of vigilantes operating outside the law?" the on-the-street reporter asked him.

"Are you kidding? These crooks have been operating *within* the law for years now. And look where that's gotten us. The police and the courts can't do anything. When their hands are tied someone has to fill the void. I wish they'd come sooner."

Two other people were interviewed. One was a small older woman who said she was outraged by the reckless behavior of the so-called Night Warriors. Bryan noted she had an accent whose origin was nowhere near Iowa. Maybe the eastern end of Long Island. The next cut was to an interview with a kid who Bryan had seen getting high in the playground. Naturally, he was no fan of the Night Warriors. "I mean, where does it stop? Do I have to be afraid they're going to jump me when I'm just, like, walking down the street?"

"If you were selling dope, you will," Bryan said to the television as he downed a glass of orange juice.

When the Night Warriors report went to the weather Bryan shut off the television.

"At least they showed one person who's for us," Shane said.

"And look at the two they picked to be against us," Charlotte said. "If there was honest reporting left in this country, I think we'd see a much different story. But no matter what they're showing, the point is that people are becoming aware that someone is actively trying to save them. That counts for something."

Bryan took a bag of ice out of the freezer and set it on his right knee while he piled scrambled eggs on a slice of toast.

"It also means we're no longer operating under the radar. We have to be more careful than ever. They'll have stepped up patrols to stop us. I don't want any law enforcement to get hurt. It's not their fault that the system is rigged against them."

"So, maybe for today we become the Day Warriors," Shane suggested. "Give ourselves the night off."

Bryan reminded him how difficult it would be to hide their identities during the day.

"Masks and hoodies. We'll just be another bunch of people who don't want to get a sunburn on their heads."

Bryan had noticed a few people around town still wearing masks outside even though COVID was almost nonexistent. The psychological damage done by the response to the pandemic was far worse than the physical. Hoodies were mostly worn by no-good thugs, especially in the summer, but then again, there were plenty of them still walking around.

It just might work.

"I think I have a way to test that," Bryan said.

Charlotte sidled next to him and massaged his sore left knee. "What about Norm?"

"He's got his orders. I told him he could wait a day or two, but once he heard there was a pretty woman involved, he got right on his horse, so to speak."

"Why am I not surprised?" Charlotte said, taking a piece of his bacon.

"L.G. thinks he knows where the next mail carrier strike might occur. Someone he stopped from trying to break into an antique store spilled the beans to avoid being roughed up. From what L.G. can tell from past robberies, it's supposed to go down close to where many of the others have over the past few months. You know how thugs love to stay close to their territory."

"When does he thinks it's supposed to happen?" Shan asked.

"As a matter of fact, today. You want to call him and Amy and have them meet us here?"

Shane pounded a fist on the table. "You bet, Boss. Let's save the Pony Express!"

Norm Hendricks had set out for Des Moines before the sun came up. He'd made reservations at a four-star hotel. Even though check-in time wasn't until the afternoon he figured he'd do a little recon.

Listening to his eclectic playlist on the drive over, a mix of bands like Weezer and Thin Lizzie and Motörhead, he kept calling up the picture of the woman he was told to find on his phone.

Boy, was she a looker. Blond and athletic, with green eyes that could melt a man's heart. The only potential issue was her age. Now, he had no problem dating younger women, especially when they were in their early twenties and out of college. The question was, would she be interested in a man fifteen-plus years her senior?

He was going to find out.

He got to Des Moines bright and early and pulled across the street from the address Amy had given him. The apartment was in a swanky neighborhood. Unlike Maverick, Hendricks thought you could actually eat off the streets here.

The trust fund baby emerged fifteen minutes later wearing bicycle shorts and a spandex top. Neither left much to the imagination. She had her hair up in a pony-tail and earbuds jammed in her ears. He watched her jog down the street, her blond hair bobbing up and down and out of sight.

Oh, this was going to be fun.

They parked the car in the driveway of an abandoned house. The blight that had befallen Broad Street had spread its tentacles to the surrounding neighborhood. The homes here were shabbier, the streets dirtier. There were broken windows in houses that were clearly occupied. Drifters and grifters hung out on front lawns or stoops holding brown paper bags that hid nothing. It didn't surprise Bryan that this had become a favored spot of the lowlifes who had taken over Maverick.

Shane sat in the front seat with L.G., Bryan and Charlotte in back. The air-conditioning was turned up high so they didn't sweat to death in their dark hoodies.

306 William W. Johnstone and J.A. Johnstone

According to L.G.'s rat, a UPS truck was supposed to be targeted this time around. All eyes were on the lookout for a big brown truck.

"These guys take porch pirates to a whole new level," Amy commented. "You'd think the delivery companies would put armed guards in the trucks to keep their drivers safe."

"That costs money, honey," Shane said.

"And you know how much they hate guns," Charlotte added.

A couple in their eighties walked by, holding hands as they slowly made their way. Bryan wondered if there was a chance that could be he and Charlotte someday. In their line of work it was doubtful.

"This could be a long day of nothing," L.G. said after a while. "We could be on the right street but nowhere close to where it's supposed to go down."

Bryan thought he'd spotted men moving about a block away and suddenly falling out of sight. Maybe keeping low to wait for the UPS truck to arrive? "You gotta have faith."

A half an hour later a boxy UPS truck turned onto the street.

Like roaches spilling out of dark corners when the lights went off, the mail thieves sprang from their hiding places.

In an instant at least a dozen men swarmed the truck from every side. One of them had a gun in his hand. He stepped in front of the truck and pointed it at the front window. The truck came to a jerking stop. Three men dashed into the side door. Another pounded on the driver's door, demanding he get out. Others went to the back of the truck.

Sadly, those who were hanging out and not part of the gang watched it all unfold, cheering it on, raising fists and whistling loudly.

Bryan had a fleeting thought that a misguided liberal would find the silver lining in all of this in that the men involved were of every shade of color, working in harmony. A true melting pot of criminal enterprise.

"Jesus Christ," Shane yelped, throwing his door wide open. Everyone spilled out of the car and ran toward the melee. They pulled on their medical masks and flipped up their hoods.

The driver was dragged out of the truck and thrown to the ground. A man with an Afro kicked him savagely in the ribs. He rolled over onto his side, clutching his midsection.

Bryan saw daylight pierce through the truck. The thieves inside had opened the back doors and were now tossing packages out to their waiting comrades.

Some of the bystanders broke out into wild applause when the boxes started flying out of the back of the truck. Others ran to the truck, looking to cash in.

It's a miracle Aaron Chisolm walked away with his life, Bryan thought. With the loiterers now joining in, his team was outnumbered four to one.

But this wasn't a numbers game.

There was only one way to get their attention, to shock the thieves out of their lust for chaos.

Still running, Bryan raised his Glock and fired three

quick shots into the sky. The successive booming concussions echoed throughout the run-down streets.

Every head turned in their direction. Men froze, their eyes wide, stolen packages in their hands.

"Get down on the ground! Now!" Bryan shouted loud enough to be heard the next county over.

Shane, L.G., Charlotte, and Amy flanked the truck, guns drawn, while Bryan faced down the man who had stopped the truck. The thief had his gun, what looked to be a .38, at his side, tapping his thigh.

For a breathless moment nothing happened. Eyes flicked about wildly, faces twisted with indecision.

The bystanders were the first to make a move. They dropped the pilfered goods and fled down the street, hopped fences, and dashed down alleyways. Nothing but opportunist pilot fish; Bryan had no interest in them.

The man with the gun said, "Who do you think you are?"

He raised his gun hand.

Bryan wasted no time burying a bullet in his thigh. Blood exploded from the wound as the mail thief's gun clattered to the ground.

"Oh hell!" someone exclaimed.

Guns were pulled out of waistbands and pockets. One of the men dropped a large box and took a shot at Amy. She spun to her left, crashing against a parked car. L.G. returned fire and the man flipped onto his back.

This was Bryan's worst nightmare. The last thing he wanted was a firefight in the middle of the street. For all he knew innocent men, women, and children were huddled in the surrounding houses. If a stray bullet hit someone, he'd never forgive himself.

Charlotte and Shane advanced on the men closest to them, shouting and cursing and doing what they could to disorient them.

Bryan managed to horse collar a man who tried to flee the scene. He drove him to the pavement, stomping on his kneecap to keep him where he wanted him.

Three thieves who had been by the back of the truck ran, firing wildly as they headed down the street. Amy and Shane whirled and fired. Two stumbled for a moment before collapsing.

Bryan, Charlotte, and L.G. delivered brutal kicks and blows to anyone else still on their feet or pointing guns. They disarmed the men while delivering as much pain as possible. A couple fought back, but their street-fighting skills were no match for trained soldiers'.

When all was said and done Bryan counted eight men cradling an assortment of wounds. It didn't appear any would be fatal.

The one howling the most was the man Bryan had shot. He scooped him off the street by his shirt. "I can put you out of your misery if you want."

Tears streamed down the man's face. "Please. Don't kill me."

"Then tell me who's in charge! If we see one more mail carrier being so much as catcalled, I'll murder every single one of you."

The wounded man blabbered incoherently at first.

Bryan had to shake him roughly to get him to slow down and speak.

"We have to go," L.G. said.

Bryan threw the man back onto the pavement. He'd gotten what he needed.

Charlotte helped the UPS driver to his feet. During the interaction, he'd hidden himself between two parked cars.

"You okay?" Bryan asked him.

"I . . . I . . . think so," the man stammered. He took in the groaning wounded littering the street.

The wail of a police siren sounded in the distance.

Bryan clapped the man on the arm. "Sorry if we frightened you. Hopefully this is the end of you having to worry about going to work."

Sweat beaded the man's face. "I'm requesting a transfer."

Bryan waved for his team to head for the car. The police were getting closer and they had to disappear.

As they jogged away, the driver called out, "Who are you?"

"Tell everyone the Night Warriors were here," L.G. shouted.

Windows and doors opened as they ran. People staggered out of their houses and were clapping.

They clambered into the car and Shane mashed the accelerator as they sped away.

Amy cradled her arm. There was blood seeping under her hand.

"Just got winged," she said. "I'm fine."

As they headed out of town, Bryan said to L.G., "'Tell everyone the Night Warriors were here'?"

His friend broke out laughing, the tension of the past few minutes exploding out of him. "You can't beat good marketing, Brother."

CHAPTER 33

Governor Alexa Bennington received the latest news with creeping dread. The more her chief of police spoke about the thwarted attack on the UPS truck, the tighter the knot pulled in her stomach.

Chief of Police Damien Arnstadt looked to be taking great pleasure in reporting the failure of his force. She wanted to swipe that smug look right off his face.

"I thought you were going to have extra patrols!" she suddenly exclaimed. Colin Farmer, who had been sitting next to her, fumbled his tablet, catching it before it hit the floor.

"We do. However, the bulk of it was planned for later in the day. This occurred in broad daylight."

Bennington rose from her chair. "How many times do I have to say this? We can't have vigilantes controlling our streets."

Six men were still in the hospital, either with broken bones or nonlife-threatening bullet wounds. The people who had taken them down were no rank amateurs. Only well-trained professionals could have a shoot-out and skillfully *not* kill anyone.

When Arnstadt didn't respond Bennington added, "Well, if this happened in the light of day, we at least must have some descriptions of who did it."

"You know scum like this would rather let their attackers run free than talk to the police. We do have some neighbors talking, and it appears all of them wore hoodies and surgical masks. However, there is a consensus that at least two of the Night Warriors were women. That jibes with what happened at the substation and other eyewitness accounts."

"Wonderful. Phantom men and women opening fire on a busy street, playing judge, jury, and executioner. We may as well just roll out the red carpet for them and give them carte blanche to blow up the whole place if it suits their fancy!" Bennington swept everything off her desk. Colin had to jump out of the way to avoid being hit in the legs.

"Actually no one is in life-threatening condition," Arnstadt reminded her.

Bennington's cold eyes flashed at him. "I know all of this is making your day."

Arnstadt's eyes narrowed. "Come again?"

"I'm not an idiot. I know you blame me for criminals getting back on the street in record time. You don't care who took these people out as long as it was done."

He put his fingertips on her desk and leaned closer. "You do understand my entire career is based on the rule of law? I don't care about the intentions of these Night Warriors. They are disregarding everything I've sworn to uphold."

Bennington mirrored his stance, not cowed in the slightest.

"If that's the case, think on this: The people of Maverick and every surrounding county think your police force is a joke. And if you can't get the job done, I guess all those calls for defunding the police were right on the money. Now, get the hell out of my office and figure out how to save your job."

They stared at each other for a smoldering span of time that felt like hours. Chief of Police Arnstadt's mouth pulled into a tight line. He backed away, straightened his lapels, and stormed across the office.

"One thing!" Bennington said. "The next time Nostrand Ganz comes to pay me a visit, you're going to be right by my side, delivering the bad news. Ganz has been known to take great joy in shooting the messenger."

Arnstadt slammed the door when he left.

Colin dropped to his knees so he could gather everything up from the floor.

"And what is with this resignation letter from Donnegan?"

"I'm not sure. It just came through an hour ago. He hasn't replied to any emails and he's not answering his phone." He put everything back on her desk.

"What the hell is going on? We can't let the inmates run the damn asylum."

"No, we definitely can't. I've asked the Denison PD to go to Donnegan's house. If he's not there, we can put an APB out for his car."

Alexa Bennington paid him no mind. She was too

busy seething. But beneath that current of anger was a deep trench of worry. Nostrand Ganz was eventually going to lose his patience. This latest development would not bode well for her, or Todd.

What it meant for the citizens of Maverick, and Iowa, mattered little.

Easy and Lori had returned from their trip to South Texas. According to Easy, he and Lori had been very convincing. Their captives from the tent city had willingly gone back over the border, though not without a few feeble threats and a handful of curses on their lives. Sure, some or most would find their way back to the States, but no one thought they'd ever darken Iowa's doorstep again.

Bryan's entire team was gathered in the old barn. Bruno Rocchio had announced that the harvest was almost done and he wasn't needed at the farm anymore. He looked happy to be done with working on the farm and keeping an eye out for trouble. At the moment Jason and David were taking turns patrolling the farm.

Lori sat close to Rocchio. Bryan noticed they were holding hands.

"Absence make the heart grow fonder?" he asked them.

"You should have heard them arguing when we were on the road," Easy said with an amiable grin. "But we all know how they roll." Lori slapped Easy with a backhand to the chest while everyone else laughed.

Norm Hendricks was back from his recon in Des

Moines. Before he could give them the full sitrep, Bryan wanted Charlotte to tell everyone what she'd discovered.

"We have a few people in custody that I've spent some quality time with," Charlotte said.

"Not if you asked them," Amy said.

"True. We found one of the men who set fire to Bryan's parents' farm. He admitted he was there and did throw a torch into the corn. The other men he was with fled that same night and haven't been seen since. They were supposed to do the same to half a dozen other farms. What's interesting is that this wasn't some random act of violence. And it wasn't revenge for not being hired on to help with the harvest. I get the feeling this guy wouldn't know the first thing to do on a farm."

"That didn't stop me," Rocchio joked.

"Bryan also had a heart-to-heart with one of the gang who was knocking off mail delivery trucks. We grabbed him when he was released from the hospital. Both men have something in common. They're getting marching orders from someone else, though they can't say who. These guys are bottom-feeders. They wouldn't know who the sharks are. Most of them are illegals, and I suspect whoever got them to Maverick is the one pulling the strings. Someone with a modicum of wealth and influence is plucking them from the border and giving them a free ride to let their criminal freak flag fly, so long as they do a few things in return."

L.G. got up from the bale of hay he'd been sitting on. "Are you implying that it could be the governor behind this? She and her husband have the money and influence."

"I had them checked out, and even though they have

tentacles just about everywhere, Mexico is a blind spot for them," Amy interjected. "Aside from a trip to Cabo ten years ago, neither has been south of the border before or since. They have no business holdings there. No contacts."

"That doesn't completely clear them," L.G. said. "They don't seem to give much of a hoot what's happening, so at the very least it's happening with their consent."

While everyone spoke, Bryan had been whittling a branch with his knife. He pointed the stick at L.G. "You recall who the Benningtons are in hock with?"

"You mean Nostrand Ganz."

"Damn straight."

"Ganz has almost as much money invested in Mexico as he does in China. Or any other struggling nation that can provide cheap labor. He even has a palatial mansion just outside of Mexico City. I hear he isn't there very often, but he does have roots in Mexican soil. It's safe to say there isn't a politician or business tycoon who isn't under his thumb south of the border."

"Same here in America," Easy said. "Why should it be any different in Mexico?"

Hendricks raised his hand. "I can confirm that Ganz is at the very least a big part of the mix."

"How so?" Rocchio asked.

"That girl I was sent to meet? Her name is Penny Hastings and she just happens to be the step-and-fetch-it for Governor Bennington. Says the governor treats her like garbage. Not surprised. Penny is young and good at playing dumb. I have a strong feeling that game has gotten her a lot of what she wants in the past. She hears and sees a lot of things. One of them being an impromptu meeting between the Benningtons and Ganz that, in her words, seemed to *scare the shit out of them.* Ganz and some other rich asshats have their sights set on Maverick and a lot of other towns like it in Iowa who are big on natural beauty and land and short on the funds to hang on to it. He wants it all. Some farms to be used as dumping grounds for all those batteries from China that we'll need to run the electric cars they're forcing down our throats in the name of saving the planet. Other farms will be tilled with Frankenseeds, all livestock tossed aside, so they can provide a healthy vegetarian solution to an obese America. Of course no one knows the long-term health effects of eating genetically modified crops on a scale never seen before." Hendricks held up one finger. "Last but not least, everything left will be turned into resorts strictly for the wealthy and foreign investors. They'll offer the locals minimum wage jobs and keep them hovering on the poverty line, all while pretending they are the only thing preventing the community from dying on the vine."

When Hendricks finished there was silence, save for Bryan's determined whittling.

"How did you get this girl to tell you all of this?" Rocchio asked.

Hendricks winked at him. "Right guy at the right time. She's been carrying this burden for months and needed a sympathetic ear to listen. She can't tell her parents because they're in deep with the Benningtons."

"This is crazy," Easy said.

"I've got a safe house in Upstate New York with her

name on it just in case," Hendricks said. "Penny doesn't seem like the type who can lie her way out of a situation if things go sideways. For the moment she's a disillusioned and frustrated employee who needs someone to vent to. I'll ride that line until I think she's in danger."

"Good call," Bryan said. "Get whatever you can out of her, but keep her safety top of mind."

"You betcha," Norm said.

"So, what we're saying here is that Nostrand Ganz is ultimately the one responsible for your mother's death," Shane said.

Bryan buried his knife in the ground and snapped the stick over his knee. "Not just hers. Too many to count."

"What do you propose we do?" L.G. said.

Staring at the ground, Bryan said, "I'm working on it. For now we just keep doing what we're doing. I'll find a way to deal with Ganz and damn the consequences. I promise, it won't be pretty."

Broad Street was slowly turning back to normal. More and more Maverick residents came out to shop or meet at the diner or Mannion's Restaurant without fear of running into trouble. Crime was most certainly on the downtick.

There was an article in the paper about an attempted smash-and-grab by three men who tried to get behind the pharmacy counter and make out with garbage bags filled with pills. They never made it out of the store as the employees, along with several shoppers, used everything at hand to stop the thieves and beat them over the head until they fled into the streets.

The playground was no longer a drug oasis. Bryan and his team made an anonymous donation to the parks department to rebuild parts of it so little children could enjoy the swings and seesaw. When word got around about the donation, gossip spread like wildfire. Clearly the donation was from the Night Warriors. To double down on their generosity, the town had banded together one weekend to thoroughly clean the park, which included repainting the benches and replanting flowers and bushes. Pride had taken root and was blossoming in Maverick.

Despite everything they'd done, there was still an undercurrent of drug abuse, though overdoses were down demonstrably. Bryan wished he could stop it altogether, but that was a pipe dream. Some people would always find a way to destroy their lives and those around them. There'd been no sightings of his old pal Jimmy. Shane thought he must have run out of town when things went south. Bryan had a pretty good handle on Jimmy. He wouldn't know what to do outside of Maverick. A local through and through, Jimmy was holed up somewhere, more than likely up to no good. Bryan hoped their paths crossed again.

Bryan's team still stalked the night, stopping petty crimes in their tracks, but it was getting more difficult as the governor flooded the streets with police patrols. There were cars from nearby towns along with state police and plenty of undercover, who stood out like sore thumbs.

The old farm had been named Hay-Q by Shane. Charlotte and Bryan had released the man who was part of the mail theft gang, as well as the two men Hendricks had brought in from the tent city. Easy had driven them, blindfolded and bound in the back of a van, to the middle of nowhere. When the wounded man had asked where they were, Easy had looked around, squinting at the sun, and said, "I'm not entirely sure. But I hope you're clear on where you'll never go again."

The man who had set fire to the farm was still in the storm cellar. Bryan wasn't entirely sure what do to with him yet.

Overall, things had gotten quiet. And that worried Bryan.

Jason stopped by Hay-Q one Sunday with a tray of chicken and rice.

"A gift from Pam," he said. Bryan's stomach rumbled just at the sight of it.

"Pam's cooking is one thing I miss dearly out here," Charlotte said as she took the tray from his hands.

"She and Dave are sticking around?" Bryan said, offering his brother a beer.

"Dad won't let them leave. They've got the farm running almost as good as when Mom was alive. And to tell you the truth, I think he's fallen in love with those kids. Lola especially."

They went out behind the barn. It was a perfect day, with passing clouds in a pale blue sky and just the hint of autumn on the wind. The sound of Rocchio pounding a heavy bag he'd set up in the barn accompanied the last of the season's heat bugs, their song of summer sounding wistful.

"Where is everybody?" Jason asked.

"Out and about." Bryan tapped his brother on the arm with his beer. "You know, Bigfoot, it's clear you have to find a woman to make an honest man out of you so you can give Dad some grandchildren."

Jason popped the top on his beer. "What about you? You and Charlotte should step up to the plate."

Bryan shook his head. "Not in the cards. We both saw to that. Having a child is a liability with our way of life. There's always a chance we'd leave a kid an orphan in the blink of an eye. That wouldn't be fair to the kid, no matter how much we'd want one. Sad to say you're the normal one, so that duty falls to you. Got anyone in mind?"

"There is this girl, Erin, I have my eye on. She was a personal trainer at the gym. It closed about a year back. I don't know what she's doing, but I see her in town every now and then." Jason picked up a rock and tossed it into the field. "My sad love life isn't why I came here."

"I thought it was to bring us food."

"Ha. No, I wanted to let you know that they're bringing back homecoming in two weeks. The high school last did it about four years ago. There are a lot of happy people making plans. That's all because of you guys. You all brought this town back to life. Who would have thought my hellion brother would be the secret savior of Maverick?"

The brothers stared off into the wild overgrown field, sipping their beers and considering all that had happened.

"We're not pulling up stakes just yet," Bryan said.

"I thought you'd be dying to get back to Pennsylvania."

"Charlotte and I have been talking about, well, moving here. I never thought I'd miss this place, but the past month has proved me wrong."

"That'd make Dad real happy. He took a shine to Charlotte. And you're okay, I guess."

"She is my better half."

"So why do you seem so wound up?" Jason asked.

"You haven't been around me for a bunch of years. I'm tense when I sleep. Got too much on my mind."

Jason found a rock and launched it into the field. "Anything you want to clue me in on?"

"Nothing you need to worry about."

"That's usually when I need to start worrying."

Bryan changed the subject. "How many touchdowns did you score at homecoming?"

Jason's face lit up. "Three. Was the school record until this monster running back broke it about seven years ago. He's on the practice squad for the Packers now."

Bryan patted his brother on the stomach. "Come on, let's try some of that chicken and rice. I see Pam's been fattening you up good."

CHAPTER 34

Easy tagged along with Jason as he helped prepare the school and football field for homecoming. With less to do as they avoided the authorities, Easy was growing restless and needed to get out. He'd never attended a homecoming when he was in high school. He was too busy trying to flunk out. The day gave him a chance to experience something he'd missed.

The most pleasant surprise was the total absence of homeless people around the downtown area. Word on the street was that Father Rooney was taking on help at St. Matthew's. They had even supplied him with enough funds to hire someone to facilitate connecting the needy with the means of getting résumés written, filling out job applications, and applying for myriad assistance programs. The idea was to get them up and on their feet as quickly as possible. For those who had entered illegally, that was a whole other kettle of fish that still needed some focus. At the moment those with honest intentions were well-cared for by the priest and his parish.

Easy snapped some pictures with his phone to show Bryan later. The man needed a reason to smile.

"You want to help paint the bleachers?" Jason asked.

"Boy, do I!"

Jason handed him a paint can and a brush. "I can see why my brother likes you. Sarcastic birds of a feather . . ."

They set to work with about twenty other volunteers, the youngest a pair of preteens wearing Metallica T-shirts and the oldest a couple who appeared to be well into their seventies. The smell of fresh paint on a clear almost-fall day was downright heavenly.

When they were done Jason and Easy volunteered to do the cleanup and put away the paint cans, brushes, and pans. The teenagers especially looked grateful.

"Where does all this stuff go?" Easy asked as he rolled up drop cloths.

"They set up pallets for it all in the gym. I'll take this," he said, lifting a mostly full fifty-gallon bucket of paint.

"I'd help you with that, but I think it's better you get to show off for the natives."

"You're a riot. Keep telling yourself you could help me if you wanted."

It took Easy five minutes to get the drop cloths neatly folded. He kicked open the gym doors because both of his arms were full.

The paint buckets and other supplies were on the pallets. No sign of Jason.

Easy's radar instantly went up.

"Jason?"

His voice bounced around the empty, cavernous gym.

When he didn't get a reply, he dropped the cloths and took out the pistol from his ankle holster.

"Jason, where are you at, buddy?"

He heard a groan to his right, just over the pallet of supplies.

Easy ran to the other side of the pallet. Jason was on the ground, cupping the back of his head. There was blood on the hardwood floor. Next to him was a man wearing a hoodie pulled so close he couldn't make out his face. The man had a hammer in his hand.

"Back the hell up!" Easy commanded. The man jerked and nearly dropped the hammer when he saw the gun pointed at him. "Who the hell are you?"

Easy reached forward, pulled away his hoodie, and punched him on the bridge of his nose. The man reared back with an agonized cry, both hands cupping his face.

"Jason, you okay?" Easy said.

Bryan's brother moaned and pushed himself until he was sitting up. He looked over at the man writhing on the floor.

"Jimmy, you son of the devil, I'm gonna kill you!"

Jason recovered quickly, though blood ran down the side of his neck. He picked up the wounded man by his upper arms and yanked him to his feet. He smashed Jimmy hard against the wall.

Jimmy's nose was bent at an awkward angle and his eyes, puffing up, poured water.

"Who is this guy?" Easy said, wondering if his next task was going to be saving Jimmy from Jason.

"The town piece of crap. He's a drug dealer, mostly dealing to kids."

When Jimmy tried to speak Jason kneed him in the groin. He melted to the floor, a high keening sound whistling from him like a screaming teakettle.

Easy picked up Jimmy's hammer and tucked it under his belt. "I take it you two don't get along."

"We're not anything to each other. He used to hang out with my brother when they were kids."

Easy put two and two together. This must be the guy Bryan had put out of business. And since Bryan was on the down-low, the misguided dealer idiot decided to take out his frustrations on his brother.

"I . . . I wasn't gonna kill you," Jimmy huffed. "Just wanted to . . . to scare you."

Jason grabbed him by the hair and dumped him on the floor. "Do I look scared to you?"

Jimmy flicked a quick glance his way, then went about holding his nose and crotch, massaging both.

"Your brother screwed up everything for me."

"Forgive me if I don't shed any tears that you're not selling poison to kids anymore."

Jimmy was reduced to crocodile tears. He was clearly strung out, now hurt and scared.

"What do you want to do with him?" Easy asked.

Jason dabbed at the blood on his head. "I don't know. I sure can't trust him. What if he comes after my father next? He's a total bum." Jason grabbed Jimmy by the chin. "Aren't you? How many kids overdosed on the stuff you sold them? And after everything that happened here, you still didn't have the good sense to run away."

"If it wasn't me, it would just be someone else. You can't blame me for people's messed-up lives. I'm just making a living, same as anyone else." Jimmy winced when he said it. Jason's fist was balled and ready to strike.

Easy put his hand on Jason's arm. He worried that if Jason punched Jimmy, he'd kill him. Jason's fists were like twin ham hocks.

Jason took in a deep breath and then relaxed. "Get the hell out of here, Jimmy. This time, have the good sense to leave town." Jason touched his head, looked at his red hand, and wiped the blood on his shirt.

Jimmy gathered himself up and shot daggers at both of them. Tears still ran down his face.

"The supply will come back," Jimmy mumbled. "Your brother didn't do anything but pause things. You think all those junkies just turned over a new leaf and can live without what I sell them? You let him know that. He's still a nothing. Only now he thinks he's better than me."

Jason's chest puffed up. Easy looked him in the eye and shook his head as Jimmy walked past them.

"Those kids helping you out there? I'll laugh my head off when the first one has a bad trip, man."

Easy couldn't believe the total lack of good sense Jimmy possessed. Then again, drug dealers were not known to be the brightest bulbs in the pack.

Striding over to Jimmy, he grabbed his hoodie and jerked it as hard as he could. Jimmy's arms pinwheeled as he tried to keep his balance.

"I have a strong feeling you're not going to run like you should," Easy said, spinning Jimmy around to face him. "Let me make your stay as unpleasant as possible."

He whipped the hammer from his belt and delivered

two bone-cracking blows, one to each shattered kneecap. Jimmy's mouth opened in a silent scream. While he was down, Easy stomped on both of his wrists, feeling the satisfying break of bone.

"Consider this *my* warning," Easy said. "You don't put Maverick in the rear view, I won't be so nice."

Jimmy writhed on the ground, his cries finally escaping his throat.

Easy and Jason dragged Jimmy out of the gym and tucked him in a corner outside, stuffing a rag in his mouth. "You tell the cops about this, you're dead. If you keep quiet, I just may call an ambulance for you. Capisce?"

Jimmy nodded between spasms of pain.

"You good to finish cleaning up?" Easy asked Jason.

Jason lightly tapped his head. "This coconut is hard to break."

They made quick work of the cleanup, and on the way out of town Easy did call an ambulance. He hoped Jimmy enjoyed learning how to walk again.

CHAPTER 35

The nighttime home invasion made the early news. A man in his midthirties with a rap sheet long enough to wallpaper a kitchen had broken into a family's home while they slept. He managed to take the jewelry box from the woman of the house's dresser, as well as her husband's wallet. He would have gotten away if he hadn't taken time to waltz into their twelve-year-old daughter's room and pull the covers off her to get a better look. She woke up screaming.

He hit her father in the head with the jewelry box when he rushed to her room and fled down the stairs. The wife hit the house alarm. Fortunately for them, with the increased patrols looking for the Night Warriors, the man was caught running out the door.

Bryan sent the newsclip to Bruno Rocchio and L.G. Iverson.

They were waiting for the thief two blocks from the courthouse. It was easy work to hustle him into the car and drive off. While L.G. manned the wheel, Rocchio took out all of his aggressions on the thief. The man tried to fight back, but he was no match.

After finding out from Amy's research that the thief was also a convicted pedophile, Rocchio mashed the man's testicles until they would never ever work again. They dumped him four counties over on the side of the road with a simple note stuffed in his pocket. It just said, RUN.

As much as Bryan wanted to catch people in the act, it was almost impossible to do night missions with the amount of police on the streets. So now they worked mop-up duty in the day, applying justice after the fact.

They fed Sam Mishra the latest news, because so much of it wasn't being covered by actual news outlets. It helped keep the turning of the tide in Maverick on her *Lying for Dollars* podcast. It had quadrupled in listeners over the past few weeks. Bryan knew the power of alternative media, especially with younger audiences, which was why he kept Sam close.

The silver lining was that crime was on a sharp decline, including in counties Bryan and his team had never visited. Maverick's unsavory element had either headed for the hills or were too afraid to ply their trade for fear of retribution from the Night Warriors. Even when immigrants were bussed into town, word got to them quickly that Maverick was not a safe haven for those with impure intentions. They hightailed it to other towns, other states that were more welcoming and willing to turn a blind eye.

Jason had filled Bryan in about his run-in with Jimmy, and how Easy had taken care of him. It was a relief to have Jimmy out of action. One less thing to worry about.

He couldn't shake the feeling that there would be another attack on the farm, which was why he had his team taking turns keeping an eye on the place. It also helped to know that Jason and David were armed and on alert.

Shane brought a flyer that had been handed to him while he walked the streets of Maverick. It was printed on orange paper with large block lettering.

"You can't beat homecoming food," Bryan said when he read the advertisement. It gave the time for the festivities and the promise of a blowout barbecue to celebrate both homecoming and the revival of Maverick. At the bottom was a P.S. It said, NIGHT WARRIORS EAT FREE. "We have to decide who goes. And no taking them up on the free meal offer."

"I volunteer," Shane said as he rubbed his belly. "I'm sure Amy wouldn't mind being my arm candy."

"If she heard you call her that, you'd be on the ground now."

"That's why I said it while she's thirty miles away."

Bryan set the flyer on the tabletop. "I wish Charlotte and I could go. It would be nice to take her to homecoming. I'd get to show her a little bit of my past."

Shane opened a water bottle and downed it in one long gurgling pull. "Your family and the Cruzes will be there, too. We'll need eyes on the farm."

"I was thinking Charlotte and I might take that shift. We'll make sure no one sees us. The rest of you minus Hendricks cover homecoming. My brother's run-in with Jimmy reminded me that not everyone is happy as a clam that Maverick is turning a page. Sad to say but it's the truth."

"We got you," Shane said. He'd been growing out his beard over the past several weeks and couldn't stop scratching at it. "Until then, there's not much to do. The crime blotter in the paper is empty."

That made Bryan smile. "Not even mentions of the cops running some kids off private property?"

"Not even that."

"Things are going much better than any of us could have expected."

"I know. It makes me nervous."

"Me too, buddy. Me too."

Penny Hastings was tasked with organizing the files crammed within a dozen cabinets. It was a tedious job, but at least it kept her busy and out of the governor's sights. Alexa Bennington was about as pleasant as a rattlesnake. And her husband, Todd, gave Penny the creeps. Every time he looked at her, she felt the need to go home and take a hot shower. He was clearly bad news, which made him the perfect mate for Alexa.

She heard the phone ring in the next room, and then heard the door to the governor's office close and lock. Bennington was on the line with someone, but her voice was muffled. Penny normally worked with her earbuds in, but she'd lost them during her run that morning. She strained to hear what the governor was saying, but it proved to be too difficult to decipher.

No matter. She had a date that night with Norman.

They had reservations at one of the nicer restaurants in town. Now *there* was a real man. He was tall and good-looking and rugged. When she spoke he kept his eyes on her, devouring every word, every motion. No man her age she'd dated had ever done that. Most of them were preoccupied with their phones or busy preening. Not Norman. Sure, he was older, but he treated her right. Like a true lady. It was easy to forgive the age gap.

The office door suddenly opened. Colin Farmer emerged pale as a ghost. He went straight for the water-cooler, poured a cup, and drank it like a shot of whiskey. He poured another and repeated.

"Everything all right?" Penny asked. She was no fan of Colin. Her father had warned her about sycophants.

"Never hitch your wagon to a bootlicker," he used to say. "Yes-men get you nowhere."

Colin looked startled that Penny was there. "Oh, um, nothing."

His hand trembled, almost spilling the fresh water in his plastic cup.

"It doesn't look like nothing," she ventured to say.

The governor's chief of staff burped into his fist and excused himself before hustling out of the room.

That was strange.

Penny slipped the files back into the drawer. Colin had left the door open.

The governor was on the phone, but she was clearly talking to her husband. She was recounting what had happened on her previous call. She'd said it was with Nostrand Ganz. Unaware that the door was open, she went blow-by-blow, clearly as rattled as Colin.

Penny, shocked at first, recovered and took out her phone so she could record the governor. What she heard frightened her to her core. When the call ended Penny slipped quietly out of the room, heading outside to get some fresh air. She hadn't realized she'd been crying until the cooler air touched the tears on her cheeks.

CHAPTER 36

Norm Hendricks could tell something was wrong with Penny the moment he saw her walk into the restaurant. At first she told him she was fine, she'd just had a long day. It took three glasses of wine to break down her defenses. By the time dinner came the dam had burst. She was terrified and sad and anxious.

Hendricks couldn't blame her.

"I can't ever go back there," she said, wiping her tears with her cloth napkin.

He reached across the table and took her hand. "I understand. This is some serious stuff. I'd be scared, too."

That brought a half smile to her lips.

"I don't know what to do. Do I go to the police? I mean, they work for the governor, right? Maybe the FBI. I . . . I'm so confused."

The poor girl was trembling.

That was when Hendricks clued her in to who he was and why he was in Iowa. The revelation shocked her out of her panic.

"You're . . . one of the Night Warriors?"

Hendricks looked around them to make sure no one

was listening. "I need you to keep that down. And to yourself."

"The governor hates you."

"Yeah, well, if we met, I'm sure it would be mutual."

He was surprised she wasn't mad that he had obviously targeted her. She was probably too shocked to put it all together.

He offered to take her someplace safe if she felt she couldn't carry on there one more day. Knowing he was a Night Warrior gave her a shot of confidence.

"Maybe I can dig around a little. Get some more solid details," she said, barely touching her food. "I mean, if it can save lives."

Hendricks moved over until he was sitting next to her and could talk close to her ear. He had to admit he was falling for this beautiful woman, and after what she'd told him, he wanted to protect her at all costs. "I'm not going to let anything happen to you. If I need more info, I'll get it out of the governor herself if I have to."

That would be a difficult task, but it wouldn't be his first. With the help of his team he could find a way.

Penny's eyes lit up. "Wait. I know someone who probably knows just about as much as the governor. Colin. Her chief of staff. He was a mess when he came out of the office. I even think he went to throw up. He's like her little pilot fish. Whatever she knows, he knows."

Feeling bolstered by the revelation, Hendricks asked, "What's his last name?"

"Farmer. Colin Farmer. I can find his address if you want. I'm sure it's close enough to the governor so he can do her bidding."

He patted her hand. "I have everything I need. Now, I say let's enjoy this beautiful food, have a decadent dessert, and then head to your place."

Penny's grin grew wide. "A night with a Night Warrior."

He gave her a long kiss on her cheek. "We'll get you packed up later."

Before the sun rose the next morning Hendricks had Penny on a plane, and he put Des Moines in his rearview mirror. He got to the farm just as Bryan, Charlotte, and Shane were making breakfast.

The moment Bryan saw Hendricks's face, he said, "What happened?"

Hendricks walked into the RV and they sat at the galley table.

"I had to put Penny on ice," he said, accepting the hot mug of coffee Charlotte offered. "She's in the air as we speak. My brother will meet her at JFK and take her to the safe house." His brother was also ex-military but had chosen a more sedate life postwar.

"What did she hear? Or see?" Charlotte asked.

"The governor got a call from our pal Nostrand Ganz. Penny said when the call was over the governor's chief of staff came out of the office looking like someone close to him had just died. He didn't tell her anything, but he left the door open. Penny heard Bennington call her husband. She was rattled. Ganz isn't happy with what he's hearing and her inability to capture us. He's going to take control of the situation."

Bryan ran his hand through his hair. "Crap. I was afraid of that. Did she talk any specifics?"

Hendricks shook his head. "Penny is sure the governor, her husband, and her chief of staff know exactly what's coming, hence their being shook up. What Penny did hear is that people are going to die. The governor told her husband she was advised to stock up on body bags. Ganz would direct her and her team how to respond, what to say, and how to act. Iowa is under his version of martial law."

"People are going to die?" Shane exclaimed. "Who? It's us they want. If they can't find us, who else is this psycho gonna take it out on?"

Charlotte's mouth was pulled into a grim line. "Anyone he wants."

"From what Amy's learned he has a considerable force of ex-military and other questionable characters from overseas in his employ. Like us, they're mostly deployed in developing countries, enforcing his rules so he can break the backs of people who build the very things that make him wealthy beyond measure," Bryan said. He looked around the table. "These men and women are pros. Now, we're pros, too. The difference is that some of them don't possess a moral compass." He got up and paced up and down the RV. "We need specifics."

"The chief of staff is a softer target," Hendricks said. "His name's Colin Farmer. I'm heading back to Des Moines to track him. Penny said he spends most of his time with the governor, one of those first-to-arrive-and-last-to-leave types. But he does eventually go home. I have his address. Who wants to come with me?"

"Definitely me," Charlotte said.

"I'll go, too," Bryan said.

"What about me?" Shane asked.

"Three is plenty," Bryan said. "Tell everyone to keep low for the moment. We need to find out what Ganz has cooked up in his twisted little mind. God knows what's up his sleeve. It's likely he's been planning this end around for a while."

The next few minutes the RV rocked back and forth as everyone got ready. Bryan and Charlotte grabbed their go bags and loaded them in Hendricks's rental. They also wolfed down toast and microwaved bacon. There was no way to know when their next meal would come.

Before they left, Bryan stalked across the field to the storm shelter. Neither Charlotte nor Shane bothered to ask what he was doing.

He unlocked the chain and threw the door wide open. The man who had been complicit in his mother's murder was on the ground, shielding his eyes from the blinding light.

"Enjoy your stay in hell."

Bryan put two bullets in the man's head. Then he flipped the door closed with his boot.

There was no point in holding back anymore.

It was time for the people who were messing with his town to see just how dangerous Bryan and his team could be.

Shane called ahead to Bruno Rocchio to let him know the latest. When he asked where Jason, George, and the Cruz family were, Rocchio said they were all in town.

"What for?" Shane asked.

"That whole homecoming thing. Jason's been working on it and the kids wanted to go. I get a feeling George can't say no to that little girl."

That was right. Today was homecoming day.

"You at the farm?"

"Yep," Rocchio said. "Lori was going to stop by, give me a hand watching over the place, until Bryan and Charlotte get here. Should be about as much fun as watching corn grow."

It felt as if an ice-cold finger ran down Shane's spine. Two words flashed into his brain.

False flag.

Governor Bennington hadn't been able to smoke them out. So Nostrand Ganz was going to set fire to Maverick.

What better place to light that spark than the very town that had overcome their sick plans to run everyone out?

"Listen to me. Screw the farm. I need you and Lori to meet me and everyone else at the high school." Shane set the phone on speaker and opened one of the secret doors to grab some weapons and stuff them in an olive-green duffel bag.

"Whoa. Slow down, brother. What has you all worked up?"

"I think Ganz is going to sabotage the homecoming." Sweat ran down Shane's face as he raced to get everything he and his team needed.

"What makes you think that?"

"We'll talk later. Just call Lori and get to the high school. And call Easy, L.G., and Amy. They need to be there, too. Whoever gets there first needs to get the family the hell out of there."

Rocchio sucked on his teeth. "What about Bryan, Charlotte, and Norm?"

"They're heading for Des Moines to take care of something that could be linked to this. I could be totally wrong, but it's better to be safe than sorry. Now go!"

Shane tossed everything into the car and laid down half the rubber on the tires as he sped out of the old farm. He dialed Bryan's number but had driven into a dead zone.

CHAPTER 37

Bryan had the call on speaker. Norm's knuckles were white on the steering wheel. Charlotte paled, shaking her head, while Shane told them about his hunch.

"We're turning around right now," Bryan said.

Hendricks cut the wheel and the car fishtailed as they made a rocking U-turn in the middle of the two-lane road. A truck speeding down the east lane nearly clipped them. Smoke billowed out from the rear wheels as they sought traction on the blacktop.

"How far out are we?" Charlotte asked.

"About twenty-thirty minutes," Bryan snapped.

"I can cut that down considerably," Hendricks said as he mashed the accelerator to the floor. They hadn't spotted any speed traps on their way out. If a patrol car decided to pull them over, they would have to follow them back to town.

Bryan got back on his phone.

"Who are you calling?" Charlotte asked.

"The school. I'm calling in a bomb threat. That should clear the place out."

The burner phone was untraceable, so he wasn't

concerned about them finding out who made the call. Even if they could, his main priority was getting everyone out of there. Sure, Shane could be wrong, but it made sense. Bryan could kick himself for being so stupid. They'd worked in foreign nations that were masters of false flags in the hopes of gaining absolute trust in the very people and institutions that were spreading fear and death.

He nearly threw the phone against the window when no one answered. They were all at the homecoming event.

Next he called the police. The phone rang until he got a recorded message.

"Are you kidding me?"

"Call Sam," Charlotte said.

She was right. With his growing audience, especially in Iowa because that was where all his stories were originating from, someone was bound to be listening.

Sam picked up and Bryan bowled him over with information.

"Wait, you're serious about this?" Sam said.

"I am. We could be wrong—hell, I want to be wrong— but we have to play it like we're right."

"I'm on it. Good luck. And be careful."

Bryan looked over at the odometer. The digital display showed they were going over a hundred miles an hour.

"Can't this thing go any faster?"

"Not without blowing a gasket," Hendricks said. "Next time I'll rent a Porsche."

They blazed a path to Maverick. Charlotte had Bryan's

shoulder in a death grip from the back seat. No one spoke the rest of the way, all lost in their troubled thoughts.

Sam Mishra stared at the phone in his hand.

If what Bryan had said was true, this was going to go down as one of the most infamous moments in US history.

But if he was wrong, and Sam got on the air basically yelling "Fire!" in a crowded movie theater, he'd have to remain in hiding . . . forever.

"You okay?" Tina asked. He'd been crashing at her place for the past week and felt as if he were overstaying his welcome, despite her reassuring him to the contrary.

He put down the phone and shook his head. "Not really. I've been asked to do something that can either save lives or destroy mine."

Tina sat in the chair opposite him and touched his chin so he could look her in the eye.

"You know what to do."

Sam rubbed his thumb against his index finger, deep in thought.

One versus many.

He'd started the *Lying for Dollars* podcast to expose the corruption prevalent in politics and beyond. Now here he was, potentially facing a life-and-death disaster that his podcast could impact.

Shooting up from his chair, he ran to the dining room where his laptop and equipment were set up.

"Can you grab me a drink? I think I'm going to need it."

Shane pulled into the first spot he could find in the high school lot. The sound of the marching band thumped from the field. All of the bleachers were full to capacity. The smells of sausage and peppers, corn dogs, and fried dough permeated the air. There were people everywhere. It seemed as if every living soul in Maverick had come out for the festivities.

"Good Lord," Shane muttered. You couldn't have dreamed up a more perfect moment to foment chaos.

He looked around the perimeter, searching for anyone who seemed out of place. If there was anyone out there, they were expertly hidden.

That didn't mean there couldn't be Ganz's foot soldiers hidden in plain sight. The problem was Shane didn't have a clue what any of them looked like. If they were here to light up the homecoming, they would damn sure make it a priority to blend in.

Shane wore a sweat jacket that helped conceal the pistols he had on each side of his waist, as well as a few cannisters of tear gas in his pockets.

Grabbing his phone from the passenger seat, he dialed Rocchio.

"You here?"

"Yeah. Lori and I are near the home end zone."

Shane looked across the field and spotted them. They stood beside a hot dog cart, along with several dozen other people.

"I don't see anything funky yet," Shane said. "But keep an eye out."

"Copy that."

He next called Easy, then L.G. and Amy. All were on site at different parts of the field. Between them, they had eyes on every access point to the homecoming.

Cheerleaders ran to the 50-yard line and began their routine. The crowd erupted as they encouraged the football team, who stood on the sidelines, to be aggressive. A few penny rockets whistled high into the air just as the cheerleaders finished.

Shane looked for Jason and his father. He texted everyone to see if they had eyes on them. L.G. said he'd just spotted them. They were in the stands about five rows up from his position.

"I need you to get them the hell out of there," Shane said.

"What do I tell them?"

"The truth. I want them scared and running like their butts are on fire."

"I'm on it."

Shane watched everything unfold and wondered what he could do to clear the place out. His hand went to his pocket and his fingers wrapped around the containers of tear gas. He only needed to toss one and that ought to do the trick. The bleachers on the visitor side of the field were closest to him. People would panic once he threw it, but that was the idea. He just had to hope no one got hurt in the stampede.

A thought nagged at him as he jogged to the bleachers. What if they were wrong?

He was about to sabotage the one bright thing that had happened in Maverick in years.

He spotted Jason, his father, David, Pam, and the kids wending their way through the stands, with L.G. in the lead.

That was one good thing.

A voice blared from the speakers. "Let's give a huge round of applause for *your* Maverick Broncos!"

The place went wild as the team took to the field. They had their arms raised and their fists were pumping. Everyone in attendance rose to their feet, clapping hands and stomping boots. Shane lost sight of the Branches.

"Come on. Come on."

Once the Branches and Cruzes were out of the area he was going to launch the tear gas.

To his surprise, he saw a few teenagers running away from the field. They had their phones in their hands and were showing other people whatever was on them, trying to pull them away. Shane had no idea what was going on, but in just a matter of seconds more and more people, mostly kids, were triggered by something and finding a way to get out.

Suddenly he was a trout swimming upstream. People carelessly bumped into him as they fled. Had something happened on the field he couldn't see? But then why were people still cheering?

He called L.G., but with all the noise he assumed his buddy couldn't hear the phone.

What everyone could hear over the cheers, the boot stomps, the band, the dozen or so people rattling cowbells, was the sharp crack of gunfire.

Cheers turned to shrieks.

Shane instinctively ducked, his head on a swivel, searching for the source of the gunfire.

The rat-a-tat-tat of automatic gunfire was instantly all around. Shane unholstered one of his guns, his back into a tree.

He heard return fire in the form of handguns against whatever high-powered weapon was being used against the crowd.

There was a burp of bullets, and Shane watched as a middle-aged couple fell to the ground, their heads and necks exploding in crimson. Some people jumped away from the bodies in terror, while others, too caught up in the panicked swell, were driven into their gory remains. They fell atop the corpses and struggled to get up as others trampled them.

Earlier he had counted eight police assigned to keep an eye on the proceedings. Looking at the ground, there were six people in uniform down. They must have been the priority.

Shane bulled his way through the crowd. He grabbed the outstretched hands of two crying teenagers covered in blood and viscera, pulling them to their feet and urging them to keep running and not look back.

Then he saw movement behind an open window in the school. A person wearing fatigues and a black ski mask fired shots into the crowd. Shane made a beeline for the school. He'd have to trust the rest of his team to find the other shooters.

CHAPTER 38

Iverson urged everyone to keep as low as they could while still running. Bullets flew overheard from every direction. He didn't try to grab his gun because he was pressed in by the crowd. Odds were if they saw it, they would turn on him. Anyone with a gun right now was the enemy, and he wasn't sure how many people packed heat in Iowa. It seemed more of a rifle/shotgun kind of town, but you never knew.

He spotted Bruno Rocchio and Lori Nicolo up ahead. They were beside a trio of metal garbage pails, scanning the field and surrounding buildings.

Up ahead, the parking lot was bedlam. Between the people streaming through the lot and cars stopped at strange angles trying to get out of their parking spaces, it was a total logjam.

"Jason, is there anywhere we can go to get some cover?"

"Yeah! My truck!"

L.G. pointed at the lot. "That's a dead end."

It was a poor choice of words because, a second later, he witnessed a young girl get cut down by gunfire. The boy who had been holding her hand let go and ran for his life in the opposite direction. L.G. knew that simple moment would haunt the kid for life . . . if he lived to see another day.

"The sandwich shop," Jason said, pointing to a closed store across the street.

L.G. nodded. It would have to do. He'd shoot out the glass door so they could get inside. Of course, a stream of humanity would follow them inside. That was fine, as long as he could find a way to keep people safe.

The constant rattle of gunfire was unnerving. He didn't have a helmet or any of his heavy-duty equipment. There was no way to pinpoint where it was coming from, so he didn't know which was the best way to go. Between them and the sandwich shop was a killing field as more and more people jerked and fell.

There was a pained shriek behind him. Jason grabbed L.G. by the back of his collar.

He looked down and his heart dropped.

David and Pam were on their knees. Lola was convulsing on the ground. Her shirt was bright red. L.G. saw the hole and knew she'd been shot in or very close to the heart.

Pam wailed as she clutched her daughter. George Branch stood above them with his hands in his hair, his face pale with anguish and anger.

A bullet whined close . . . too close . . . by L.G.'s ear.

Rocchio and Lori burst through the crowd. Their eyes went straight to Lola. The pain on their faces was clearly visible.

"We have to get them to the sandwich shop," L.G. said.

Rocchio reached into his pockets and had a gun in each hand. He said to Lori, "Help Pam and get the hell out of here!"

It took some doing to get Pam to budge. Her grief was beyond measure. L.G. saw that Lola had stopped shaking. She was clearly dead. He grabbed David by the arm and pulled him forward. As they ran to the sandwich shop, Rocchio fired across the field to give them some kind of cover.

Rocchio saw a man in fatigues jogging down the field. He had what looked like a Colt M16 and used it to shoot people in the back. The man spotted Rocchio and turned his weapon toward him.

Dropping to the ground, Rocchio rolled over twice, came to a stop on his stomach, and fired. The bullet caught the man in the upper thigh. He grasped his leg, falling sideways onto the turf.

Wasting no time, Rocchio sprinted to the downed man. He straddled his chest and rained fists to his face, feeling the man's cheekbone crack. He pulled the black ski mask from his face. The man had a deep scar running from his forehead to the bridge of his nose. His hair was buzzed short and he had some years on Rocchio.

"You working for Ganz?" he shouted at the man.

Blood bubbled from the man's lips.

Rocchio went to town on the man's kidneys with a

flurry of rabbit punches that knocked the breath from his lungs. Bullets traced over his head, but Rocchio didn't care. He grabbed him by the throat.

"How many of you are there? Tell me their positions."

To Rocchio's surprise, the man gave a smirk.

He saw red. Here was this man, shooting at innocent men, women, and children, and all he could do was smile?

The punches came without him knowing he was delivering them. The pain in his knuckles refused to register as he whipped the man's head from side to side with each blow. He only stopped when he realized there was no more solid bone left in the man's skull.

Chest heaving, Rocchio spat on the man's ruined face.

The first bullet pierced his side. It didn't hurt much. Just felt like he'd been pricked by a hot needle.

He looked around for the shooter.

There was a man in the now empty stands, rifle raised, pointed at Rocchio.

Rocchio lifted his gun.

The second bullet hit him square in the chest before he could pull the trigger.

For a split second he thought he may have shot his attacker as he heard an echoing crack. The soldier flipped onto his back and his rifle flew out of his hands.

The world spun. Rocchio struggled to breathe, to stay erect, as he watched Easy approach the soldier he'd shot. Easy ran in a crouch toward Rocchio.

"I'm . . . okay," Rocchio wheezed.

Then all he saw was the sky, followed by black.

* * *

As soon as they saw the crowd of panicked people clogging the streets, Bryan knew they were too late. Hendricks brought the car to a screeching halt. They left it in the middle of the street and sprinted to the high school. All had handguns with them, but from the sound of things they would be no match for whatever hell was being unleashed at homecoming.

By the time they got to the field they spotted Easy and Amy trapped in a doorway. Bullets reduced the brickwork to dust as they took turns blindly returning fire.

Three men dressed in black-and-white camouflage raced across the field. They picked up one man who was lying beside another, dragging him back to the stands and out of sight.

What Bryan saw made his stomach drop.

Bruno Rocchio was on the 30-yard line, and he wasn't moving.

Gunfire erupted in the school. Bryan looked up just in time to see a man go flying through the window. He landed headfirst, his neck breaking at a nauseating angle.

Shane's head popped out of the window to assess his work. He spotted Bryan, Charlotte, and Hendricks. "The school's clear!"

The automatic gunfire continued, but it was fading in the distance as Ganz's troopers retreated.

There were bodies everywhere. Some were splayed

across the bleachers. Others littered the field, either dead or close to dying.

Bryan had never seen anything like it on American soil. He did a quick assessment, counting almost fifty dead or wounded.

When the automatic fire ceased, Charlotte and Easy ran to the nearest victims, checking for a pulse, then doing what they could to stanch the bleeding for those still alive.

"Have you seen my father or Jason?" Bryan asked Amy.

She shook her head. "Ever since the shooting started I was trying to find where it was coming from. I found a couple of men in a van by the field. I think I hit one of them. The side door slammed shut and the van sped away. There were others on the rooftops over there, but I'm pretty sure they're gone now." She was breathless but in control. "We need to check on Bruno!"

They ran to Rocchio. It was clear they were too late. Amy felt the side of his neck and did chest compressions, but that only pushed more thick blood from the wounds. Bryan had to pull her off.

Where were the sirens?

By now the entire place should have been crawling with first responders and ambulances.

The sudden silence was bone-chilling.

"We have to get him out of here," Bryan said.

Hendricks helped him and Amy carry Rocchio to the edge of the field.

"We need help!" Charlotte cried. She pointed at two

boys, probably no more than fifteen, crying and cradling gunshot wounds.

Bryan looked to Amy. "Go. We've got this."

Hendricks raced to get the car, pulling up just a minute later. Together they loaded Rocchio's body into the back.

By the time they were done, the first squad car came racing to the scene on the other side of the field.

Heavy doors clanked open. Shane walked out of the school, looking distraught.

"Where's my family?" Bryan asked, more harshly than he'd intended.

"I don't know. Have you seen L.G. or Lori?"

They scanned the sea of bodies.

"We'll find them," Shane said.

"Rocchio's dead."

The flesh on Shane's face pulled taut, and a brief fire burned in his eyes.

"He's in the back of Norm's car."

After a beat Shane said, "We'll deal with that later. First let's see if there's anyone here we can save."

It wasn't difficult to find someone in need of help. They did what they could, waiting for wide-eyed paramedics to arrive. No one asked them who they were. They simply took over.

The police were busy establishing some order, which was no easy task.

Terrified people streamed out of the businesses across the street. Bryan saw broken windows and doors. Aaron Chisolm cradled a young woman who had a hard time walking because of the bullet hole in her leg.

When Bryan saw his brother and father he felt as if he was going to collapse. L.G. and Lori were with them.

Then he saw David, Tomás, and Pam. The parents cradled what, from the distance, looked like a broken doll.

Bryan's heart stopped at the sight of little Lola.

He couldn't hear or feel Shane tugging at him, telling him it was time to go.

CHAPTER 39

Governor Alexa Bennington shook two pills out of the bottle into her palm. Todd and Colin Farmer sat on either side of her. There wasn't much to say. At least not privately. The press conference was scheduled to begin in ten minutes.

Bennington wasn't sure there would be enough time for the Xanax to take effect. If it didn't dull her enough, she'd have Colin go out and tell them she would be a few minutes late.

Nothing could have prepared her for this. It was one of the worst mass shootings in American history. And she had let it happen. Now she was about to go out there and lie through her teeth about it.

This was no time or place for an attack of good conscience. Nostrand Ganz had proven in one fell swoop that he could do anything he wanted with impunity. She and Todd were far from the only people he owned in one way or another.

Todd sat ashen-faced, staring at the conference table. When she'd suggested they cut and run he'd quickly reminded her there was no place on Earth where they would be safe. If they defied Ganz, he would find them, and they would die.

Colin checked his watch. "Five minutes. Are you good?"

Normally she would have snapped at him for even suggesting she wasn't on top of her game. Today she didn't know what to say. Her hands shook so much she had to place them under the table so neither Todd nor Colin could see.

Before her was a stack of printed index cards with everything she needed to say during the press conference. It had been prepared either by Ganz or one of his team. She was strongly advised not to stray from the message.

Hell, she wasn't even sure she could get the pre-written words out, much less go off script. But then again, to do such a thing was a death sentence.

There was a knock at the door.

Damien Arnstadt, the chief of police, looked as if he'd aged ten years overnight. He wasn't in on the plan, so he took full blame for the lack of police presence and a proper response.

"It's time," Arnstadt said.

Bennington took a deep breath, stood up, and straightened her skirt. She didn't bother looking at her husband as she walked out and to the podium. The room was packed with press, many of them men and women she'd never seen before; every national station was there for coverage.

The low murmur of voices hushed when she organized her index cards. Arnstadt adjusted the microphone for her.

"Today is a dark day not just for Iowa but America as well," she said, her voice quivering just a bit. "The entire country's thoughts and prayers are with the victims and their families as they wake up to a new day without the ones they love. Their worldview will never be the same, and they will never forget what they suffered through yesterday, and will continue to grapple with, all the days of their lives."

She took note of several reporters, men and women, with tears in their eyes. All but one of them was local.

"Unfortunately this is just another case of a growing sickness in America. The proliferation of powerful firearms and those with misguided principles is a deadly yet sadly common combination. In this particular instance, we now know that a group of white nationalists was behind yesterday's attack. They are the same group of vigilantes who have been referred to as the Night Warriors." She took a sip of water, hoping no one saw it tremble in her hands, then thinking showing such raw emotion would work in her favor. "This particular faction of domestic terrorists spread their roots in the town of Maverick, gaining people's trust just so they could take advantage of it. Little did anyone know what their ultimate plan could be. People lost faith in law and order and due process. Now death has come to Maverick. Some of the first to fall were four members of the Maverick Police Department.

"I want this to be clear: We will find every single one of these Night Warriors and bring them to justice.

And we want your help. If you see anything, reach out to your local authorities. We may not have the death penalty in Iowa, but rest assured when we capture the monsters who took the heart of our state away, murdered our children, mothers, fathers, and friends, we'll make sure to provide the next best thing."

Tears ran down Bennington's cheeks. She didn't bother wiping them away.

All eyes were on her. She could see she'd captured every heart, every soul, every human need for retribution.

She hoped Ganz saw that as well.

The tears were not for the fallen.

They were tears of fear . . . for her own life.

Bryan, Charlotte, and Shane stayed at the family farm.

Charlotte had given a pill to Pam to calm her down. She was asleep in bed, peaceful for the moment, but they all knew it wouldn't last.

David was quiet, sitting on the chair next to the bed, lost in his own thoughts.

Charlotte did her best to comfort Tomás, who was feeling the loss of his sister just as hard as his parents. He kept breaking into tears. Charlotte would hug him until he cried himself out.

In the living room Bryan, Jason, their father, and Shane had just watched the governor's press conference. George Branch was on his third whiskey. He looked old and frail and beaten.

"If Ganz were here in this living room, I'd kill him with my bare hands," Bryan said.

"Don't spare her," Shane said, pointing at the television. The live coverage of the press conference was giving way to nonstop reporting on the massacre.

"I still can't believe it happened," Jason said. An empty whiskey glass sat on his knee.

"Ganz and Bennington are wild dogs, and that's an insult to wild dogs," Shane said.

Bryan found it hard to talk. At that moment Lori was driving Bruno Rocchio's body to New York. He had no family, no one to mourn him. They all had left explicit instructions on what to do with their remains should they die in the line of fire.

Rocchio had a cabin in the Catskills that he used for rest and recovery. It was also where he hunted and fished and learned to love life again after the war. Lori, who was heartbroken but not beaten, was going to bury him there, by herself. She said she'd be back when it was done. There was unfinished business that needed to be attended to. Of that they were all in agreement.

Rocchio. Bryan had met few people with his fiery spirit. They'd all been saved by him more than once.

"So now what do we do?" Shane said.

Bryan ground his teeth until he tasted blood. "Hendricks and I are going to Des Moines to grab her chief of staff. If there's anything else in Ganz's plan, we need to know."

"I'll keep an eye on things here," Shane offered.

Right now little Lola's body sat in a cold locker at the funeral home. Bryan had told David he would pay for the funeral. No questions asked. He wasn't sure David had even heard him. Charlotte would have to go with them to the funeral home later today. He'd need Shane to stand guard at the farm. During the melee none of them had hidden their faces. They could all be targets now. It was why Amy, Easy, L.G., and Norm had checked out of their hotels and headed for Hay-Q.

"Thanks. Dad, are you going to be okay?"

His father finished his whiskey. He'd barely spoken in the past twenty-four hours.

"Kill them, Son. I don't care who it is or where they are. You need to make them pay."

Bryan took his empty glass away and grabbed onto his hand. "I plan on it."

CHAPTER 40

Knowing Colin Farmer would be pulling a late day considering all that had happened, Bryan and Hendricks decided to break into his house and wait for him. Farmer rented a tidy condo in an area full of up-and-comers and those in the political machine. Everyone was out, addressing the mass shooting, so getting into his place was not a problem. Any door cam or security camera they spotted was taken out with a BB gun Hendricks had brought along for just such a thing. The shots were quiet and did the trick.

Nothing was out of order in Farmer's place. In fact it barely looked like anyone lived there at all. His color palette was, as Bryan remarked, cowlike, with every-thing either black or white. His bed was made and the sink was clear of dishes. There were no photographs on the wall or books on shelves or night tables. It looked to them like a model home for a real estate agent. This was the dwelling of a man who did his living else-where.

Time passed with inexorable slowness. Bryan had to stop himself from checking his watch every minute. His nerves hummed and his brain was on fire. He needed to take all of this pent-up energy out on someone. It looked like Colin Farmer had drawn the short straw.

It was going on ten o'clock at night when they heard a key inserted into the front door lock. The condo was pitch-black. Hendricks hid in the kitchen while Bryan waited behind the couch. A light flicked on in the foyer and keys clanked in a ceramic bowl.

Farmer walked up the five stairs into the living room, unbuttoning his shirt and loosening his tie.

Bryan leaped from his hiding spot and tackled Farmer to the ground. Norm hustled out of the kitchen in case Bryan needed help.

Farmer curled into the fetal position. "Please! I don't want to die! I don't want to die!"

Bryan jerked him to his feet and tossed him onto the white leather couch. Hendricks zip-tied his wrists behind his back. While Farmer blubbered, Bryan smacked him across the face. Once. Twice. Three times, to get his full attention.

The living room was still in darkness, though some of the light from the foyer bled through so Bryan could see the snot pouring out of Farmer's nose.

"Please. I didn't say anything. I promise!" Farmer blubbered.

"Who do you think you're talking to?" Bryan said.

"I don't know. I won't tell anyone."

Bryan lashed out and grabbed Farmer by the throat. "You think we're some goons sent by Nostrand Ganz?"

Farmer took in a deep breath. "Wait. What?"

"That's right. We know all about Ganz and the

governor. And the parts we don't know you're going to tell us." He applied more pressure, choking off Farmer's sobs.

When he eased back Farmer spluttered, "Who are you? Are you the Night Warriors?"

"The people you framed," Hendricks said from behind him. He found a pressure point in Farmer's shoulder and dug his thumb until the chief of staff yelped. Bryan clamped his hand over his mouth.

"What else does Ganz have planned?"

Farmer shook his head. "I can't. He'll kill me."

"How about *we* kill you now?"

The familiar scent of urine filled the room.

"Tell us everything you know," Hendricks barked.

Farmer screwed his mouth up tight.

"Do you want more blood on your hands?" Bryan hissed. "Eight children, all of them under ten, were killed yesterday. And you and the governor knew about it. I hope their ghosts haunt you until the day you die. You want more on your conscience? Or do you want a chance at some redemption? You're still going to hell, you pissant, but try to do some good before you get there."

Panting, Farmer said, "I really can't. You saw what he did. He won't stop at me. I have a brother and sister. Parents."

Bryan loomed over the political assistant.

"You help us and you won't have to worry about the safety of your family."

Colin's eyes were as big and white as golf balls in the meager light.

"How can I know you're telling me the truth?"

"You can't," Bryan said. "So you either trust me or we get what we need out of you in ways you don't want to think about. You'll wish that Ganz got his hands on you."

It didn't take long for Farmer to break down. Hendricks took out the phone and recorded everything. When Farmer was done Bryan knocked Farmer out with a blow to the head and joined Hendricks in the kitchen.

"If he's telling the truth, I mean, sheesh," Bryan said.

Hendricks grabbed two bottles of expensive water from the refrigerator. "I can say we've faced worse before, but I'd be lying. We have to take on the world's richest most untouchable man. Right away. If we don't, too many people to count are going to die. Some right away. Others slowly."

There was no time to waste. Bryan used his water to splash on Farmer's face to wake him up.

"Let's go pack," he said to Farmer.

"Where are we going?"

"Wherever I say. And let me tell you one thing. If you're lying, I'm going to take great joy in making you suffer before I end you."

Sweat broke out all over Farmer's face. "I'm not lying. I swear."

Bryan shoved him into his room and allowed him to pack a bag.

The clock was ticking and there was a lot to do. Farmer had just confirmed their worst fears.

It was do-or-die time. How did you thwart a man

who had pockets deep enough to own every politician and one-percenter in the country?

Bryan had to remind himself that Nostrand Ganz, when you stripped away all of his money, was just a man.

And a man could die any time, in more ways to contemplate in a day.

"Where's the governor's chief of staff?" Charlotte asked as soon as they returned.

"I stuck him in a no-tell motel the next county over. I told him if he tries to slip away it will be the last thing he'll ever do. He's chicken-hearted. He'll do what he's told."

There was a somber air in the house impossible to miss. Charlotte said she had just gotten back from the funeral home with the Cruzes. David, Pam, and Tomás were in town looking for clothes to wear to Lola's funeral. Charlotte had to stop herself for a moment, her hand covering her face as she fought back tears. Bryan pulled her close. "I'm sorry. It's just that she was just a little girl. She had her whole life ahead of her."

He ran his fingers through her hair. "Unfortunately she's not the first innocent child we've seen murdered. All we can do now is stop it from happening to someone else."

Hendricks set his phone on the dining room table. "You have paper and a pen?"

Bryan directed him where to find it. Hendricks turned his phone on low and transcribed what Farmer had blubbered.

There was heavy clomping down the stairs. Jason popped in looking as if he hadn't slept in a week.

"We need to get everyone here," Bryan said.

"I'll do it," Hendricks said.

"How did it go in Des Moines?" Jason asked.

"We have a lot to share. I'm not going to hide it from you this time. Ganz declared war on Maverick. The only way to survive is to know what's coming."

Within the hour Amy, Easy, L.G., and Shane were at the house. Everyone looked ragged. They sat around the dining table with very little to say. Shane asked where George was. Jason said he'd gone out for a long drive to clear his head.

L.G. said, "I got a call from Sam. His podcast has been taken down because it was promoting terrorism. He says he's gotten at least fifty death threats. It's a good thing we have him hidden in Nebraska because someone broke into his apartment in Iowa and trashed the place."

"There goes the one avenue we have to promote the truth," Easy said.

"It doesn't matter anymore," Bryan said. "Fighting with words is over. We now have one mission: take out Ganz. The second we do, all of his plans fall to pieces."

"That's a pretty tall order," L.G. said.

"Yes, but not impossible. Entirely necessary but not impossible."

"Okay," L.G. said, "what does Ganz have planned?"

Bryan nodded for Hendricks to read his notes. Hendricks read them in a monotone, trying to keep the facts straight and not let his emotions get the better of him.

"My God," Amy said. "Ganz is certifiably insane."

"He's used to getting his way. We put a monkey wrench in his plans. Now he's like a spoiled child throwing a temper tantrum. Except this kid has the means to destroy everyone and everything in his path," Easy said.

All told, Ganz had outlined a five-step program to seize back control of Maverick and the state. The similarity to Mao's five-year plan wasn't lost on any of them. One lunatic offering an homage to another.

The first step had already been enacted with the massacre at the homecoming. In one stroke it demonized the Night Warriors, instilled crippling fear in the population, and took out the podcast. All trust was now funneled to Governor Bennington and the very police who people were decrying just a couple of years ago.

"We can't let them get to five," Charlotte said.

"We won't," Bryan replied. "Their next target is the food supply. That's supposed to happen tomorrow."

"Where is it again?" L.G. asked.

"Over in Gatling. It's a central hub not just for food production but trucking. He's going to blow up the whole damn thing and cut off food to most of western Iowa," Bryan said.

"How are they planning to do it? It would help to know so we can figure out a countermeasure," Amy said.

"Farmer didn't get any specifics. That kind of intel would only be for Ganz and his men. Now, the third operation is the one that sickens me. They're going to stage a slaughter at St. Matthew's Church. It's supposed to happen five days after the attack on the food supply, but I'm not counting on Ganz to sit on his hands that long if we stop them on step two. There are special masses being held every day now since the mass shooting, so each one is a potential window of opportunity for him."

There was a knock at the door. Everyone went silent.

Bryan crept to the living room window. Aaron Chisolm stood on the porch, not in uniform.

"Bryan, I know you're in there," he said when he knocked again. "I just want to talk."

Bryan looked over at Charlotte, who simply nodded. He opened the door.

Chisolm didn't seem surprised to see a dining room filled with strangers. He said hello to Jason.

"What can we do you for?" Bryan asked warily.

Chisolm, his face still bruised, looked Bryan in the eye and said, "I want to help. And it's not just me. We lost some very good people the other day. One of them was my daughter's godmother. We know this was a setup. Most of us were signed up for mandatory training on the other side of town. Now I know why. Detective Meyer was in charge of the training session. That skunk." His gaze drifted to someplace far away as his jaw muscles worked. "I saw you and some of your team there, stopping the shooters and saving lives. I know who you are, Bryan, and what you've been trying to do. Slaughtering innocent people isn't one of them. Now they have you pegged as the worst domestic terrorists in history. What can we do to help change that?"

No one spoke for an interminable amount of time.

Finally, Shane said, "Can we trust him?"

Bryan nodded. "Yes. Take a seat, Aaron. I just hope you're prepared. Your life will never be the same again."

CHAPTER 41

Lori Nicolo had called to let Bryan know Rocchio's body was where it belonged. He filled her in on their plan to stop Ganz's sickening five-point plan. She said she would be on the next plane out. She wouldn't get there in time for the offensive at the food processing center, but she would be at St. Matthew's.

The way Bryan figured it, if they were successful in stopping Ganz's men from blowing up the plant and trucks, he would immediately step up his timetable and send some men to St. Matthew's right away to murder everyone there and make citizens believe that even their religion, their very faith, couldn't protect them.

There was a mass scheduled for seven each night. The governor had put a curfew in place in the interest of keeping the citizens safe from the Night Warriors, who were still on the loose. Everyone had to be in their homes and off the streets by eight p.m. Ganz could attack them in the church or while they were racing to get home before curfew.

That meant Bryan had to divide the teams, which had grown considerably now that Aaron and seven other members of the Maverick PD had sworn to help. Bryan warned Aaron to tell his people to keep a tight lip. Not even spouses or significant others could know. One slip and everything could be ruined. There was no telling how many tentacles the governor and Ganz had spread throughout the town.

Shane drove the RV headed for Gatlin, which was a few hours east of Maverick. Charlotte, L.G., and Amy sat with Bryan around the galley table. Hendricks said he would meet them at the Park Valley plant, which provided the majority of canned goods through Iowa and its surrounding states. Canned food were essential items in times of crisis. Other parts of Ganz's plan were to strike at the power infrastructure once again. Fresh meats, fruits, and vegetables would spoil quickly. Without stockpiles of canned goods, the people of Iowa would starve. And who would they implore to save them? The very government that was complicit in their starvation.

Easy Campisi had stayed behind in Maverick and would coordinate things with Aaron and his people.

They did catch one break. Amy found out that Ganz did not have any type of ownership in Park Valley, which meant his team wouldn't have special access. It would be difficult but not impossible for his private army to waltz right in and hide bombs throughout the plant.

"Unless he's had this plan in motion for a while and has people already implanted there, I think we're safe in assuming his goons are going for an all-out strike today," L.G. said while he cradled a cup of hot coffee in his hands. The RV hit a bump in the road and some of it sloshed on his fingers. He didn't even wince.

"From your lips to God's ears," Charlotte said.

Taking the garish RV was essential because it was stockpiled with just about everything they'd need. They planned for the worst and hoped for the best.

They were a mile out from the plant and trucking station when Shane pulled the RV to the side of the road, which was littered with signs announcing that Park Valley was just up ahead. Diesel trucks passed them by in both directions.

"Busy day," Shane said.

"Nonstop. There are always a lot of mouths to feed," Bryan said.

He stepped outside the RV with his field glasses and used them to scan the sky. It was a clear day with barely any clouds. A slight breeze tickled the back of his neck.

Farmer hadn't given them a time. Just a day.

Bryan had assumed the strike would happen in the daytime, when things were at their busiest. They would also want witnesses to swear that it was the Night Warriors who had caused yet more destruction, even though they hadn't a clue what the Night Warriors looked like.

"See anything?" Charlotte said, suddenly beside him.

He put down his binoculars. "Nada. Looks like we just have to wait for them to make a grand entrance."

"I agree," L.G. said. "The flashier the better."

Bryan said, "This is the only road to the plant. When Ganz's men attack they'll have to pass us."

"But how will we know it's them?"

L.G. patted her shoulder. "Like I said, flashy."

They went back inside to do a full weapons check. If a patrol car pulled over to inquire if they were having any trouble, Bryan was prepared to subdue the officer. There was no room for interference at this point. Shane kept an eye on the road.

Bryan set four M16's with grenade launchers mounted below the barrels in a row. They also had one bazooka that he never dreamed they'd need while in Iowa. He still hoped it wouldn't be needed.

The RV was alive with the sound of sliding metal and the smell of gun oil.

They also took one opportunity to study the plant from images taken by Google Earth. Bryan had printed several of them and tacked them on one of the RV's walls.

They were ready.

Everyone's nerves were on edge. No one said a word. Amy went outside to get a better view of the road.

Even though it was a relatively cool day, sweat trickled down Bryan's face. The anticipation was always the worst.

Suddenly Amy slapped on the side of the RV and jumped inside.

"I think it's them," she said excitedly.

Everyone but Shane ran to look out the back window. He needed to get the RV running.

Bryan saw what was coming down the road and said, "I'll be damned if that's not them."

Four black Hummers, keeping very little space between them, zipped past the RV. The wind they kicked up rocked the bus.

Shane let them get ahead for just a little bit before pulling onto the road.

"Are there any more?" he called out.

"Just the four up ahead," Charlotte replied.

Bryan dialed Hendricks. "Where the hell are you? We have four Hummers a mile out from the plant."

"I'm right behind them," Hendricks said.

Bryan ran to the front of the RV and saw a yellow Corvette between them and the Hummers.

"You brought a Corvette to a gunfight?"

"I have my reasons."

Bryan ended the call. "Suit up. The party's about to begin."

Bryan and his team put on their Kevlar vests and masks. They wore olive drab overalls so they wouldn't be confused with Ganz's team. It was assumed that his soldiers for hire would stick with the camouflage that they'd worn at the homecoming massacre. That had become the unofficial uniform of the "Night Warrior terrorist group."

As they got closer to the plant, the Hummers picked up speed. Hendricks pulled to the other lane and let the RV overtake him.

"I'm thinking these guys don't have passes to get in," Shane said, pushing down on the accelerator.

"Always more than one way to get through a gated entrance," Amy said.

"Everybody buckle up."

"There aren't any seat belts back here," Charlotte said.

"Then hold on to your butts!"

Bryan saw it unfold:

The first Hummer smashed through the wooden gate, sending shards in every direction.

The second clipped the guardhouse, crumpling the metal. Whoever was inside would be lucky to be alive. The third and fourth passed through the obliterated gap with ease.

"Keep close to them," Bryan urged Shane. He assumed Ganz's foot soldiers had tunnel vision at the moment: just get to the plant and destroy it.

Unfortunately, once inside the perimeter, the Hummers split into two groups. Two of them went around toward the back of the plant itself. The other two headed for the enormous lot where the trucks were kept.

Bryan dialed Hendricks and told Shane to stop. The Corvette pulled up alongside the RV. L.G. flung open the door and handed Hendricks an M16 and a duffel bag of other things he might need.

"I'm going with you," L.G. said. "We'll take out the Hummers going to the truck lot."

Norm had the Corvette going before L.G. could shut the door.

The Park Valley grounds were a hive of frantic activity. An alarm bell sounded off in the distance and people came running to the front entrance to assess the damage. Shane almost clipped a couple of security guards as he sped around them.

The plant itself was massive. It could easily double

as a hangar for multiple dirigibles, jumbo jets, and more. They raced along its west side, looking for the black Hummers.

"There they are," Shane said, pointing out the front window.

Sure enough, the Hummers had stopped close to one of the loading docks.

Eight doors opened simultaneously.

The men who clambered out were, as Bryan's father would say, *loaded for bear*. Hand grenades were strapped across their chests. All carried heavy weaponry. Bryan saw grenade launchers on their rifles as well. They were wearing the same camo gear they had at the homecoming massacre.

What they didn't have were eyes on the backs of their heads.

Bryan, L.G., Amy, and Charlotte were out of the RV before it fully stopped. Charlotte fired tear gas in the direction of Ganz's soldiers.

People working at the plant saw them and the men in camouflage and went running.

Amy fired more tear gas at the soldiers for hire.

Bryan and his team flipped down their masks so they weren't affected.

Smoke filled the space between them.

A random shot was fired. The window of a nearby truck exploded.

Bryan's team took cover behind cars and trucks, all while rapidly advancing.

One of Ganz's men was down, gasping for air. He

saw Bryan and struggled to lift his rifle. Bryan took him out with a shot to the head.

With so many people running about, they had to be precise about who they were shooting at. Yes, the tear gas was good at slowing the men down, but the ensuing fog added a layer of difficulty they could do without.

Shane was the first to get close to one of the Hummers. He fired at the tires, puncturing them. The windows did not break at first. Although a few rounds from an M16 at close range was enough to finally shatter the bullet-proof glass.

Amy snuck ahead and went about disabling the other Hummer.

Keeping low so they could see the legs of Ganz's men, Bryan and Charlotte dropped to their bellies and aimed for ankles. Three men went down as geysers of blood erupted from their calves and ankles.

A harsh wind came out of nowhere, clearing the area of smoke.

Four men turned to face Bryan and his team. They fired at them in desperation. Bryan rolled behind a car and saw a man in a suit who had been running away grab his lower back and fall face forward.

Things turned into a standoff, with both sides exchanging fire.

Whenever there was a slight break Bryan could hear the echo of gunshots in the distance. He hoped Hendricks and L.G. were all right.

Shane was nestled behind the lead Hummer. He caught Bryan's eye.

"Any civies over there?"

Bryan did a quick check before bullets banged off the roof of the car he was crouched behind.

"Looks clear," Bryan said.

Shane pulled the pin on a grenade, popped out from behind the Hummer, and tossed the device at the men. One of them spotted Shane and fired.

Bryan's friend spun and went down.

The grenade went off. Bryan looked up just in time to see two men tossed in the air.

At the moment he didn't care about them. He ran to Shane.

A rain of bullets chewed up the asphalt lot, cutting a path straight to Bryan. He kept running, adrenaline masking the pain in his bad knee, pushing him forward.

Amy and Charlotte opened fire on the remaining men, giving Bryan good cover.

A man screamed in agony. The shooting stopped.

"Shane!"

His friend was unconscious. Bryan looked for blood but couldn't find any. But he did see a hole in Shane's overalls. He'd taken a bullet to his chest, but the Kevlar vest stopped it from burrowing into his heart. He must have hit his head when he fell and knocked himself out.

"Clear!" Amy shouted.

Charlotte stood over Bryan and Shane, still keeping an eye out.

"Is he . . ."

"He's fine. I think. We need to get him back to the RV."

Charlotte set her rifle on her shoulder and helped Bryan drag Shane to the RV.

Amy came running to them. She was shouting, "Everyone, get out of here! Now!"

There weren't many people around, but a few, brave and curious, had come to see the aftermath now that the shooting had stopped.

Bryan popped open the RV door and lugged the top half of Shane inside.

"What's going on?" he asked Amy.

"One of the Hummers is loaded with explosives. It's about to blow."

Charlotte and Amy pushed to get Shane inside. Bryan jumped into the driver's seat and keyed the ignition. "Hold on!"

He slammed the gear in reverse and plowed through everything in the RV's way. He made it about thirty yards before the Hummer went up in a mushrooming fireball. A shard of metal from the hummer hit the RV's front window. It blew out the glass and smashed the closed door to the back bedroom.

The exterior of the plant was charred. Nearby vehicles were on fire, but it looked as if the car bomb hadn't done any structural damage.

Bryan cut the wheel and made a 180-degree turn.

"We're not done yet."

CHAPTER 42

Hendricks pulled the Corvette between a row of trucks. Then he and L.G. jumped out and ran at the two Hummers. All of the Hummers' windows were down with muzzles poking out of them.

L.G. fired at the Hummers. Small holes pockmarked the back windows, but they didn't give in. Hendricks dropped to a knee and strafed the vehicles with his AR15.

A hail of bullets screamed their way. They had to tumble until they were hidden behind a row of cars.

"No time for games," Hendricks said.

"Nope."

They leaped from their hiding place, firing grenades at the Hummers.

Both lifted off the ground for a moment before crashing down in a fury of black smoke. A couple of doors flew open. Several men spilled out, clutching their weapons and looking for a target or just plain dazed. L.G. and Hendricks picked them off before they could regain their senses.

"I bet they thought this would be like shooting fish in a barrel," Hendricks said.

"Sometimes the fish shoot back," L.G. replied.

They cautiously approached the damaged Hummers.

Inside, men coughed and struggled to regain their bearings. One driver was bleeding from the head and clearly in shock, his eyes locked on the cracked steering wheel.

L.G. took one Hummer and Hendricks the other. They fired into each until every man was dead.

All around them people were screaming and running.

"They're going to think we're the bad guys," L.G. said.

The high-pitched whine of multiple first responders sounded off in the distance. Before they knew it, this place would be crawling with police.

"We'd better make like trees and leave," Hendricks quipped.

They turned to run back to the Corvette when Shane's ridiculous RV came barreling down the lot. Hendricks offered up a silent prayer of thanks.

Charlotte jumped out of the side door when the RV stopped.

"Did you get them all?"

"Did you doubt us?" Hendricks said. "I have a date later. I can't afford to fail."

L.G. rolled his eyes.

Just then they felt and heard the steady whump of a military helicopter. When they looked up they spotted what looked to be a matte black Apache Guardian.

They had taken into account the possibility of Ganz

making an air attack. The combination of ground and air forces would guarantee the total destruction of the facility.

Bryan and Amy jumped out of the RV carrying a pair of rocket launchers.

"Where is it?" Bryan shouted.

Hendricks and L.G. pointed to the north. The chopper was seconds away from flying directly over their heads.

Bryan and Amy got to their knees and steadied the rocket launchers on their shoulders. In the desert Hendricks remembered Amy was a crack shot with rocket launchers, but then, she was shooting at tanks. Hitting a fast-moving object overhead was no easy task.

"Let's help them out," Hendricks said.

He, L.G., and Charlotte aimed at the Apache and started firing. Hopefully a shot might take out the rotor and send the helicopter into a death spiral. The biggest concern was where it would crash. There would be destruction, of that there was no doubt. If they were lucky, it would be minimal, especially compared to what Ganz had in mind.

With twin whooshes, Bryan and Amy set their HEAT rounds at the Apache just as it passed over them.

Bryan's shot went wide, just missing the helicopter.

Amy's hit it dead center, piercing the armor plating.

The Apache exploded from the inside out in a rain of fire, smoke, and sparks.

The forward momentum of the helicopter hurtled it over the processing plant as the Apache spun, flinging off parts in every direction.

They watched it descend, hitting into the back corner

of a parking lot that seemed to be mostly empty save a few cars. The ground shook when the Apache smashed and broke apart. Oily black smoke billowed into the air.

Bryan was on his haunches, staring at the smoke. "Please don't tell me there are any more."

Hendricks checked the sky. It was clear.

He fished in his pocket and tossed a set of keys to Bryan.

"What are these for?"

"The Corvette. You and Charlotte get back to Maverick as fast as it'll take you."

L.G. took the rocket launcher from Bryan's hands. He was about to stow it in the RV when Shane stumbled down the steps rubbing the back of his head. "What did I miss?"

The whine of sirens from police cars, fire trucks, and ambulances were very close now.

"We got 'em," Bryan said.

Shane's face went from a grimace to a grin. "Time to erase our tracks."

"I'll get us a truck," L.G. said, dashing down the row and opening the door to the first truck he saw.

"We're going to Maverick," Bryan told Shane.

"We'll see you there."

"Don't let him drive," Bryan said to Hendricks. "He's still woozy."

"You bet. Now go."

Bryan and Charlotte piled into the Corvette. Just as he peeled out, there was a tremendous boom. He saw the RV explode in his rearview mirror in a great ball of flame.

"He loved that RV," Bryan said.

"Yes, but I think he wanted to hit the self-destruct button even more," Charlotte reassured him. "Like something out of one of his comic books."

Part Two of Ganz's master plan had been foiled. Now Bryan hoped he could get to Maverick in time to stop the next.

CHAPTER 43

Easy Campisi met Lori at the Branch farm. She looked exhausted, with dark bags under her eyes.

"How're you holding up?" he asked her.

"I'm standing," she replied.

"You good to do this?"

She patted his chest. "Don't worry about me. I'm good. In fact, I need this."

Easy saw the blisters on her hands from digging Rocchio's grave. Yes, she did need this.

He looked back at the house as he pulled away. He didn't know where the Branches and Cruzes had gone. They weren't there when he'd arrived an hour ago. He didn't need the extra agita. His nerves were keyed to the max without losing track of Bryan's family.

He'd gotten word that they had stopped the attack on the food processing plant. Charlotte had sent a quick text to let them know they were heading to Maverick.

The news was crammed with stories of an attack on the Park Valley Processing Plant. So far there was one reported dead employee, the front gate guard, and several injured. Reports were confusing as to the nature of the attack. For now, the throughline was that the Night Warriors had struck again.

That was quick, Easy thought.

No one spoke about the soldiers for hire that Bryan and the team had cut down. Would they eventually say the corpses were those of the Night Warriors? Easy would bet good money that would be the case.

They pulled into St. Matthew's Church lot. There were several cars already parked there.

Aaron Chisolm emerged from his car and waved Easy over.

"I heard the radio. Sounds like one hell of a fight out there," Aaron said.

"Yeah, well, the good guys won. Not that you'll probably ever hear that part."

Lori stared at the giant cross on the peak of the church. "Of all the places for a lunatic to want to destroy."

"Madmen with no religion, no morals, have been trying to tear down the faith of the people for as long as there's been hope," Easy said. "You ready for this?" he asked Chisolm.

"Yep. I have four of my people stationed at the shelter. We have everyone in the bathrooms for now. Sturdiest rooms in the building."

They walked to the church's double oak doors. "Good. We don't know if Ganz will strike there, but we can't take a chance with so many women, children, and elderly."

"Agreed."

The doors opened and heads turned in their direction.

Easy's guts coiled like a snake. Lori groaned beside him.

"You can't be here," he said, his voice pinging off the church walls.

Jason and George Branch, David and Pam Cruz sat in a pew together. This was the last place they were supposed to be. If Bryan knew, he'd take Easy behind the woodshed.

"This is our church. Our town," Jason said. He lifted the shotgun he'd had by his feet. "It's time we did some fighting for it."

Easy looked around. "Where's Tomás? Please don't tell me you brought him here."

"He's safe," Jason said. "I dropped him off at a neighbor's house."

Easy shook his head at them. David and Pam stared back unapologetically.

"You've all put me in a tight spot."

"We're sorry about that. But it's our decision and it's final," George said.

Easy scratched his head and did his best to hold back his frustration. After pounding his fist against the back of a pew he said, "Okay, Lori, you stay at the door and wait for either my sign or the sound of anything out of the ordinary."

She patted her AR15 and headed for the narthex.

Father Rooney approached them from the altar. He made the sign of the cross over Easy and Chisolm. "Do we know for sure it will happen tonight?" he asked.

"No, Father," Easy replied. "It's a hunch based on dealing with other megalomaniacs in the past."

The priest looked around the pristine church. "She may never be the same, will she?"

"We'll make sure they don't make it inside. I can't guarantee there won't be damage to the exterior. The most important thing is that your parishioners are safe and we stop this maniac."

Without hesitation Father Rooney said, "Yes. You're absolutely right. Officer Chisolm said I should go to the shelter until everything is over."

"That's for the best. And please make sure you stress to everyone to stay where they are when they hear the sh . . . it . . . I mean you-know-what hit the fan. We don't want anyone taken out by a stray bullet."

The priest nodded gravely. "Of course. Of course."

"Now, let's get everyone on the same page," Easy said to Chisolm.

Easy told them he would stake out a position outside the church. Everyone else was to stay inside until it was time to spring their trap.

Ganz would surely push up the timeline for the church attack. The maniac would need it to heal his wounded ego.

Easy wished the rich snot were here, right in front of him. He'd fix his wagon but good.

He was jolted from his ruminations by the arrival of

a white van. Its windows were tinted so dark, he couldn't see inside. Never a good sign.

The van parked in a handicap spot and idled.

Another van, this one black, turned into the lot and found a spot by the exit. It too idled, exhaust spiraling from the tailpipe.

He slipped his finger on the trigger.

"Come on, show yourselves," he muttered. He had the white van in the sights of his AR15. If anyone looked slightly suspicious, he was opening fire.

Time passed by like cold molasses. Easy took deep breaths and settled himself. Being too amped when you had to pull the trigger was bad for a shooter's health. Easy pictured himself taking everyone out before they got a foot on the first step.

Envision success and it was sure to follow.

Easy read the setup. The men in the white van would storm the church. Those in the black van would cut down anyone who tried to leave.

It was Easy's job to stop the white van from making it inside the church. Once the shooting started, everyone in the church would take care of the rest.

The side door of the white van slid open.

A man wearing gray and black camo jumped out, an assault rifle in his hands.

Looking back at the church Easy thought, *You have to protect this place. Don't let them get too close.*

Allowing the soldiers for hire to get closer would have been the tactical move. But St. Matthew's meant so much to the rebuilding of Maverick, he had to take the hard way.

Easy didn't waste any time. He fired at the man's neck, sure that he was wearing Kevlar to protect his center mass.

The man fell back into the van, blood spurting from the wound.

For a breathless moment there was silence.

Then five men burst out of the van firing in Easy's direction. The assault was thunderous and unrelenting. The stone wall he'd hidden behind rapidly chipped away. Easy raised his gun and fired blindly in their direction.

Just as suddenly the gunfire stopped.

Easy took a quick look and felt his blood turn to ice.

He barely had time to duck before the grenade screamed his way. He felt the impact for just a moment before everything went dark and numb.

Lori heard the buzz saw of automatic fire and grabbed one of the door handles. Wood splintered as a round went through the door.

Everyone in the pews ducked.

"Get ready, everyone!" she shouted.

Chisolm and his four fellow police officers, none in uniform, along with the Branches and Cruzes, gathered their weapons and hustled to the narthex. They waited breathlessly as Lori held up her fist, making eye contact with everyone. She almost preferred handling the rest on her own. Worrying about the lives of everyone was something she'd have to push to the back of her mind.

Chisolm got his hand on the other door handle. On the count of three, they threw the doors wide open.

Several men in fatigues, armed to the teeth, were running to the front steps.

The defenders spilled out of the church firing away.

A soldier taking bullets but still on his feet jogged forward with a grenade in his hand. Lori took off the top of his head before he could pull the pin.

Both sides exchanged fire. One of Chisolm's men cried out and rolled down the concrete steps, leaving a trail of blood.

Four of Ganz's men littered the ground, leaking blood from numerous holes. Three others broke off and ran around either side of the church.

"We'll cover the back," David Cruz said. He tapped his wife, George, and Jason, and had them follow him into the church. There was a back door to the sacristy that would be easy to break through. Lori thought she saw blood on Pam Cruz's arm.

Where the hell is Easy? Lori thought. The answer was obvious and not one she could linger on.

"You take that side with her," Lori said to Chisolm, pointing to one of his officers. She grabbed the other one, a tall man with forearms replete with tattoos. "You, come with me. Be quick but cautious. They may be waiting for us to pop our heads around the corner."

Taking the lead, Lori kept her back to the church façade and did a quick peek. Two of Ganz's men were partially behind a pair of trash cans, guns pointed her way. A shot rang out, and Lori's face was hit by shrapnel from exploding brick.

"Damn."

She was thinking about a way to sneak up behind them when she spotted the black van.

It reversed for a few feet, then headed straight for the church.

Lori fired into the van. The bullets didn't penetrate the windshield.

It kept on coming.

Lori and the police officer let loose.

A man sitting in the passenger seat rolled down his window and returned fire. It went high over their heads. He adjusted, and just as Lori dropped to the ground, the officer's head went back as he was hit.

Lori kept her ground, aiming for the tires.

She spotted a yellow Corvette out of her periphery. It came screeching across the parking lot. Seconds later it smashed into the van, pushing it off course and into a parked car.

Charlotte and Bryan jumped out of the crumpled Corvette. The airbags had deployed, and it looked as if it had broken their noses.

Bryan and Charlotte, backing away from the van, opened fire on the gas tank.

The van exploded, the back end flipping up until the van collapsed on its roof. A man was thrown from the side door. Charlotte shot him before he could get up.

The rest burned with the van.

Lori's head whipped around at the crack of gunfire behind her. Taking a chance, she stepped from the safety of the building to look down the alley. The soldiers that had been waiting for her were down. One of the stained glass window panes was flipped open. She saw the barrel of a rifle retreat back into the church.

"Are there any more?" Bryan asked when he spotted Lori.

"Maybe one. He might be on the other side of the church or in back by now," she replied. "I also can't find Easy."

There was a crackle of gunfire reverberating within the church. Lori, Bryan, and Charlotte ran up the steps and burst through the open doorway.

Jason and George Branch were in the center aisle with their rifles pointed at the altar. One of Ganz's men lay in a crumpled heap beside the baptismal font.

Pam Cruz had a foot in her husband's hand and was being lowered from one of the side windows. When he set her down he tore off his shirt to wrap it around her bleeding arm.

"What the hell are you doing here?" Bryan asked.

"Just following your lead, Big Brother." Jason wrapped Bryan and Charlotte into a bear hug.

George Branch dropped his rifle and grabbed Bryan's shoulders. No words were spoken, but everything that needed to be said was conveyed loud and clear.

A shadow passed over them. All turned to see someone standing in the narthex. The man fired at them with a pistol. Jason grunted before crashing into a pew.

George Branch lifted his rifle and fired back. The figure doubled over seconds before collapsing face-first.

Bryan dropped to his bad knees to check on his brother.

"It burns," Jason said, wincing. "I thought getting shot would hurt more."

"Welcome to the club, Bigfoot. Just stay still," Bryan

said, pulling off his shirt and folding it up so he could apply pressure. Outside, they heard sirens. "You're gonna be okay. Ambulances are on their way."

George Branch touched the top of Jason's head, made sure he was going to be okay, and then turned to Lori.

He walked to the narthex as if in a dream. Lori followed him.

Dead on the ground was a middle-aged man. Lori saw the badge clipped to his belt.

"Detective Meyer," George said. "Can't say he didn't earn this."

George turned away from the cooling corpse and rejoined his family while Lori went out to look for Easy. She found his mangled body, fell to her knees, and wept silently.

CHAPTER 44

Governor Alexa Bennington and her husband Todd sat numbly across from each other, nursing their drinks. The news from the previous day had rocked them to their core.

As much as Bennington had spent the day pushing the message that the Night Warriors were responsible for all of the death and destruction throughout Iowa's darkest day, people still questioned the story.

If the Night Warriors had tried to bomb the food plant and church, what group had stopped them? Despite Bennington praising the quick thinking and brave actions of the police, acting on an anonymous tip in each instance, implying the Night Warriors had a traitor in their midst, a quick poll showed that people weren't buying it.

"Lousy Farmer," Bennington seethed.

Colin had not shown up for work. Conveniently, he'd disappeared right before Ganz's plans had gone to hell. It didn't take a genius to put it all together. She wondered now if District Attorney Donnegan had flipped as well.

She couldn't wait to serve the traitorous cowards to Ganz on a silver platter.

Anything to take the attention off her.

Penny Hastings was gone as well, but that wasn't a bad thing. Her email stating she couldn't handle the stress was just about right for her generation.

"I'll say it again, Todd. We need to get the hell out of here."

Her husband rose from his leather chair and poured himself another drink. "And I've told you a thousand times, there's nowhere to go. We just need to do whatever Ganz asks of us."

She leaned forward. "I'm no bleeding heart liberal, but Lordie, this is insane! And I'm the one who has to keep showing my face, toeing this ridiculous line, while you sit back here and drink yourself to death. Why don't you be a man for once?"

"Acting hysterical won't get you anywhere," Todd said. "We're in this until the end. The only way to get to the end is to go all the way through, no matter how unpleasant it is."

"Hell, if I could deed the entire state to Ganz, I'd do it with pleasure and just be done with this."

"I'm sure you would."

The man's voice startled them. Todd Bennington dropped his glass.

"Who the hell are you?" Alexa Bennington demanded.

A man and a woman entered the study. They had surgical tape over their bent noses and black eyes. The woman closed the door and kept her back to it.

"Why, we're the white nationalist terrorists who want

to upend democracy," the man said. He motioned with his hand for Todd to take a seat. "Now, let's all have a nice talk."

Bryan wished he'd taken a picture of the Benningtons' faces when he and Charlotte traipsed into their cozy study.

He'd been right to assume Ganz would have some of his men posted at the mansion. In fact there were two. One was posted outside, patrolling the grounds. While Charlotte distracted him, acting like a political protestor, complete with a sign demanding Bennington tell the truth about what had happened, Lori came up behind him and slit his throat.

Bryan and Charlotte subdued a kitchen worker when he came out to throw away the garbage. Hendricks hefted the man on his back and carried him away.

They found the other Ganz guard in the hallway. He had his finger on his earpiece and was calling for the soldier for hire they had taken out.

When Bryan and Charlotte stepped into the hallway the man spun, gun in hand. Even with silencers, they worried the multiple rounds they put in the man would alert the staff or Bennington.

"Must be nice to have a house so big you can't hear someone getting shot," Charlotte said as they grabbed his body by the ankles and dragged him to a closet. Using towels they found in a nearby bathroom, they mopped up the blood as best they could.

Now it was just them and the pathetic Benningtons.

"Is there a lock for this door?" Charlotte asked.

Alexa looked at her as if she'd spoken an alien language.

"We would like to lock the door," Bryan said. "Tell us how."

The governor narrowed her eyes at him and then pointed at a desk. "There's a key in the top drawer."

Bryan pulled his pistol from his pocket. "First things first. If you scream, I'll shoot you both. We clear on that?"

Both heads nodded.

Charlotte found the key and locked the door.

"What's your name?" the governor asked with a bit of steel in her voice. He had to give her credit, she had some balls.

"That's none of your business."

"The Night Warriors sounds a tad ridiculous, don't you think? Sounds more like a bad B movie to me."

Bryan grinned, and that clearly wiped the cocky look off her face. "I have a name for you that you need to be very, very concerned about."

She arched an eyebrow. "Oh? And what's that?"

"Nostrand Ganz."

Her cool veneer cracked. Todd Bennington swallowed audibly.

"I have it on good authority that he's on his way here. And the men he left to guard you? They won't be able to save you between now and when he arrives."

Alexa's face paled.

Amy Thomas was able to track Ganz's private plane through some very deep channels. So deep, she'd told

Bryan, that she'd used up every favor with that contact. The plane had landed about an hour ago. His car and security detail should be there any moment.

"You and I both have a problem," Bryan said. "Ganz is unstable. For all his successes, he destroys far more than he builds. We know he wants Iowa. Hell, he wants every state under his control. You thought you could benefit from his ambition, but I have a sneaking suspicion you're now aware that an invading disease like Ganz consumes everything it comes in contact with."

Alexa Bennington said nothing. He wondered if she thought he might be wired. It didn't matter.

"First, I need you to dismiss your staff right now. When Ganz gets here you're to let him in as if your lives don't depend on it."

"You think two of you can take on his goon squad?"

Bryan pointed his gun at Alexa Bennington's forehead. "Who said there are only two of us?"

Todd Bennington erupted from his chair. "Get that gun away from my wife!"

"Sit down!" Bryan barked. Todd Bennington complied quickly, visibly relieved that he had played the part of the protective husband without getting killed in the process. "Now, contact your staff and tell them to clock out for the night."

The governor's husband fumbled with his phone, texting, while Charlotte stood over his shoulder to make sure he wasn't sending any messages for help.

Now all they could do was wait.

"You look nervous. Have a drink," Bryan said, pouring whiskies for the Benningtons.

"Are we supposed to pretend you're not going to kill us?" Alexa said, her hand trembling slightly as she brought the glass to her lips. "We've seen your faces after all."

Bryan sat on the edge of a table. "We're here for Ganz. We free you from his grip, you forget we were ever here. And you may want to consider resigning as governor ASAP."

"It's that simple, is it?"

"It can be. Depends on you."

After an interminable wait the bell rang downstairs. No one moved.

"Are you going to answer it?" Charlotte asked.

Alexa and Todd looked to each other, the fear in their eyes paralyzing them.

Bryan waved his pistol at the governor. "Time to get up." He took the glasses from their hands.

Alexa rose from her chair while Charlotte unlocked the door. Todd was shaky, but he managed to follow his wife.

Bryan and Charlotte followed them, stopping at the top of the winding staircase. The governor paused on the first step and looked back at them.

"Go on," Bryan said.

They looked like two inmates walking death row.

The doorbell kept chiming.

"Someone is impatient," Bryan said to Charlotte.

"That makes two of us."

Alexa Bennington opened the door.

"Nostrand," she said in a serious tone.

Four men in black suits poured through the door. The

almost-trillionaire hustled past the couple, surrounded by his men.

"I am not happy. Not happy at all," Ganz hissed through gritted teeth. "Do you know how many men I lost? How much this is going to cost me to keep the truth from coming out?"

Bennington flicked a glance to the stairway. Bryan caught her eye.

"The Night Warriors are here!" she shouted, pointing at them.

Bryan and Charlotte had been waiting for that.

Ganz's men opened fire. Bryan heard a round whine just past his ear. He and Charlotte ducked, peppered with shrapnel as the automatic fire demolished the wall behind them and the staircase railing.

Bryan took a quick look into the vestibule. One man had draped himself over Ganz like a human shield while the other three reloaded. They were all clearly wearing bulletproof vests. The Benningtons had fled the scene.

In the brief silence he heard Ganz shout, "Kill them! Kill them!"

He wasn't sure if Ganz meant him and Charlotte, the Benningtons, or both. Most likely it was both. Kill a couple of Night Warriors and the governor and you could wrap the whole thing with a tidy bow.

Bryan stood up. "Hey, Nostrand. You hire *The Gang That Couldn't Shoot Straight*?"

Three rifles jerked up in his direction.

Three men jittered as their bodies were strafed from top to bottom before hitting the floor.

L.G., Amy, and Hendricks stormed into the mansion.

The guard protecting Ganz stood up. L.G. took him out with a clean head shot.

All that was left was Ganz.

He stood up, looked about at the chaos and destruction, and adjusted his sport coat.

Craning his neck to address Bryan, he said, "You must be the leader of your Night Warriors, or whatever you call yourselves. I have to admit, despite my anger at the situation over the past several weeks, I am impressed. I would like to hire you, seeing as you've bested my own lacking team of soldiers."

"Not interested," Bryan spat.

"Don't say that before you hear my offer. I can make all of you richer beyond your wildest imaginings."

Bryan raised his Glock. "Can your money bring my mother back?"

Ganz cocked his head, confused. "I'm sorry. What are you talking about?"

Bryan squeezed the trigger, and Ganz's arms splayed as the side of his head exploded. He fell on his back in a Christlike pose.

Hendricks kicked Ganz's arms to his sides. "That's more like it."

Bryan and Charlotte descended the stairs. The clock was ticking. Even though the mansion was a good distance from any neighbors, someone had to hear the shooting and call the police.

The clatter of footsteps caught his attention. Lori

marched Alexa and Todd Bennington to the bloody vestibule.

"I found a couple of runners," Lori said, deadpan.

Todd Bennington stared at the bleeding bodies in complete shock. "You . . . you killed Nostrand."

"I sure did," Bryan replied.

"You'll never get away with this!" Alexa Bennington said. "Do you think you can murder the richest man in the world and just waltz out of here? The president will hunt you down for the rest of your lives."

Bryan looked at his wife. "I didn't vote for him," Charlotte said.

"Me neither."

And then Alexa Bennington did something no one expected.

She whirled around and managed to pull Lori's rifle from her hands.

Before she could turn the weapon on Bryan and his team, Charlotte pulled her trigger twice. The Benningtons hit the floor, collapsing in a tangle of limbs.

Bryan looked down at their bodies, piled so close to Ganz. "I'd feel bad about lying that we'd let her and Todd go, but when a dog goes rabid, there's only one thing to do."

Shane ran into the mansion and eyed the chaos. "I heard on the scanner that the police are mobilizing. We have to go."

"Anyone left outside?" Charlotte asked.

"Not anymore. Burn it?" Shane asked.

"Like the biggest bonfire in Iowa history," Bryan said. He took Charlotte's hand in his and walked to the great lawn while Shane and the others got to work. Thirty seconds later the house went up with a great whup.

Standing in the grass for a moment, they watched the purification of his home state and beyond.

CHAPTER 45

Three weeks later, the murders of Nostrand Ganz and Governor Bennington and her husband were still at the top of the news. As were the Night Warriors. The usual sides were either for or against their actions. Without Ganz or the Benningtons around to control the narrative, stories of their sordid pasts started to infiltrate the news streams. Ganz especially was beginning to look like the monster others had been claiming him to be at the risk of their reputations and livelihoods when he was alive.

Bryan paid little attention to it all.

In those three weeks they had laid Lola Cruz to rest. Many tears were shed, and the healing seemed to have a long way to go to even begin.

Pam's injury was minor, the bullet digging a furrow into her arm. Her grief didn't allow for the pain to register.

George Branch told the Cruzes his home was their home for as long as they wanted. He spent long afternoons with Tomás, teaching him how to build a birdhouse,

mend the fences, and do any kind of general repair
around the house and farm.

"Busy hands help heal wounded minds," George said
to Bryan one night. "That harvest saved me when your
mother died."

Jason was recovering from his bullet wound and
wore a sling. Bone chips had to be removed from his
shoulder and there was talk of reconstructive surgery,
but that was for a later day. For now he used his survival
at the church shoot-out to woo Erin, the former fitness
coach. It seemed to be working because he'd taken her
out on three dates in the past week.

"You have everything packed?" Charlotte asked
Bryan. He looked at the open suitcases on the bed.

"Whatever I forget I can always replace."

Charlotte shut the window behind him. The air was
getting chilly and the sun was out without a cloud in
the sky.

She put her arms around him.

"I'm going to miss this place."

"I am, too. Funny how I never thought I'd want to be
here again. And now all I want to do is stay."

Since the shoot-out they had kept themselves within
the confines of the house, careful not to be seen by
anyone who might come by the farm. The only person
to pay them a visit was Aaron Chisolm. He and his
surviving officers were to receive medals of commen-
dation from the interim governor for stopping Ganz's
men at St. Matthew's Church. As far as the official
statements went, the Night Warriors were nowhere to
be seen that night. Bryan was sure it pained Father

Rooney to lie, but it was for a worthy cause. That was what confession was for.

"Is it strange to say I'm going to miss you and be glad you're gone?" Chisolm said to Bryan.

Bryan could only laugh. "Nope."

They had a beer and Aaron bid them goodbye.

Charlotte closed up the suitcases and stared out the window. "I keep expecting to see Shane's hideous RV out there."

"Not unless some of those pieces blew all the way over from the food processing plant."

After secreting Easy's body away, Shane, Lori, L.G., and Hendricks had slipped quietly out of Iowa. Before they left they had a sort of retirement party at the Last Rodeo Bar and Grill. The absence of Rocchio and Easy was impossible to ignore. They toasted them round after round, recalling some of their wilder exploits. Lori wavered between crying and laughing. When the night was over they hugged one another, knowing it would be the last time for quite a long while, if not forever.

With so much attention on the capture of the Night Warriors, they had decided it was time to retire. That meant each was heading off to a safe quiet foreign destination that had always been part of their plans.

Bryan and Charlotte had to head back to Pennsylvania to sell the shop and their house before heading for Spain. Bryan used to look forward to the suburbs of Valencia. Now, staring out at his family farm, he wasn't as excited. But it had to be done.

"Come on," Charlotte said. "One last thing before we go."

Charlotte went throughout the house, asking everyone to follow her to the flagpole. The procession donned coats and followed her out of the house. Bryan held her hand. Pam and David had their arms around each other's waists, a sign that today was a better day for them.

"I hope this is quick," Jason griped. He wore a thin T-shirt under the windbreaker he threw over his shoulders. "I'm freezing already."

"You need to grow your winter coat, Bigfoot," Bryan said.

"Thanks, Gimpalong Cassidy."

George Branch's burned and tattered flag flew at half-mast.

Charlotte opened a cardboard box that was next to the flagpole. She took out a plaque, holding it with two hands so everyone could see.

There was a picture of Bryan's mother at the top. It was taken when she was a younger woman, smiling as she balanced her two small boys on her lap.

Beneath it was a photo of beautiful Lola, wearing the dress she donned for church that first Sunday at St. Matthew's.

Beneath them were initials carved into the wood.

Bryan's chest tightened when he saw E. C. and B. R.

Finally beneath that was a quote:

May we think of freedom,
not as the right to do what we please.
But as the opportunity to do what is right.

—*Peter Marshall*

*Forever in our hearts, we love you
and will forever miss you.*

George Branch stepped forward to take the plaque from Charlotte. All were silent as he read from it.

The wind snapped the flag and the scent of rich soil was all around them.

Visit our website at
KensingtonBooks.com
to sign up for our newsletters, read
more from your favorite authors, see
books by series, view reading group
guides, and more!

Become a Part of Our
Between the Chapters Book Club
Community and Join the Conversation

Betweenthechapters.net